PHOENIX ASCENDANT

BAEN BOOKS by RYK E. SPOOR

Digital Knight
Paradigms Lost

GRAND CENTRAL ARENA SERIES
Grand Central Arena
Spheres of Influence

THE BALANCED SWORD SERIES
Phoenix Rising
Phoenix in Shadow
Phoenix Ascendant

BAEN BOOKS by RYK E. SPOOR & ERIC FLINT

Boundary
Threshold
Portal
Castaway Planet
Castaway Odyssey (coming)

"Diamonds are Forever" in the anthology *Mountain Magic*

PHOENIX ASCENDANT

Ryk E. Spoor

PHOENIX ASCENDANT

A Baen Books Original

Baen Publishing Enterprises
P.O. Box 1403
Riverdale, NY 10471
www.baen.com

ISBN: 978-1-4767-8129-7

Cover art by Todd Lockwood
Maps by Randy Asplund

First Baen printing, March 2016

Distributed by Simon & Schuster
1230 Avenue of the Americas
New York, NY 10020

10 9 8 7 6 5 4 3 2 1

Pages by Joy Freeman (www.pagesbyjoy.com)
Printed in the United States of America

ACKNOWLEDGEMENTS & THANKS

As always to my wife Kathleen, for giving me the time

To Toni Weisskopf, without whom Kyri
would not have completed her quest

To Tony Daniel, for guiding Kyri to her final destination

And to my Beta-Readers, for invaluable
support, feedback, and nitpicking.

This novel is dedicated to my daughter Victoria and my son Gabriel, who have both been waiting to see the end of Phoenix Kyri's quest.

CONTENTS

Map of Zarathan — x

Map of Moonshade Hollow — xii

Map of Evanwyl — xiii

Previously in The Balanced Sword series — xv

Phoenix Ascendant — 1

Gazetteer of Zarathan — 323

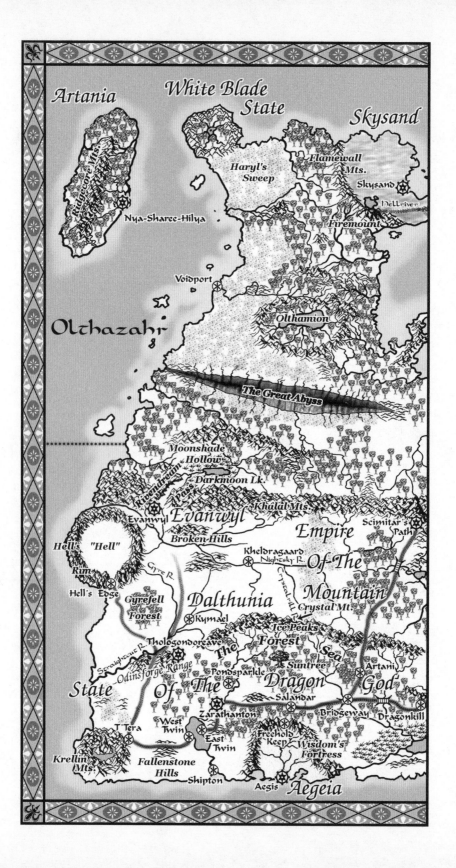

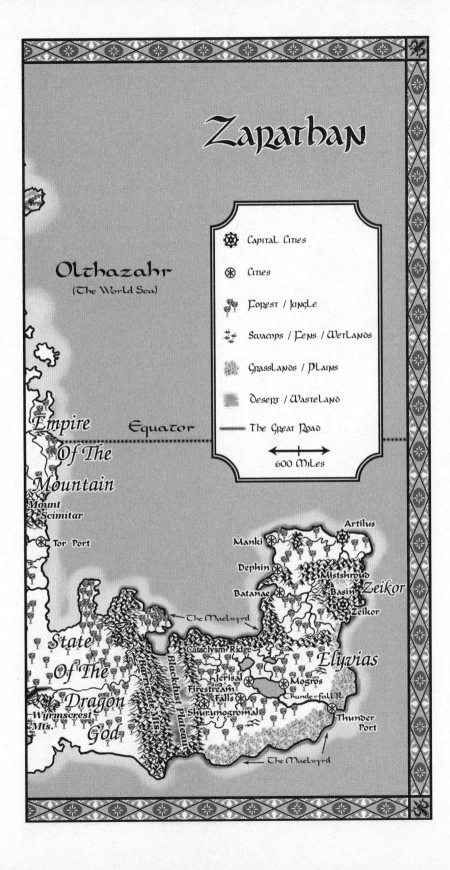

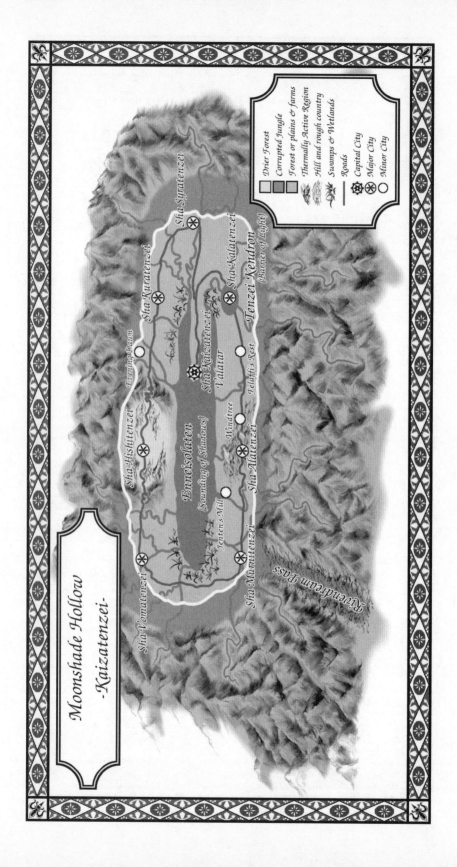

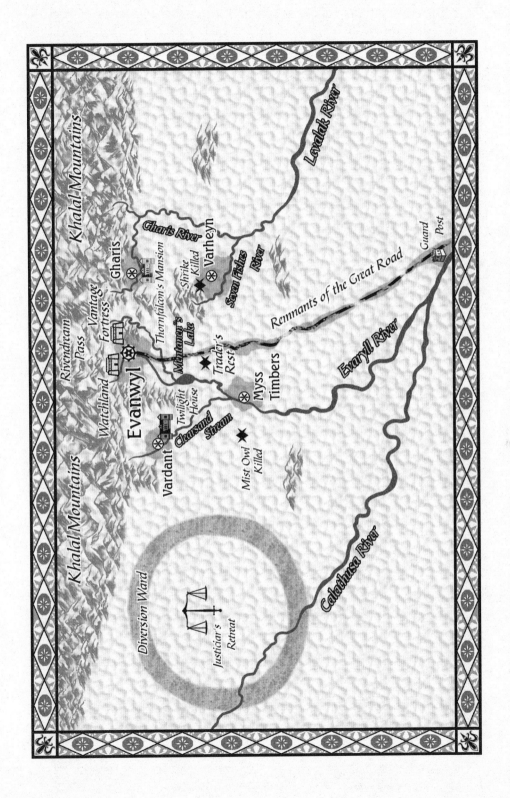

Previously in The Balanced Sword series

Phoenix Rising

Kyri Victoria Vantage lost her parents to unknown attackers some years before. Even the Justiciars of Myrionar, God of Justice and Vengeance, the patron deity of her country Evanwyl, were unable to discover the identity of the assailants. But she has moved on, and her brother Rion has become a Justiciar himself. Then tragedy strikes a second time, and during a sudden and monstrous attack on Evanwyl, something kills Rion, tearing his soul to shreds.

Shocked and now worried that her whole family is in peril, Kyri leaves Evanwyl with her aunt Victoria and younger sister Urelle, travelling to far-distant Zarathanton to begin a new life. But a chance discovery there reveals the hideous truth: that it was the *Justiciars* who were responsible, the supposed holy warriors somehow betraying everything they stand for. In rage and shock, Kyri demands Myrionar explain itself—and the god answers. Something far worse is happening; Myrionar is weakened, perhaps dying, but It promises Kyri that if she will be true to Myrionar—will become the one true Justiciar—then she will one day have the justice and vengeance she seeks.

Meanwhile, Tobimar Silverun, youngest prince of the country of Skysand, is forced to leave his country in search of the origins of his people—a quest that is thrust on his family once in a generation, and which amounts to exile for twenty years...unless he can discover their ancient homeland. The mysterious mage Khoros, once Tobimar's teacher, also warns Tobimar that the next Chaoswar is about to begin, and that this is connected to his quest.

Tobimar's search leads him to Zarathanton, greatest city of the world, and to a startling meeting with Poplock Duckweed, a diminutive Toad adventurer who has already disrupted the plans of one of the *Mazolishta* demonlords, Voorith. The two seek an audience with the Sauran King, only to find that he has been assassinated moments before they enter the Throne Room!

Having accepted Myrionar's offer, Kyri realizes that if she is to be a Justiciar, she must obtain the magical and powerful Raiment—the armor of a Justiciar—that both symbolizes and protects a Justiciar, and sets out to find the half-legendary Spiritsmith who can forge the Raiment. After managing to discover him—and pass his lethal tests—she convinces him that she is indeed the first of the new Justiciars, and takes the name Phoenix as her new title (as all Justiciars have the names of birds).

As refugees from the Forest Sea begin to pour into Zarathanton in massive numbers and word of revolutions or wars in distant lands begin to arrive, Tobimar and Poplock realize that they are seeing part of a vast, coordinated plan to destroy the State of the Dragon King and perhaps the peace of the world—certainly part of the Chaoswar that Khoros warned them of.

The small clues that Tobimar had for locating his country suddenly come into clear focus when he realizes that the god Myrionar's symbolism and location fit everything he has heard, pointing him and Poplock to Evanwyl. In the company of a new ally, Xavier Ross of Earth, they head for Evanwyl, confronting demonic pursuers along the way.

With her new Raiment and accompanying sword, Kyri begins her work of undermining the false Justiciars and preparing to confront them. She attempts to convince the first, Mist Owl, to change sides and help her, but he fears the force behind the false Justiciars too much to do this, and dies at her hand. A second Justiciar, Shrike, afraid that she will convince his adoptive son, the Justiciar Condor, to follow her, which might lead to Condor's death, also fails to kill her. Realizing that her confrontational approach is making it almost certain that she must fight each one, she chooses to try another way: to approach them not as a Justiciar, but as their "little sister," Kyri Vantage. For this, she selects Thornfalcon, the least martial of the Justiciars.

At the same time, Tobimar and Poplock have arrived in Evanwyl, having parted ways temporarily with Xavier. They hear the rumor of a false Justiciar named "Phoenix" who has killed at least one of the real Justiciars, and as this fits with the sort of thing they've already encountered more than once, offer their services to help hunt down Phoenix. They come across Shrike's body and deduce where Phoenix is headed next—although they do not realize the truth yet.

Kyri makes contact with Thornfalcon, who seems open to her approach... until he reveals the trap he has set for her. He was the one who killed her brother, and who has directed most of the operations of the false Justiciars (although there is someone or something above him).

Tobimar and Poplock arrive at Thornfalcon's just in time to prevent him from murdering Kyri, and instead find themselves in a fight to the death. But Kyri escapes her imprisonment and joins them. Together the three kill Thornfalcon despite his nigh-demonic powers, but are then caught in a trap that is unleashing an apparently endless horde of monsters into the midst of Evanwyl. At the last minute Xavier shows up, and together they locate the source of the monstrosities. Kyri calls upon the power of Myrionar and destroys the gateway through which they are coming.

Once all four have been introduced and understand each others' stories, Kyri, Poplock, Tobimar, and Xavier make their way to the Temple of the Balanced Sword where they confront two more false Justiciars, Bolthawk and Skyharrier, and reveal them for what they are.

The truth has been revealed, but they know that there are more mysteries—who was truly behind Thornfalcon, how a god's chosen emissaries can be corrupted, and how this all connects to the rise of war throughout the world. With Xavier now gone on his own quest, it falls to the three of them to find the answers...

Phoenix in Shadow

In a prologue, the unnamed true enemy examines the aftermath of the battle against Thornfalcon, and realizes the identity of the Phoenix, as well as deducing more of the nature of her companions than she might suspect. It then returns to the corrupted Justiciar's Retreat, just ahead of Aran Condor.

Aran demands their patron find some way of giving him the power to confront and destroy the Phoenix. Their patron calls on Kerlamion, King of All Hells, greatest of demonlords. Addressing the patron as "Viedraverion," Kerlamion agrees to provide the power Aran seeks... if Aran comes before his very throne to request it.

Meanwhile, Kyri and her friends have done their best to help and restabilize Evanwyl after the terrible shock of discovering the other Justiciar's corruption. Finding Tobimar's weapons heavily damaged after the battle against Thornfalcon, Kyri leads them to the Spiritsmith's forge. The Spiritsmith agrees to forge appropriate weapons and armor for Tobimar.

As they are talking, something monstrously *wrong* happens, shaking the earth, darkening the sky, and in horrified shock the Spiritsmith points to a shadow that now stands on the horizon; the Black City of Kerlamion has somehow come *to* Zarathan, and the King of All Hells now walks the living world.

The Spiritsmith completes the forging of Tobimar's gear, and also contacts the legendary Wanderer to assist the travelers in determining their destination and understanding the forces arrayed against them. The Wanderer confirms—as they had guessed—that they must journey through corrupt and deadly Rivendream Pass to Moonshade Hollow, and that much of what is happening he knows, but cannot tell them. Kyri says: "A prophecy. You have a prophecy."

The Wanderer responds with a strange smile, and answers, "Not...precisely. Though, perhaps, close enough for your purposes."

He gives them only a few cryptic hints, emphasizing that while he would very much like to tell them more, doing so could jeopardize everything they are all trying to accomplish—but that Myrionar's promise that they *can* succeed is very much true.

Aran Condor has made his way through the wastelands nicknamed "Hell," and then finds himself confronted by the real thing—standing before the doors of the Black City itself. His anger and need for vengeance (barely) overcomes his more sensible fear, and he continues forward. Kerlamion gives him the Demonshard Blade, a piece of Kerlamion's own sword, a weapon of tremendous demonic power that the Lord of All Hells says should be capable of destroying anything—even the Phoenix Justiciar.

The three heroes make their way through Rivendream Pass,

which is even worse than they had expected. During this trip, Kyri and Tobimar finally (with a bit of pushing by Poplock) admit their attraction for each other. Shortly after entering the corrupted forest in Moonshade Hollow, they come across a small figure about to be attacked by a monster.

The diminutive, beautiful girl introduces herself as "Miri, Light of the Unity," and leads them through a barrier wall into a land she calls "Kaizatenzei," translated as "the Unity of the Seven Lights."

Impossibly, Kaizatenzei seems to be not only not corrupt, but in actuality a haven of purity, a supernaturally *right* place where it is almost impossible to imagine the existence of the evil that lies just outside of its walls. The people know nothing of the world beyond the corrupted forest and are astounded by the three new arrivals. Miri is the right-hand servant and troubleshooter for "Lady Shae," the Lady of Seven Lights. Lady Shae bids the group travel to their capital, Sha Kaizatenzei Valatar.

The three are joined in their travels by Hiriista, *mazakh* "magewright"—master of magical talents tied to more physical sources, such as alchemy and the discipline called "Gemcalling." Despite his species, Hiriista appears to be very much on the side of good and develops an unexpectedly strong bond with Poplock.

The group learns that Hiriista has noted some oddities concerning the "Unity Guard"—the combined police and military force of Kaizatenzei, a group that includes Lights, Colors, Shades, and Hues, with Lights such as Miri at the top. These oddities fit with a few unsettling feelings Phoenix has had around Unity Guards.

Unbeknownst to the adventurers, Miri and Shae are the demon-lords Emirinovas and Kalshae, and they have some plan which requires Tobimar Silverun, whom they refer to as "the Key," and also the assistance of the cold and calculating researcher named Master Wieran.

Aran Condor enters Kaizatenzei in pursuit of the Phoenix. The purity of Kaizatenzei breaks the corrupting hold that the Demonshard Blade had gained on Aran's mind, and Condor successfully defeats the blade in a contest of wills. Miri, as asked by Viedraverion, meets Aran and sends him traveling around the central lake in the *opposite* direction from Phoenix and her companions.

Miri is stunned when, during their travels, Phoenix manages

to summon the power of her god to heal children who should be unsalvageable (infected by a soul-damaging parasite). She also fears that her constant contact with the magic that has made Kaizatenzei so pure is corrupting her demonic essence.

The travelers reach Sha Kaizatenzei Valatar, and all seems perfect—except for a momentary flash of sensation by Phoenix, where she detects two dark presences, one filled with anger and hatred, the other cold and amused.

Tobimar is allowed to approach "the Great Light" in the Valatar Tower, and its response to his approach proves beyond any shadow of a doubt that the Great Light is the Sun of Terian, one of the greatest artifacts of one of the most powerful gods of good, and because of that Tobimar now knows that Kaizatenzei is what is left of the true homeland of his people.

Miri discovers that she *is* totally corrupt—or, more accurately, purified—when she finds herself drawn physically and romantically to Phoenix.

As a celebration is prepared for them, the adventurers notice a much larger number of Unity Guard entering the city, and recognize that this whole setup could be a trap. Their attempt to escape fails, and they are captured and Tobimar placed on a sacrificial altar; Miri is also caught out and captured by Kalshae.

As Wieran's and Kalshae's ritual is nearing completion, Tobimar connects the events with the last advice Khoros gave him, and realizes that an old childhood prayer is in fact the key to accessing the power of the Sun of Terian. For a moment, Terian himself manifests through the body of Tobimar, freeing and healing the Skysand Prince and his friends. Kyri and Hiriista leave the room to rescue Miri, while Tobimar—with more than mortal power—and Poplock confront Kalshae.

Kalshae is defeated when Poplock tricks her into triggering a summons of herself, and Kyri reaches Miri in time to keep her from being locked away. The group confronts Master Wieran in his laboratory, but cannot fight him directly—his Great Array includes hundreds of tubes in which are still-living human beings. Poplock manages to play on Wieran's ego and desire for an audience, distracting him long enough for Hiriista to notice a secondary magical array and damage it, releasing *something* which has been sealed up beneath the central lake for millennia.

This disrupts Wieran's attempt to attain something even beyond the godhead, and Wieran barely escapes; worse is the fact that what is rising now is Sanamaveridion, an Elderwyrm or evil Dragon of incalculable power.

Aran Condor, who has been performing small acts of heroism in his travels around the lake, uses the Demonshard Blade to disrupt the tsunami thrown up by Sanamaveridion's emergence, while Kyri does the same on the other side of the lake with the power of the Phoenix. Aran cannot do more at this point, but is now certain that where the Elderwyrm has risen, the Phoenix *must* be waiting.

The heroes confront Sanamaveridion, and after a tremendous pitched battle defeat him through the combined efforts of Tobimar, Kyri, and Miri, with an inspired last-minute summoning by Poplock finishing the job.

Miri attempts to recover the communication scroll she has used to contact Viedraverion—this turns out to be a trap. Miri discovers that "Viedraverion" is not what it seems, but is instead some other terrible being, one she calls by the name "Lightslayer" before it erases her memory of key facts.

The remaining Unity Guard, now no longer under anyone's mental domination, confront the group for answers once the immediate search-and-rescue after the battle is complete. To the surprise of everyone, Miri confesses everything, and Lady Shae reappears—having been herself purified by the Light of Terian. With the entire party, including Hiriista, now supporting Miri and Shae's redemption, the Unity Guard accept them as leaders once more.

But the now-unknown adversary has seen everything going according to Its plan, and in the final scene it has also reached beyond the grave to bring back three of the old Justiciars in preparation for the final confrontation...

PHOENIX ASCENDANT

CHAPTER 1

"Lady Shae!"

Kyri shouted even as she realized that Shae could not possibly react in time, and lunged forward, shoving the taller woman aside. Her gauntleted hands caught the sagging beam, gripped so tightly that the hardwood dented beneath her fingers, and she braced herself, throwing all the Vantage strength into keeping the monstrous mass of stone above from moving so much as one more inch.

By then, Shae had caught herself against the corridor wall. "Phoenix? By the *Light!*" Immediately the red-haired ruler of Kaizatenzei raised her voice. "Tanvol! Miri! Braces, *quickly!*"

Kyri felt her arms starting to give. *Myrionar, no!*

Another presence next to her, and a glow of blue-white power enveloped Tobimar Silverun as he used his newfound strength to reinforce hers, the two of them keeping the roof of the corridor from collapsing until the two Lights of Kaizatenzei—Tanvol with his massive frame, bushy black beard, and booming voice, and Miri, tiny, delicate, and golden blond—arrived and levered their braces into place.

"Whew!" Kyri said in an explosive breath, and leaned somewhat shakily against the wall. "That was..."

"...far too close, Phoenix," Shae said, and looked at her with concern. "Are you all right? Do you need to rest?"

I can't afford *to rest.* She didn't say that—it would trigger an argument from all her friends who would then insist she needed

1

to sit down. "No, I'm all right. Besides, we're almost there. We can't stop now!"

She saw Miri bite her lip and gaze down the last few steps of the staircase to the doors of Master Wieran's great laboratory, which had shut behind them when they had left to confront the Great Dragon Sanamaveridion. It wasn't hard to guess what was going through her mind—the almost ethereal girl was still coming to terms with the fact that she was no longer a demon but . . . something else, a something else that still remembered, and felt terrible responsibility for, the evils she'd committed and assisted before awakening to the Light she'd been pretending to serve.

Kyri put her hand gently on Miri's shoulder. "Come on. Let's save them."

Miri looked up and swallowed, then smiled and nodded bravely. "Yes, of course."

"Oh, *bottommud!*" Poplock Duckweed cursed from the door. "Stupid things *locked* themselves."

"Do we have to break through?" Shae asked, looking apprehensively at the already-cracked stone above. "I do *not* look forward to trying anything so forceful here."

"Ease your mind, Lady Shae," Hiriista said with a rippling of his crest that conveyed a smile. "I and the Toad will unravel these seals momentarily. Wieran's major defenses were broken; these should prove little impediment, and then we can leave the doors open to provide their own bracing—just in case."

True to his word, after a few minutes of muttered consultation and inscribing of various symbols, there was a muffled *clack* and the doors began to swing open.

The great laboratory looked far different than it had when last Kyri had seen it. Great shards of stone, many with sections of the Great Array still glinting on their surfaces, had plunged down into the ranks of tubes that encircled the forty-nine levels of the laboratory, and smashed much of the fabulously complex machinery and sorcerous designs which had filled the center of the immense room. Sharp smells of chemicals, the sulfur tang of broken stone, the tingling scent of sparks, and underlying stenches of more ominous nature were set off by the eerie and irregular lighting. Some of the lightglobes spaced around the laboratory were still intact, others crushed to dark powder, and other devices and runes flickered with blue or green or purple light. The ordered hum was now disrupted, uneven, but still present.

"Careful!" Poplock admonished in his surprisingly powerful voice. "We know what's at stake, but Hiriista and I have to check these tubes out first. The fact that you Unity Guards are mostly still moving tells us that old Wieran's systems weren't so fragile that a few falling rocks would do them in, but we don't know what kind of traps he had on them, or how independent they are, or how hard it is to get someone out of one of these things alive."

Kyri restrained herself with difficulty; she could only imagine how hard it must be for the others, most of whom had friends—or, in the case of the Unity Guard, them*selves*—somewhere in those shadowed rows of coffinlike tubes.

"He *seemed* to be able to put people in or take them out very easily," Shae said in her warm, steady contralto. "I've seen him do it."

"Alas," Hiriista said, as he and Poplock cautiously approached one of the intricately sculpted tubes, "that means little to nothing. Weiran may have carried a charm that allowed him—and *only* him—to safely open and close the tubes, or have previously unlocked some safeguards before you observed him, or any of a number of things which would make it far, far more difficult for anyone else."

Kyri stood a considerable distance away from the two as they worked. There was no point in crowding them; she knew almost nothing about magic, while Hiriista was probably the greatest magewright in the country and Poplock, for all his protests that he was a mere amateur, had an uncanny insight into the workings of mystical devices, especially from the point of view of someone trying to undo any locks or defenses on such devices.

Lady Shae was herself a magewright of no small skill, but Kyri watched her eyes first narrow, then widen, and then saw the ruler of Kaizatenzei rise quietly and move away, shaking her head. "I am older than everyone in this room put together," she said with a rueful smile. "Except for Miri, of course. And I have studied magical works, off and on, for centuries. But those two..." She shook her head again in disbelief. "You say he's only *twelve*?"

"That's our guess," Tobimar said. "Of course, for the Toads it's not the same; by the time he was a year and a half old he was close to the size he is now, and already talking at the level of an eight-year-old. Toads grow up fast. But even so . . . yes, he's something unique, isn't he?"

"My body and spirit remember *how* unique very well, yes," she assented wryly, referring to the way in which Poplock had defeated and nearly killed her with her own magic, before Shae had followed Miri and changed her mind about which side she was on.

"Does that mean that he's not going to live as long as a human?" Miri asked, worry in her voice.

"On average, Toads don't live as long as we do, no," Tobimar said quietly. "On the other hand, if someone really *wants* to live longer, there are ways, and I'm sure Poplock will find one."

Kyri chuckled. "Yes, I think he will."

Tanvol and his usual companion, the Light Anora (who was taller than Miri but even more pale-skinned and with hair so blonde it was nearly white), came to stand near them. Kyri smiled at the pair. It had seemed at first that Anora had met her end when Tobimar had cut her Eternal Servant body in twain during his duel against Shae, and even more when the Tower was shattered by Sanamaveridion.

Instead, two of the Guard had found her remains amongst the debris, and Poplock had not destroyed, but merely removed, the crystal assembly that made Wieran's artificial constructs "alive"; replacing that assembly triggered the astonishing self-repair capabilities, knitting both halves back together and returning Light Anora Lal to the ranks of her comrades . . . living now on the same borrowed time as the others, if they could not retrieve her real body along with the rest.

"I've told the others to spend their time putting up more bracing all along the stairs," Tanvol said. "Give them something useful to do while we're waiting."

Kyri grunted. "You know, I think I'll do that too. I have no idea how long this will take."

Tobimar nodded and followed as she started out of the room, and the others came after them. *No one really wants to just* wait *without being able to do anything.*

There was a *lot* of bracing to do. Most of the three-hundred-forty-three-step staircase had cracks running across the ceiling, showing where the combat against the miles-long Sanamaveridion had transmitted its shock and violence down, hundreds of feet into the living rock. Miri could summon temporary bracing columns of stone, but more permanent timbers of wood, or supports of metal, had to be put in place to ensure that the path would remain clear.

On the positive side, after a good night's rest there were a total of eighty of the Unity Guard still present and active, and eighty of those borderline-superhuman warriors could do a *lot* of work. Orders were bellowed, relays of materials and workers and water were organized, and strong, regular ranks of bracing and beams began to spread up the stairs like frost across a windowpane, a smooth and inexorable blooming of perfect symmetry. Kyri let them direct the work; these people knew each other and trusted each other, and she was the outsider—respected and perhaps more, but still not one of them, and not able to respond as they could to a hint or a gesture.

But finally she heard Hiriista's steamkettle whistle.

"Well?"

Poplock spoke up from the mazakh's shoulder. "Good news. There *were* some boobytraps, but Hiriista and I think we've got 'em all. The good news there is that they were *universal* traps—once we broke them, they're off *all* the tubes, and each tube is self-sufficient. I don't think there's anything else on them; let's face it, Wieran had plenty of other security and he didn't have any reason to expect anyone would ever get the chance to try to take away his human batteries."

"I have to wonder," Tanvol rumbled, "just what will happen to, well, *this* me when *that* me," he gestured vaguely to the dimness in the laboratory, "well, wakes up."

"Not sure, honestly," said Poplock. "But that question isn't something to answer right now. The tubes have to be opened carefully and we don't know what shape the people inside will be in. From what we know of Zogen Josan, he was in perfectly good shape, but they knew he was retiring a couple months ahead of time, so they could have spent that time preparing his body for release. We're going to have to take all the tubes out of here as fast as we can; there's *no* way to brace that ceiling, it's a dome a thousand or more feet across and hundreds high—it's a water-clear *miracle* it didn't all collapse right away. But—"

There was a clatter and hiss as fragments of rock spattered from the floor a short distance off.

"—but, as I was saying, that could happen any time now."

"Enough with the bracing, lads!" Tanvol thundered. "Everyone, we're moving the tubes containing our people—and us—out of here! In relays, everyone, we can fit three across the main entrance, so I want teams of three. The strongest here—Lady Shae, Phoenix, and Miri, with of course Tobimar Silverun's assistance—will remove the tubes as fast as they can, while we run a rotating relay to carry them to the Valatar Throne."

That's . . . twenty-seven teams, plus the three of us. She heard a faint groaning of the stone overhead, and rock dust sifted down. *I hope that will be enough.*

"It *has* to be enough," Tobimar said, and she realized she'd spoken aloud.

"It *will be* enough," Miri said. She reached down and detached one of the tubes—taller than she was, weighing over a hundred and fifty pounds *without* the man inside—and heaved it up, carrying it easily to the first three-man team. "We will *make* it enough."

Kyri watched them lugging the massive tube and frowned, even as she hauled the next tube out of its socket and walked heavily over to the next team. *Twenty-seven teams. Three hundred forty-three steps, then down a good stretch of corridor, then up the fifty or sixty steps to the Valatar Throneroom . . . that's a ten-minute operation even if they don't start to get exhausted right away. Twenty-minute round trip. We have to get one a minute or so.* She looked around the room. Even leaving aside the ones that had been crushed by falling debris, there were *hundreds* of the tubes. How long could they keep up the relay?

She saw by Tobimar's grim face that he'd been doing the same internal calculation; Poplock was also silent on his shoulder as the Prince of Skysand used the power of Terian to carry the next tube over.

"There's no way we can keep this up, and ordinary citizens won't be of much help; carry something weighing hundreds of pounds up hundreds of steps? No, that just won't work," she muttered to herself. "But we *have* to do this." She pulled up the next tube, not looking at the deathlike face barely visible within. "I can do this three, four, five times, but even I'm going to get tired." She handed that tube over, then sighed as she passed Tobimar. "If only we could make them lighter, somehow."

"That would be . . ." Tobimar trailed off, and then exchanged a wide-eyed glance with Poplock on his shoulder; just as the idea dawned on her, the little Toad drew in a huge breath.

"Tanvol!" shouted Poplock. "Phoenix just got a great idea! Send a couple teams up to pry off as much of that floaty-rock as they can from the broken bridges, and bring it down with some nets! We can use that to *float* these tubes up!"

Tanvol froze for a moment, and then his thunderous laugh threatened to bring the roof down. "By the *LIGHT*, that we will!"

The next half-hour was agonizing work, as they kept hauling out the massive tubes and dragging or carrying them to the teams that would somehow lug them to the surface. But then a crowd of the citizens of Kaizatenzei flooded into the laboratory, carrying nets filled with the mysteriously buoyant stone and metal that supported the flying bridges that had spanned the city. It took many of them to hold each set of stones down, but hooking them onto a tube made the tube easy for even an ordinary man to guide and carry up the stairs.

The hours blurred together; the work might not have been quite as backbreaking, but it was painstaking, tedious—and dangerous. A massive boulder dropped from the ceiling three hours into the operation, crushing eight more tubes beneath its mass, and causing one Hue to drop instantly to the ground; the human body that had supported Hue Surura Saval was dead, and without that body and spirit there was nothing left to move the artificial shell. For a moment all the Unity Guard stood silent, shocked; then Miri snapped "*Move!* That's what will happen to *all* of you if we don't get your tubes out of here—and we don't know which ones are yours!"

More hours passed, tubes pulled from sockets, rubble cleared from paths, chains and rune-ropes untwined to allow more tubes to be removed, a quick drink of water, a bite of food, then back to the work. It was harder because Wieran had not simply filled all of the spots starting from a given location; the individuals were spaced according to a complex pattern that made it difficult to be sure you had found *all* the tubes in an area, and forced you to go much farther, on average, to reach the next tube.

Finally, Kyri realized that they actually were nearing the end. "We've . . . almost reached . . . the far side of the room," she said, sliding the current tube into a floating sling.

"Yes," Miri said, exhaustion in her voice. "Let's get the next one."

The "next one" was a tube isolated from the others, near the central area where Wieran had done his most complex work. She was about to grab it when Hiriista hissed a warning.

"That one...is different."

"Yeah, and different could be bad," Poplock said. "Different makes me suspicious. Let's take a look at this one."

"You know anything about this?" Kyri asked Miri and Shae.

Miri shook her head; Shae tilted hers, then nodded slowly. "That one...is relatively recent. I remember it showed up there a year or two ago. It surprised me; I knew we hadn't had any new...recruits in that time. When I asked about it, Wieran said it was a special delivery from his patron; that was as much as he'd say."

"Well, that one *was* locked and trapped. Good catch, Hiriista. I don't think Kyri really wanted a bath in acid."

She shuddered. "No, thank you." Kyri moved cautiously up to the presumably harmless tube, which was also slightly larger than the others—perhaps built to be moved more easily? It had been shipped here, if what Weiran had said was the truth.

Kyri leaned forward, squinting at the clouded glass in front. *What's inside this one?*

She realized there was one way that might show her; she picked up the tube and tilted it towards her.

The shadowy shape within swayed and moved a few inches forward, revealing the outlines of the face for just an instant.

Kyri staggered back, dropping the tube, which was barely caught by Lady Shae. She couldn't speak, she couldn't *think. It's impossible! Impossible!*

But then the face became visible once more, as Shae lifted the tube back up, and Kyri lunged forward, without thinking, screaming out the name:

"RION!"

CHAPTER 2

Tobimar caught at Kyri's arm and pulled her back. "Don't! We don't know how these open, remember?" He caught her gaze, staring steadily into the huge, gray eyes, waited until they focused on him. "You all right?"

She closed her eyes and then nodded slowly. At that point, the recognition of the name she'd screamed hit him. "Wait. *Rion? Your brother?* But...he died in front of you, didn't he?"

"Yes...yes, of course. You're right." She cast an agonized, confused glance at the tube as Lady Shae slid a floating cradle under it. "But...but that looks like him. I mean, it *really* looks like him."

"You're looking through a not-perfectly-clear window at some guy floating in whatever-that-stuff-is that Wieran filled these tubes with," Poplock pointed out. "Your eyes might be tricking you. Shae's got that one; let's finish this work up. We're not opening *any* of these things yet, so there's nothing more to do with that mystery anyway until we're done here. Right?"

Kyri tore her attention away from the receding, mysterious tube with a visible effort, then gave a rather forced-looking smile. "Of course, you're right. As usual."

The two of them worked in silence for a few minutes. Tobimar couldn't help but think about the bizarre event. *What could that mean? Kyri's got really good senses, and if* anyone *would know her brother, it should be her. What if that is Rion?*

"Could be another trap," the little Toad muttered in his ear, making him twitch.

"What? Are you reading *minds* now, Poplock?" he murmured back.

"Not hard to guess what *you're* thinking about. Probably what she's thinking about too."

"I suppose. Yes, it could be a trap. But for what purpose?"

"That's the murky part, yeah. It's not an illusion in that over-sized jar, I can tell you that; if her eyes weren't just confused, then whoever's in there must look awfully like her brother."

"But *looking* like him would be pretty useless."

"Very useless," Kyri's voice spoke from behind them, making them *both* jump. "Sorry to startle you."

"We were trying not to..."

"I know. But it isn't as though I'm not thinking the same things." She shook her head as they started maneuvering yet another sealed tube up and out. "I watched Rion *die*. An impostor won't fool me for a second."

Poplock made a face. "Don't be so hopping sure. We couldn't even tell that Miri and Shae were demons until they dropped the masks. We're dealing with great demons and gods—they can fog even *Myrionar's* sight, and you know it."

Tobimar could see Kyri try to come up with a countering argument and fail. "An Eternal Servant maybe?" he suggested. "Like the Unity Guard?"

The Phoenix Justiciar shook her head. "Possible, I suppose, but it makes no sense. Why put one of those artificial things in a suspension tube? They don't age on their own and I can't think they'll be better off soaking in liquid than operating. And what good would such a thing be without the original alive anyway?"

"I don't have answers there," Tobimar admitted. "But I'll tell you what: once we've got every tube out of here, that one will be the first to be opened. We know the tubes are stable, so the Guards will be okay as long as they're out of here, and your tube constitutes a mystery that we really want to solve."

Kyri smiled gratefully at him. "Thank you, Tobimar. You know it would eat at me if I had to keep waiting."

"Well, assuming that Shae or Miri or Hiriista don't come up with some really convincing argument that we *should* keep waiting, I'll go along with that idea," Poplock said. "But remember that this *is* their country and...Oh, *drought*."

"What?" Tobimar suddenly became aware of a faint hissing

noise in the background. He whirled, seeking its source, and found it; a grayish line shimmering from the far wall. *Water. The wall has finally sprung a leak.*

Kyri ignited in golden flame. "*Move it,* everyone! I know we're exhausted, but the wall holding back Enneisolaten is giving way!"

Muttered oaths echoed around the room and the exhausted salvage crews redoubled their efforts, yanking the tubes from their foundations, desperately dragging them to floating cradles, sprinting out with them. Kyri placed herself against the far wall, which had begun to crack across its surface, and auric-orange flame spread, dug in, anchored, refused the movement, denied the water entrance. But Tobimar knew that her power would not last forever, or even for terribly long. Both of them had drained their reserves almost to nothing in the battle against Sanamaveridion; he saw the strain on her face already.

He saw Poplock scuttling around the wrecked mystical machinery at the center of the Great Array, shoving various things into his neverfull pack. *Don't know what he's doing, but there isn't too much he can do to help in carrying these things, so I suppose he's doing whatever he thinks is best.*

There was a cracking, grumbling noise from above, and part of the ceiling sagged.

"Everyone out!" bellowed Tanvol, his deep voice echoing around the room. "We've done what we can! Phoenix! Phoenix, *run!*"

But instead of running, Kyri *walked,* backing away from the far wall a step at a time, golden fire streaming from her arms, covering the wall, trying to climb higher, to grasp the bulging ceiling above.

Poplock bounded to Tobimar's shoulder. "Come *on,* go, go, go!"

"I should help—"

"She knows what she's doing! You don't have enough control of your power yet!"

Tobimar gritted his teeth but couldn't argue. He could use the power of Terian to reinforce himself, and to deliver incomparable strikes against his enemies, but controlling that power to reach out and hold something without possibly making it worse...no, he didn't know enough to do that.

But Lady Shae and Miri knew how, and did. The two former demons flanked Kyri and their power—white and aqua—reached out, building columns and braces of temporary might and evanescent energy. The workers were streaming out, Tobimar now passing most of the stragglers, glancing over his shoulder at the three women, still methodically retreating, holding uncountable tons of stone and water at bay through unbending will as much as immortal power.

Tanvol was surveying the room himself, making sure all the others were getting out. "Lady Shae! Miri! Phoenix! We're all out! No more time to waste, *come on!*"

Tobimar, Poplock clinging tightly to his shoulder, and Hiriista ran through the open doors of Wieran's lab, hearing a creaking, ripping rumble starting, shaking the stone below them. Light Tanvol and Anora Lal sprinted past them with Unity Guard speed.

Tobimar couldn't keep from turning around.

A blaze of white-gold light appeared in the entryway, and he saw all three women *flying* towards him, Kyri's gold-fire wings stretched out and nearly touching the sides of the corridor, while Shae and Miri streaked through the air seemingly by will of light alone.

And a rumbling roar echoed out behind them; dark-roiling movement seethed into view.

"Great *Desert!*" he cursed, and ran.

Kyri caught up with him after only a few strides and caught him up, speeding up the stairs, weaving between the support columns. Behind them the water roared like Sanamaveridion's rage, and Poplock gave a terrifed, wordless squeak. Cold, foul-smelling wind blew past them and Tobimar saw to his horror that the water was *catching up*, channeled by the tunnel into unspeakable velocity, reaching, hissing spray vaporizing from Kyri's flaming wings, and then—

—water caught them, coiling, grasping, filled with stinking bottom-mud and shards of stone, propelling them onward—

—smashed into a wall, a stunning blow, Poplock torn from his shoulder—

—and again, forward, unable to breathe, lungs beginning to protest, tumbling over and over, hammered by pebbles and rocks and timbers torn from the bracing below, racing at unguessable speed—

—breath burning from being held in, unable to see, water dimming even the brightest lights, or perhaps there *were* no lights anymore...

Tobimar felt darkness greater than that surrounding him

starting to close in on his consciousness, a red-tinged blackness that meant death; once he gave in, he would try to breathe, and the vile water would fill his lungs. But he couldn't hold on much longer. *Poplock...Kyri...*

Abruptly he struck stone, rough but symmetrical, cut and ordered, and the headlong flight had slowed, the water was becoming sluggish, hesitating, going *backward*. With the last of his strength he reached out, grabbed hold of the stone beneath, and held on as the water streamed by, first slowly, then faster and faster, as knives seemed to be impaling his lungs and his grip weakened. He felt his fingers starting to slip—

—and a massive hand closed around his and yanked him up.

The gasp of pure air was the most wonderful thing he had ever felt. For a moment he simply hung there, letting the air force back the reddish-black haze that had nearly taken him. Then he managed to open his eyes again.

Tanvol was holding him half-suspended in air, the huge Light gasping for breath himself, draped across a brace that was jammed diagonally in the stairway that ascended to the Valatar Throneroom.

"Thanks," Tobimar managed.

"Think...nothing of it...Prince of Skysand," Tanvol replied slowly. His grip slackened. "Glad to...have been able...to provide a last...service."

A sliver of ice pierced Tobimar's heart. The massive, boisterous, inexhaustible Light seemed to be...fading. "Last...what do you mean?"

"It appears," Tanvol said, with his brilliant grin wan and regretful, "that one of the few capsules...we failed to retrieve...was my own." His eyes were clouded. "I...see two places at once... here, and...a dark place, with vague shimmering against glass before my eyes, and it is cold."

"T-Tanvol? No, *no, no!*" Miri was stumbling up the steps. "No, I won't let—"

The rumbling chuckle was a ghost of its former self, but the humor was there. "Alas, my one-time demonic comrade, I fear you...cannot forbid...death." The black eyes blinked, glazed, the head was drooping, even as Lady Shae and Phoenix staggered up. "I see...cracks forming. Slow enough...to allow a farewell...swift enough to not draw out the pain. It...was a good life...Lady Shae...Miri...do not mourn, but...sing for me. The Light...awaits me. I see it now...Light beyond here...beyond the glass...that drips water upon...my unmoving face."

Tanvol's eyes closed, but he was smiling, and the lips parted once more. "...and with...such glory ahead...who wants...to live...forever?"

The massive Light's body sagged, and Tobimar caught it as it slid, now lifeless, to the ground.

CHAPTER 3

Poplock gave his own little salute from atop Danrall's shoulder as Tanvol's body, clad in a pure white robe with the pattern of the Seven and One embroidered on it in gems and gold thread, was borne towards the shores of Enneisolaten by seven people: Lady Shae, Miri, Anora, Herminta Gantil and another Color whose name Poplock didn't quite remember, Hiriista . . . and Tobimar. Tobimar had insisted he be the Seventh, and none had argued with him.

The Unity Guard had been silent as the body was prepared and the seven had stood. But as Tanvol passed the last in line, they began to sing, a solemn and powerful chant, and turned as one to march behind the seven bearers. Looking behind, Poplock saw most of the population of the city, thousands strong. They were following, some grim, some sad, some crying silent tears, but all of them following with proud and measured pace.

As the procession reached the shore—a shore more broad and low than it had been before the Great Dragon rose from beneath its depths—the Unity Guard began to fan out, spreading towards other white-wrapped bodies waiting on simple rafts at the edge of the great lake.

Tanvol would not depart alone.

At that, we were lucky. Even counting the Unity Guards, less than a hundred people died in Sha Kaizatenzei Valatar. There had, of course, been at least thirty-five other tubes that had been crushed along with four other Unity Guards, and Poplock

15

suspected a lot more had died in outlying areas—the ones actually struck by Sanamaveridion's ravening fires—but while the main city had suffered much physical damage, its people had mostly survived. Poplock hopped from Danrall's shoulder and, after a moment, bounced back to Tobimar and climbed back to his accustomed place. *I owe Tanvol too; I ... wouldn't want to be doing any of this without Tobimar.*

Lady Shae yielded the place of honor next to Tanvol, Light of Kaizatenzei, to Tobimar, and instead became honor guard to Light Dravan Igo, the one Kyri had killed in freeing Miri. The others took up places at the side of the fallen, Unity Guard or merchant or mother or, in two heartbreaking instances, child, and stood tall and straight, looking west towards the setting sun.

"Lady Phoenix," Shae said, "we await you."

Kyri stood at the very edge of the water, at the farthest point of land remaining. "I do not know your rituals well..."

Lady Shae shook her head. "I was the speaker for the Light, but in this disaster I had a terrible hand; I will not speak our words. You know us well enough, Phoenix, and your friend and companion stands as Final Guide to his savior. I trust you will find the words and gestures of your own that say what needs be said."

Poplock nodded. Shae carried too much guilt for these deaths to feel comfortable giving the last rites, and the same went for Miri; it made sense that she'd give the position to the next most visible hero, the Phoenix who had shattered the wave and withstood the Dragon with wings and sword of flame that had been seen even from endangered Valatar.

Kyri took a deep breath, and when she spoke, her voice was unnaturally strong, but not a shout; it merely *carried* like a shout, like a crack of thunder, yet spoke quietly, softly, warmly.

"We stand here on the shores of Enneisolaten, at the border between land and inland sea, to say our farewells and give final salutes to those who have crossed the greater border from this world to the Light in the Darkness," Kyri began. "I will not tell you not to grieve, for grieving is a part of loss; even if we are all to meet beyond death, still it is the departing of friends, of family, of children and teachers and lovers and protectors.

"But they would be happy to know that most of us remain, that their hopes and dreams were not destroyed—that Sha Kaizatenzei

Valatar still stands, and will rise again. The Tower is fallen, but the Light endures within us all, and lives most strongly of all in those who gave of themselves that we might live."

She turned and faced the sun, now a blazing sphere sitting atop the surface of the great lake, drawing a glowing path across the water to where Phoenix stood. "I cannot speak for the Light in the Darkness, for Terian; but I can speak for Myrionar, his ally and friend, and I stand ready to send them on their journey to the Light. Let Tanvol, Light of Kaizatenzei, lead your people to the Light, and I hope and pray that Myrionar will be his guide."

Poplock held on as Tobimar shoved the little raft out, and it floated free, slowly drifting on the water. Kyri pointed her sword, and golden fire reached out and caressed the wood of the raft, pulling it forward, guiding it to drift outward along the path of gold-shimmering water, flames of the same color beginning to dance along the edges of the raft.

More scrapes within the silence, and the other rafts with their white-wrapped cargo began to drift from the shore. Kyri's red-gold flame flowed down both shores, directing the drift, and setting each to glow with the same fire.

Flame leapt higher on Tanvol's raft, which was now drifting farther away. "Terian the Infinite, in the name of Myrionar I commend these people, the fallen of Kaizatenzei, into your care. I ask you—I beg you—to hear me and bring them to you, receive them into the Light, for though they knew not your name, they served you and have held your Light in their hearts for all their lives."

Kyri bowed her head, and then raised it, gazing steadily at the armada of fiery rafts, all flickering with the golden fire of the Phoenix.

Then Poplock felt Tobimar's shoulder stiffen beneath him, even as his own little hands gripped suddenly tighter.

The setting sun ignited in blue-white fire, spreading star-bright light across the water, a path of gleaming silver and sapphire that stretched to meet the oncoming fleet, and as it did so their flames turned to argent and sky. Silhouetted against the now brilliantly-blazing orb was a tiny figure, cloak or cape streaming in a distant wind, arms outstretched as if to welcome friends and family home. The pure, brilliant fire rose higher, dazzling all of the watchers, so that Poplock turned away and even Phoenix raised her hand to shield her eyes.

And when the light faded, there were only the calm ripples of Enneisolaten glittering ruby and amber in the last rays of the setting sun; of the myriad rafts and their fires there was not a trace.

For long moments, none spoke; even Kyri was staring in disbelief.

Then Lady Shae gave the great spread-armed bow to the Phoenix Justiciar, lowering herself until her forehead nearly touched the shore, and there was an echoing rustle up and down the shore as everyone from Hiriista and Miri to the entirety of the gathered crowd followed her lead.

Only Tobimar and Poplock stood unbowed and looked into the gray eyes that still showed Kyri's wonder that she, *she* of all people, could be the focus of such gratitude and awe...and the heavy awareness of the responsibility that placed upon her. *And now she's become a symbol all over again, to these people, as much as she was to Evanwyl. Oh, Tobimar's got some of that too, but she's got the presence...and the god* acts *through her. They'll remember the Phoenix of Myrionar first and always.*

At last Shae rose. "We—we *all*—thank you, and through you Myrionar, for Its intercession on our behalf, and give praise to the Light, to Terian himself, for taking our fallen to his side." There was a murmur of agreement, echoing gratitude that covered the peninsula. "We can now return to our city with the sure knowledge that those we had lost await us in the Light, and wish us all joy and strength."

The stars had begun to shine out above, the clarity of the sky resonating with the purity that still somehow persisted about Sha Kaizatenzei Valatar, and as they began to move towards the broken, beautiful city, Poplock glanced back, and saw Kyri silhouetted against the fading crimson of the sunset.

Above her, just visible against the coming night, the stars of the Balanced Sword shimmered.

CHAPTER 4

"Ready," said Poplock.

Kyri looked around the large, rectangular room and saw Miri, Tobimar, and Lady Shae in combat poses. "Do you actually think he's going to lunge out of the tube to kill us all?" she demanded, feeling a somewhat unreasonable annoyance at this suspicion. *We don't* know *it's Rion,* she reminded herself. *It really can't be him. Can it?*

"Expect, no," Hriista said from beside her. "Think it is a possibility not to be utterly discounted, yes. You yourself admit that you *saw* your brother killed, were present when your priest failed to keep him alive due to his soul being torn apart. It is, therefore, vanishingly unlikely that this is indeed your brother. It is thus rather more likely that this is some form of trap. I am still unclear as to what the nature and purpose of such a trap would be, and the fact that apparently this tube was present for well over a year prior to your arrival argues against it being a trap in the conventional sense. But such caution is wise, would you not agree?"

"I . . . yes, I do," she admitted reluctantly. She sighed and looked down at the shadowy face behind the glassy port of the tube. "What do I have to do?"

"If this *is* your brother, it is obviously best that you be the first person he sees," Hiriista said. "By your account he was a formidable warrior, and awakening without warning to an unknown group of people could be . . . unfortunate for all concerned. Physically it appears that these tubes have provisions to keep the being within in good health for some indefinite time; we know that this should be the case as Zogen Josan was able to be retrieved and returned to duty as his living body relatively quickly without anyone noticing anything particularly odd. But I would still doubt that he is actually going to emerge with all faculties and physical capabilities at full strength."

He pointed to a series of three gold and blue catches. "Release those three—first this one, then the one on the other side, then the third—and then you can lift the cover up. Poplock and I have performed all other preparations; you may proceed when you are ready."

Kyri found herself hesitating, her fingers trembling as they rested on the first catch. *Am I afraid of finding out it's not him, or am I afraid of what it will mean if it* is *him? What* will *it mean if it is?*

With an effort she banished the questions. *They'll be answered once I open this thing.* With swift, precise motions, she unsnapped the catches, the smooth *clack* of their operation echoing around the laboratory that was currently being borrowed from one of Kaizatenzei's best alchemists. Taking a breath, she threw the cover back.

The top of the casketlike tube was hinged in the vicinity of the figure's feet. As soon as the cover had risen nearly vertical, it seemed to trigger something within; the cloudy liquid with its faint, sharp smell began to drain out the bottom of the tube, running swiftly towards the drain set in the floor. Slowly the liquid level dropped and the figure within was revealed; lighter-skinned than she, blond hair matted, and features she knew almost as well as her own. *It's Rion! No . . . it's Rion's* face, she corrected herself. *I've heard it said that everyone has a double in some other town. Maybe this is Rion's double, someone I've never met and never would have.*

But the coincidence that this "double" would have been sealed in a tube "a year or two" ago—perhaps, even, the same time that Rion had died—how likely was that?

Liquid dribbled from the figure's nose; a blue-green light shimmered from the sides of the tube and the liquid *fountained* from his nose; the chest suddenly rose and fell.

With abruptness that startled her, blue eyes snapped open and the figure half-sat up, a weak, pathetic scream wheezing from the mouth that was open in a horrified "O." The eyes blinked, then focused on her. "K-Kyri . . ."

It was her brother's voice, speaking her name. She *couldn't* forget that, couldn't possibly be mistaking it for any other voice. "R-Rion?"

He took a deep breath, then coughed, reached up a hand to grip her arm shakily, spoke, staring at her with horror still written across his face. "The . . . Justiciars . . . Kyri, they're corrupt . . . it was *Thornfalcon*, Kyri, Thornfalcon who . . ."

His other hand moved to his stomach and froze. He tore his gaze from her and looked down, then back up in disbelief. "What . . . was it a nightmare? I . . ."

She didn't know what to say or how to respond. It *sounded* like Rion, it *looked* like Rion, it was saying what Rion would say if, somehow, he had been brought back from the moment of his death, yet . . .

In that moment it seemed that the young man became aware of the surroundings. "W-w-where am I?"

"You're in the city of Valatar in the country of Kaizatenzei," Miri said, apparently having decided at least for the moment that he wasn't dangerous.

"What do you remember last?" Hiriista said.

Rion (Kyri couldn't help but think of him as Rion now) blinked and his brow furrowed at the sight of the mazakh, but then he shrugged slowly. "I . . . had finally found the proof I needed that the Justiciars were not what they seemed, and I was running home, when Thornfalcon caught up with me. We dueled, but he—"

His gaze snapped back to Kyri. "Kyri, he's a *monster*, he's not even *human*, I couldn't beat him, even Myrionar's power was—"

She found herself laying a hand on his arm. "Rion, it's all right. It's over. Thornfalcon's dead."

"*Dead?*" He stared with comical disbelief. "*How?*"

"I killed him myself. Though not without a lot of help."

"You . . . ?" His eyes finally seemed to focus on what she was wearing, and the horror drained away, slowly replaced with dawning wonder. "By . . . the . . . *Balance*. You? A Justiciar? My little sister, a *Justiciar?*" He started to rise, but his arms wouldn't support him enough to let him stand. "But . . . I don't recognize that Raiment."

"You found out the Justiciars were corrupt," she said. "So once

Myrionar answered my prayers...well, actually," she blushed, remembering, "once Myrionar answered my *demands*, I had to go get the Spiritsmith to make uncorrupted Raiment."

He burst out laughing, and it was Rion's laugh—weak, interspersed with fits of coughing, but Rion's laugh, oh, so very much. "You *demanded* something of Myrionar? And then went and found the Spiritsmith to...*how long has it been?*"

She thought back over what had happened: Rion's funeral, packing and traveling over the Great Road to Zarathanton, confronting Myrionar in the Forest Sea, finding the Spiritsmith and gaining her Raiment...killing Mist Owl and Shrike and nearly being killed by Thornfalcon...then all the terrible and wonderful adventures since that took them through Rivendream Pass and Kaizatenzei to where she sat now..."Almost two years, Rion."

"Two *years*?" He fell silent, staring first at her, then looking around the room, studying everyone and everything with the careful, considered gaze that she remembered so well. "Where is Urelle?"

A pang of worry that she had repressed for months resurfaced. "I...I wish I knew for sure. We left Evanwyl—went to Zarathanton, and...well, after I was chosen and headed out..." she stopped. "Oh, gods, Rion, it's too much to explain right now."

"Especially," said Tobimar, stepping up, "since we have much more important questions to be answered. I'm sorry, Kyri," he said to her, and she could see his genuine sympathy, "but we can't hold off on this."

Rion raised an eyebrow, then glanced up. "I suppose you know what you are doing here. More than I do, at any rate. But could I get out of this...elaborate coffin and get some *clothes* on?"

Miri burst out giggling. "Our apologies!" she said. "Poplock, could you..."

"No problem." The little Toad hopped onto the edge of the tube, Rion regarding him with bemusement, and did a mumbled gesture that caused a rainbow mist to march from Rion's head to his toes, leaving him—and the interior of the casket—perfectly clean and dry. Hiriista handed Rion a robe. "That will do for now, I trust."

"Sufficient to be acceptable, yes," Rion agreed, and slipped it on and tied it before standing slowly up; he wavered and Kyri caught his elbow, steadying him. "I guess I am *not* entirely myself," he muttered.

She guided him to a table on the other side of the room and let him sit down; the others followed and took their own seats around the table. She remained standing for a minute, worrying, before she forced herself to sit.

"Before we do anything else, I need to introduce you," she said. "Rion, this is Tobimar Silverun, Seventh of Seven of Skysand. The Toad on his shoulder is Poplock Duckweed; together with another friend of theirs, Xavier Ross, they saved me from Thornfalcon's trap and helped me finally kill him and wipe out the monsters he had brought into Evanwyl."

Rion bowed from his waist. "Then both greetings and my thanks, Tobimar and Poplock, for helping my sister avenge our parents' deaths—and I suppose my own—and making my country a cleaner place."

"Believe me," Poplock said, "it was our pleasure. Some people just need a lot of killing, and Thorny there, he was about top of the list."

"Yes, he was," Rion said, not even a trace of a smile visible.

"The *mazakh* with the magnificent crest is Hiriista, finest magewright in Kaizatenzei, and a wonderful companion to have on any journey."

Hiriista shook his crest in pleased embarrassment as Rion acknowledged him.

"And this is Miri, Light of Kaizatenzei—that means one of their protectors and warriors, like the Justiciars back home—and one of my new and best friends."

Miri nodded and blushed at Kyri's praise, but Kyri felt it was important to emphasize her position both personal and professional. It couldn't hurt to make sure that an ex-demon remembered why they decided to make that change, and more importantly would help prevent unfortunate reactions when they had to discuss her nature in front of Rion.

"Finally, this is Lady Shae, the Lady of Light, ruler of this country."

For that Rion *did* rise and do a proper bow of respect. "You should have introduced her *first*, sister. Don't you know etiquette at *all*?"

She giggled, and Shae laughed and responded, "Nay, young man, she introduced the saviors of my country first, and so I, being the ruler who made certain…errors that led to it being in danger in the first place, am truly the last that needed introduction."

Rion looked at her with half-disbelieving eyes. "Savior of another country—that I never heard of—*after* managing to become a Justiciar *and* killing off Thornfalcon? You've been awfully busy, little sister."

"Yes, she has," Tobimar agreed. "But we have to turn to the more serious question of whether you have the right to *call* her 'sister.'"

Rion's head snapped around. "*What?*"

"Well, that was a little more blunt than *I* would have recommended putting it," Poplock said with a kick of reproof to the blue-eyed Prince, "but, yes, basically. See, you died two years ago in front of your sister and that nice old priest Arbiter Kelsley, who practically killed himself trying to put your soul back together—and *failed*. You had your funeral and everything, and your body was there for it all. So...how can you be here *at all*, and still be Rion Vantage?"

His wide blue gaze returned to her, eyes now wide with shock. "Kyri? Is this...true?"

"Yes," she said, and restrained the impulse to comfort him. *My heart thinks this is Rion...but my head can't see how that's possible.*

"Well." He sat in silence for a few moments. "I certainly see the problem," he said finally. "If my body, or what's left of it, is back in Evanwyl, and I died in front of Kyri...then I shouldn't be here. But by the Balance, I sure *feel* like Rion Vantage!"

Hiriista leaned forward. "You mentioned what happened to you, Rion—for I suppose that is the best name for us to use for now, provisionally. Think back. Think *carefully*. Tell us the details of your last thoughts, and I especially want you to pay attention to those which may seem nightmare or delirium; this may provide us with key insight as to what truly happened to you...or what was used to create you."

Rion shuddered. "I...suppose so. But while it has been two years for you, for me it was...just moments ago, by my memory." He paused. "And yet...yet it feels longer. As though my death was far in the past."

"Go on," Miri said gently.

Rion drew in a deep breath and let it out. "All right.

"I was at the Justiciar's Retreat, trying to find the last piece of evidence I needed to prove what I had come to suspect—that the Justiciars were, somehow, false. I don't have to explain *that* to you now, I guess, but do you realize how *hard* it was for me to even *think* of it?"

Kyri would have laughed, but it hurt too much. "No, you don't, Rion. Even after you...died, they fooled us again. I only found out the truth almost by accident."

"Well...The problem for me was that while everyone *acted* as though Mist Owl was supposed to be the leader, he would often put off a decision and then come back with his orders an hour or a day later. He usually excused this as his preferring to think on things, and at his age that took time, but somehow it *felt* as though he was going to ask someone else for advice and coming back with his orders later. And every once in a while it seemed that he would glance at someone else—usually Thornfalcon—as though seeking confirmation.

"So I managed to enter the sanctum, where the leader of the Justiciars is supposed to hold council in case of emergencies, special events, you know the kind of thing. I'd done this as carefully and quietly as I could, even praying to Myrionar for the ability to hide myself and pierce illusions. And as I said, I managed to get the door of the sanctum open and looked in.

"It was very dark, with only a faint light about a quarter of the way across what was a much, much bigger room than I'd imagined. But there was a person outlined against that faint light, and I could recognize the thin, tall figure easily: Thornfalcon. He was talking to one of the other Justiciars—Skyharrier, I'm pretty sure—and the bit I heard mentioned my name in a tone that wasn't positive.

"Honestly, I hadn't expected anyone to be in that room, or that if anyone *was* there that they'd be in the dark. Even as I heard my name, Thornfalcon glanced around and I knew he couldn't possibly miss me outlined in the light from the hall. I slammed the door to as soon as I heard Thornfalcon's sword sliding out of its sheath, and threw a sealing prayer at the lock, then ran like Hell itself was after me."

His face was even paler. "I think it was, then. I called on Myrionar, and I was *fast*, so fast that even Mist Owl barely had time to turn and gape as I passed him and was out into the forest. I knew that all I had to do was get to the temple. I was sure in my heart that Kelsley was still untouched, still a man of the Balance, and so I didn't have to hold back, just run, run faster than any man, so fast with the power of Myrionar that they would never catch me.

"And... I thought they wouldn't. I was sure. It takes many hours to get to the retreat normally, you know that, but I think I was almost home in two, the jungle *flying* by, Myrionar's power buoying me up, and I had hope, Kyri, I was sure that Myrionar would not fail me—

"—and then I saw Thornfalcon step out of the shadows ahead of me, smiling."

Kyri shuddered herself, and saw both Tobimar and Poplock shiver. They had faced more powerful adversaries... but she wasn't sure that any of them, even the parasitic *itrichel*, could have matched Thornfalcon for sheer, vile malevolence.

Rion looked at them and managed a faint, wan smile. "I don't suppose I need to describe how I discovered that I was outmatched."

"No," Hiriista said. "But you *must* describe your final moments, to the very end, in as much detail as you can. Because there we may find a clue as to whether you are an impostor, or in some wise the true Rion, impossible though that would seem."

"Of course." Rion's shoulders hunched, part of him trying to crouch, to hide and protect himself from the hideous memory. "Could I... have something to drink? Stronger than water, please."

Kyri reached into her neverfull pack and brought out a bottle of Gharis Sunset—an ale that was one of her favorites, but that Rion really didn't like at all. "Here."

Rion took the bottle, pulled the seal aside absently, and took a swig. Immediately he made a face. "Oh, *Balance*, I should've guessed you'd have packed some of that swill along," he muttered. "Oh well... it's better than nothing right now."

If he isn't really Rion, he's incredibly well-trained.

The blue eyes were haunted as he continued. "Thornfalcon and I exchanged several passes of blades. I'd sparred with him before, but I knew even before we drew swords that he had been holding back. Then again, so had I, some.

"At first it looked like we might be even... and that meant that with the Vantage strength and my endurance, I had a good chance,

I could wear him down, eventually hammer Skytalon right through his guard. But then I heard screams in the distance and I saw him *smile*—the coldest, most bone-chilling smile I've ever seen."

Kyri couldn't repress another shudder, remembering that smile herself.

"I remember demanding from him what he'd done, and he explained very calmly that the entire idea was to arrange my death in a way that none would ever associate with the Justiciars." He drew a shaky breath. "And then he...he *changed*. This huge, dark *shadow* seemed to grow out of him, a shadow with moon-blank eyes and huge claws and spectral fur, and I suddenly felt my sword sagging, feeling as though it had become a dozen times heavier."

His hands tightened on the bottle, and there was an abrupt *crack*; loam-dark ale foamed across the table as Rion jumped back with an apologetic curse.

Poplock rolled his eyes, but repeated his cleansing spell; the table and Rion were neat again, though there was a sparkling mass of broken glass in front of his seat.

Rion smiled weakly. "Wasn't even aware I was doing that."

"Don't concern yourself with it," Lady Shae said, and gestured; the glass vanished. "Continue, please."

He nodded. "Of course." He swallowed, then went on. "I called on Myrionar, of course, and for a moment I felt stronger...but as we fought I felt my power *draining* away and I finally understood what kind of a monster Thornfalcon was. But that was far too late, and his sword started carving me apart—one cut at a time, and with every cut I felt my strength departing, my endurance failing, the night growing darker, with him laughing, laughing all the time..."

He paused. "...or was he? Part of me says he stopped laughing at the very end, but another part says I heard that laughter for a long, long time."

"You don't remember me reaching you? I talked to you, Rion! You tried to tell me what was going on, you just couldn't before..." Her voice wavered and she stopped.

Rion's brow furrowed and he was silent a moment. "N-no. I'm sorry, I can't remember a thing. And I *wanted* to see you, so much, Kyri. You and Urelle and Aunt Victoria. But it just went black, with that laughter..."

He trailed off again, but this time thinking. "The laughter *did* go on a long time. But then...I don't know how long, I wasn't really *conscious* I think; these are more impressions than memories, if you know what I mean?" He looked anxiously at Hiriista, who gave a slow assenting nod.

"So after a long time the laughing faded, and I felt cold, *icy* cold, and...I don't know, I felt as though I had suddenly been brought into a gigantic chamber, a chamber filled with the essence of ice. But there was fire, too. And it wasn't either. Myrionar's *Blade*, I can't say what I mean."

"You mean to say that these were impressions, analogies, not literal truths," Hiriista said. "You do not, for instance, believe you were brought into an actual giant chamber."

"Yes, that's it. I'd been somewhere...warm yet deadly, with laughter, and now I was somewhere huge and both hot and lethally cold, and instead of laughter the cold was amused and then..."

Kyri was so tense she realized her nails were digging into her palms. She forced her hands to relax. "Then?"

Rion stared into unguessable distances. "Then...I was forgotten, I think. Or put aside? I don't know. I can't make *sense* of these sensations. My words just aren't...it's something I *feel* but it wasn't real, not like here. But after some time I can't guess I finally I felt something change around me, more darkness, but with feelings that weren't all dark and laughing and hate-filled, and then everything faded away completely..." he glanced to her, "...until I opened my eyes and saw you."

Kyri didn't know what to think, and from his frown neither did Tobimar. But Poplock and Hiriista were exchanging glances, and she saw both Miri and Lady Shae nodding slowly.

"All right, it seems that made sense to most of you," she said finally. "What did that mean? What happened? *Is* he Rion?"

The four looked at each other, then the others nodded at Hiriista, who rose and bowed slightly.

"There are...tests I would like to do, but I believe that we all have a good idea what happened...and if we are correct, then he is, indeed, Rion—or a part of him."

"A *part* of me?" Rion echoed.

"A new body—manufactured from what I cannot be sure—but with a fragment of your soul placed within, to grow and heal. If we interpret those images correctly, Thornfalcon had taken parts of your soul, but instead of simply consuming them, gave them to someone else, I would presume this Patron—"

"Who is almost certainly Viedraverion," Miri put in.

"—as I said, his Patron, possibly the Demonlord she has named, and certainly a being of far greater power than Thornfalcon. The Patron kept your spirit-fragment intact within himself or possibly some sort of spirit container, and eventually placed it into the body you now wear and shipped you off to Wieran. For what *purpose* I cannot fathom, but this would appear to be the likely scenario."

Rion was studying his arms and hands as though they would give him a clue as to how this had all happened. Kyri was, however, more interested in something else. "Miri, who is 'Viedraverion'? You've mentioned him to us earlier but in all the other work we've been doing we didn't have time to talk."

"Viedraverion," Lady Shae answered, "is one of the most powerful Demonlords—a Child of the First to Kerlamion himself. In fact, Viedra is supposedly the *actual* first child of Kerlamion, which would make him vastly more powerful than any Child of the Second and even most other Firsts."

"He...helped us a lot," Miri said hesitantly, something which caused Rion's head to snap up in consternation.

"Sorry, Rion. You're not the only mixed-up entity here," Poplock said. "Our two good friends over there *used* to be Demonlords themselves before they changed their minds. And that wasn't all that long ago."

Rion blinked. "*Used* to be Demonlords?"

"It's a long story," Miri said uncomfortably. "And I'll tell it to you, later. But let me finish. He was...well, not a *direct* ally, but a resource. He sent Weiran to us, let us know you were coming, verified that Tobimar was the Key, all that sort of thing, but that's not really the important thing. The *really* important thing is that he's the architect of Kerlamion's grand invasion."

Kyri felt her mouth drop open. It took a moment to close it again. "Wait. Are you saying that...that the monster responsible for making Thornfalcon, for corrupting the Justiciars, is *also* the one who arranged the Sauran King's assassination, the invasion of Artania and Aegeia and—"

"—yes. I am saying exactly that. He has been living in Evanwyl most of the time, and I think his private project is there, somehow, but he's been directing almost everything that Father and his forces have been doing."

"Terian's *Light*," Tobimar murmured. "I remember talking with King Toron about all this; we couldn't figure out who was responsible for the coordinated unrest; we even contemplated it being one of the Great Wolves that assassinated the prior Sauran King, because of the perfection of the disguise."

Poplock bounced assent. "But we knew that couldn't be the case because this was an assault by demons and lots of other nasties, all across the continent, and the Wolves don't work for anyone except—"

"Yes," Miri said. "Except the Godslayer, Virigar, their own king. They do not work with any other creatures, which is just as well."

"But it being the first child of Kerlamion, one of the most powerful of all demons? That fits, especially with the tricks he might have gotten from Master Wieran along the way. And this all connects to Evanwyl somehow."

"I presume so," Miri said. "I've seen his current human guise many times; would you like to see it?"

Kyri's hands tightened into fists. "See the monster responsible for all this? Oh, yes. I want to know him when I see him."

Miri concentrated for a moment, then touched one of the gems set in her left armlet.

Light shimmered in the air between them, coalesced into a human figure.

Kyri found herself on her feet, her chair clattering away unnoticed, feeling as though a terrible abyss had opened at her feet; Rion had risen too, and Tobimar as well, all of them staring in disbelieving shock. "Oh, *drought*," Poplock finally said, and his tone was utterly devoid of his usual humor.

Before them, floating perfectly defined in midair, was the handsome, blond-haired figure of Jeridan Velion, Watchland of Evanwyl.

CHAPTER 5

"It makes all too much sense," Tobimar said quietly.

He saw Kyri nod, still pale under her dark skin. Rion had nearly collapsed after that last revelation, and it was clear that he needed rest badly. Now he and Kyri stood at the edge of Valatar, and he rested a hand on her shoulder.

She started at that, then nodded again. "Of course. And fits perfectly with that *sensation* I had around him—the one that first led me to be suspicious of the Unity Guard."

"That's right, you sometimes really liked him and sometimes got a creepy feeling about him," Poplock said, nibbling on a beetle he'd caught bumbling by.

"Exactly. Just like the Unity Guard when they were being switched from their real selves to their other . . . mode of operation, I guess?"

"But if that's the case . . . this Demonlord isn't a simple Eternal Servant type simulacrum or anything," Tobimar said, trying to make some sense out of the situation. "What does this . . . two sided sense mean?"

Kyri shook her head. "I can't say for sure. Just . . . there were times that I'm absolutely sure that the man I was talking to *was* a man, and one who sincerely cared about me and my family. Perhaps the demon possesses him on occasion? Maybe this Viedraverion has trapped the soul of the original Jeridan? I don't know, but I'm sure that it's not as simple as the demon simply *pretending*."

"I'm sure too." Tobimar remembered how accurate her senses were; he wasn't sure if that was *because* she was the Justiciar of Myrionar, or if one of the reasons Myrionar had chosen her to begin with was that she had such a keen ability to see through deception. "Though Thornfalcon fooled you."

"That's been *bothering* me a lot, too," Kyri admitted. "But I *think* I know why. I'd been raised with him around—much more than the Watchland, too—and with everyone treating him on face value. I think I'd learned to shove those warnings away even when I was very young, because it was *obvious* that he couldn't really be a bad man. And by the time I was older, he'd really perfected his role and, maybe, could use his powers to hide his very nature."

He saw her face suddenly lighten with surprise. "What is it?"

Kyri looked both angry and sad. "Just remembered another clue that I missed. When the Justiciars came into the house and gave me their . . . apology, something I guess was almost honest for some and less so for others . . . they kept glancing back, through the door, watching someone else. I thought it was just worry about privacy, and later I wondered for a while if it was Mist Owl they were watching . . . but now I realize it was the Watchland."

She looked up towards the green-shadowed leaves of the trees before them, slightly touched with gray as a huge cloud changed the sunlight to dusk. "We can't wait much longer."

"No, we can't," agreed Poplock. "Tobimar's solved his riddle, you've paid us back for our help, it's time for us to help get to the bottom of yours. And with what *we* just found out . . ."

Tobimar cursed. "Great *Terian*. The Watchland's in charge of your entire *country*, and we just left him there while we walked off into what everyone thought was a deathtrap!" He had a sudden vision of what could have happened to that tiny, isolated country with a Demonlord in charge, one who now had no one to hold him back and whose plans were now well underway. Even Kyri's *Sho-Ka-Taida* Lythos would be no match for such a creature; Tobimar remembered the other people he had met and come to know during the weeks he'd remained in Evanwyl—Arbiter Kelsley, priest of the Balance and one of the most truly *holy* men Tobimar had ever been privileged to meet; little Sasha Rithair, Evanwyl's resident Summoner and all-purpose magician who'd done her best to teach Poplock her craft; Master of House Vanstell, dryly competent and faithful retainer; Minuzi, tall, dark-haired apothecary and housewife who despite her business found time to visit Kyri often as a neighbor and family friend rather than someone looking for the "Justiciar Phoenix."

The thought of them under the rule—or worse—of the demonlord who had planned the assassination of the Sauran King was almost more than he could bear. "You're right, we have to get back. With us out of the way, there's no telling what he's been doing since we left."

"Yeah," Poplock agreed, "and even our friend Xavier might be in trouble. He *said* he'd be trying to meet up with us once he finished his trip, right?"

"*Balance*, you're right. And he started out weeks before we left for the Spiritsmith. If he actually *made* it to the Mountain..." Kyri trailed off. "Well, he either did or he didn't. But he could easily be on his way back *right now*. And if he gets there and doesn't know what Jeridan is..."

"...things could get *real* ugly," the Toad finished. "Lots of reasons to go, not too many to stay."

Tobimar could see her hesitation, and took her hand. "I know—Rion. Don't worry, Kyri. Do you think I'd tell you to just leave your brother—if that's what he really is—behind?"

She looked embarrassed. "I...don't want to make other people wait just for—"

"It's *not* just for you. Or him, for that matter," Tobimar said emphatically. "His presence here can't be a coincidence. Maybe what they planned was to have him sent back to Evanwyl at a certain point. Wieran would have been able to implant all sorts of directives in him without him even knowing. But Wieran never got around to it, not with his main project consuming his time. Maybe Rion was a backup plan. But there's no way this doesn't connect to you, and we're not ignoring it, or making you ignore it either."

She looked at them both gratefully, and then hugged him tightly; Tobimar could see one of her hands give Poplock a pat, including him in the embrace. "Thank you both. And if you're right...if Hiriista's right, and that really *is* Rion..."

"...then we'd be plain *stupid* to leave behind another real honest-to-gods Justiciar of Myrionar when we're going to face down a demonlord," Poplock finished for her. "If their country didn't need 'em so bad right now, I'd be begging Miri and Shae to come with us."

Tobimar thought of that and smiled. "And I think we could probably convince them even so; they owe us a lot, and I can tell that Miri, at least, would rather like to see Evanwyl and the rest of the world as it is now, rather than the way it was thousands of years ago." He shook his head. "But that wouldn't be the right thing to do."

"No," agreed Kyri, still not quite letting him go. "Kaizatenzei *does* need them, and I think *they* need Kaizatenzei."

"Oh yeah," Poplock agreed. "We don't want them away from the bright shininess and going back to being demons. They only changed their minds a little while ago. Let that set a bit, I think, kinda like pourstone. 'Course, I don't know how long that shiny perfection's going to last now that the Sun's gone poof."

Tobimar shrugged. "You're probably right that it will fade in time," he said, finally stepping away from Kyri after a quick kiss. "But I'd guess that'll take quite a while, especially since the force that was causing all the corruption beneath was probably Sanamaveridion, and he's *gone*."

"I hope so," Kyri said, looking out at the peaceful shining of stars above the city. "I'd like to think it will always be like this."

"So do I," Poplock said, but his tone was serious. "But that's sure not gonna happen if we wait much longer."

Tobimar nodded. It had been a wonderful, terrifying, and in some ways *healing* journey through Kaizatenzei. But now they knew that they had left the architect of the world's disasters— of what in fact must be the next Chaoswar—behind them, and Viedraverion was surely not idle.

Time was running out.

CHAPTER 6

"They...they seem to be exactly as they were," Bolthawk murmured, in a tone of mingled fear and awe.

It followed the false Justiciar's gaze to where Mist Owl stood in conversation with the earlier Silver Eagle, Gareth Lamell, and Skyharrier. "Oh, indeed, they *are* exactly as they were." It chuckled. "I suppose your surprise comes from your first reintroduction to your fallen comrades?"

Assured by its tone that this was not a dangerous subject, Bolthawk nodded. "They stank of the grave, their eyes were dull, they seemed graverisen, nothing more. But over the last week..."

"Yes, they *have* perked up quite a bit since then, haven't they?" It gestured for Bolthawk to take a firmer grip on the damaged piece of Silver Eagle's raiment which was currently on the creature's workbench, and then began gently hammering on the metal; faint ripples of green and shadow flickered from the armor as the being worked on it, bringing the armor back together. *Ahh, Spiritsmith, your work is supernal; a shame it had to be marred so. My repairs will be serviceable, but hardly up to your standard. Then again, you would rather they were not repaired at all than serving my purposes, so I suppose that's as you'd prefer it.*

"The fact is that for one such as myself, bringing the dead back *fully* takes a bit of time," it said, continuing the discussion. "The body must be either repaired or in some cases rebuilt, the soul brought back, and the connection between the two must

35

heal as the body...*learns*, I suppose is the best term, how to live again. By now, that process is quite complete."

"You mean...they are not just wraiths or revenants?"

"They are as fully alive as they were before they met their deaths, yes. If I were somehow felled tomorrow, they would not collapse and turn to moldering corpses or anything of that nature. They are not imitations of their prior selves, Bolthawk. They are precisely who they appear to be...just with some rather unique experiences that you have been fortunate enough to avoid thus far."

Bolthawk's expression was a delicious mingling of awe and fear. "Never have I heard of anyone reviving the dead after so long a span of time, in the case of Gareth, many years indeed. Not even the gods."

"It does, in truth, require some rather unique circumstances, I admit. But more than that you have no need to know."

"Where is Thornfalcon, then? Surely you would have wanted *him* back more than the rest of us."

Your stolid exterior, Child of Odin, is rather misleading when you show so clear an evaluation of the world around you. "You are of course correct, Bolthawk; he had the best overall...mindset for the job as I envisioned it. Unfortunately, and rather ironically, his journey along the path to become one of *my* people led to him meeting the *final* death, one from which even I could not retrieve him."

"That path gave him a weakness, then?" Bolthawk's face suddenly went pale; it could tell that Bolthawk was realizing that the question itself was potentially dangerous, one that could draw an immediate and fatal reaction.

Instead it laughed. "Certainly it did, Bolthawk. Of course poor Thornfalcon, being so new to his power, was far more vulnerable to that weakness than I; I would have been wounded by the same strikes, but not slain, let alone had my soul shredded irretrievably. All things have their weaknesses, even the King of All Hells...or me. But while I might, if it amused me, tell you *his* weakness, I think I will leave mine for others to guess."

"I would expect nothing else, sir."

It grinned again, and straightened, looking at the now almost invisible seam. *Almost done.* "It wouldn't do you a *great* deal of good, Bolthawk; the oaths you and the others have sworn would make it inadvisable for you to plan a rebellion, even if I not only told you my weakness but allowed you to prepare to make use of it. It's more a dramatic preference than anything else; all things must be done *properly*, you understand?"

Bolthawk started to nod, then cocked his head, and shrugged. "I can't say I do, sir."

"I suppose not. If you live long enough, perhaps we shall have this conversation again and your answer may change. But—"

A signal touched its consciousness in a way another might have described hearing a faint but significant sound. "Ah. I have something to attend to. Clean this up and lay it aside; I'll complete the work later."

It took only a few minutes to reach the inner sanctum of the Retreat and place the silver-and-gold scroll on its pedestal. "Yes?"

The scroll did not show a face; the person on the other end did not have the capability to make a full connection. "Initial attempt complete. Progress as expected."

"Good. Do not contact me more often than once every three weeks. The more you disturb the matrix, the greater the chance you will be discovered. Let its truth hide your own."

"Understood. I will only act under the agreed-upon conditions."

"Correct. Thank you for your report."

It leaned back in the chair with a smile. Placing agents at the right places, with the right preparation, could be *so* much more effective than sending armies or monsters. And—as with Miri, the poor girl—it wasn't even necessary that the agent understood what their true goals were, or even that they follow its literal instructions. Many agents, again including Miri as well as Master Wieran and Kalshae, were best when they thought *it* was *their* agent, or at most ally, and thought that by disregarding its instructions they would foil its plans.

But if you knew how such people thought, you could make sure that even their betrayals were *part* of the plan. So far, everything was going according to that plan. The most dangerous—and by the same principle, most entertaining—parts were coming soon, however.

But, it reminded itself, even the most careful manipulator could also be manipulated. And as the endgame approached, it had to watch the board more carefully than ever. Even the smallest piece—like, say, a Toad—could upset plans years in the making.

That would be extremely costly for it; setting up these precise conditions had taken more years than even Thornfalcon would have believed. It certainly did not want to lose *this* particular game.

And yet...if that were to happen...wouldn't that be *exciting?*

Smiling broadly, it turned and strode out to rejoin the Justiciars.

CHAPTER 7

"You know, I really *hate* to say goodbye," Poplock said, as he shook Hiriista's extended claw between his forepaws.

"As do I, more than I can express. We make excellent team-mates, all of us, do we not?"

"Beyond any doubt," Kalshae said with a laugh. "I learned this to my sorrow ... and my joy. A strange yet satisfying end to many things, despite our losses."

"And one that's resolved so many of our questions," Tobimar said. "Not just my quest, but some of Kyri's as well."

Poplock bounce-nodded. "Including where all those monsters came from."

The experimental laboratory where Wieran had worked on his life-shaping had been—as Poplock had suspected—down the third portion of the underground portion of the Valatar Palace, the branch to the right as one came down the stairs from the Throneroom. Shae and Miri had both verified that it was a place that contained almost uncounted monstrous things—both "successes," like the enhanced *itrichel* they'd encountered in Jenten's Mill, and far more failures—which were the things that had come through the gateway at Thornfalcon's estate.

"Wieran had some way of controlling them, preventing them from tearing each other apart—mostly," Miri had said. "I asked him once why he didn't just destroy them, and he looked at me—as he often did—as if I were an idiot, and gave two reasons: first, that they represented *data* that he might want to reexamine, and second, that even the failures might serve a purpose."

"Yeah, like being cannon fodder, as Xavier once put it, for someone like Thornfalcon," Poplock had responded.

But whatever might have been down there before, it was no more. The third corridor, and whatever lay beyond, had collapsed. Uncounted thousands of tons of rock had obliterated Wieran's third laboratory.

Poplock bounced again, shaking off the memory. "Definitely good to have those answers, but now that we've got the one answer about who the Big Bad is, we *really* need to get moving."

"I'm sorry we have to go—" Kyri began.

"*Light*, will you stop apologizing?" Miri said with exasperated fondness. "You came to our country, woke me to the light, defeated our enemies—including the Elderwyrm himself—and helped us get back on our feet. You've got to take care of your *own* people. Of *course* I wish you could stay—so does all Kaizatenzei. But you need to go."

"Shame old Wieran's upper workshop got ruined," Poplock said. "We might've been able to get a couple of those teleport gems and cut weeks off the trip."

Tobimar shook his head. "Do either of you really think you could have figured out how he did all that—even if his lab was intact?"

After a hesitation, Hiriista shook his head and hissed a sigh. "No. No, he was far, far ahead of us. He had clearly mastered aspects of magic that I have not an inkling of."

"Shame he was a total nutcase," Poplock said. Then he sat up higher on Tobimar's shoulder. "I guess you guys let everyone *else* know we were leaving?"

Kyri stopped dead on the top step of the mansion they had been staying in while part of Valatar Castle was restored, and stared in consternation.

A cheer so loud and deep that it became a roar shook the air, and the gathered people of Sha Kaizatenzei Valatar waved and cheered again. "Kyri! Tobimar! Poplock!"

Miri and Shae laughed at Kyri's expression. Poplock had to admit that she looked pretty funny. "Oh, how, now?" Shae said with a broad grin, and then gave Kyri a sisterly hug that almost tipped her over—Shae being significantly taller and bigger than

Kyri. "Did you think we would let you leave our city without the people knowing, and at least telling you with their voices how much you will be missed?"

Her face three shades darker than normal, Kyri muttered, "I had *hoped* you would..."

"Come *on*, Kyri!" Miri grabbed her hand and started pulling her down the stairs. "You're leaving now, but we've got something to show you on the way."

"Something to show *me?*"

The crowd had looked disorganized to Poplock, but as the two women approached it parted in a straight line up Dawnlight Way, the central street of the city. The rest of the little party followed Kyri and Miri; Poplock glanced to his right.

Rion returned his glance. "I still can't believe my little sister's come so far, so fast."

"She had a lot of motivation. And a little help," Poplock said. Inwardly, Poplock still wasn't completely convinced that "Rion" was who he appeared to be. Oh, the story made *sense*, and it was hard to imagine that someone could have planned out the sequence of events that put him in their party...but Poplock felt that there was an awful lot of evidence that the head baddie—this "Viedraverion"—was just exactly that good. Still, Rion had passed all the tests they could figure. There *were* a few minor quirks of magic around him, but since there was no telling yet exactly how his new body could have been supplied, that wasn't very informative.

"Still..." He gave a disbelieving chuckle. "I thought *I* was the one who was going to be the Justiciar in the family, the hero to bring our parents' murderers to justice. And here's my sister doing the job for me, while I was...dead? Or something close to it."

The crowd closed in behind them, not quite close enough to be intimidating, but following the group as they moved up the street.

"Just be glad she and the rest of us did, or you'd still be in that tank. Anyway, as I understand it, you're something pretty darn tough yourself. We can use all the help we can get."

Rion ran his fingers through hair vastly lighter than his sister's; according to Kyri, Rion got all the traits of their mother, while Kyri and their little sister Urelle both took after their father. "I'm pretty good, yes—and now that I'm feeling more myself, I'll be able to help." He glanced down at the armor he was wearing. "This stuff isn't *bad*, and I'm grateful to our hosts...but I need to get better armor and weapons. If we're going up against the other Justiciars..."

"We'll keep an eye out, but from what he said, the Spiritsmith was heading out a little while after we left, so I don't think we can get you a real replacement for the one you lost."

"I didn't *lose* it. I was killed *in* it." When he spoke with the angry iron in his voice, Rion *did* sound very like Kyri. "And I plan to get it back from the people who took it from me—the ones that played at being our friends."

Poplock bounce-nodded. "That's our plan, too." He glanced up. "Ooo, looks like we're almost to the show-and-tell—whatever it is."

Miri and Kyri were standing in front of a building that Poplock thought, thinking back, had been some kind of large storefront before the big battle. Now the front was covered with a huge piece of cloth held in place by a few ropes; the little Toad squinted and was able to make out a few people standing on either side of the building, holding ropes. *Ah, it's an unveiling. They'll pull those ropes, and the cloth gets pulled apart like a giant curtain.*

"What's going on here?" Kyri asked, staring at the cream-white cloth as it rippled in the breeze coming down the street. There was a similar ripple in the chuckles that ran through the crowd.

"We wanted to make sure that you all saw this before you left." Shae raised her hand, and the veiling cloth fell away to each side.

Poplock stared, then wished he could grin as widely as Tobimar.

The face of the building had been reworked, its front now in deep sky blue with touches of silver and gold, and over the doorway, the symbol of the Balanced Sword. And clearly visible inside, by light shining down through what must be a skylight, was a statue of a tall woman holding an immense sword aloft—a sword that was suspending two great balance-pans on its point, one pan on each side.

Considering how they had to be doing this in little spurts of their spare time, probably dozens of them—they got her pretty well. The fall of the hair, the overall shape of the armor, and the stance—that was, beyond a doubt, Kyri Victoria Vantage, the Phoenix Justiciar.

"Oh, great *Balance*..." Kyri murmured, managing to combine joy, embarrassment, and shock into a single expression.

"I see we succeeded in hiding it from you," Hiriista said proudly.

Poplock looked over to the *mazakh* magewright narrowly. "And you didn't tell *me*?"

"Ahh, my friend, your first loyalty is to Tobimar and the Phoenix; I would not have strained your discretion so."

"Bah. It would clearly have been worth it."

"But you already *have* your own temples of the Light," Kyri was saying. "You don't need—"

"We don't *need* to," interrupted Shae gently. "We *want* to. Within the first *day* after the disaster I had *thirty-six* requests for a temple to your god Myrionar, to honor Its emissary on our behalf."

"But you put *me* as part of the *Balance*! That's... that's too much, it's using me to symbolize Myrionar. Please... Please, if you must, keep the statue, but... but put up a plain Balanced Sword, all right?"

Miri started to laugh, then saw the deadly seriousness of Kyri's face. "You mean it."

"Yeah, she does," Poplock said, bouncing to the Justiciar's shoulder. "It's a big thing in the religion—I've learned a lot about it, traveling with her. The fact that there *isn't* a face for Myrionar is important. Makes it so there's no arguing that Myrionar *really* favors humans, or *mazakh*, or Children of Odin, or Toads. It is purely for justice for all. Right, Kyri?"

"Yes, that's it. Thanks, Poplock. I...I don't want to offend any of you, it's... its so incredibly touching, I never expected this, but that *statue*, it's just too much..."

"Understood," Shae said firmly. "We shall move the statue to a place of honor that is not at the altar, and place the simpler sword and balance symbol above. We have only begun to understand your ways—most of what we did here came from Miri and Hiriista, who were present when you prepared your more extensive teachings for those in Jenten's Mill. We didn't dare ask you for similar writings at the time, not if the surprise was to remain a surprise."

Kyri smiled more naturally—it was easier to relax, Poplock guessed, if you weren't worried that your image was being used in a sacrilegious representation of your own religion. "I guess not. We were leaving now, but..."

"Fear not; as you know, the Unity Guard are now preparing to return to their customary cities. I will have one of them—Danrall, I think—go to Jenten's Mill and acquire a copy for use here in Valatar."

"No, leave that to me," Kyri said. "It's my *job* to spread Myrionar's faith, and we did plan to stop at Jenten's Mill so that Zogen would know that he had been right to worry...and does not have to worry any longer. Maybe he'll even bring it himself, and rejoin the Unity Guard."

"If you would do that for us, we would be very grateful," Shae said.

"*I* will be grateful," Kyri said, face darkening with several shades of embarrassment anew as she looked back towards her statue, "for you give Myrionar new life, so don't thank me anymore. Just...let us finish this quest. We'll come back, I promise!"

"*If* we survive," Poplock observed pointedly. "But yeah, all three of us will want to visit you again. Don't think you've seen the last of us."

Miri and Shae laughed and then bowed low. With a whispering rustle, the entire crowd echoed the gesture, a bow that rippled outward through the city like a wave. "Then be on your way, Phoenix Kyri, Tobimar Silverun, Poplock Duckweed, and Rion Vantage. May the Light shine upon you and illuminate your souls and the blessings of Kaizatenzei follow you always. Good luck," and Shae's face suddenly acquired a fierce grin, "and good *hunting.*"

The crowd rose and parted, and the four companions turned, walking towards the risen sun, from the steps of the Temple of Myrionar.

CHAPTER 8

With a slight groan of effort, Aran heaved himself over the sharp edge of the black-glass scar across the land. Ahead, he could see that the Necklace continued down a gentle slope a short distance away. If he'd been willing to walk down the dark-polished miniature canyon for another quarter mile, it would have ended due to that downward slope. But the slope rose again in the distance, and Aran Condor could see the smooth-crescent bite that had been carved out of the hill, directly in line with the glass valley.

Looking back, he could not repress another shiver of awe. The Elderwyrm's rage had carved the land like a sword straight from the forge, in lines from the battleground that cut irresistibly through everything in their path for incredible distances. This glassy ebony mark on the land ran past Syratenzei and, he thought, had even left a mark on the far-distant mountains ringing Kaizatenzei itself; depending on how the ground rose and the curve of the earth had presented itself, it had reached depths of *hundreds* of feet at points along the way, at one point boring straight through the earth as a vast black tunnel that was slowly flooding from both without and within.

And the Phoenix—and her companions—defeated this thing, surely, or the Dragon would reign supreme here ... if he had not simply leveled everything for a hundred miles.

The thought was beyond merely daunting—it was sometimes almost enough to make him reconsider his mission. Even the Demonshard Blade had hesitated at the thought of facing the

Elderwyrm, and it was really the Demonshard that offered Aran his only hope to overcome the Phoenix and, finally, get his vengeance for Phoenix's murder of his friend and adoptive father, Shrike.

He shook his head and took a grip of his courage. *It's a little late now. You asked the King of All Hells for his help hunting the Phoenix down; you'd been serving his son Viedraverion for the years before. Do you think there is any* other *way out of this?*

Morbidly he mused that the *best* outcome might be his own death following immediately after striking down the Phoenix Justiciar.

Then he shoved that thought, too, away. *I've done* good *since then. I have! Maybe I can't ever make up for what I've done... or what I will do... but I can make the cost less. I can be remembered for something other than evil. There's people here who won't hear my name and spit, even when the truth comes out. At least I hope so.*

As he got farther from that vile dead wound in the earth, the shining peace of Kaizatenzei returned, and with it some of his own spirit. He'd held off the Demonshard's influence in this place, forced it to serve *his* ends, helped rebuild Sha Kuratenzei and Syratenzei after the disasters, rescued others along his way. He smiled wryly. "And I've been calling myself the Condor Justiciar of Myrionar. Who knows, there may even be a believer now somewhere along my route."

Which would in its own way be quite a blow against his so-called master. Aran felt the smile tighten to a near-snarl. *That* was the real reason he couldn't afford to die even after taking down the Phoenix. Phoenix was a *personal* issue. But the "Patron" of the false Justiciars? He—or to be more accurate, *it*—was the *cause* of the whole issue, and wouldn't it be *just* indeed for the creature to meet its downfall at the hands, not of its greatest known enemy, but someone it thought was its puppet?

Aran reached the crest of the hill and looked down upon Sha Kaizatenzei Valatar.

The legendary Valatar Tower was fallen; most of the floating bridges that had crossed the town in lines of crystal and dream were shattered. Yet the beauty of the great city remained, and for a few moments Aran, the Condor Justiciar, could do nothing but stare, drinking in the shining rose-sunset tinted loveliness and feeling it ease, for at least a few moments, the tension and guilt and fear.

Finally he shook himself and moved down the last stretch of the Necklace towards the town. *Evening now. Tomorrow... tomorrow I think I'll have to go to the current palace, whatever they're using while rebuilding the Valatar Palace, and see if I can get an audience with this ruler, Lady Shae. She* must *know where the Phoenix is... if the Phoenix isn't still here.*

There was of course a considerable danger in meeting up with the Phoenix *here.* Presumably the city knew—had probably *watched*—as the Justiciar of Myrionar and companions had done the impossible; they'd be uncontested heroes and any assassination attempt would probably result in him getting lynched. So he'd have to be somewhat circumspect until he discovered whether the Phoenix was still here. If his target had left recently, though, Aran could probably catch them on the road with no witnesses...

The gates were still wide open as he approached. He nodded to the two guards standing attentively at the sides, but evaded conversation. A quick glance at the buildings ahead showed him one with a sign—the Dawning Light—that was clearly for a travelers' inn.

Aran hastened his steps slightly as he neared the inn. His legs ached—*all* of him ached, actually, because climbing in and out of the scar and walking down the slick glassy surface had been what he'd done for most of the day, and was *far* more wearing than ordinary walking. *A meal and a good bed will do me a lot of good.*

Arranging for a room took a little longer. Refugees had taken many spaces, and apparently Lady Shae and her right hand— Light Miri, whom he'd met earlier—had decreed that refugees be housed and fed at the inns (expenses, he heard, borne entirely by the Lady of Light). But he was able to get a small corner room finally, and sat in the quietest corner of the downstairs dining room that he could find.

In the middle of finishing his *gyllidat*—an interesting grilled dessert pastry he'd never tried before—he became aware of someone standing near his table.

Glancing up, Aran saw it was a young woman of about his own age. "Yes, miss?"

"Excuse me, sir, but... would you be named Aran?"

What in the Balance... "Why do you ask, miss?"

She tilted her head, studying him. "Because you fit the description. The armor you're wearing, like a great condor?"

Cautiously now... "What description?"

"I was given a letter to deliver to you, if you ever arrived in Sha Kaizatenzei Valatar. Told that if you were coming, you'd show up in one of the inns soon. *If* your name is Aran."

His heart felt as though it was sinking through his chest. Who would act in this fashion to get a message to him? Not the Phoenix. Not anyone he knew of an ordinary sort. But Viedraverion? Quite likely. "Yes, my name is Aran," he said, trying not to sound too angry. It wasn't *her* fault she was being used as a messenger. "Do I have to pay...?"

"Oh, no, sir—paid half in advance, I will be paid again once it's delivered."

And how will it know...

As he took the thick parchment envelope, he was surprised by its weight; more than ordinary paper was within. The seal on the envelope was also complex, and now Aran understood; once the seal was broken, whoever sent it would know the delivery was complete. "Thank you, then."

She bowed and moved off—apparently with other deliveries. *They have a delivery service in the city for messages? Well... yes, I suppose they must. We didn't need any in Evanwyl, but I did see something of the sort in Sha Kuratenzei.*

He finished his dinner first; there was no particular reason to rush, and the contents would be likely something he didn't want exposed to public view. Once he was done, he went up to his small room, set as many wards as he reasonably could manage, and only then sat at the tiny wooden table and placed his hands on the seal. "Aran Condor," he said, and bent the seal; it popped with a flash of green and eerie yellow.

Undoubtedly our Patron, he thought grimly, as the contents slid into view: a polished mirror-scroll, silver trimmed with gold. He remembered with a chill his last viewing of such a scroll—the mirror-finish replaced with the pure-black face and dead-blue eyes of Kerlamion himself.

With a sigh, Condor picked it up and held it before him. "I am here."

There was no immediate response, and Condor had a sudden hope that there *would* be no response. Maybe something had happened in the intervening time. If his Patron was no more...

But if that were the case, he would have known; the powers it gave them would have faded away.

On his third attempt, the silver faded suddenly, replaced with the cheerful smiling face of their Patron. "Ah, Condor! How wonderful! You've made it all the way to Valatar."

"Not without incident. I still haven't caught up with Phoenix, always just a few weeks behind them, and in the meantime this... place almost got destroyed—by a Great Elderwyrm, no less!"

"Yes, indeed, Sanamaveridion himself. But about Phoenix—I'm afraid we were both a bit misled."

"What do you mean?"

"I mean that you would be *very* ill-advised to go talk to the lovely rulers of Kaizatenzei and bring up the subject; you see, while I had *thought* they were—in a general sense, mind you—on my side, both Lady Shae and Light Miri betrayed my cause, and that of the King of All Hells." He looked sincerely apologetic. "I am afraid that while you thought you were following the Phoenix, they were just laying a false trail. The Phoenix was going the *other* way around the lake."

For a moment Aran sat still, dumbfounded. *Tricked? Following a false trail all that way? Hundreds of miles following NOTHING?*

Then he cursed and turned away. "Myrionar's *Balance*, how *stupid* could I be. Of course, that makes sense of *everything*."

"Really? What does it make sense *of?*"

He gestured vaguely. "I kept running into problems—real people problems, monsters, kidnappings, all that kind of thing— that it seemed *obvious* to me were the kinds of things a real Justiciar would have to deal with. It passed belief that the Phoenix would just pass them by unless there was something just incredibly immediately important driving them on, but I never got a hint of what important thing that could be.

"But now I know I was just getting whatever false hints they wanted to keep me going in the direction I was already headed. *Thunder and Fire!*" He kicked the wall so hard it left a hole, and winced. *Great, I'll have to pay for that.*

"Yes, I see. Quite correct, of course. From what little I got from Miri when she severed our relationship, Phoenix did indeed get involved in such things along the route the party actually took."

"Do you at least know if Phoenix is still here in Valatar?"

It smiled apologetically. "I am afraid not. You are now, in actuality, in the position you *thought* you were in earlier—a few weeks behind the Phoenix. The last symbol of Myrionar is now on its way home—to Evanwyl."

Aran closed his eyes and counted from fifty backwards to zero. This kept him from cursing again, at least, and saved the walls and furniture from more abuse. "At least I know where Phoenix is headed. I should be able to make up distance, unless they're pushing forward on a hard march."

"They shouldn't be; they have no reason to think it is necessary, and why would there be? Everything's fine at home." The smile was suddenly just a hair too sharp and shiny, and Aran shivered. "Get your rest tonight, Aran. You will catch them this time. I guarantee it."

"And if I don't? If they reach Evanwyl? I—"

"Aran, Aran, I understand your oath completely. I assure you, none of us will stand in your way." Its eyes lit up with sudden amusement. "In fact, I think we could help you."

"What?" He was immediately—and, he felt, justifiably—suspicious.

"What do you think the Phoenix is going to do when he—or she—arrives in Evanwyl?"

"Now? After what they've done *here?* Come after you, of course!"

"But how will they *find* us?"

"They...oh." He paused. "Oh, I see. If I work it correctly, I could lead them *to* you. And then..."

"And then," agreed the other with a chuckle, "You can get your vengeance and we can...deal with the Phoenix's companions so that no one interferes with you at all."

The idea worked. If Phoenix had companions, and they'd even *lived* through that last battle, they'd be dangerous, dangerous adversaries. Having his Patron and his old comrades taking on those adversaries... "Agreed. If I don't catch and kill Phoenix before we enter Evanwyl, I'll find a way to get them to follow me." He felt his lips twist in an ironic smile. "Given that Phoenix will want to kill me about as much as I want to kill them, that probably won't be too hard."

"No, I wouldn't think so. Well, then, Aran, I leave you with wishes for a peaceful night's rest. Good night!" It hesitated before making the final cutoff gesture. "Oh, this scroll—break it after we are done, please."

"As you wish, sir."

"Farewell, then." The scroll went blank. Aran immediately picked it up and bent it double. It split and cracked down the center, and instantly began to evaporate. *A summoning or temporary creation... maybe a functional duplicate of some original our Patron has elsewhere?* He'd never really studied magic in detail. The important point was that no trace of the mirror would remain in a few moments.

He grinned suddenly. *Yes, an excellent plan, Patron. Bring your most powerful enemies to our stronghold, where they will be most vulnerable.*

But you will be in greatest danger there, too, for there will be nowhere for you to hide... and once Phoenix is dead, no reason for me to wait.

CHAPTER 9

Poplock caught a *tenzili* on the wing and crunched down. The glowy-stuff the little insects used gave them a particular tang that he liked.

"That's . . . kind of eerie, Poplock," commented Tobimar.

"What is?"

"When you eat those things you end up with a glowing mouth for an hour or so. So I just see this little floating smile and sudden flash of you gulping something else down."

"I didn't realize that! Sounds neat!"

Tobimar chuckled. "In a creepy way, yes, I think." The Skysand Prince finished putting the supper dishes away and then went to sit beside Kyri on the other side of the camp.

The Toad noticed Rion looking pensively at them. The one-time Justiciar shrugged and frowned, then turned to look out into the darkness surrounding the camp. "If no one objects," he said, "I'll do a scout around camp before we all turn in."

Kyri and Tobimar glanced around, both with some reluctance. Knowing what was on their minds, Poplock bounced up onto Rion's shoulder. "I'll come with you." The relief on the others' faces was obvious.

So was the wry smile on Rion's, even in the near-blackness under the stars above Kaizatenzei. He walked a few moments in silence, moving easily and quietly through the brush. "Not letting me out of your sight yet, are you?"

"Would *you*, in our position?"

Rion didn't answer right away; finally he let out an explosive sigh. "No, I suppose not."

"Part of you was counting on that."

"What?"

Poplock gave him a gentle kick to the side of the head. "I saw you looking at them. You're not comfortable with that, are you? You figured one or the other would insist on coming with you."

The blond-haired head dropped down in unmistakable embarrassment. "I...look, for me it's two years ago. My sister hadn't even *noticed* anyone aside from Aran and the Watchland, and now suddenly I find she's...well, *serious* about this so-called prince I've never met before. Of course I'm a little worried." He raised his head and cocked an eyebrow at the Toad. "And given what I *now* know about those other two, I think I have a little bit of a reason to be cautious about her judgment there."

Poplock snorted. "Okay, you might have a point. 'Cept it's still not really your business."

"No," Rion conceded after a moment. "But after our parents died...I guess I still want to take care of everything. That's stupid, though; she's obviously taking care of herself perfectly well. Better than I took care of her *or* me, for that matter."

"You got kinda suckered like everyone else. She still thinks you're the greatest thing living; you don't *know* how hard it is for her to let us stay suspicious of you."

A quiet chuckle. "About as hard as it would be for me, I would guess." He paused, then smacked his sword against a nearby bush; something hissed but scuttled swiftly away, recognizing Rion was *much* too dangerous to confront. "Can I ask you something?"

"Sure. Don't guarantee I'll *answer* it, but you can ask."

The one-time Justiciar hesitated again. "No one...no one really told me the results of your analysis, just that you had decided that I really was at least a part of Rion Vantage. Could you please tell me what you found out?"

Poplock considered. He obviously *could* tell Rion everything. The question was whether he *should*.

After a moment's reflection, he decided that there was no real reason not to. It had been a few weeks. If Rion had a deeper game he was playing, it clearly wasn't time for him to move yet, and nothing that they'd discovered would be a surprise to *him*.

"You're not exactly human. I suppose you probably guessed that."

"My human body was left in Evanwyl. I had *hoped* that it had been re-created here. No?"

"The samples we took...well, you were saturated with magical energies, no surprise *there*, and there were components that were human, some that were probably demonic, and...well, there's no *nice* way to say this...some that were graverisen."

Rion looked at him with faint horror. "I'm...*graverisen?*"

"There's a *part* of some type of walking dead there—can't tell what type, though. Plus demonic power and essence, and human. That all isn't surprising, though. They probably took part of your original corpse as a pattern, and this Viedra guy used his demon-power to build you a new body." He hesitated, because the next part was worse.

"What? Come, Toad, don't stop now."

"Okay, but you'll really hate this one. He still needed a living human body as a base, something to take that fragment of your soul—something like making a new flickerflower bush by grafting a branch from it onto a simjin root. So—"

"Oh, great Balance." Rion's face, always much lighter than his sister's, looked almost white in the starlight, and he stopped walking. "I...I'm wearing someone's reshaped body?"

"And," Poplock said, "one whose soul was used to rebuild yours. At least, that's our guess. Wieran, or Viedraverion, or both were involved, and they're like *way* out of my league and even out of Hiriista's. What we found...could mean something completely different. But that's our best theory."

Rion did not move for several minutes. Finally he gave such a shudder that it nearly pitched Poplock off the tall man's shoulder. "*Myrionar's Mercy.* Someone was *erased* just to make an imitation of myself. For what *purpose?*"

Poplock gave a bounce-shrug. "No idea, really. We kinda hope that they just weren't *done* with you, so you're pretty much who you appear to be—"

"—but maybe I'm not at all, and I'm going to turn on you at some point. I may not even *know* I will."

The Toad stared up at the sparkling sky, the edge of the Balance just visible above the trees. "No, maybe you won't. Wieran sure managed to do that well enough with the Unity Guard, and if we're right *you* were a special project for his biggest patron."

Rion nodded, and began walking again—but more slowly.

Poplock could feel the heaviness in the stride. "Poplock...just so you know...if that turns out to be the case, I want you to know ahead of time—I don't care what happens to me. Just keep me from hurting Kyri. However you have to. Okay?"

"Trust me, if you try to hurt either her or Tobimar, I'll stick Steelthorn through your ankle and then cut your throat as you hit the ground. Just so we're clear on that."

"That's comforting to know." The attempt at humor was weak but sounded genuine.

"But," Poplock said.

"But?"

"But I *do* think there's something of the real Rion Vantage in there. And if that's true?" He looked straight into Rion's startled eyes. "Then I've seen your sister in action, and if there's one thing I know about her, it's that there is *nothing* that she'll let stop her from doing the right thing. So if you're the brother she thinks is so incredible, then *you* should be able to fight any control anyone puts in your head. Don't ask *me* to keep you from hurting Kyri. Do it yourself."

Rion looked away, then looked back with an almost sheepish grin. "I...I guess you're right. What kind of a Justiciar would I be if I let someone else turn me against my friends?"

"Not much of one, that's for sure."

They moved on for a few moments before Rion spoke again. "Thank you, Poplock."

"Just speaking the truth as I see it. But you're welcome."

"But," Rion said, pausing as he reached a small clearing that gave a view to the East and the faint red glow of Ajaska, the westernmost of the three volcanic vents ringing Sha Alatenzei, "if I'm really something other than what I seem...aren't you taking an awful risk just having me with you? Without anyone else?"

Poplock knew Rion wasn't just referring to the current situation—the little Toad alone with Rion—but to the small four-person party itself. "A risk? Sure. An *awful* risk? No."

Rion raised an eyebrow at him. "How do you figure *that*? If I am a time-destruction spell or something, I could be—"

"—worse than what we've faced?" Poplock swayed side to side in his equivalent of a headshake. "If you think I haven't already planned out how to take you out *right now*, you're making a really big mistake. As for all three of us—we killed Thornfalcon.

Me and Tobimar beat the hell out of Lady Shae. We survived an *Elderwyrm*. Tobimar will cut you from a hundred feet away and Kyri will level the whole *forest* to get you, if you backstab us. *Maybe* you could kill us... but I know which side of that bet *I* am taking."

Rion threw back his head and laughed long and loud, the sound disappearing into the trees. "Well said, Poplock Duckweed. Well said. Then I say that if I *am* who I think I am... I am very, very glad my sister has gained such friends."

"And if you are... I'm really glad you're here, because she's missed you. A lot."

His face softened. "I know." The little campfire was now visible again ahead of them; the two figures sitting near it were so close that they seemed to be one.

Rion smiled. "But not so much she closed her eyes. Good enough."

CHAPTER 10

Zogen Josan stared at them from wide eyes. He hadn't moved for several seconds.

It is, Kyri admitted to herself, *an awful lot to take in at once, even if some of it tells you that you weren't crazy.*

Reflect Jenten also had the glaze-eyed look of someone hit in the head *hard* during sparring. He was the only other person they'd brought in to hear the story of what had happened in Sha Kaizatenzei Valatar. The ruler of Jenten's Mill had a right to know the truth, but none of them wanted to deal with the questions the whole town would be asking.

Not entirely to her surprise, Zogen recovered first. "By the Seven Lights, Phoenix. You...you swear to us that this is all true?"

"As true as anything I have ever said, Zogen," she said emphatically.

"It is...still so hard to believe. Our rulers *demons*? Yet demons who changed their minds? A Great Dragon of legend? Master Wieran the enemy?" He shook his head.

"Yet we have our own evidence for her story," Namuhuan Jenten said with a nod in her direction. "For did not many of us *see* her, blazing with golden fire, stopping a moving mountain of water? Did not the Temple of Myrionar itself come awake in blue and gold and silver in that moment? Lady Phoenix, we must once more thank you and your patron Myrionar; it seems that you did not come merely to unravel small mysteries, but to set right things vastly darker."

59

I'm at least getting used to the compliments so that I don't blush all the time, but it still *makes me feel so . . . so . . .* fake *sometimes.* "Thank you, Reflect. I hope you will understand that we intend to continue on as soon as possible."

"Of course," Zogen said, with a nod to the Reflect. "You have said nothing directly, but both the Reflect and I can hear beneath the words; you have a terrible task awaiting you on the other side of the mountains."

"Terrible enough," she agreed. "I felt that we had to tell the two of you the truth ourselves, though. I have only one other task here: I must speak with those who have chosen to serve in the Temple of Myrionar."

Zogen glanced at the Reflect, who smiled. "Of what must you speak?" the former Unity Guard asked. "For while I may be a very poor imitation at the moment, I have undertaken to become a servant of Myrionar, and have been studying your writings—and praying—for the proper guidance. It may be very long before I might call myself an Arbiter, but perhaps I might claim the title of *Seeker* Josan without being entirely arrogant."

"*You?*" She felt a huge grin spreading across her face, and heard Tobimar chuckling behind her. "Oh, Zogen, that's . . . I'm so honored, I—"

"Oh, enough of your humility! Take the credit for being such an example that I had not a choice but to follow you if I were to keep my self-respect." Despite the sharpness of his words, Zogen's smile was affectionate. "Now ask."

"Well . . . they have chosen to found a Temple in Valatar. They need the full copies of the writings I have given you—and I promise you that I'll send copies of the *real* holy writings as soon as I get home—so if you could possibly . . . ?"

"Transcribing the words and principles would seem an *eminently* reasonable thing for me to do, my lady Phoenix; I will learn the words more clearly, and achieve your goal. Worry no more on it, then. I will make sure that a proper and full copy of your words reaches Valatar as soon as possible."

"So, I guess that means you're not going back to being a Unity Guard, huh?" Poplock asked.

Zogen shrugged. "Immediately? Certainly not; I must focus on this new path until it is as clear to me as the Necklace. But later . . . perhaps. There will still be much work to do. Unless," he turned to Kyri with sudden concern, "there is something in the Way of Myrionar that would forbid me to do so?"

Kyri thought. "No, I don't think so. It's clear that Terian himself has accepted the title of the Light as you view him, and Terian is one of Myrionar's oldest and most renowned allies. Your ultimate loyalty would of course have to remain with the Balanced Sword, but I cannot see that properly serving the interests of the reawakening Kaizatenzei, with its rulers now serving the Light for real and true, could in any way conflict with Myrionar's goals." She smiled and looked over at Tobimar.

He returned the smile and turned to Zogen. "Kyri and I even discussed the possibility that someone who serves another— Terian, of course, in my case—could become a Justiciar; there seems nothing that forbids it. Myrionar, Terian, Chromaias, and the Dragon King himself all accept and work with each other; they expect us to do the same here on Zarathan. I think that Myrionar would consider it an honor to have a servant of Terian choose the calling of Justice and Vengeance . . . and that Terian would be equally honored to have a Justiciar choose to follow him in prayer and worship."

"Then . . . perhaps I shall return to the Guard, one day. Once I feel I have truly understood the new calling I have chosen." Zogen rose and bowed to both of them. "I thank you again, Phoenix, Tobimar. Rest assured, I shall myself carry the transcribed materials to Valatar."

Kyri rose and took his hand. "Thank *you*, Zogen. To know that someone like you has taken up the Balance . . . it means a lot to me."

"And to all of us," agreed Reflect Jenten. "He's gone from our strange recluse to our new holy man, and we have needed one. Now go, go. You traveled far out of your way to come here, and you don't need to be mobbed by all our citizens and slowed again. Take the side door from my mansion; no one's likely to see you there."

"If you don't think it will be a problem—"

"Oh, there's plenty who will be disappointed. Just promise me you'll return here to visit once your mission is complete, and I'll explain it all to our townsfolk."

She smiled, relieved. "That I can promise. Tobimar and I very much want to come back."

"Then it is done. Go, now, and may the Light follow you."

As they exited the meeting room, Rion looked up from where he had been playing cards with Poplock and Nimally. "Done? Just as well. These two have succeeded in halving my meager resources."

"Oh, just a little luck," Poplock said unconvincingly, as he scraped coins into his little pouch.

"I begin to suspect that there is no such thing as 'luck' where you are concerned," Nimally said. "I cannot believe you hid your nature for your entire passage across Kaizatenzei."

"Not entirely. Old Hiriista figured me out almost at a glance. Sharp old lizard."

"That he is," Nimally agreed. "And a kind healer, as well. I followed his advice and I am finally healed."

She said these words with only a hint of a shudder. *I don't think I could speak of it so casually if I'd been through her ordeal.* Nimally had been the host of the master-itrichel, the horrific mind-parasite that had used the children of Jenten's Mill for its brood. *The nightmares she must have; I would never wish that on anyone.* "It is very good to see that you *are* healed, Nimally."

"Thank you. I see you are leaving already?" She sighed. "And I was just thinking of the appropriate seating arrangements for the banquet."

"Not another banquet!" said Tobimar in mock horror.

"Get on with you, then," Nimally said with a smile. "The side door's just that way."

As the Reflect had indicated, there were none to see them leaving from the side door; a few minutes brisk walk took them into the woods, and an hour of more sedate progress led them to the road that would bring them back to the Necklace.

"I don't think you'll escape a banquet in Sha Murnitenzei," Rion said. "From what I've heard, anyway."

"No," she agreed, "we probably won't. That's the first city of Kaizatenzei we saw, and the last one before we have to leave and enter the corrupted forest and go through Rivendream Pass. They'll want to hear something of our story and celebrate, and—honestly—I'll want one more night here in Kaizatenzei before I have to go back into...that."

She shuddered. Rion reached out and touched her shoulder. "Is it that bad?"

"You have *no* idea, Rion. It's...it's like..." She paused a moment, searching for a way to describe the hideous *wrongness* of Rivendream Pass that her brother could grasp. "It's like... that moment when Thornfalcon let you see what he *really* was? That instant when something normal and safe and sane suddenly turns to be completely, utterly corrupt and evil? *That.* Imagine the entirety of nature, every tree, every beast, every *insect*, the very *air* itself being as corrupt and hostile and lethal as Kaizatenzei is pure and uplifting."

Rion frowned as he tried to imagine what she described. She saw a slight shiver. "If it's *that* bad, I'm amazed you got here."

"I wouldn't have without Tobimar and Poplock." She nodded at the other two, walking some distance ahead.

"So...do you love him? Really?"

I must really believe he's Rion, because that question doesn't feel like an intrusion. More like Father questioning me. "Yes, I do. Really. I know it seems abrupt to you...and I guess in a way it was. He and Poplock saved me from Thornfalcon."

"Hm. They tell the tale slightly differently. Tobimar says you saved *him.*"

"Well...both are true. If Tobimar and Poplock hadn't arrived just in time, Thornfalcon would have...tortured and sacrificed me." She saw no point in detailing just *how* Thornfalcon had obviously intended to carry out the torture, but Rion's expression showed that he could probably guess. "Then when I got free, I guess I did save them. And then all three of us barely killed Thornfalcon. After that it took all of us plus Xavier to deal with the gateway of monsters Thornfalcon had left behind."

He looked at her, then shook his head again with a smile. "And they say you did it by yourself, with the power of Myrionar. My little sister...a Justiciar." Rion looked at her armor. "But why Phoenix?"

"You ought to know *that.*"

"Well, yes. Rebirth."

"And...?"

He looked...*blank* for an instant, then smacked his head. "Ugh. I'm not quite...perfect, I guess. Whatever they did to bring me back. Took me a second to remember. Things are foggy..." He blinked. "But...yes, of course. You were always the Phoenix and I was the Dragon."

She felt a slight creeping chill. She had almost managed to forget the macabre nature of Rion's reappearance, but this brought the disquiet back in full force. The association of Dragon and Phoenix went back to her youngest memories. *It's Rion . . . but is it* all *of him? Or is there something* else *there as well?*

"Does this mean you'll be having a whole new set of Justiciars?" Rion continued, apparently unaware of her thoughts. "Dibs on being Dragon, then."

Kyri forced the thoughts back. *No point in second-guessing. He's still Rion. Just maybe a little . . . injured.* "If you meet the qualifications."

"Oh, ouch. Am I going to have to go through all the Trials again?"

"We'll see. If we all live through this, I think that'll probably *qualify* as trials."

"You're likely right." He looked up to where sunlight trickled in green-tinted gold through the canopy. "The old Justiciars were named after birds; you're going for, what? Legendary flying creatures?"

"Makes sense to me. Phoenix, Dragon, Thunderbird, Eonwyl— if I can get the blessing of a temple of Eonae, anyway—Griffin, things like that." She made the sign of the Balance. "We need a clean start, and the old Raiments will at the least need to be reblessed and probably reforged by the Spiritsmith."

He looked at her with the fond smile she remembered so well, and the cold discomfort faded almost entirely away. "And reforged in the image of our old toys."

She realized that he was right; that set of figurines hadn't just had the Dragon and Phoenix but all the others she had named, and more. "Oh, by *Myrionar*, did I actually *do* that?"

He laughed and impulsively flung an arm around her, hugging her close. "Of *course* you did, little sister. But with perfectly good reason and symbolism even a god couldn't complain about . . . and," he looked serious again, "with the *heart* that a Justiciar needs. I'm not a Justiciar now—I've tried, but the power isn't there—but if one day I am . . . I know my sister's made an example for *me* to live up to."

She hugged him back; for now, things were exactly as she'd hoped, and she thanked Myrionar for that. "And I know you *will* live up to it."

CHAPTER 11

Once more the scroll remained silvery, blank, even as the voice spoke from it. "A few weeks only, now."

"Really? You have made good time. The matrix remains intact?"

"Astonishingly so. I need only focus on my intended path and impression, and it brings forth the words, the posture, the gestures... everything I need." The voice paused, and in the silence it read something else.

"You sound troubled, my friend."

"It brings forth... feelings, as well. I cannot fight those any more than the thoughts, without risking discovery. Yet..."

"You are not being... *affected* by these feelings, are you?"

The hesitation was a far clearer signal than the answer. "I... I am trying not to be. I know the penalty for failure. But... she was... very important to him."

"Of course she was. But you *must not* allow this to affect your own emotions. You know how dangerous that would be—and not merely because you might be discovered." It was just as well that its unseen agent could not see it either, or it might have found the broad, vindicated grin the creature wore to be incongruous, even eerily unsettling, in comparison with the concerned, warning tone of its voice. *Perfect. He will hold out for a bit longer, but fall eventually—as I have expected.*

"Yes, I know. I will not allow it to affect me. Other than that, everything seems perfectly on schedule. They..." A pause, in which the creature could hear some other distant sounds. "... sorry, I must go."

The scroll went inert, now a simple metallic object. It leaned back and laughed, then shook its head. *Only a few weeks? I will have to prepare soon!*

It stood and began to leave, but it had taken no more than two steps when the scroll chimed an emergency alert—something *most* unusual. It immediately returned to the table and passed its hand over the surface. "I am here."

The face revealed on the scroll was of Chissith, a sand-demon of moderate power but excellent tactical skills, second or third in command of Yergoth's forces—forces that were supposedly in the process of crushing Skysand.

Chissith did not look like someone who was busy crushing a country; on the contrary, the congealed, unshifting mess on one side of its normally fluid visage looked like someone else had been doing the crushing. "L-Lord Viedra... help me..."

"What a surprise, Chissith. I hadn't expected Yergoth to hand this scroll over to anyone else." It smiled broadly.

"Yergoth... dessstroyed," Chissith said, voice slow, hissing and moaning like the wind over sand in pain and disbelief. "Moss-sst of the forcesss... annihilated..." It glanced away, as though fearing pursuit.

"Dear me. And last I had heard there was just 'a little unexpected resistance,' and 'we are assured of victory shortly.' What terrible powers *could* have intervened there, Chissith? Did one of the gods violate the Pact?" It couldn't keep its grin from widening yet more.

"No... gods... jusssst two—" The sand-demon's remaining eye widened. "Noooooooo—"

There was a momentary flash of movement that to the creature's eye looked like a river in flood, and the connection abruptly ceased, leaving the scroll as reflectively blank as ever.

Well, well. That was a bit of a surprise. Not entirely, true, but I would have expected something not quite so utterly overwhelming. But... the same sort of thing seems to have happened at Artania. Balgoltha's forces were abruptly shattered just yesterday and none of the survivors gave a coherent account of what actually happened.

It seems that the plan is—

Without warning, the scroll darkened, to show a figure visible only as the darkest outline within darkness, the eyes blank wells of brilliant blue fire; an eerie, sussurant howl accompanied the vision. "Viedraverion."

"Ahh, Your Majesty, I had been expecting your call."

Kerlamion's rumbling, echoing voice, the sound of an endless fall and the destruction of air, held no trace of levity or amusement; it was filled with tightly leashed rage. "You would do well to moderate your tone, Viedraverion. I have tolerated your behavior due to your successes, but I now see a series of failures, and the armies of the Empire and the Dragon both surround my walls."

"We knew that turn of events was to happen already, however." It was still smiling, and the blue-flame eyes narrowed dangerously.

"*That* turn of events, yes, but *your* plan also included other events—ones that would also have freed other forces to act, and assist against this siege. Instead, I have heard a litany of failures!"

"A *litany*? How terrible."

The shadowy figure leaned forward, and the unseen lips drew back in a snarl that showed the same deadly glow within the mouth. "Have a care, Viedraverion! Neither your record nor your blood makes you immune to my wrath, and I near the end of my patience! This very moment I felt the fall of Yergoth of the Endless Desert; a short time agone, Balgotha fell and his spirit has not been seen in my halls; no word has come from the Academy, and I have heard stirrings from far Aegeia that things are not all as they should be. Explain yourself, or you shall suffer my anger first!"

As good a time as any; the King will be most busy from now until at least a few weeks hence ... and it seems that a few weeks is all I will need. "Explain myself? Very well, Kerlamion. The explanation, really, is quite simple. I gave you a plan that stood a reasonable chance of success on its own, and allowed you to follow it, as your success—or failure—did not matter at all to me, but keeping you occupied with *something* did matter. Now, however, I have no more need to waste time with your puerile dreams of conquest, which are—as I expected—coming apart at a rather startling rate."

Kerlamion leaned back slowly, glowing eyes narrowing. "You are not insane. Yet these actions would seem to shout of insanity. You say the plan had a reasonable chance of success, yet it is failing almost simultaneously across all of Zarathan. Why would you do this? To weaken me? Are you entertaining a mad belief that you could usurp *my* throne?"

It laughed long and loud. "Oh, Lord Kerlamion, I have not the faintest interest in your throne. I said the plan had a good chance of success *on its own*. But many other factors are involved besides that one plan—most particularly, perhaps, Konstantin Khoros. I think you can lay the blame for the debacle of Skysand and Artania at his door, and perhaps that of Aegeia as well, though I would be unsurprised to discover that the Lady of Wisdom had a hand in it as well; that is, after all, her territory. But I have other, more pressing matters to attend to, matters in which your Hells mean really nothing at all."

Kerlamion suddenly stood, glowering down at his own scroll. "You...*who are you?*"

"And *now* you begin to understand, Kerlamion. A bit slow to realize, but then, I *have* had some practice in fooling others."

"What have you done with my first son?" The King of All Hells clenched his fists, and the air howled in blue agony.

"I? Found him nigh-dead already, defeated in his mission, humiliated by his own plans, and took what remained for my own purposes. But that was long, long ago, mighty Kerlamion, long before it was reported to you that his task-in-exile was complete."

It allowed itself to smile broadly as Kerlamion sagged back into his throne. "You have been playing my own son for *four hundred thousand years?*"

"I have. And you have only suspected now because I have allowed you to."

The massive black form bent forward, and the mouth was a blazing slit with jagged fire for fangs. "I will destroy you, whatever your true form. I will seek you out with all the power of the Hells, and there will be no place in all the myriad worlds, in all the universes beyond the Veil, where you can hide." Kerlamion's voice rose to an echoing thunder. "I will call forth the hosts of the Black City to search for you, yea, for a thousand times a thousand years if I must, even if I give up all I have gained and more! I will discover your name and erase you and it from—"

"Oh, but you *know* my name, little one," it said, and dropped the human guise, grinning now with a mouth of blades and eyes of its own inhuman flame.

Kerlamion's eyes widened and he staggered back. "*Lightslayer.*"

A light laugh. "How charming; the second time I've been reminded of that lovely old nickname. But yes, you know me now, Kerlamion. *Now* do you think you can threaten me?"

The huge dark head shook slowly from side to side.

"Excellent. Then I will not have to listen to your bluster anymore." It began to rise.

"*Wait!*" Kerlamion's voice shook with restrained rage. "You *planned* for my failure. Why?"

"Oh, no, Demon-King. Even now, it may be that you will find victory. My plans were sound, so far as they went, and while it is true I did not intend to stay the course, so to speak, you *have* managed to accomplish what has not been done in ages: bring the Black City here to Zarathan, and this time without the other gods to intervene. You have the best chance to achieve your conquest that you have ever had."

"Why did you do all of this? What do you seek?"

It raised an admonishing finger. "Oh, now, where would be the fun in *telling* you? Some questions should remain unanswered. I'm sure you'll learn when the time comes. Fare thee well, o King of All Hells; I doubt we shall speak again, at least in *this* age."

It passed its hand over the surface, erasing the visage of the furious and shaken Kerlamion, and threw back its head for a thundering, inhuman laugh that shook most of the Retreat.

And so the endgame is begun.

CHAPTER 12

Tobimar heard the triple *twang-twang-twang* as Poplock's clockwork crossbow fired. *"Behind you!"*

Tobimar whirled, silver-green swords out, slashing across the shadow wraith which was already burning white in three places, shattering it to fading shards of night. "Close."

"We're not done!"

Two more shadow wraiths, graverisen affected by the dark powers in Rivendream Pass, had materialized from the dimness beneath the twisted trees—trees that were now ripping their roots free of the soil and bending towards them. One wraith raised a hand and gestured, carving symbols of light in the air. *It's a mage! What—*

The symbols blazed up, and instantly a roaring sphere of flame streaked towards the little party.

To Tobimar's surprise, it was Rion who acted first. Bracing and focusing on his sword's edge, Kyri's brother cut down and split the attack, both fiery pieces passing harmlessly to either side. *Justiciar or no, he's damned good. The skill to cut enchantments isn't something learned easily.*

That pause had given Kyri her chance. She charged out from behind her brother, Flamewing carving straight through an outstretched, coiling branch, and bore down on the shadow wraiths. *"Myrionar!"* she shouted, and the immense sword burst into its own golden flame. The shadow wraiths flowed back, trying to disappear into the gloom, but the fire of Myrionar left precious little to hide in.

By then Tobimar had caught up. He sprang across the remaining distance, focusing his awareness and strength *through* the swords the Spiritsmith had forged, and felt the essence of the creature resist, then fail. It, too, exploded in fading mists of night. Rion harried the third while Kyri kept the hostile trees at bay; then Poplock put another of his alchemical flame-darts into the shadow wraith's half-substantial head and Rion's swords finished tearing it apart.

With that, the trees shuddered, sinking slowly back into the ground, moaning and leaning away from the terrible flaming sword, one of them beating ponderously against its own branches that had caught fire. Gradually the poisonously green, dimly lit jungle subsided into its eerily watchful near-silence.

Rion wiped his brow, shaking slightly. "I had wondered . . . if you were exaggerating. I started to think you had not when we left Kaizatenzei. Now I know you did not describe this abominable place well enough."

"To be fair," Poplock said soberly, "I don't think *anyone* could describe this place well enough. You have to *be* here to understand. And honestly, I wouldn't wish that on anyone."

"Oh, there's a few I would wish it on," Kyri said grimly, looking around warily. "If I wasn't afraid they'd find it pleasant."

"I don't suppose we could go back to Sha Murnitenzei?" Rion said with a wan smile. "It's only a day and a half. They'd probably welcome the chance for another party."

"We'd just have to come back out *here* again," Tobimar said with an answering grin, as the little party began to move cautiously up the slowly increasing slope of Rivendream Pass. "And I don't know about you, Rion, but I think I'd find it worse, having gone back into Kaizatenzei for but a day or so."

"I can't disagree," Rion said after a moment, with another shiver. He looked up the tangled slope where only the faintest of trails was visible. "How far is it?"

Kyri answered, though her eyes were still scanning the brush as they moved upslope. "Well, we didn't *measure* it . . . but that's the pass through the Khalals, so we're crossing through a mountain range, at least partly—even if this valley sort of dents the Kalals in. A hundred and fifty miles? Two hundred? Weeks of travel, anyway. Maybe we can move a *little* faster since we've done this before, and we've got you with us, but . . ."

Rion's eyes widened, then his jaw set. "Weeks. In *this* place.

Myrionar's *Mercy*. And you three came through here without even knowing that Kaizatenzei was on the other side? Maybe I *wasn't* really worthy of being a Justiciar, because I'm not sure I'd have had the courage to do *that*."

Kyri flashed him one of the smiles that seemed reserved for her big brother—filled not just with affection, but admiration that only a younger sibling could have for their older, better brother. "You would've done it alone, if you had to. I know you, Rion."

Rion glanced at Tobimar, as if to say *well, if she says so*, and then chuckled. The sound was both a relief and somehow alien in Rivendream Pass. "I suppose if anyone does, it's my sister. So..." he glanced around, including Poplock in his survey, "...do we have a plan as to our next moves?"

Poplock shifted on his shoulder; Tobimar caught Kyri's eye; she nodded. At that, Poplock relaxed slightly. "Okay," the little Toad said. "I guess we should bring you up to date. Sorry, but we've done those kind of discussions mostly among us three. We should probably include you from now on."

Rion shook his head. "I can't blame you. I wouldn't entirely trust me either, yet."

"*I* trust you, Rion," Kyri said firmly.

"*You* are prejudiced," Poplock said just as firmly. "And you know it. It's good you trust him. Just as long as you know we don't, yet. Honestly, until we've dealt with this Viedra guy, I'm not going to relax."

Kyri sighed, then stuck Flamewing into a suspicious-looking bulge on a tree root; the bulge screeched and splayed multiple clawed legs before collapsing. "Agreed. You shouldn't."

"All right." The Toad shifted to the shoulder nearest to Rion. "So, our next moves—after not dying in Rivendream, that is. The plan's pretty simple, based on what we've learned. Oh, first—that other figure that Thorny was talking to when you caught them out. Could it have been the Watchland?"

Rion thought, then shook his head. "No. My gut feeling was Skyharrier, and the height and build...they're not right for the Watchland." He looked apologetic. "Of course...there's no certainty that I remember everything right either."

"No, there isn't," agreed Tobimar. "Given that you're at least in some way a construct, there's a lot that Wieran could have changed, especially with a major demon helping."

Kyri frowned. "So, no evidence one way or the other on the Watchland there."

Tobimar shrugged. "No, but honestly? Miri's evidence is *more* than enough, if we trust her—and I do, and I think the rest of us do, too." Kyri nodded.

"*Any*way," Poplock said with a slight emphasis, "the plan is first to scout out Evanwyl—see if everything looks okay. If it is, we'll sneak in a little farther, see if Xavier and any of his friends have shown up." Poplock gave the broadest grin his not-terribly-mobile lips allowed. "They'll kinda stand out, so that's not going to be too hard."

"If they are there?"

"Well, we make contact right away, clue 'em in. Believe me, if we can get Xavier in on the party, we *want* him in on it. You'll like him, he's a neat guy, warrior, looks kinda like your sister Urelle, fights like Tobimar."

"Except better," Tobimar said.

"*Different*," Kyri corrected him. "You both learned the same basic discipline, but he was taught different parts. It's true he has a couple of pretty frightening tricks, though."

Poplock looked at them like a sage interrupted in a lecture. "If I could *finish*?"

"Sorry," Tobimar said contritely.

"So, as I was saying, if Xavier and his friends are there, we make contact. Might have to spend some time talking with them, get to know 'em—you can't work well with people you don't really understand, after all.

"After that, or if they're *not* there, we'll be ready to start the dangerous part of the operation—the parts that might or will tip off our enemies that we've got 'em pegged. First, we go to the Temple of Myrionar and see if Arbiter Kelsley will let us dig through the Temple records. *Somewhere* in there they've got to have some idea of where the Justiciar's Retreat is."

Rion nodded. "We can't confront our enemies if we can't find them."

"Right. So, whatever comes of that, our next stop is the Watchland himself. Preferably not in his home, of course."

"You're going to confront him before going to the Retreat?"

"Of course," Kyri said firmly. "There's only three possibilities, Rion. The first is that I'm right that there're two sides to the Watchland, good and bad—and maybe we can use the good side against the bad. The second and third possibilities come from the chance that either I'm wrong, or whatever's good in him can't really stand up to Viedraverion. In that case, either he will decide to take us on immediately, or he'll decide to run for the Retreat. I am *pretty* sure that no matter what tricks he may have in place, he will *not* be able to keep me from finding the Retreat if I'm following him closely enough. If he leads us to the Retreat, or we beat him and can find our way there with Kelsley's help...well, then the final chapter of this plays out one way or the other."

Rion nodded. "I see. But what if...well, he's made his move? What if Evanwyl...isn't Evanwyl?" He was obviously tormented by the thought, and Tobimar couldn't blame him; Tobimar probably had the same expression when he wondered what had happened to Skysand in the time he'd been gone.

Kyri's face was suddenly cold and hard as stone. "Then we go straight for the Watchland, no pauses, no chance for anyone to raise an alarm or prepare. At the most we try to scout things out as carefully as we can beforehand, but we *can't* take a risk of alerting them. There's only four of us; we can't afford to give them time to get a larger force against us, even if we're stronger individually. And yes, Rion, Tobimar, I understand that depending on...what Viedraverion is, and what allies he may have and powers he may use, we may end up fighting our own friends." She held them all with her gaze. "If that's the case...we try not to hurt them. But we have to win, or this was all for nothing. We continue until we are all down...or we've won."

The three others looked at each other, and then nodded. "Agreed."

Rion touched her arm. "You know...that means we might have to fight *Lythos*."

She nodded. "I know."

"He could kill us."

She looked momentarily infinitely sad. "No, Rion. I don't think he could. Not me, anyway. Oh, he's a better *warrior* than me—than probably all of us put together. But if you remember, Lythos himself told us 'enough skill can overcome power. But enough power can overcome skill. Those who have both...*they* are the masters.' Well, Tobimar and I fought an Elderwyrm and lived. I think we're . . . well, out of his reach, no matter what his skill."

Rion stared at her, then shook his head with a grin. "I . . . still have a hard time grasping that."

Tobimar snorted. "So do *we*. There are times it still doesn't seem quite real. Even though we fought it, and you and I crossed the scars on the landscape the monster left. I don't think our minds are really *meant* to be able to comprehend something on that scale."

"Oh, it happened," Poplock said calmly. "Otherwise I'd still have that crystal, and wouldn't have had to replace that Gemcalling matrix." He patted the elaborate ring around his upper arm, a ring with a glittering blue-purple gem set in it. "And wouldn't have the scars where my arm got shattered."

"In any case . . . don't worry about it, Rion," Kyri said, and hugged her brother. "Time enough for that when we get there."

Tobimar agreed with her. Right now, they had to stay alive— though that really should be easier now, given the powers they'd learned to use. But no point in borrowing trouble from the future.

Whatever was waiting for them . . . wouldn't be waiting much longer.

CHAPTER 13

"Gharis again," murmured Tobimar.

"Appropriate. It *was* the easiest of the outlying towns for us to get to from Rivendream," Poplock said. He was feeling perhaps unreasonably cheerful and optimistic; getting out of the vile, sanity-eroding *nastiness* of Rivendream had that effect. Maybe Evanwyl wasn't the sparkling perfection of Kaizatenzei, but compared to Rivendream Pass, well, close enough. "How do you want to do the reconnaissance?"

Tobimar frowned. "People there might recognize me, so I can't go too far in."

"Neither of us can even get close," Rion said reluctantly. "We are...*were*, in my case...known throughout Evanwyl, and there's no one that would mistake us for anyone else unless we try disguises."

Kyri shook her head. "And against the forces we're worried about, I don't know if disguises would help. You're not really much better off, Tobimar, except that you're not so tall that you'll stand out."

"That's why I'm going to only go in close enough to be able to hear if things go too badly wrong. It's really going to be up to Poplock."

"Yep," agreed the little Toad, checking his pack and making sure it was well settled and its subtle camouflage was working. "As far as I know, no one except maybe the Watchland himself ever twigged to the fact that I was something more than a pet. And I'm small enough that people often don't even notice me."

"True," Kyri said. "All right; Rion and I will stay back here and wait for you two. *Do not* take any chances you can avoid, Poplock. I don't want an alarm *or* a fight if we can evade it."

"Hey, I don't stab people who don't deserve it. Trust me." He gave her a pop-eyed smile so she knew he wasn't really annoyed; she returned the smile and bowed, then kissed Tobimar quickly.

It wasn't a rainy night, as it had been the first time they approached the little town. Poplock pointed out a dark street that led to a tiny copse, a sort of park, not even a stone's throw from the Southern View, the main inn and gathering spot in Gharis. Tobimar nodded. "Okay, I'll wait there. Good luck."

"See you in a bit."

Poplock dropped from the Skysand prince's shoulder and scuttled through the grass. He *could* make better time bouncing along the main road, but that would make him more visible. Toads didn't stay on streets often, not when they had a choice.

A few minutes took him to the wall of the Southern View. Constructed of large logs carefully fitted and laid in an interlocking pattern, the inn also had verminseal wards on it, with some security webbing in place as well, as he could see by looking at it through one of his special lenses. But it hadn't changed since the time they'd come here searching for Thornfalcon, as far as he could tell.

He squinted up. Sure enough, there were a couple of vents under the eaves. That allowed air circulation through the building, which could get stuffy otherwise. He climbed swiftly up to the roof using the log ends, which were also the anchors for the security and verminseal wards; this meant their outer edges weren't inside the wards, but normally that wouldn't matter much; the only vermin that attacked big wood blocks were kept out by the preservative paint.

Fortunately, the fact that they were relying on the cheaper security webbing meant that there were significant gaps in the coverage—significant to a Toad who was less than four inches across. The webbing had a six-inch spacing, which made it almost easy to get through and enter the vent.

Remembering the *mazakh* ducts, Poplock looked carefully inside, but this wasn't even really a duct, just an opening to permit good air circulation through the building; he just had to remove and replace the grating that kept debris like dust and leaves from entering.

The attic was filled with various dry goods—beans, gravelseed flour, smoked meats hanging from the ceiling, and such. It didn't take long for Poplock to figure out how to ease his way into the gaps at the side of the floor and drop down, first to the second floor and then to the first. *They build everything so* open *in Evanwyl. Almost unfairly easy.*

He reminded himself that he was just about to hit the *hard* part of this job. He was now hanging upside down, looking into a pantry with a half-open door through which came the sounds of cooking, someone moving about, stirring something, rattling of pans. "More tineroots, and where's the roast for Gillie?"

"Coming!"

Poplock poked his head back up, found that—as he had hoped—the ceiling down here was a thin layer of boards concealing the supporting beams and braces. It was only about six inches high, but that was more than enough space for him. He scuttled along, following the sounds of movement and the structural components until he figured he was over the common room where most people would gather. *Hopefully I'll get some idea of what's going on around here.*

For the first time he had a problem. Listening was all well and good, but *seeing* people was really important. Words could say one thing while expressions, gestures, and body posture said another, something that old Hiriista had proven when he figured out that Poplock wasn't an ordinary toad.

The problem was that the ceiling boards were really well fitted. There was barely a hint of light seeping through them. That left only a few choices. He could try to lever one of the boards so that there was a gap he could look through; he could bore a hole through the wood and peek through, either by eye or using a small mirror; or he could take a chance at being spotted and just go to the edge of the ceiling and peek down from between the gap between the ceiling and wall.

After turning the possibilities over in his mind, he opted for the last. Levering boards you hadn't fitted yourself could break them or cause obvious sounds or movement. Boring a hole could easily end up with splinters or shavings dropping down where someone could see them.

He scuttled quietly over to one side, which he thought would give him the best view, and then very slowly and cautiously lowered himself until he could *just* make out the room below.

The initial glance was encouraging; there seemed to be about as many people in the little inn as he remembered from their first visit, which meant that business was reasonably good. People's expressions also covered the gamut but were tending towards good cheer, something he would definitely not expect had, say, a Demonlord announced its overlordship of the country and begun crushing the citizenry.

A young man and young woman—both black-haired and dark-skinned, like the majority of people in Evanwyl—were waiting tables and taking orders, directed partly by an older woman with graying hair who was also going in and out of the kitchen. *I remember her... Gam, I think it was?*

The man who had been here on that visit, of course, was gone; Vlay had been a collaborator with Thornfalcon, one of the few who knew of the Justiciar's very *un*heroic tastes and assisted him in the procurement and disposal of people when necessary. *Gam must not have known, if she's still here.*

Poplock settled himself down and listened. *Tobimar knows I'll be here a while.* You couldn't gather good intelligence if you weren't patient. Momentarily, Poplock wondered about Kyri and Rion, but shrugged. Rion had had plenty of opportunities to betray them before. If he was really in league with their enemy, his best bet was probably to just go along with them and then backstab the party when they were already in battle with Viedraverion. If he wasn't, well, the two had plenty to talk about; sometimes even in Rivendream Pass they'd ended up discussing their younger days to the point that Kyri almost seemed to have forgotten Tobimar was there.

"Hey, Pingall, how goes it? Have a few days next week?"

"Ah, so it's the harvest you're ready for? Sure, I have a day or three. Good weather we've been having."

"Not like three years ago. Remember that drought? Like to have lost the whole crop."

"Oh, yeh, that was bad. Now, not as bad as the one in 2112, though..."

Poplock moved around from point to point along the edge of the rafter space. Most of the discussions were like that—talk of crops for farmers, shipments and manufacturing points for merchants and smiths, a few children out with their parents demanding treats, an apprentice mage of some sort trying to study while her larger companion kept interrupting with questions that showed that he wasn't perhaps bright enough to understand her answers.

Then he heard something that would have made his ears prick up, if that was something physically possible for a Toad. "...war's not going well, I hear."

"Oh, have you heard something since the last quarter-year?"

"My son works the road to the south, you know, and a runner came through—about beat, he was, too. Seems the rumors are true."

Silence; Poplock noticed the whole inn had suddenly quieted. The protests of the youngest child at the far table were being shushed.

"You mean..." the questioner's voice dropped to a penetrating whisper, "the *Black City*?"

"That's what he said," the first person, an older woman, answered. Her tone was that of someone both horrified, and incredibly pleased to be the one bearing important news. "Said that the City's sitting right in the center of Hell itself. Said that the Sauran King marched an army right through Hell's Edge, had them open the gates that were never opened so they could pass through."

"Great Balance, Enn. That sounds like..."

"Chaoswar, so they say," Enn continued, with that same horrified relish in her voice. "And that's not all. He says the *Empire* sent an army through right after. Both the Dragon and the Archmage are on the move. What does *that* say?"

"I don't believe it," a deep-voiced man said, though his tone was uncertain. "The Black City's the center of All Hells, not something sitting on *this* world."

The debate went on below. The bit about the Black City wasn't news to Poplock; he, Kyri, and Tobimar had been at the Spiritsmith's when it happened, and the Spiritsmith himself had told them what they had seen. But the idea that the massed armies of the Dragon and of Idinus of Scimitar himself had gone together to face the threat...that was news, and not really good news. Well, it was good that someone was facing the forces of Kerlamion, but Poplock had a bad feeling that once the King of All Hells had a foothold on Zarathan he wasn't going to be easy to kick back off.

The smiles were fewer and the atmosphere of the inn had changed. The discussion of a Chaoswar that might already be upon them had thrown a pall over the entire crowd. Some were already leaving.

Then Poplock caught a fragment of another conversation.

"...to believe. Haven't been any travelers through Evanwyl in months."

"Not quite true. There's that group of youngsters that showed up over to the Balanced Meal."

"Strange ones, those are. Though they say the one boy's been here before."

Been here before? Could that be...

"Oh, aye, I know the one. Looks like he could be a by-blow of old Kyril Vantage, eyes just like Miss Kyri he has."

Poplock felt his broad face trying to split into a grin.

Xavier's back!

CHAPTER 14

Once more, Tobimar found himself hiding in shadows, watching an inn. A misty, warm drizzle of rain wet his hair and dripped from the eaves above. Poplock was on his shoulder as they stared at the Balanced Meal from the darkness of a narrow alley between a clothier and a farrier's stables across from the main inn of Evanwyl proper. "This is going to be difficult," he murmured.

"Why in Blackwart's name aren't they at the Vantage estate?" Poplock complained. "I'm sure Vanstell would vouch for Xavier, right? And it'd be *so* much easier that way."

The problem was that they still didn't want Evanwyl at large to know they were back. No telling what their enemy might be watching for or planning as a sort of welcome-home present. They could have gotten to and into the Vantage estate without anyone noticing easily enough—even Tobimar and Poplock had been there long enough to know the less-obvious ways inside— but walking into the Balanced Meal would be practically hiring a crier to announce their return.

"Because he's too polite to do that," Kyri said quietly from next to Tobimar; Rion was all the way at the other end of the alley, watching in case someone seemed likely to intrude. "He wasn't entirely comfortable staying at the estate even when it was just him; I'm sure he'd feel that he was imposing far too much if he showed up and asked Vanstell to put up not just him, but four other friends of his as well."

That fit with Tobimar's memory; Xavier was, from his point

of view, a bizarre mixture of the formal, casual, and utterly alien who was nonetheless one of the best friends the Skysand prince had ever had. "We'll have to do *something* soon, though." Tension made him feel as though he were being watched, and he glanced around, then looked back at the inn. "We know they're in there, but not how long they're staying, or if they're watching the area . . . or if someone *else* is spying on them. Probably is. We were lucky to get this close without being seen, but who knows—"

"—what evil lurks in the hearts of men?" asked a voice that was, impossibly, behind him.

Even as he spun, swords unsheathing in a single motion, a part of him recognized the voice, and by the time his blades were parried in mirror-perfection, he was grinning from ear to ear, feeling a startling joy surging through him. "*XAVIER!*"

The gray-eyed, black-haired boy grinned back, his swords crossed before him in the exact same pose as Tobimar's. "You really have to stop saying 'hello' with your swords, dude. Someone could get the wrong idea."

"Xavier!" Kyri said it quietly, but still stepped forward, caught up their friend, and hugged him so emphatically that he gave a little *oof!* sound. "I'm *so* happy to see you!"

"Same here," Poplock said, bouncing onto Xavier's head and looking down. "What was that stupid line you just said?"

"Oh, it's a quote from some old show and comic my mom and dad had around. I'll tell you later, it's kinda cool. Anyway, who's the guy down there?"

Kyri gestured to Rion, who was looking in their direction, but still at his post. "Come on down, Rion."

"How in the name of the *Balance* did someone get *past* me?" Rion hissed as he approached.

"We'll show you later," Tobimar said with a grin, sheathing his swords. "Rion, this is Xavier. Xavier—"

But as Rion's face came into the dim light of the street, Tobimar saw Xavier's face go gray beneath its olive complexion. "M-*Michael?*"

As they stared at him in confusion and consternation, Xavier's face slowly started to regain normal color. "No . . . no, you're not Michael. But, *Jesus,* you look like him. I mean, you *really* look like him. Even sound like him, I think. Holy crap. I'm kinda freaked out here. Who is this again?"

"This is Rion, my older brother," Kyri said. "Rion, this is Xavier Ross—who helped us clean up Thornfalcon's final revenge, and helped Tobimar get to Evanwyl in the first place."

"Pleased to meet you, Xavier. Balance and Justice be with you."

"And you," Xavier said, shaking his hand. He squinted at Rion narrowly, and without warning there was something else in his gaze. His voice didn't sound different, but Tobimar was suddenly sure he was looking at something that the rest of them could not see. "Wait a minute. *Rion*. Your brother. Your *dead* brother?"

"Yes. In a way, anyway. It's a long story and not suited for an alleyway. Is there any way for you to get your friends to come meet us at the Estate?"

Xavier hesitated; he glanced to Tobimar, and in that wide gray gaze Tobimar saw both a question and worry that surprised him. "Is something wrong, Xavier?"

The native of Earth looked back up at Rion, then at Kyri. "Do you know that he's . . . not normal? Not like an ordinary human?"

Kyri was startled. "How can you . . . Oh. That sense of yours."

"Yeah. I wasn't really *looking* at him before, but now that I do . . . there's something *wrong* there."

Poplock bounced back to Tobimar's shoulder. "We know there's something weird about him, yeah. Like she said, long story. But do we want to go through that now?"

Xavier studied Rion a moment longer, then gave a shrug. "I guess we can wait if you're cool with it. As for the Estate, yeah. We've been . . . well, arguing a lot, and letting them know you're back will end a lot of the argument."

Tobimar saw the embarrassed-yet-defiant expression and leapt to a heartwarming conclusion. "You've been keeping them here. Waiting for us."

Xavier looked down, and his cheeks were a shade darker. "Yeah. We've got important stuff to do . . . but I tried checking out that Rivendream Pass, and knowing you guys went *there*, well . . . I didn't want to go without knowing what happened to you, no matter what else was going on."

Kyri beamed at him. "Thank you, Xavier. So yes, can you get them to meet us there . . . perhaps in two hours, if you're all willing to stay up a bit later?"

"Ehh, sure, most of us don't go to bed all that early anyway. And they'll really want to meet you." He glanced speculatively at

Rion again, then nodded to Tobimar. "Okay, see you in a couple hours at Kyri's place."

With that, he closed his eyes and vanished. Rion gave a startled curse. "Invisible . . . no, more than that. I can't sense him at all."

"Nope. As far as I know, no one but me's ever been able to sense him," Tobimar said, now leading the way cautiously back up the alley, and trying to figure out the quickest way to get to the Vantage estate without being seen.

"And why *you*?" Rion asked, eyebrow raised.

"Because both of us were trained in the same discipline, called *Tor*."

Rion stopped in his tracks for a moment, then resumed walking; but Tobimar thought that his face had looked *shocked* for a moment. "*Tor*? The name's very vaguely familiar," Rion said, in a voice that sounded faintly brittle, tense. "Is that what gives him the ability to do that trick?"

"Yes," Tobimar said, trying to figure out what those reactions—if they were real reactions, and not just a figment of Tobimar's imagination—meant. "He learned it in a different way than I did, from a different teacher, so each of us knows different parts of the art."

Rion seemed to be walking normally now, and his next words sounded perfectly at ease, so Tobimar wondered if he had actually seen and heard what he thought. "Well, whatever that art is, I'm *very* impressed. I would have sworn no one could pass me unawares, not a magician, not a spirit, nothing. Yet he apparently did."

"Or he just stepped through one of the walls without even going past you," Poplock said. "He can do that kind of thing."

Rion looked even more impressed.

Between the four of them, it took about three-quarters of an hour to work their way to Vantage Fortress. There was no one in sight of the front gate, but they weren't planning on taking chances, so they went to a rear entrance concealed in an area of brush. Walking through the short tunnel, they emerged into a small courtyard that Tobimar remembered fondly from hours spent practicing and sparring.

A door opened at the far end of the courtyard, a tall, slender figure visible holding an unsheathed blade. "Who enters Vantage Fortress unannounced? Speak, or you shall pay a short and bitter price for trespass."

"Lythos!" Kyri said, her joy clear in face and voice.

The gleaming blade vanished, and the *Artan* master of arms, or *Sho-Ka-Taida*, ran lightly across the courtyard to stop and bow before her. "Lady Kyri," he said. "I had hoped for your return, but not looked for you to enter your own home as a thief in the night."

"We have reason for caution, Lythos, as we'll tell you shortly," Tobimar said.

"I will expect to hear every detail, Lord Silverun," Lythos said calmly. "Now, I—"

The *Artan* stepped back, his blade materializing in his hand as if by magic; only the tension of his voice and a slight widening of the eyes showed how shocked and startled he was. "...You cannot be what you appear. Name yourself truly, or be destroyed."

"Lythos," Kyri said sharply. "This is Rion, as best we can determine."

"That is *impossible*," Lythos said coldly, his blade a literal hair's breadth from Rion's throat; Rion stood frozen, his eyes wide and staring at his former teacher. "I saw his body, I prepared it for its final rest myself, I helped the Arbiter perform the final rites. Rion Vantage died and passed from this world. I say a second time, name yourself truly!"

"Stop it, Lythos," Tobimar said emphatically. "We *know* there's something wrong here. We know there are questions we haven't answered. But—"

"Tobimar, you will stand silent, guest though you are. I am *Sho-Ka-Taida*, and I am also the guardian of House Vantage, and now thrice I say to this one: *name yourself truly!*"

Rion swallowed, and then said, slowly, "Rion. Rion Vantage, Lythos. It is me. I don't know how, I don't know why, but it is me."

For a long, long moment Lythos gazed straight into Rion's eyes, and Tobimar was tense, hands gripping the hilts of his swords. He knew that Kyri would act to defend Rion if Lythos chose to act, and that the tableau could abruptly dissolve into incredible violence. Despite Kyri's earlier words in Rivendream Pass, he was not at all sure of the outcome of a duel between Kyri, himself, and *Sho-Ka-Taida* Lythos.

But the *Artan's* blade was sheathed again, and Lythos bowed. "There are mysteries behind your eyes, Rion, and I think there are some not yet spoken. At the same time, I see you, and ask that you forgive my caution."

Rion laughed. "There is nothing to forgive, Lythos; you were protecting my sister and our home."

"Well enough, then. Welcome home, all of you—including you, oh mighty Toad."

"Thanks!" Poplock bounced onto Tobimar's head and bowed. "Now, we'd better get ready."

"Ready?" Lythos looked at them questioningly. "For what?"

"For a council of war," Kyri said. "Our friend Xavier and his four companions will be here shortly, and we all have much to tell one another. And then I will have to speak of our true enemy." Her face was once more the cold vision of Vengeance. "And you will not be pleased to hear that truth, Lythos."

Lythos studied them an instant, then bowed again. "Then I shall tell Vanstell to prepare. Your room, Rion, has been maintained since your ... death, at the wish of your sister and aunt; as they accept you as Rion, so shall I, and thus you know where you may go to refresh yourself. I shall await you all in the grand dining room."

He bowed and left, and the four of them left by one of the other courtyard doors. Tobimar felt tension rising in him.

The final preparations were about to begin.

CHAPTER 15

Kyri gave a full, formal Armed Bow to the five young people—all of them definitely younger than she was, Xavier's age, sixteen or seventeen at the most. "Welcome to my estate, all of you." She was dressed in the Raiment; not only was this an official council of war, with hopefully new allies, but also if somehow their enemy realized what was going on, she wasn't going to be caught off guard.

Her companions clearly felt the same way; Tobimar had cleaned up and probably had Poplock help, but he was in traveling gear, Poplock was on his shoulder, and Rion had simply added one of his old traveling cloaks to his armor. Lythos stood to one side, watching, his sword-hilts visible on the left and right.

The newcomers bowed back, emulating the bowing pirouette, but aside from Xavier none of them appeared to be armed; fortunately, she wasn't a Sauran, so she wasn't going to take offense. *But how in the world could they have traveled so far and seen what must have been a great deal without weapons or, as far as I can see, armor of any significance?*

Xavier stepped forward. "Thanks, Kyri. Let me introduce my friends here."

Seeing the five close up, she was once more struck by their impossible beauty. In their own way both the girl with white-blond hair and the taller one with locks of forest green rivaled Miri and Lady Shae in appearance, and that was without the shining rightness of Kaizatenzei to help the perception along.

Similarly, the other two boys—one with hair as straight and black as Xavier's but with brilliant blue-green eyes that seemed to take in everything about him at a glance, the other tall as Rion with golden-blond hair and exotic violet eyes—were almost otherworldly in their beauty. *I had gotten somewhat used to Xavier's appearance, but seeing all of them together is still strange.*

Apparently oblivious to her musings, Xavier proceeded with the introductions. "This is Nike Engelshand," he said, gesturing towards the silver-blond girl whose crystal-blue eyes were set off by the unusual golden-pale skin, tanned yet far lighter in shade than almost anyone Kyri had met except Miri. "The emerald-haired girl's Aurora Vanderdecken, this guy who stole my hair is Toshi Hashima, and the too-tall fashion plate there is Gabriel Dante. Guys, this is Kyri Vantage, Rion Vantage, and my real good friends Tobimar Silverun and Poplock Duckweed."

"Xavier's told us a *lot* about you," Gabriel said, and his violet eyes twinkled at her in a way that reminded her, with a pang, of Condor—Aran—before everything changed. "I must say his words failed to do you justice, Lady Kyri, although that is perhaps not so much his fault as that of words themselves."

Kyri noticed Aurora give him a gentle jab in the ribs with an elbow; Gabriel grinned and slipped an arm around her waist. *Together, then.* "I see you have someone capable of flattery, if not diplomacy, in your group. But please, all of you, come in. We've laid the table for all of us to sit and eat and talk."

"Eating and talking sound like a good idea to me," Nike said.

"But there *is* one other issue first," Gabriel said, and his gaze was on Rion. "Xavier, I see what you mean."

"And?"

Gabriel turned to Kyri. "You are aware that he is not human; are you aware that he is demonic, and something else—undead, I believe—as well?"

"Well, *mudbubbles!*" Poplock said in chagrin. "You know, it took *days* for me and Hiriista to analyze all that, and you and Xavier can just *look* at him and see it? *How?*"

"Let's leave 'how' for later," Gabriel said. "We have very good reason to be suspicious of such creatures. Demons do not just hunt your group, they are hunting ours as well, and the unliving even more so. What of this...being you are calling your brother?"

Kyri started forward even before she knew she was doing it,

but both Rion and Tobimar caught her arms. "Kyri, calm down. Let me answer them."

She couldn't keep from glaring at Gabriel Dante, but forced herself to control the anger at his words. "All right." *I am overreacting. I knew people would be wary of Rion's nature, to say the least. Why am I so . . . touchy over what I already expected?*

Tobimar faced Gabriel. "Your suspicions are perfectly reasonable, and echo our own when we first discovered Rion." He quickly summarized the situation. "Do we *know* that this is really Rion? No. He *could* still be a spy or worse, but if so he knows Rion's past and personality to an incredible degree—enough so that Kyri has no doubt that it *is* him. Either way . . . we had no choice but to bring him with us. And with that, we've had to trust him in our counsels or we might not have gotten out alive. If he's what we believe, then Rion lives again, and we will be using one of our enemy's creations against him. If he's not . . . well, at least he's not out of sight."

Nike nodded, smiling wryly. "I see. 'Keep your friends close, and your enemies closer.'"

Gabriel bowed. "A perfectly reasonable position. I apologize, Rion; I meant no offense."

"None taken," Rion answered with the smile she remembered so well; she felt herself relaxing as she saw that Rion wasn't bothered by the situation. "It was the right question to ask. But now, I think we should take our seats."

"I'm starved," Xavier said, heading for one of the chairs nearest the largest roast.

Toshi spoke only after everyone had been seated and served. "Xavier has, as Gabriel mentioned, told us a fair amount about you. I think it's only fair we tell you something of us."

"You're right," Aurora said suddenly, "but first—Tobimar, you're from the country called Skysand, right?"

She saw Tobimar quirk an eyebrow. "I am—technically in exile, though don't take that negatively." He flashed a brilliant smile. "And that will end soon enough, if I can only get home."

"I just had to be sure. We just came from Skysand, and—"

Instantly Tobimar was up, leaning eagerly—and fearfully—across the table. "From my home? What has happened? Even the Sauran King could not get word—is my mother all right? The city? How—"

"Whoa, slow down!" Xavier waved a hand. "Dude, get a grip. She was going to *tell* you and now you're like all freaky."

She watched Tobimar take a deep breath and then looked at Xavier. "I can't blame him," she said, realizing how Tobimar's reaction echoed hers about Rion. *We're both tense.* "I'd feel the same way if I hadn't been to Evanwyl in a few years."

"Can we do this in some sort of *order*?" Toshi said, looking slightly put out.

Nike's laugh was a light *glissando*, a sparkling sound in keeping with her looks. "Oh, Toshi, you know how crazy everything gets. But you're right, we should do things in order or it'll all get confused."

Tobimar seated himself slowly, and Toshi looked around the table before speaking again. "All right. First...what has Xavier told you about us?"

"Not *too* much," Poplock said. "He said that he actually hadn't known you guys all that long to begin with, but that you were all from *Zahralandar*—what you call Earth—and that Khoros had brought you all together and dumped you here."

"And that Khoros somehow expected you to find a way to break the Great Seal itself, or you'd never go home," Tobimar continued; at that statement she saw Lythos give a noticeable start. "We were at the Dragon's Palace when everything went to the Hells, so we ended up seeing something of your conversations in the cells— though," he paused and nodded to Toshi, "you should know that Willowwind Forestfist was exceedingly impressed by the way you made it almost impossible to drag meaning out of those recordings."

"Almost?" Toshi looked crestfallen. "I'd *hoped* I had made it *actually* impossible."

"Take it as a compliment," Poplock advised. "Willowwind is one of the best there is, and you managed to really mess up most of his reconstruction work. Don't get all hung up on it not being perfect."

He shifted on Tobimar's shoulder. "So, anyway, you got caught, broke out of prison, and scattered, leaving Xavier to watch everything and decide if he could talk to anyone. I think that's pretty much it. Oh, yeah. You're elementals of some kind—Willowwind figured that out—and we know Toshi's gotta be Air, and Xavier's obviously Spirit." The little Toad squinted. "Somehow Aurora just *screams* 'Earth,' to me, which makes Gabe and Nike the last two.

I'm gonna make a guess and say that just because she looks cool as frost that she's probably actually Fire, and Gabe's Water."

Toshi raised an eyebrow and looked over at Xavier, who was wearing a vindicated grin. "That Toad *is* good," Toshi said finally.

"You have *no* idea," Kyri said. "But I think that *is* pretty much we know about you. Do we need to know more?"

"*Need*, I don't know. But there *is* a lot more to know. You are aware, I presume, that all of the simultaneous assaults around the world were part of a larger war launched by Kerlamion?"

"Yes. We also know who planned it—and that he's here in Evanwyl."

"The man behind the man," Xavier breathed, leaning forward. "You know who was pulling Thornfalcon's strings."

"We do." She saw that Lythos was also standing straighter; they had not yet told him, since they planned on explaining everything all at once. "His real name—at least, the name that anyone will speak—is Viedraverion. He is rumored to be the first son of Kerlamion himself. And..." She hesitated, finding that saying the last part was surprisingly hard—painful, in truth.

Lythos stepped from his position near the door. "And...?"

"And he is known to us as Jeridan Velion."

"Oh, crap," Xavier muttered. "The big boss of this whole country? The *Watchland*? He seemed like a pretty cool guy while I was here."

Lythos had simply closed his eyes as though in sudden pain; when his eyes opened, they had clear understanding. "Of course. It answers many mysteries. But you do not look as I might expect you to look, having finally found the architect of this evil."

"Because I am also sure that there is a *real* Jeridan Velion, Lythos. That many of his words and deeds are as honest and true as those of any in this room."

Toshi's head tilted. "Possession? A duplicate?"

"Something possibly more complicated than that," Tobimar said. "Look at Rion for one possibility. I think we will need to tell each other our stories, since at least the time that Xavier left us, and ours might be the more urgent here. But, please," he looked intensely at Aurora, "tell me at least—my mother, my brothers and sisters—are they all right?"

Aurora looked at Gabriel for a moment, then shifted in her seat. "Your mother Talima is well. Most of your brothers and sisters are also. But . . . Terimur and Sundrilin fell defending Sky-sand. Sundrilin . . . defending me." She looked down. "I'm sorry. It was my fault."

Kyri's heart felt pierced through as she saw the stricken look on Tobimar's face. Then as his expression relaxed, with an effort only she could sense, she thought the pain was worse from her love for him in what he said next.

"Aurora . . ." A hesitant glance up. "Did Sundrilin know what she was doing? Did she *choose* to do what she did?"

"I . . ." Aurora's swallow was audible across the table. "Yes. Yes, she knew what she was doing, and why."

"And did she achieve what she hoped?"

For an instant, Aurora's face was transformed, to one of anger and certainty. "Yes. Oh, yes, she did."

"Then do not apologize." The hint of tears in Tobimar's voice could have torn Kyri apart, but there was only gentleness in his voice. "We are *Silverun*. We are the defenders of our people, of our lands. We know our duty and the peril of our lives, and the most any can ask of their deaths is that they gave their lives *well*. And it sounds to me as though Sundrilin died well."

"As did Terimur," Gabriel said. "Both of them died very, very well, and gave us the time we needed."

"That *I* needed," Aurora said quietly. "Gabe, I know you'd like to take part of that responsibility, but it *was* my fault." She looked up, eyes shimmering with tears, but she smiled. "But . . . thank you, Tobimar."

"You are welcome." Tobimar sat down slowly, and his head bowed; Kyri saw Poplock pat his friend's head gently.

"More of that story in its place," Lythos said. "Kyri, I believe you were going to tell us all of what has passed since last we saw you."

She took a deep breath. "Yes. Well, first we traveled back to the Spiritsmith . . ."

The tale was long and involved—longer, now that she had started, than she had realized. As time passed and dishes were cleared and refilled, Tobimar roused himself from his private grief and began to help, giving his keen observations, with Pop-lock adding key insights along the way. Even though the five visitors—for the most part—listened quietly, it was still a long time before she was finished.

In a way, she was reminded of the night they had first met Tobimar, and each had told their stories to the others. *It is similar. We are on the same quest, in a way, and guided by Khoros' phantom hand, and I think now is one of the most crucial moments of all our lives.*

Finally she reached the climax, the duel against alchemy and madness culminating in a battle of gods and magicians, and then the recovery and rebuilding where it was possible. "...and then we made it back through Rivendream and, well, here we are."

For a few moments, the room was silent as it had not been for over two hours. Nike broke the quiet with a sudden laugh. "Well, I thought *we* had had something of an adventure, but I'm not sure it compares. Mad scientists and dragon-gods!"

"It compares," Toshi said calmly. "I think we are of rather equal footing overall—which is frightening in its implications." He looked at the others. "Our own stories might take even longer to tell. There are aspects that I think would be best kept to ourselves, as well. Meaning no offense," he looked at Rion, "but if there is even a *chance* that one of the people here could be—willingly or not—a spy, there are details we shouldn't discuss. I am presuming Rion was already familiar with your own story, so it was not an issue there."

Kyri wanted to protest, but...Toshi was *right.* There weren't that many secrets *she* had to hide from Rion, but these five... "Understood. But there is one question I want to ask Xavier first."

"Sure," said Xavier.

"When you saw Rion, you called him by another name. Who—"

"Michael," Xavier said quietly. "And jeez, I still see Mike over there if I don't look carefully."

"Hold a moment," Kyri said, suddenly dizzied. "Xavier... Michael, of course, I'd forgotten...*that* was the name of your brother? The one you were planning to avenge?"

"Yeah." Xavier cast another incredulous glance at Rion. "Here, lemme show you."

He dug through his pack for a moment, then held out a leather wallet which he flipped open to show a small picture. "There, that's Mike."

"Great Balance," she murmured.

Michael Ross did indeed look very, very much like Rion Vantage. The hair and eyes were identical; the faces shaped much the same, the smile was very like Rion's; even the build of the two men was very similar. She could see some small differences—the darker shade of Rion's skin, the slightly narrower cheekbones of Michael—but the effect was startlingly similar; the two could have been brothers, almost twins.

"Terian's *Light*, no wonder you thought it was him come back from the dead," muttered Tobimar.

"Lady Vantage—"

"Oh, Kyri, *please*," she said, glancing over to see that it was Toshi addressing her.

"Kyri. Just so I understand—you had an older brother who died, and for whom you swore vengeance against his killers, yes?"

"Yes."

He glanced to Xavier. "And you are one of three children."

"Yes."

"And you and Xavier share eyes of a rather unique shade of gray." Toshi considered. "Your brothers are startlingly similar in appearance as well as circumstance. There seem many peculiar parallels here."

"Want another?" Poplock said. "Xavier's middle name is Uriel, right?" A nod. "Well, Kyri's little sister's name is Urelle."

"Fascinating." He looked over to Nike; the silver-blond haired girl nodded.

"Does it *mean* anything?" Aurora asked.

"I think it means *Khoros*," said Nike bluntly. "We know he manipulated our lives—our *families'* lives—for as far back as we can count. And we know he can travel between the worlds. So it makes sense he's doing the same thing here."

"Still, one has to wonder what the purpose is."

"I don't think it matters at this point. Perhaps one day we shall have the chance to ask him," Gabriel said reasonably.

Nike shrugged. "Perhaps. Now, we have to tell you our stories... maybe with a little less detail and a little faster."

"I'll trust you to tell ours," Toshi said.

The white-blond girl raised an eyebrow. "You *do*?"

The blush was *just* visible under Toshi's skin. "I *have* learned a few things."

"We'll both tell ours," Gabriel said. "Different experiences and perspectives. But Toshi will probably hush us at points."

"And then I'll tell mine," Xavier said, "since I was the only one there."

Kyri glanced at the clock. "We lack only a few minutes of midnight. Does everyone still wish to go on? You could rest here—"

"Not unless you're too tired to listen," Toshi said. "We are in a hurry—not a desperate one, but a hurry nonetheless—and finishing this will help you understand that, just as we now understand what you might need of us."

"All right," Tobimar said. "But I need a few minutes to visit, er—"

"Yeah, we all need a bathroom break, I think," said Xavier bluntly. "So, what, let's all take a break, let Vanstell and the others clean up our mess, and meet up back here in fifteen?"

"Agreed," Kyri said, smiling at Xavier's straightforward handling of the situation. "In fifteen minutes, then, you'll tell us *your* stories."

CHAPTER 16

Poplock watched from his perch on one of the unlit candleholders, nibbling on a thimbleberry, as the others slowly filtered in. Xavier practically leaped back into his chair and started eating. "You know," said the Toad, "you seem to eat like twice as much as everyone else."

"Yeah," Xavier mumbled around a mouthful of crispwing, "my *sensei* said something about that being a consequence of burning more energy than everyone else. Then there's Rion, who doesn't seem to eat much at all."

"We figure that's because he's, well, not human."

"Makes sense. Maybe an advantage in some ways." Xavier reached out and poured himself more water.

Gabriel and Tobimar came in from opposite directions, while Lythos finally seated himself rather than standing and observing. "These matters run deep and strange," the *Artan* warrior observed. "And I suspect your stories will prove even stranger."

"I can't say for sure on that, sir," Gabriel said. "As Nike observed, I would hardly have expected their tale to include what we would call a classic mad scientist—which surely fits your Master Wieran to perfection—so they already have from my view something of an advantage on us."

Most of the others had returned and gotten settled. Nike nodded at Gabriel's comment, and smiled at Xavier; Poplock noticed that Xavier's gaze often strayed to Nike even when he was talking to someone else. *Which, if there's mutual attraction, would leave Toshi odd man out.* He couldn't tell if there was a mutual attraction, though; Nike's demeanor was calm, professional most of the time, even with those she traveled with. *Xavier said she was raised by guardsmen—police—so she obviously takes after her parents.*

"Where's Rion and Kyri?" asked Toshi.

"I think they were out getting a little air before coming back in," Tobimar answered.

"Huh. Dude, I would've thought *you* would be taking her out for a walk, not her brother."

Tobimar laughed. "He *was* thought dead for two years, and she always...well, rather idolized him. Besides, he's been confronted with his nature a couple of times tonight, they're probably talking some of that out. He's...not happy with it."

"Yeah," Xavier admitted, "I wouldn't be too comfortable finding out I was a half-undead demon-duplicate either."

"*Please* don't say stuff like that casually, especially around Rion," Tobimar warned him.

As Xavier nodded his understanding, Poplock saw the two remaining people coming in from the front entrance. Without her habitual helm to conceal her face, the Phoenix Justiciar seemed noticeably more tired than usual, but cheerful, greeting the room with one of her flashing smiles. Rion looked also more relaxed than he had before they left; as per usual habit, he waited for Kyri to seat herself next to Tobimar before taking the seat on her other side.

"Okay," Poplock said. "We're all here. It's you guys' turn to tell us what you've been up to."

The five young people looked at each other, and then Gabriel nodded. "Aurora and I will go first.

"You all know that we managed to escape from the prison under the Dragon's Palace. When we did that, it was agreed that we would split up; I believe that Xavier has already told you that Khoros had apparently foreseen this?"

"Yes," Poplock said, searching his memory for the exact wording. "So you could, um, '...find answers to the tasks before you, the powers within you, and the doubts that surround you,' right?"

Aurora snorted, her expression an odd blend of fury and gratitude. "Yes. I will still kick that old bastard in the balls before I thank him, though."

Gabriel shook his head. "I think the first may be difficult to achieve. In any event, we were agreed that we had to go our separate ways to minimize the chance of all of us being recaptured. So we attempted to...flee as quickly as possible." Toshi had glanced at him during the last sentence. "Exactly how is one of the things we won't detail. We found ourselves, eventually, in a desert, something which was most distressing to me as I am—as you so correctly observed—inherently of the Water element. But with Aurora's support we were able to travel until we came in sight of a city, which turned out to be Tempestward."

"*Tempestward*?" Tobimar repeated. "You traveled from *Zarathanton* to the northernmost desert of Skysand in such a manner you knew not where you had gone or how?"

Poplock was at least as stunned. *Thousands of miles, in what they imply was an extremely short time, without knowing the territory they passed through? But teleportation's severely limited these days. Makes sense as to why they don't want to explain just how. Big useful secret there.*

"We did," confirmed Aurora. "And then we were chased into the city by something that we figured out later was a demon. Which did at least get the attention of Sundrilin." Her face fell.

"You were friends with her, weren't you?" Tobimar asked quietly.

"Eventually...once I stopped being paranoid about everything. She brought us to Skysand, the capital, and that was when the real trouble started..."

Poplock saw Kyri reach out and take Tobimar's hand in hers as Gabriel and Aurora continued their story—a story that included mystery and intrigue and even betrayal within the capital city, a siege, and eventually a counterstrike against demonic forces that seemed endless and unstoppable...

"...We *had* to fight for them," Aurora said, and by now there were tears in her voice, her eyes wet. "I'd been...we'd both been...difficult to deal with. But your mother and Sundrilin and your other brothers and sisters...they had patience, they helped keep us *alive* in more ways than one. And then these *monsters* were trying to wipe out your people, it was a planned assault, and time was running out..."

"The demons were, of course, beings of fire and sand, taking advantage of the terrain," Gabriel said. Poplock remembered the sand demons that had ambushed him, Tobimar, and Xavier, and thought about what an army of such monsters would be like. "We tried to fight them . . . did fairly well . . . but while demons of fire are certainly things I can fight well, those of sand could sap my strength easily; not so much Aurora's, but she did not have any particular advantage against them, and many of them seemed able to ignore ordinary blows entirely."

Aurora swallowed, then sat straighter. "And then the royal family took the field." She looked directly at Tobimar. "Be proud of them all. They were *amazing*. They rallied everyone—including us—and drove towards the leaders. I was . . . not fighting as well as I should."

Now it was Gabriel's hand taking Aurora's, even as the girl forced herself to continue—even as Toshi shot them another warning glance. "I . . . I can't tell you everything. But I was . . . fighting myself, I guess, my own mistrust. My parents . . . kinda screwed me up without meaning to, and I made things worse. But even with us not doing our best, me and Gabe . . . were pretty obviously dangerous targets, so they sent a force against us . . . and when one of them almost had me, Sundrilin . . ."

She stopped, unable to go on, not that she had to; Poplock had seen more than enough battles to understand the rest.

"And then?" Kyri asked finally.

"And then . . . we found the key we had been searching for, the answers that Khoros had spoken of," Gabriel said grimly, "and we scoured the desert until not one of the monsters was left standing."

Rion stared at him. "By . . . by *yourselves*?"

Aurora gave a predatory, vicious smile from beneath her tear-streaked face. "Oh yes. By ourselves, then."

There was a short silence as Poplock and the others took that in. "Okay," Poplock said finally. "I guess you *are* playing on the same level as we were, there. Ouch. How'd you end up back here?"

"A few weeks afterward, the *Nomdas*—the high priestess of Terian?—called us and said that she had been sent a vision by her god, a message that was clearly for us. Once Gabriel unraveled it, it basically said for us to head to a particular place and we'd find what we were looking for. And sure enough, when we got there, we ran into Xavier."

"Which means it's time for *our* story," Nike said, "since we ran into all three of you a little while later."

Poplock saw both Tobimar and Kyri take some *havaja*, an herb and fruit brew that helped maintain alertness, as Nike and Toshi related their own adventures—with the same vagueness on key issues. Even so, Poplock could pick out the same basic threads and implications of the narrative. The two had arrived in a forest filled with dangerous demonic things and barely managed to escape to a city under siege—the city named *Nya-Sharee-Hilya*, Surviving the Storm of Ages, capital of Artania, home of the *Artan*. Lythos listened to their story even more intently than he had the previous one—a story with similar complexity, subterfuge, espionage, and danger, culminating with a battle against the forces of the Demonlord Balgoltha—a battle that ended with yet more vague generalities.

"Then, sifting through what was left of the besieging forces' materials, we came across a reference to Evanwyl that seemed promising," Toshi said.

Nike raised an eyebrow. "Boy, you make that sound easy. Took both of us to piece together that—"

Toshi held up his hand, and Nike paused; Toshi continued for her. "Anyway, we decided to go. Queen Mithras felt she owed us, um . . . pretty much anything we wanted," for a moment he looked embarrassed, "so we got passage on the fastest ship she had and they sailed us up the Nightsky River as close to Evanwyl as possible."

"And ran into our friends a little before actually reaching the city," Nike finished. "Xavier?"

"Heh," Xavier said, dropping a bone into a plate already stacked with them. "Mine wasn't nearly as combat heavy. Kinda funny, since only me and Gabe really started out as fighter types." He leaned back and took a drink. "Anyway, I set out to get to Mount Scimitar, like you guys already knew. Unlike my friends here, I don't have some super-fast trick for travelling, so that was a long haul. Had to dodge around what looked like a big force headed for the Broken Hills, then hiked pretty much straight East for a long time. Spent a lot of my time invisible, figured that'd make me harder to track and keep me out of trouble. Still, there were times . . ."

Xavier had continued through most of the Empire of the Mountain, occasionally running into people who needed the kind of help he could provide, and getting better directions from them in turn. Eventually he'd gotten close to the legendary Mountain.

"Man, that's a *different* place. Scimitar's Path, that is—the capital of the Empire? It's sorta like I figured Vatican City must be like, everyone all religious and faithful and like that, except that the god they're worshipping isn't somewhere beyond the sky, he's *right there* at the top of the mountain." Poplock didn't *exactly* get the "Vatican City" reference, but he remembered well enough that on Xavier's world the gods didn't ever seem to act, at least not the way they did here.

Xavier went on, "And it's kinda creepy; he's got all kinds working for him, including undead, some demons, other pretty shady types, but they don't cause trouble in the city.

"I figured I could just head on up the mountain by myself, but the only decent path up had a big temple straight across it. I *could* sneak around, but . . . well, anyway, I started asking around, and it turned out that anyone could *try* climbing the mountain, but no one actually knew *anyone* who'd gone above a certain point, basically where there was a little shrine, and come back alive. There were a few stories—but always the 'a friend of a friend' kind, where you can't actually *find* the friend of a friend who reached the top. Turned out that I couldn't even get a good idea of what this Idinus guy really looked like."

Xavier had finally set out on his climb, and found that even with his unique powers it was *hard* to progress. It took him a couple of months, he said, and there was a trick to it that took him most of that to figure out. "And I felt kinda stupid when I did, but anyhow, I got to the top finally."

Tobimar stared at him, then shook his head in disbelief. "Really? You got to the *peak* of Mount Scimitar? And . . . was he there?"

"Idinus?" For a moment, Xavier's usual breezy, casual manner vanished; he was deadly serious, his eyes seeing something beyond the room they sat in. "Oh yeah, he was there. Scariest son of a . . . gun I ever met, except maybe my sensei if he got mad. Never raised his voice, barely moved most of the time, but he didn't have to. But . . . he told me what I needed to know."

"The location of the Great Seal?"

"Yeah." He glanced at the others; Toshi gave a nod. "It's in the center of the Black City—probably in Kerlamion's throne room itself."

"Great Balance," whispered Kyri. "You mean that you . . ."

". . . have to find this Black City, get into it, find the throne room, and *then* somehow break this seal, yeah," Xavier confirmed. "And the longer we wait, the stronger those guys are getting, the more their grip on this world tightens, at least as I understand it."

For a moment even Poplock couldn't speak. These five people— five *children*, really, not even as old as Kyri and Tobimar—were supposed to invade the fortress of the King of All Hells, enter his castle, and then undo his greatest work, a work that had endured for half a million years. *What in the name of Blackwart is Khoros* thinking? *I mean, these kids obviously have got* some- thing *or they wouldn't have survived what they did, but that's... way, way out there.*

Finally he bounced, shrugging off the mood. "Well," said Poplock, "We know that the Empire *and* the Dragon have armies there, so Kerlamion's invasion isn't proceeding without a hitch. He's *not* going to just brush the Sauran King and the Archmage aside, no matter what he's set up. Plus if I don't miss my guess, what you guys did has *seriously* messed up his plans; I'll bet he was planning on having both Skysand and Artania totally dealt with, so he could be calling in the forces he had there to help him with the main battle—and from what you said, he's not even getting most of 'em back even in retreat. Still..."

"We understand why you do not wish to wait for long," Tobimar said. "But now that you know that the *architect* of these events is here in Evanwyl...what we need to know is can you stay at least a little while to help us?"

Toshi looked at his friends. "For a *little* while. What we need is to figure out a route to the Black City, preferably one as quick as possible. We *could* go to the city of Hell's Edge, but that is a long, long way from here, and we have good reason to suspect that using any of our...quick methods of travel would get us noticed immediately, especially as we get closer to our goal, now that the City is actually manifest here. Also, taking the expected route will mean a route that is under constant observation. If we can determine a better route, it will be worth some time."

"Besides," Nike said, "Your group's also been guided by Khoros. We've got a mission in common along the way, I think."

A wrinkle appeared on Toshi's forehead, then cleared. "*So desu*," he said. "In both our stories, one thing stands out: *noth- ing* like our meetings is left to chance. Khoros has mapped out every encounter both of our groups has had. The fact that Kyri

did not meet Tobimar and Poplock in Zarathanton, but rather
only in desperate need at the end of their journey; the way in
which Tobimar and Poplock first met; the exact ways in which
each of us was...brought in by Khoros, the encounter between
Xavier and Tobimar that brought him here twice before—Khoros
obviously *planned* that.

"Given that, it's completely ridiculous for us to think he
didn't plan this encounter, and the only reason I can think of
for that is that he wants us to help you, and maybe something
else, something we haven't thought of. Maybe you even have a
way for us to shortcut getting to the Black City."

Poplock blinked at that. *You know...maybe we do. Not one
I'd recommend to anyone else, but...I'll talk about it with Kyri
and Tobimar later.*

"So..." Toshi went on, "...unless there's an objection, yes,
we will stay for a while."

"What do you have in mind that we can help with?" Gabriel
asked immediately.

Poplock gave his widest grin. "Be our backup when we pay
a social call...on the Watchland."

CHAPTER 17

The Watchland's Fortress lay in front of them, only a few hundred yards distant. Of their dual group, only Rion was not present; he had remained behind with Lythos at Vantage Fortress. His presence would have vastly complicated the entire issue. Kyri looked to the five younger people. "Ready?"

Toshi nodded. "This should not be complicated, only potentially dangerous. For our purposes, there are really only three scenarios. First, we discover the Watchland is our enemy immediately, and the battle is joined; at that point I would *hope* that all of us together will be able to overcome pretty much anything."

Remembering the Elderwyrm Sanamaveridion, Kyri shuddered. "Maybe. But we can't just use the full powers we've talked about here. Jeridan has a staff of at least twenty people; we're not very far from the center of Evanwyl. If we fight a battle anything like the one we fought in Kaizatenzei—"

"Lady Kyri," Gabriel interrupted, "please—we understand. We very much understand." She saw in his eyes that he, too, was remembering something devastating. "But if you are right, your ultimate enemy is the *cause* of most of this. We are choosing to confront him here; that leaves the possibility that such a battle may be *fought* here."

"You wanna abort?" Xavier asked. His expression was serious, not judging her, just asking a question. "Drop it and try something else?"

In her mind's eye, Kyri saw her golden fire contesting with

107

night-black destruction, shattering hills, blasting buildings, igniting fields. *Can I even* possibly *risk that?*

Tobimar and Poplock were silent; neither seemed willing to advise her to either go forward or retreat.

Myrionar, guide me. Do I move forward, or back? Do I risk this, or is it wiser that I do not, and seek another course?

She waited, but there was nothing, neither an omen of danger nor something drawing her forward. *Even Myrionar is saying to me 'this is your choice, and yours alone.'*

The fortress ahead gleamed white and silver in the afternoon sun, a structure whose design made massive walls and watchtowers seem delicate and airy, faced with polished white marble and enchanted steel. She remembered the Watchland from her youngest days, always present yet always moving, and remembered their talk at Rion's dance years before. With a shock, she realized that the towering older figure she remembered from her third year must have been a youth, someone no older than Gabriel or Xavier. *He's been protecting our country since he was younger than me, since his father died fighting something out of Rivendream.*

That, somehow, decided her. *I have faith that I am right about him, and that it will not come to destruction, not here.* "Come on," she said quietly. "It's time."

The others followed in silence. As they approached the Watchland's Fortress, Kyri saw the guards at the gate snap to full attention and bow. "Phoenix! By the *Balance*, you're *back*?"

"Hello, Renthas, Yomin," she said with a smile at the pair, one blond, solid, and cheerful, the other tall, dark, and deceptively dour. "We are indeed. Would the Watchland be available? I would like to introduce him to some important visitors."

"It would be extremely improbable that he would *not* receive you," Yomin said, a rare smile flickering on his long face, softening the expression of disbelief that had also been there. "Give me a moment to check, of course." He stepped into an alcove with a speaking tube, while Renthas kept watch; the guard's gaze scanned the group with abject curiosity, but no suspicion. *I'd be stunned if there was, actually. My advantage here really is being utterly above suspicion. And hopefully, there is no need for suspicion.*

Yomin emerged and nodded. "The Watchland says he would

be most pleased to receive you and your friends; go straight in, you know the way. He's in the library."

Kyri felt her heartbeat accelerating as they approached the dark-red polished wood of the library doors. *Please let me have made the right decision.*

Jeridan Velion rose as she entered. "Kyri! You've returned from beyond Rivendream?" Before she could answer, he strode forward and embraced her. "Oh, welcome home, welcome *home*, Phoenix Kyri! And Tobimar! By Myrionar's Blade, I had begun to give up hope that you had survived!"

Kyri felt unexpected tears welling up. *This isn't an act! I can . . . feel him here. Not distant, not cold hiding behind a warm face! This is the Jeridan I was hoping to find!*

She returned the embrace, but at the same time felt tension rising in her. *But that's just my feelings, and it's what I wanted to find. It really depends on what the others see . . .*

"We did, Jeridan—not easily, I admit. And that's a long tale that you'll have a hard time believing," she said. "But first, I want to introduce you to our visitors."

Watchland Velion immediately straightened and gave the customary Armed Bow, allowing all to see the straight, double-edged sword in its sheath on his hip as he completed the turn. "My apologies to you; all of us in Evanwyl have been concerned for Kyri on this venture, and to know she was well—"

"Don't worry about it, Watchland," Xavier said with a grin. "I was just as glad to see them."

"Xavier Ross! I admit this is a pleasant surprise."

"Jeridan, you recall that Xavier mentioned he'd come here with four friends?"

"Indeed." The golden-haired Watchland raised an eyebrow. "Then these are your lost companions?"

"Yep!"

"Jeridan, allow me to present to you Gabriel Dante, Nike Engelshand, Toshi Hashima, and Aurora Vanderdecken," Kyri said. The natives of Earth, being somewhat close together and not practiced in the idea, didn't do the Armed Bow but instead bowed from the waist.

"Welcome, all of you," the Watchland said, his blue eyes studying the newcomers keenly. He also clasped hands with each of them. "All from the legendary other world? A momentous occasion for my fortress, I must say. Please, come with me to table, I will have some refreshments brought and we can talk a bit before I must tend to other duties."

"How could we refuse?" Nike said. "We'd be honored."

"I assure you, the honor is entirely mine. There must be a grand story behind your arrival here as well, and I look forward to hearing something of it."

As the Watchland led them to his private dining room, Kyri glanced quickly at the others.

Gabriel gave her an emphatic nod, but raised one eyebrow; Xavier gave a thumbs-up gesture which she knew meant "yes," then also shook his head. Poplock also bounced once on Tobimar's shoulder.

Relief surged through her again, this time so strongly she felt herself momentarily weak. *He's nothing monstrous. But they've found something else. Now we find out if he can be saved.*

It took only a few moments for everyone to be seated. "Once more, welcome, old friends and new. I will call to have us served—"

"Wait, please," she said. He paused, hand reaching for one of the gems that would have brought servants in to take direction. "There is something we would rather say to you in private, now."

"Ah. Something more than a social call, then? I should have suspected as much, since I had heard no word of your coming, despite having heard that there was a small group of strange youngsters at old Kell's place." Instead of touching for a summons, he passed his hand over another, which was meant for privacy; Kyri felt a faint wash of magic. "As you wish, then."

The others looked at her. *This is all mine; they're right.* "Jeridan...Do you trust me?"

He opened his mouth to answer instantly, but then paused, seeing her expression. "Completely and without reservation, Phoenix Kyri Vantage," he said quietly, after a moment. "Speak, then. I gave you my trust that day in the temple, and you proved me right. I shall *always* trust you."

She took a deep breath. "Then I must tell you that—somehow—your...likeness, at least...has been used and is perhaps still being used by our enemies."

Jeridan's eyes narrowed. "How do you mean?"

"She means," Tobimar said, "that the architect of not just the fall of the Justiciars, but of most of the current troubles of the world, has been wearing your face, Watchland. We found yet another part of the plot beyond Rivendream Pass, in a country called Kaizatenzei, and one of those high in the counsels of the enemy was able to show us the likeness of this master manipulator. That likeness was yours."

Watchland Velion was on his feet, and his face was dark with anger. But there was no anger in his voice when he spoke to her. "Kyri Victoria Vantage, do you trust *me?*"

"I do . . . now," she said. "Jeridan—Watchland—understand, we have already seen evidence of the ability of our adversaries to work through others, so that sometimes they were . . . themselves, and sometimes not. I had reason to believe that this was true of you. I know that—at least for now—you are the man I have always known."

The Watchland slowly examined those seated at his table. "I see. What is your purpose in this visit, then?"

"Initially," Toshi said, "to examine you at close range and determine whether you were a monster hiding in the guise of an ally, or the man you appeared to be."

"And have you found that I am who I appear to be?"

"Yes," Gabriel answered. "But not one without mysteries about him. There is a complex enchantment woven about you; I can see it, but I do not yet have the knowledge to interpret what I see fully."

"Right," said Xavier. "There's a layering of something through your soul, but from what and what exactly it does, I don't know."

"We think at least part of it is memory implant," Poplock said, causing Jeridan to jump.

"So you *are* a member of their party, Poplock Duckweed, not merely a pet!" he said. "I had wondered about that more than once. What do you mean by 'memory implant'?"

"Do you remember what you said to me, when you came to bid Aunt Victoria, Urelle, and myself goodbye?" Kyri asked.

"I confess that I do not remember it in detail, no."

"I do, though. You said '. . . for many of the last few days I have felt almost outside myself, watching what I have been doing, seeking to make it all right, yet . . . not able to let myself . . . truly reach those who needed me most . . . .'" She met his gaze. "Do you understand what I am saying?"

Jeridan Velion's gaze dropped, and he was silent for a moment. When he looked back up, she saw something bleak and frightened there. "Yes," he whispered. "Yes, Kyri. I've...felt that many times over the years. I would awaken one morning, and remember what I had done over the past days or weeks, and yet it would feel...*flat*, cold, colorless, as though I were trying to remember someone else's dream. The facts would be there, the images, but the feelings, the *connection*, would be wan, dim, cold."

"As though you had not, in fact, done it," Toshi said. "That someone had instead effectively given you the memory, but without the associations that make living memories so rich and strong."

"And you are saying that this is exactly what has happened to me?"

"Yes. The very nature of the memories confirms it," Toshi answered, after a quick glance at Poplock. "Our adversary could certainly give you memories of what they had done—but those memories, to be innocuous to you, would either be entirely synthetic, made-up, and thus expected to be thin and less convincing, or would be actual events but stripped of our enemy's actual thoughts and reactions, which would have been far too revealing."

Kyri put her hand on his shoulder. "Jeridan, where we came from, our enemy had effectively made duplicates of people, ones they could leave acting as though they *were* those people and then take over whenever needed; they described similar symptoms. We need to find out what, exactly, has been done to you—and if our enemy has any hold on you, to break that hold."

"And can you do this without our enemy being aware of it?"

"Probably not," Poplock said. "But we're getting ready to go after him and he *is* probably aware of that. Making sure he doesn't have you as a battlesquares piece? That's worth it."

Kyri saw Jeridan looking with grim curiosity at the group, and she knew what he saw; children, mostly, with her an unusual and still very young exception. "When you say this being who has been using me is the 'architect' of the current troubles... what exactly do you mean? Is he..."

"...responsible for the Black City arriving? Yep," said Poplock. "According to our sources, he planned the whole thing, including the assassination of the Sauran King, the attacks on Artania, Skysand, Aegeia, all of it. He arranged a trap for us, too, in Kaizatenzei. And he is the one behind the False Justiciars, the corrupter of the order. He is the son of Kerlamion, called Viedraverion."

Jeridan shuddered. "That name...I...*feel* something, something terrible, when I hear it." He raised his head, looked into her eyes. "I trust you implicitly, Kyri, the Phoenix of Myrionar, the one who tore the mask from Thornfalcon and the other fallen Justiciars. And this...this explains other things, veiled comments, occasional odd looks I recall from the Justiciars. Yes, Kyri." He straightened. "If you must do something, then do it. Even if it is something less...gentle than you imply."

"Less gentle...?" For a moment she wondered what he meant, and then saw the bleak acceptance in his eyes, the stiff rise of the chin. "Oh, Myrionar, *no*, Jeridan. I did not come here to kill you."

"If in *any* way I can be used against you—against *Evanwyl*—you *should* kill me," the Watchland said, hands clenched at his side. "I—"

"Let us try something less drastic first, sir," Gabriel said; the very slight smile was apologetic.

"Yes," Poplock said, interrupting the Watchland before the man could more than open his mouth. "We *know* that anything Viedra put on you will probably be mud-sticking hard to break, but we've got a couple advantages. First, he probably doesn't know we're going to try that *now*, and second, I don't think he knows *anything* about our friends, and even less that they're here. His daddy's opposing forces got pretty much wiped out without a chance to report, and no one's going to believe they all got here from there so quick anyway. And I've learned a few tricks since we've been gone, too."

Jeridan Velion looked at them with dawning curiosity, and then smiled weakly at Poplock. "Well, I recall being warned by Adjudicator Toron once, many years ago, to never underestimate a Toad. It seems I might do well to remember that advice."

"Yeah, you should. *He* forgot it and had to slap himself later," Poplock said dryly.

"Then the moments pass no less swiftly; can you perform whatever spells or rituals you envision here and now?"

"If you'll let us move the table and chairs out of the way, Jeridan, yes."

"*Burn* them if you must!" The vehemence of Velion's outburst made them all stare. "My apologies," he said, face dark with fury. "I am not angry with you, Kyri, nor with any of your friends and allies. Only at this monster who has used me as a tool. Any price is worth paying to free myself of that."

"Understood."

Kyri dragged the massive table to one side as the others gathered up the chairs and stacked them; Xavier locked all the doors and Poplock put a seal on them to prevent any possible interruptions.

"Now what?" Toshi asked. "We're not magicians, Poplock, so this part is up to you."

"You're right that you're not magicians," Poplock said, "but you're something even better. You're *elementals*, and not just any elementals, but ones probably designed by Khoros himself. For a guy like me, that makes you, um, how would Xavier put it—oh, yeah! Makes you the biggest batteries *ever*."

Aurora looked suspiciously at Poplock. "You're not going to drain us or anything, are you?"

"Well, yes and no," Poplock said, his voice somewhat muffled as he was digging through his neverfull pack at the moment. "I'm not going to rip out your spirits to fuel a dark spell or anything, but I *am* going to be tapping the power of all of you in this. Might leave you tired, but shouldn't hurt anyone." He emerged with various ritual tools, including colored sands and drawing materials.

"Elementals?" Jeridan looked intrigued, even as Poplock chivvied him to the center of the room and started drawing a complicated circle around him. "Truly?"

"Probably more than that," Toshi admitted. "We're trying to figure all that out ourselves, but at least one of our allies said something about also having virtues associated with us—"

"Oooo, that makes sense!" Poplock said. "But keep the conversation down, please—if you distract me I might put the wrong symbols down and that would end badly."

"Should we get the others set up?"

"Please do. I'll give you some guidelights." Poplock muttered and gestured, and suddenly a pyramid of light appeared, each of the five points glowing a different color: white at the apex, then light blue, crimson, green, and violet around the perimeter of the base.

Xavier looked up, nonplussed. "I suppose I can get *up* there, but if I'm in my not-here mode I don't think I'm going to, well, *be* here."

"*Trust* me," Poplock said. "I've thought of that. Just jump up there—pretend there's a little platform up there, because there is. You just can't *see* it."

The gray eyes closed. "Oh, yeah. I can see it now." Xavier gave a somersaulting leap that took him fifteen feet up, brushing the ceiling, to come down atop what looked like empty air. "On station!"

Toshi nodded as the rest took their places. "The color associations are common?"

"Here, yeah."

"Will I need to do anything?" asked the Watchland.

"Just... don't move. I've got your circle done here, and you know that damaging a ritual circle can be a bad thing, right?"

"Yes, I've seen the results of one that was damaged during the ritual. 'Bad thing' indeed." Jeridan looked carefully around him and then removed his sword, then sat down on the polished wood floor. "Now it should be safe."

"Good call."

Kyri watched the remainder of the preparations, the Toad carefully drawing complex circles around the four positioned at the points of the pyramid, and felt tension once more return. Poplock was much more skilled than he had been when first they met, there was no doubt of that. And if even half the stories of Xavier and his friends had been true, they would represent an immense amount of power.

But on the other hand, if they were right, Poplock was trying to break the bonds of one of the most powerful demonlords... bonds in use for years.

"Ready for you too, Kyri, Tobimar."

Two more circles had been drawn—one on each side of the Watchland, a line facing towards the rising sun, if the room had been open to the sky. Kyri could recognize symbols for Myrionar, Terian, Chromaias, and the sketched pop-eyes of Blackwart, and saw others scattered through the symbolic pyramid. *He's invoking just about everyone on the side of Light in this. I think that double lightning bolt is the symbol of the Three Beards, and there's the Triad, and definitely that's the Hammer and Spear.* The little Toad gestured with a tiny wand, sketching more mystical symbology into the air itself, following the lines of the pyramid and encircling Xavier as the boy sat in meditation. The others of the Five had also seated themselves. Only she and Tobimar stood, facing each other and the Watchland between them.

"Almost there," Poplock said gravely. "Once this starts, though, it's going to get *dangerous*. I can sorta *see* the enchantments in Jeridan, and they're gonna be tough."

"I can see them clearly," Gabriel said. "They are strong. But I do not think they are stronger than we are."

"Bet on it," Xavier said. "We're ready."

Nike nodded. "Ready."

"So am I," Toshi said.

"Do it already!" Aurora said.

Poplock bounced a grin at that. "Okay! Watchland, get ready. This might hurt, or might not, but I can't promise anything."

The figure of the Watchland tensed.

Poplock Duckweed began to intone a ritual. It was a strange, patchwork ritual. Some of it, Kyri could tell, was in the peculiar language of the Toads, sound and motion interspersed. Other parts were in the more common language of Zarathan. Some words of Ancient Sauran were used, and even a few ancient phrases which clearly came from the old language of Kaizatenzei. Poplock invoked gods ancient and new, recited words of reinforcement and strength, murmured pieces of ancient prayers, and, once, touched the Gemcalling matrix on his arm, sending a glitter of power through the symbols.

The pyramid began to glow brighter, the previously invisible faces of the figure shimmering with five colors in constant interplay. White light surrounded her and Tobimar and the Watchland, flowing and shifting and running through the dozens of symbols invoking both magical power and deific assistance. *Myrionar, stand with me*, she prayed. *Help to free the Watchland, my friend, your servant, from the grasp of our enemy*. She could see Tobimar's eyes also focus on something beyond him, praying.

Suddenly the Watchland gave a gasp and a grunt, and dark, sharp-edged mists swirled from within him, darting, slashing like knives of shadow or swarms of black, vicious insects at the circle enclosing him. She saw Poplock stagger, then hold Steelthorn up and shout words she did not understand in a tone that reminded her of Hiriista, the Magewright of Kaizatenzei.

Red-gold fire ignited in her circle, blue-white flame erupted from about Tobimar, the two channeling into and reinforcing the circle around the Watchland. At the same time, the circles around the five from Earth blazed to life, pure white from Xavier streaming out to encircle the entire pyramid, outlining its shape as the colors of the others welled out to the walls, lambent solidity manifesting.

"Got you!" Poplock shouted. "Living binding, master-ward, seal of the soul—I banish you from Jeridan Velion! By earth, by air, by fire, by water, by spirit, I abjure you! By passion and knowledge, judgement and trust, by truth I cast you out!"

The swirling, sawtooth-edged blackness surged, making the lines ripple, and a line of dark vapor streaked out, clawing and ripping at Poplock, who barely caught it on the shining silver blade of Steelthorn. For moments Poplock dueled what she now realized was a sentient, fighting *spell,* dueled it with nothing but a mystical blade and his own will, cuts appearing by malign magic across his brown hide. The shadow-darkness rose higher, split in three, struck like a snake; Poplock evaded it, then reversed, barely keeping himself from crossing one of the mystic circles. A keening, hungry sound rose from the eldritch thing as it slashed out again, the Toad's blade only barely parrying the razor-sharp gloom.

But then Poplock somersaulted *over* the next lunge and slammed Steelthorn down. To her astonishment the enchanted steel *impaled* the shadowy, half-living construct of sorcery. "To the Circle and then oblivion!" the little Toad bellowed, his voice far louder than Kyri would have believed possible. "By the power of the Five Elements and Five Virtues, be you *sealed!*"

There were gasps from the five around the pyramid, and Kyri saw that they were sagging, visibly weakening, as the energy was *pulled* from within them to streak to the circle surrounding Jeridan; with a subliminal shriek of fury, the black-bladed shadow was drawn back to the dark storm within.

Blood streaming from a dozen places, Poplock levered himself upright on Steelthorn, then raised his sword high; he no longer looked small or innocent or funny—he *towered* within the space of the pyramid, and his voice was filled with fury. "Begone and be obliterated by my will, by my magic, by my friends, by my teachers, by my name! Myrionar and Terian are with me, and by the Companions and Blackwart the Golden-Eyed himself, you are *ENDED!*"

The light of the circle *imploded,* crushing in on the seething darkness within, and the scream was not soundless. A detonation echoed out from that nexus, and Kyri was flung backwards to crack against the wall with stunning force. She made herself scramble to her feet, grasping at her sword, afraid for a moment that something new and terrible had been born.

But instead she saw Jeridan Velion, slowly raising his head from where he was sprawled. His eyes were wide, surprised, but clear, and they warmed when they met hers, and she knew it was the man she had come to save.

"Poplock? *Poplock!* Are you all right?"

Tobimar was crouched over the limp form of the tiny Toad. "C'mon, Poplock!"

Vaguely, she could tell that the others were barely able to move; Xavier had fallen from above in the detonation, to land a short distance from Jeridan. The others, like her, were around the perimeter of the room.

She ran painfully to where Poplock lay. "Move away, Tobimar, please."

She touched the little body, felt the faint pulse of life. "He's alive, but very weak." She heard her own relief echoed in Tobimars sigh. "I can take care of that."

The healing power of Myrionar came in red-gold light and Poplock opened one eye. "Are we done here? Because that really hurt."

As concerned shouts and pounding began from the locked doors, Jeridan Velion began to laugh.

CHAPTER 18

Tobimar watched as Xavier and Rion sparred. Rion wielded what Tobimar thought of as an *Odinsyrnen* sword and some others called a knight's weapon—a fairly long one-handed blade, double-fullered along most of its length, with a dragon-motif hilt—and a small shield, slightly larger than a buckler, and wore chain armor with some plate elements. Xavier, of course, wore no apparent armor and used two swords. As usual, Poplock had put safecharms on the blades so they wouldn't kill each other.

The two circled cautiously at first, but Xavier chose to go on the offensive quickly, striking out to disarm or create an opening—and nearly getting a sword in the face for his trouble. But Rion's attempt to follow up on that ended up catching nothing but air, as Xavier backflipped rapidly away and landed in the *Tor* combat pose, prepared.

Rion is good, Tobimar realized. He'd seen Rion in combat in their trek through Rivendream, but here he was watching Kyri's brother dueling Xavier, someone whose skills he knew well; the two of them had practiced together, sparred frequently, both during their travel from Zarathanton to Evanwyl, and in the few months Xavier had remained after Thornfalcon's defeat. Rion was holding his own against an increasingly serious assault by the Earth native.

Rion was grinning at Xavier. "You're not even *trying*. Where's your real skill, your real strength?"

"Dude! I'm not trying to *kill* you here, and I want to leave Kyri's house intact, too."

119

Rion blinked, as did Tobimar; for Rion, the blink was more costly. *Ow! That blow to the ribs must have stung.* "Are you joking with me, Xavier?"

The gray-eyed boy glanced at Tobimar, then looked back to Rion, catching his opponent's sword on one blade and turning aside a shield-bash with the other, then dodged back, leapt completely clear. "I can keep up with my friends. And your sister. So no, not joking."

A sudden bright grin. "But that doesn't mean there isn't *something* I can do!"

The swords slashed down, ten feet distant from Rion; but pearl-white light streaked out, extensions of blades and spirit. Rion's eyes widened and he brought up his own sword and shield barely in time. Even so, the impact sent him sprawling; he rolled badly, turned aside to evade Xavier's follow-up, and found his neck touching one of the bright leaf-green blades.

Rion flinched away from the blade surprisingly violently, but then laughed. "I asked for that, didn't I? Well struck, Xavier."

"Well, we'll try that again when you've got your Justiciar mojo back; I'll bet it won't be so easy then." Xavier's eyes narrowed. "Hey, Rion, did I cut you? I swear I was careful—"

Rion's hand came up, touched the bright red mark on his neck. "No, I swear you barely touched me." His face darkened. "Is there...a special virtue in those blades you carry?"

"Well, Khoros said that I wasn't ever going to find *better* blades. My *sensei* gave them to me. And Idinus seemed to think they were interesting." Xavier started to hand them to Rion, glanced at the red mark and obviously thought better of it, settled for holding the slightly curved sword where Rion could study it.

Tobimar was, of course, intimately familiar with the weapons, which both Xavier's *sensei* and the Spiritsmith called *vya-shadu.* At the base of Xavier's blades was a symbol, parallel swords and seven stylized towers; the ones the Spiritsmith had forged for Tobimar incorporated a similar design but used the Seven and One of Skysand.

Rion's eyes widened as his gaze focused on Xavier's swords. It was a momentary thing, almost instantly hidden, but Tobimar was sure he had seen it. However, all he said was, "They're beautiful. And I think I can sense...something there." His gaze dropped. "I was made by...monsters. From monstrous things.

Perhaps the reason I'm not a Justiciar again is because the holy power would *burn* me."

"Might be right," Poplock murmured to Tobimar. "You notice his—"

"Yes. Talk later."

Xavier had put his hand on Rion's shoulder. "Hey, c'mon. Maybe you're right, but I'm sure you and your sis will work through that somehow. Your god's into Justice, and it wouldn't be fair if you couldn't get back into your old profession, right?"

Rion looked at Xavier and gave a snort of laughter. "An unbeliever reminding me of the basics. All right then, no need for me to dwell on that."

"Maybe we should do something less strenuous, anyway. I have a—"

At that point Toshi poked his head through a doorway into the practice yard. "Oh, *here* you are. Come on, we have something to discuss with everyone."

Poplock gestured and a twinkle of light showed he'd dispelled the safewards. "Looks like we'll be doing something a lot less strenuous, sitting in chairs."

"Probably not as boring as a conference on Earth," Xavier said cheerfully. Rion followed them, still not looking entirely happy.

Can't blame him, Tobimar thought. *What must it be like knowing you're the creation of your own enemies?*

Once more the table in Vantage Fortress was laden with food, and there were plenty of seats already filled by the others. "We're all here, Kyri," Toshi said. "Can we back up a little and let everyone know what we're talking about?"

"Of course, Toshi," Kyri said. She waited until Tobimar and Rion had seated themselves on either side of her, and Xavier had decided which dishes he wanted to be sitting near. "Toshi and I were discussing the critical time problem. If they were to set out immediately but had to go through Hell's Edge to get to the Black City, it would take them several months; the distance is almost as far as getting to the Fallen Hills, and the last part of it would be going through Hell itself."

"Although with two armies having gone through there recently," Poplock said, "that probably wouldn't be so much of a slowdown as it might be otherwise. I'd bet both the Empire of the Mountain and the State of the Dragon King are keeping supply lines open, too."

The Toad scratched his head. "You *might* have trouble convincing them to let you through Hell's Edge, though. You can't just walk through..." He trailed off, seeing Xavier grinning broadly at him. "Okay, no, that won't be a problem."

Remembering how Xavier had been able to use his power to help him and Poplock literally walk right past Dalthunian guardposts, Tobimar had to grin along with Xavier.

"But I realized that there might be another solution, if you can manage to scale a few *really* difficult mountains."

"Hey, wait," Poplock said, and Tobimar continued, "Kyri, you won't be able to escort them."

"I don't think it will matter," Kyri said.

"Begging your pardon, Lady Kyri, but it might make things clearer if you finished telling us about this other solution," Gabriel Dante said.

"Sorry, Gabriel—and Aurora and Nike. Poplock, can you get out a map for us?"

"Hold on...yes, here you go!" The Toad pulled a scroll of paper out of his neverfull pack—a scroll several times longer than the Toad and pack combined, a sight that always looked peculiar even though Tobimar ought to be used to it by now.

Unrolled, the paper was a detailed map of the known continent of Zarathan, with Artania also up in the northwest corner. Kyri leaned over it, pointing. "Evanwyl's here; we're just about in the center of that star-shape that marks the city. Way down here is Hell's Edge. You do *not* want to go through the Gyrefell Forest; no one does. Even the Dragons warn against it.

"So you have to either go right along the base of Hell's Rim until you get to Hell's Edge, which will be a *very* rough journey, or you have to go south, catch the Great Road, and travel along here until you reach the Odinsforge Range and can take the northwest fork. That will be faster, although Dalthunia's hostile territory and there's no telling what you might run into there."

Nike nodded. "Yes, we're generally familiar with the map, although talking to someone who's actually *been* through those areas will certainly be helpful."

"Hey, *I* was through there not all that long ago," Xavier pointed out. "But they're right about it not being safe."

"In any case, you can see that's a long trip. But when I had my Raiment forged, and Tobimar got his new swords, we visited the Spiritsmith, and he lives *here*." She pointed to a point on Hell's Rim which was slightly north of the easternmost part of the circle of mountains, and thus part of the section of mountains not too far from Evanwyl.

"But he's still on *this* side of Hell's Rim, right?" Aurora asked.

"Technically, probably," Poplock said. "But Kyri's on to something. From one part of the plateau the Spiritsmith lives on, you could *see* straight into Hell, and we did see the . . . black glow, whatever you'd call it, when the Black City manifested."

"That might work," Toshi said slowly. "If you can actually *see* into this place you call Hell, then the mountain range must be considerably narrower there. Still high enough to serve as a bulwark against the things you mention live there, but if we can reach this plateau . . . Between me and Aurora, we could probably get us down from there with minimal noticeable power, avoiding calling attention to ourselves."

"But he's notorious about not wanting visitors, Kyri," Tobimar reminded her.

"But he's not *there* now," she said. "Remember, he was packing to leave when we left. He's gone with the army by now. Oh, his forge itself is probably all secured, but there weren't any signs of any traps or enchantments or wards on the plateau itself. Poplock?"

"No, no sign of any, or any sign there'd ever been any. I think he considers it pretty secure as it is."

"Can you give us clear enough directions so that we can get there ourselves without you having to lead us?" asked Aurora. "Because Xavier's never been there either."

Kyri glanced at Tobimar and Poplock. Tobimar thought back to the trip they'd made, then looked at Poplock for confirmation. "I think so. The three of us could work out the route to Waycross, and from there it's a pretty straight walk following the split-peak landmark."

"How far from that plateau would you guess the Black City would be?" Toshi asked.

Tobimar shrugged, looking at Kyri, who also shrugged. Poplock rolled his eyes. "You guys can't even guess that? Figuring elevation at around twenty thousand feet, and the fact that the city itself was still over the horizon, something over two hundred miles, I'd guess."

"Twenty thousand feet!" Nike was startled. "Good Lord, Toshi, you'll need to be providing us with oxygen or something."

"It's not *that* difficult to breathe up there," Kyri said. "Though it is colder than down here."

"Hmmm," Toshi said, frowning. "But this planet has similar gravity to Earth and apparently similar diameter. Why would the scale height be so much different?"

"They call it *magic* for a reason, dude," Xavier said.

"But *why*? Why would the magic do this?"

"It's possible that the *Spiritsmith* arranged it," Poplock pointed out. "He needs air for his forge, and probably doesn't want any visitors keeling over just because the air's too thin."

"Might be," conceded Toshi. "Which might mean that it's no longer in force when he's gone. But Nike is also right that I could manage to address that problem. So this seems a very viable alternative and one that would reduce our journey, even taking into account the need for a very slow and cautious descent on the other side, by at least two months, possibly more."

"In that case, I think we should stay for at least a couple of weeks," Nike said, "and see if they or the Watchland can some-how locate this 'Justicar's Retreat.' If they can do that before we leave—"

"—we'll go in with you and help kick this guy's ass," Xavier said firmly. "Which for all we know might make things easier all around, if he's been the guy pulling all the other strings."

"You don't have to—"

"Of course we don't," Gabriel said immediately. "But you and Tobimar and Poplock are Xavier's friends, and we now know what a terrible enemy you will be facing. We do indeed have our own rendezvous with destiny...but you have shown us a shorter way to that destination than the one we would have taken. It is only just, as your own god would say, that we devote some of that time to you. And a few weeks of rest, after what we went through, also sounds attractive."

Toshi bit his lip, then gave a little bow. "Agreed, unless Aurora has an objection?"

Aurora smacked her fist into her open hand; the concussion shook the conference room. "I would *love* to punch the guy who put that *disgusting* spell on the poor Watchland. Two weeks, maybe three."

"Done, then," Toshi said. "Do you have any leads on *how* to find your target?"

"I'm going to talk with the Watchland again tomorrow," Kyri answered. "You—any of you—could come if you like. I'm hoping that we'll be able to draw out some repressed memories of the Retreat. Either the Watchland has been there, or he's been *repeatedly* possessed by a being that has. It seems at least reasonable to think that somewhere inside, Jeridan knows how to find it."

"Right," Tobimar said. "Poplock and I are going to go talk with Arbiter Kelsley; it seems to me that the remaining high priest of Myrionar and his temple might have some clues, even if they don't *know* they're clues, so to speak."

"And at the least I might get an idea of how to get through the diversion wards they must have set up," Poplock said. "Since they'd *have* to be real similar to the original wards."

"Diversion wards?" Aurora asked.

"Enchantments to keep people from reaching a certain spot," Poplock said. "You get diverted around it, no matter how hard you try. Gets more and more blatant as you fight it harder. If you don't know it's there, what happens is that even if you *started* going straight for whatever-it-is, you just gradually change your course. If you're following a compass, you'll keep misreading it until you're well past, and so on."

Poplock rocked side-to-side, frowning. "Real hard to get through unless you're either a *lot* more powerful than the person who put them up, or you know whatever the trick is to get past, or if you're able to focus a counter-diversion ward and get through. That's what I'm probably going to have to do if we can't figure out how to just walk there . . . and I'm guessing that Viedraverion set it up so that only False Saints can get through."

"But that's *tomorrow*," Xavier said. "We're not getting any of that done now."

Gabriel raised an eyebrow at him. "And you have something else in mind?"

"Well, I'm not saying people who have more deep thoughts can't keep talking, but I'm not planning on it. Instead—partly because he reminds me of Mike—tonight, I'm gonna teach Rion, and anyone else who wants, my brother Michael's favorite card game."

He produced a pack of cards of a type that Tobimar had never seen before. "Time for this world to learn five-card draw poker!"

CHAPTER 19

"You wish to see...what, precisely?" Arbiter Kelsley asked.

"Well, that's part of the problem," Poplock said. "We're not sure."

Kelsley jumped. "By the Balance...were you *always* able to talk?"

"Yep," he answered. It *was* still amusing to see people suddenly have to revise their *entire* evaluation of him in an instant.

"Then why...ah. Because you were a far more dangerous weapon when not suspected. Obvious, really. But why reveal yourself to me now?"

"Because we know you are not one of our enemies, but an ally that we can trust, sir," Tobimar said. "It makes it much easier to discuss things with you, and I think that by now his secrecy is no longer terribly useful. Our enemy probably has guessed his nature by now."

Kelsley nodded, contemplating the little Toad with an amused smile. "Well enough. Can you at least tell me the *sort* of thing you are looking for in our records?"

"We're looking for any clue as to how to find the Justiciars' Retreat," Poplock answered. "I know it's probably not going to be so simple as finding a map and following it, but this *has* been the center of the faith since the beginning. *Somewhere* in those records might be a clue, and we're just about certain that the Retreat is what our enemy's using as a base of operations, along with the fallen Justiciars."

"Of course," Kelsley said, his cheerful face turning grim, as Poplock suspected it always did when reminded of how the representatives of his faith had been corrupted. "I recall no such traces in my readings, but I will admit that I have never *sought* such knowledge, so it may be that you are correct. Come."

He led them from the main temple through a smaller door at the back of the stage where the rituals of the Balance were enacted. This opened into a set of well-lit, wide corridors with several doors opening onto each. Kelsley led them straight on, deeper into the temple, until they came to a set of unadorned doors of polished *olthawin*, a deep blue wood that Tobimar had only seen once or twice before and never in such large pieces. The doors were clearly ancient, worn in gentle curves where untold thousands of people had passed over the centuries.

The twin doors swung open, revealing a wide, sweeping semicircular room on the right and a doorway on the left. The semicircular room was lined with bookshelves, and other books, scrolls, and artifacts were also in cases spaced around the room.

"These are the archives of Myrionar," Kelsley said slowly. "It is said that some of the artifacts, if not the records, go back to the days of the founding of the church, Chaoswars ago. A few other valuable records and manuscripts are kept here, in my office," he opened the door on the left and showed them a large office, with a broad desk, lamps, chairs, and a safe inset into one wall. "Normally," he went on with another smile, "those not of the Faith would not be brought here, but you are an ally of Kyri and have already done our temple a signal service, and continue that service. It is only just that we provide you with all the support we can."

He crossed to the safe, touched it; the solid metal shimmered, and the door opened. He extracted the contents and placed it on the desk. "You are welcome to search as long as you like, just be appropriately careful with the more ancient and fragile materials. I will be tending to temple business most of the day, and services this evening, and I will give directions that no one disturb you here."

"Thank you, Arbiter," Poplock said sincerely. The holy man was certainly going all the way to be helpful, and he certainly could have tried to be a bit sticky about showing any of the really valuable or old materials.

"You are more than welcome. I only hope you find what you are looking for."

For the next two hours, Poplock and Tobimar scoured the archives. Most material could be instantly dismissed as not bearing on their search, but there was still a lot to look at. Finally, Tobimar brought two stacks of books and papers that seemed to have a fair amount to do with the Justiciars and their activities, and the two settled down to start looking.

After a while, Poplock said "So...what do you want to do about Rion?"

Tobimar started, then looked up from the huge tome he was leafing through. "What? What do you mean, 'do about Rion'?"

"You've noticed a couple of oddities—like me. Right?"

Tobimar shrugged. "Poplock, we *know* there's plenty of 'oddities.' He's a *construct*, made from a piece of Rion's soul and at least a couple of other things to create his body. It would be pretty much unbelievable if there *weren't* oddities."

"I'm not talking about that kind of stuff," Poplock said, hearing a slightly injured note in his own voice. He found it was more annoying when Tobimar didn't get what he was saying than it was when other people didn't have a clue, probably because he was used to the two of them being in accord. "I'm talking about the little signs he gives of either not being himself, or of knowing things I don't think he should."

Tobimar got a thoughtful look on his face; he was silent for a few moments, paging through the book. Poplock continued perusing the large scroll he'd unrolled, hopping from point to point.

"All right, what little signs are you talking about?"

"You first. You *must* have noticed at least one."

Tobimar sighed. "Yes. Xavier's swords."

"He recognized them."

"Or that symbol, anyway. Which bothers me, because I've never seen that symbol before; it's similar to the one the Spiritsmith put on mine, but I've not seen it, or its like, anywhere else. And Kyri's seen those swords, and never said anything about that symbol. So where did Rion see it before?"

"Right. So, my turn; he recognized the name *Tor* for you and Xavier's fighting style, and it gave him a jolt."

"You're right. I remember, he stopped for a split second. A good recovery, but not quite perfect. Anything else?"

"When we were leaving Jenten's Mill, remember that he and Kyri were talking a little ahead of us?"

"Yes."

"Well, I was able to catch some of that, and at one point Rion went...kinda blank on her. Couldn't remember something that was obviously a big deal when they were younger, the roles they always played as kids; she was a Phoenix, he was the Dragon."

Tobimar stretched, obviously thinking. "Well, he *was* just a soul fragment, and one slashed from the original by a monster. I think it's kinda surprising he's as intact as he is."

The Toad had to concede that. "More like astonishing, I'd say. Like someone who knew him did the repair job."

"Well, if Viedraverion's been playing Jeridan Velion, that might be the case."

"Hmph. True enough. But about *Tor*—remember when we were helping put things back together, both Miri and Shae told us that *Tor* was something that scared demons half to death. Why would *Rion* get all startled hearing about some martial art no one ever mentioned before? He should have been just thinking 'oh, some new name I have to remember.'"

He could see *that* stopped Tobimar for a bit. There was a furrow between the Skysand Prince's brows as he continued searching through the tome before him.

"Well," Tobimar said at last, "we know he was made from something demonic, too. What if the soul that was used to provide the structure for Rion wasn't just a human, but part of a demon? Then he might have some faint memories or reactions from that."

"Ooo. You know, I hadn't thought of that." Poplock pulled a dried beetle out of his pack and chewed thoughtfully for a bit. "Might be true. On the other hand, it might not, which would mean...what?"

Tobimar waited, obviously wanting Poplock to continue; when the Toad simply kept looking at him silently, he cursed. "*Shiderich!* Fine. It means that there's at least part of something in there that's afraid of *Tor*, a demon probably, and that means that at the minimum Rion isn't just Rion."

"And at worst it's a demon somehow pretending to be Rion. One that somehow can hide its deceptions from both Kyri's truthsight and Gabriel's senses, which Aurora says are pretty darn impressive."

Tobimar's blue eyes narrowed. "One that's listening to a lot of what we're doing."

"Most of it, actually. Kyri trusts him—and I can't really blame her. She might be the big ol' Phoenix Justiciar, but she's no less a person than the rest of us, and I know *I* would probably really, really want to believe that someone I loved that much had come back."

"That's why you waited until we came here to talk."

"You see clearly with those squinty eyes. After what happened with Xavier's sword, I knew Rion wouldn't want to take a chance on what might happen to him if he walked straight into the actual Temple of Myrionar. And that meant we could have this talk and be absolutely sure neither he, nor Kyri, heard it."

"Don't tell me you don't trust *Kyri!*"

"When it comes to acting sensible about her brother? Well... yeah, I guess I do trust her, *if* we can present a good case. She's honest with herself that way."

Tobimar looked somewhat mollified. "All right. But *Sky and Sand*, what a mess this could be. What do you think we should do? Confronting him won't do any good—we've accepted him for a while, and there's perfectly good excuses for any of these issues, I'm sure. I'd be disappointed by our adversary if there *weren't* provisions to explain little lapses."

Poplock grimaced, rolled up the scroll, dragged over one of the books and started paging through it. "You're right. Confronting him would be useless unless he's dumber than a dung beetle, and he's not." He thought for a bit, while looking for Justiciar references. *They talk a lot about how awesome the Justiciars are, but not much about the practical stuff.* "I guess all we can do is make sure he's *never* not being watched. Unless he's a telepath or mindcaster mage, he's not going to be able to communicate with his boss while around us without us noticing *something*—and I'm pretty sure he's neither of those."

"True. So does that mean we make sure he's always accompanied?"

"No, no. We need, as I heard a fisherman say once, to let him wade out far enough to hit the dropoff. If he tries to go off on his own, someone has to follow him and watch him. And as far as I'm concerned, that 'someone' has to be me, you, or Xavier. I'm not trusting anyone else."

"Xavier likes him a lot, though."

"Saw that, playing that poker game. It's that brother thing; he knows Rion isn't really his brother, but he can't help but feel like there's a connection there. Still, I think Xavier will go along with it. If he won't, well, it's me and you. You in?"

Tobimar hesitated, then nodded. "I'm in. I hope we catch him doing nothing more interesting than taking walks."

"You and me both, Tobimar, believe me," Poplock said. "Because if he's up to something bad, our enemy's got all the info he needs to trap us."

CHAPTER 20

"You *lost* him? *You*?" Tobimar couldn't keep the incredulity from his voice. There was a part of him that felt almost *betrayed*, and he finally identified it as the same feeling he'd had the first time he realized his mother *couldn't* fix everything. Poplock had always been the one who got things done when other people couldn't.

The diminutive Toad couldn't meet his gaze. "Yeah. I lost him."

"Where?"

"He'd taken a walk into town—stealthily, but that's no surprise, since we'd all agreed he wasn't supposed to be seen. *Drought!* I was *sure* he didn't know I was following! But he turned down that same alley across from the Balanced Meal, and when I got there and looked down it, he was gone."

Tobimar glanced around to make sure his door was closed. "Have any idea how he did it?"

Poplock sighed, then finally faced Tobimar and wrinkled his face. "It was only a few seconds; even if he'd been *running* I should have seen him going the other way. Hm. Well, he *could* have gone *up*, to one roof or the other."

Tobimar frowned, thinking. "You're assuming he was limited to ordinary speed. If I use my *Tor* meditation, or Kyri used her Justiciar power..."

"You're right." Poplock smacked his own head with a small hand. "If he's actually not who he appears to be, he's probably got a lot of power he hasn't shown us yet. Stupid."

Tobimar pushed open the window. "Come on. We have to see if we can locate him."

"Tell Xavier or Kyri?"

"We haven't got anything to *prove* our suspicions, yet," Tobimar said, and jumped lightly to the ground ten feet below. Poplock followed, landing with a *thud* on Tobimar's shoulder. "*Oof!* You're heavier than you look. Anyway, without proof we'd be getting into an argument that wouldn't go anywhere."

At least we *don't have to be subtle,* Tobimar thought. *Everyone knows we're back.* Poplock was silent on his shoulder, and the walk to Evanwyl proper was ten minutes of quiet worry.

It wasn't just Rion, either. Searching the temple's records—which hadn't been fast or easy—had turned up just enough to confirm that Justiciar's Retreat was located to the west, several hours' travel at least, and a vague description of the Retreat itself. But nothing about the defenses or the diversion wards.

Kyri and the others hadn't had any better luck with the Watchland; if the location of the Retreat was somewhere in his mind, it was buried deep. Toshi was of the opinion that only the right conditions would trigger the memory, and of course they had no idea of what those conditions would be.

And they were running out of time. The research, interrogation, and experimentation had used up two weeks. The five natives of Earth would be leaving soon. Neither Tobimar nor Kyri could argue that their friends' mission was less urgently vital than their own, not when said mission would be a direct assault on one of the most ancient achievements of the King of All Hells. No, the five would have to leave, and soon.

The familiar sign of the Balanced Meal was visible ahead. "Okay, where do you want to start?" asked Poplock.

He nodded towards the nearer building across from the inn. "Up top. We'll get a good vantage point of a lot of the city that way."

"Okay. But what if he's running off to the Retreat?"

"Then we've totally lost him. But I'm pretty sure he hasn't."

Poplock's grip tightened as Tobimar—after a quick glance around to make sure no one was watching—sprinted up the side of the small warehouse. "Not saying you're wrong, but why?"

The roof was flat and solid, one of the few stone structures in a town made mostly of wood. It was a perfect observing platform, and Tobimar began a swift circle of the perimeter, looking out over Evanwyl in its somewhat disordered tangle of roads and houses and buildings, shading out into farms in the distance.

"He hasn't been caught yet," he said, answering the Toad's question. "The Retreat's hours away; he'd never get back in reasonable time. So if he's headed for the Retreat, he's throwing away all his work in staying with us, for what? A report that we're still in the area but haven't found anything? I can't see that being enough to justify the loss."

"Can't argue that, I guess." Poplock gazed out, large eyes seeming wider in the darkness. Tobimar knew that the Toad's natural sight was better in the dark than a human's, but he had his own trick; after so much practice in the last few months, it was just a matter of closing his eyes and focusing for a moment to bring up the High Center.

There was a *clarity* to the world now; it was dark, but at the same time it was as bright as day to the senses that High Center gave him. The shadows beneath trees were luminous with possibility, with the vectors of what was and what could be, and even what had been.

Almost instantly he saw something he had not before: a tall shape, kneeling in an alleyway over another figure, with a sense of danger lingering above it. *Even if it's not Rion, that's* something *we'd better look at.* "There!"

Poplock squinted. "Got it. Yeah, let's move."

With High Center already up, he could channel the strength and speed of his soul, leaping from the roof to the ground in a single motion and hitting the street at a sprint, ignoring the mist of rain and fog.

"*Rion!*" he said as they came up.

The figure, that he could now definitely recognize, jumped at his name, but as he turned Tobimar saw to his surprise an expression of relief, not guilt or anger. "*Tobimar?* Thank the Balance. Help me, would you?"

He was kneeling over an unconscious young woman.

Good actor? Or what? "What happened?"

Rion stared out into the darkness. "I was just looking around the town—hiding, as we agreed, since we're not announcing that I exist yet. And then just as I was heading up the cross-alley toward Mizuni's, I heard a sound like a faint scream or gasp.

I got up there," he pointed back, to the very roof that Tobimar had just been on, "and I saw Helina struggling with...something. Dark and shadowy. Couldn't make it out exactly. But I figured that my secret wasn't worth risking her life, so I charged toward them. The thing..." He suddenly shuddered. "It looked sort of human, but the *eyes*...yellow, hungry, and the hair was pale white. Dark *clung* to it, like it was covered with shadow, but it looked almost white under the shadow.

"Still, I had my sword out and took a cut at it. It was dead silent, didn't even hiss or anything, but it fought back and I don't know how long I was dueling it. Finally...I drove it off, and it disappeared into the darkness. Helina had collapsed. I don't know why, though, and she won't wake up, and I couldn't figure out what to *do*."

Poplock was scuttling around the area that Rion had indicated the duel took place; Tobimar knew what he was looking for. But in the meantime... "All right, Rion, we'll take care of it from here. You go back to the estate—and I mean *straight* back."

Rion paused, then his gaze dropped. "Of course. You're wise not to trust me. I just hope...hope we can find a way to get rid of that doubt. Somehow." He got up, sheathed his sword (which had been on the ground near him) and headed up the deserted streets towards the Vantage estate.

Tobimar waited until Rion was well out of sight. "Well?"

The little Toad made a wrinkled face. "Mostly his own boot-prints all over...but they *do* look like a fighting pattern. Like he was fighting something that wasn't leaving prints. Right there," he pointed to the wall, "there's a cut that's pretty much certainly from his sword, like he cut at something and it ducked. What about her?"

"She's...cold. Not dead, though. Unconscious. Don't know why."

Poplock hopped back to the girl Rion had called Helina. "She's not much older than you."

"I don't think she's *as* old as me. Maybe younger than Kyri." He looked at her hair, which was as black as the night but otherwise similar to Kyri's. *Not surprising. I would guess that if you go back generations enough, everyone's related to everyone in this small a country.* "I think I'd better get her to the Temple. You go after Rion and make sure he's headed back."

As Tobimar picked her up, though, the girl stirred, and suddenly pushed away with a weak scream. It was all Tobimar could do to keep her from dropping straight to the pavement. "Get away! Get a..."

Helina's eyes focused, and widened. "...oh! Oh, Lord Silverun!"

Tobimar found himself being almost strangled by a desperate embrace, and could feel Helina shaking. "Ugh! Um, it's all right, Helina. I'm going to take you to the Temple."

She nodded, but only fractionally released her grip.

"What happened? Do you remember?"

For a few moments she was silent, still gripping him tightly, then slowly, slowly, she released him. "I...I was walking home from the Balanced Meal," she said, and swallowed. That gave Tobimar time to place why she looked somewhat familiar; she was one of the servers at the inn, he'd seen her several times before.

"And...?" he asked quietly.

"And..." she drew a long, shuddering breath, "and...suddenly someone stepped out in front of me, at the end of this alley. I thought it was maybe Mizuni out for a walk, but then I saw the *eyes.*" She swallowed again, and almost collapsed. Tobimar could tell she was still terribly weak—far weaker than a mere fright would explain. He helped her put an arm over his shoulder and started walking with her to the Temple of Myrionar. "Yellow, glowing *eyes.* I wanted to run as soon as I saw them, but my legs wouldn't move!"

So far this fits with Rion's story. Part of him was disappointed, another part cautiously optimistic. "Anything else?"

"Oh, Balance, yes. There were...shadows crawling over it, darkness *stuck* to it like cobwebs when you push through them, and it came closer and I..." she bit her lip. "I...found myself almost *relaxing,* like it was all right, all the fear fading to the back, and it reached out and everything went all hazy." She frowned. "The last thing I remember is a shout, a distant shout, and falling."

"I'll go look and see if I can find this thing," he said. "But here we are at the Temple. Seeker Reed!" he said, seeing the young priest-trainee. "Take Helina in; she's been attacked by *something* which seems to have drained her in some way. She's terribly weak."

"Myrionar's Justice! Here, Helina, sit down." Reed drew out one of the benches. "I will call the Arbiter immediately."

"Good. I'll be looking for whatever did this."

He returned to the alley, but pretty soon came to the conclusion

Poplock had. Rion's bootprints were scuffed all over the end of the alley in a way that *could* indicate a combat, but there wasn't any trace of another combatant except a few marks that showed sword blows gone astray, presumably aimed at this enemy.

That *sort of* argued against Rion's story, but not entirely. There were quite a few monsters, ranging from hungry spirits to vampires to things from beyond other veils, including demons, that could fight you without leaving obvious traces.

There was a scuffling in the alley behind him. He glanced back, saw Poplock bouncing towards him. "Well?"

"He went straight back to the estate," Poplock confirmed, reaching his accustomed position on Tobimar's shoulder. "Didn't even go slow, went as fast as he could manage and still stay hidden."

Tobimar kicked pensively at the dirt. "Her story fit his."

"Hmph. That's interesting. Though depending on what Rion really is, convincing someone to believe a particular story isn't hard to do." The Toad shifted his weight. "The *real* problem I have with his story is timing. Took too long, from the time I came back to get you to the time we found him. I can't believe the fight he described took fifteen, twenty minutes. Can't believe it took *half* that. Most fights are measured in *seconds*."

"I know what you mean," Tobimar agreed, as he started retracing their steps to the Vantage estate. "And that would mean he spent an *awfully* long time, relatively speaking, in that alley with Helina. He could've picked her up and carried her somewhere."

Poplock grimaced. "Of course, he could argue he was frozen with indecision—carrying her anywhere would reveal his presence, especially if she woke up, and since we haven't decided whether he *is* the real Rion, we've been pretty emphatic about him hiding it. Heck, this wandering around at night is pushing it, no matter *how* good he is at hiding and how well he knows the land."

"I guess. But I don't know that I'd swallow that argument. If we don't, though...what was the point? What did he do to Helina, and why?"

"You took her to the Temple, right? Maybe old Kelsley will have answers for us."

Tobimar nodded. "We'll have to check in tomorrow. But we'd better get answers soon. Won't be long before Xavier and his friends have to leave...and then it'll be you, me, Kyri... and Rion."

CHAPTER 21

"A *vampire*?" Kyri repeated in shock. There hadn't been a vampire of any type in Evanwyl for *years*, maybe decades, at least as far as she knew.

"And it might be Rion," Poplock said.

She found herself half out of her chair, hammering her fist down on the table. "*Rion is NOT...!*" Then she realized how ridiculous her reaction was. *These are my friends and best companions. They wouldn't say things like this to me idly.* She sat back down slowly, not looking at either of them as she took a drink of water from the glass nearby. Then she looked up at them, deliberately meeting both Poplock and Tobimar's gazes. "I'm sorry. Please, tell me what you know and why you think... think Rion might be involved."

"Well..." Tobimar looked hesitant. Poplock took over.

"We've been keeping tabs on him all along. You guys decided to let him walk around if he kept himself out of the public eye, but—sorry!—we don't trust him all the way yet. So me and Tobimar have been watching him. We were also thinking of having Xavier in on it, but him and Rion have gotten to be pretty tight." She noticed a small furrow in Tobimar's brow at that. *I don't think he's aware of how he's a little jealous of that; he and Xavier spent a long time together and got to be good friends, too.*

The realization her friends had decided to follow her brother around—and not tell her—was a bit of a jolt, but she didn't need to be told the logic. And since Xavier's group was leaving this afternoon, they couldn't hold off on telling her any longer, either. "Go on."

"Well, most of the time we didn't see something too suspicious. But then a few days ago there was that attack on Helina..."

"Helina? What does she—"

"If you'd let me *finish* you wouldn't need to ask!" Poplock said acidly. "Like I said, there was that attack on Helina, but the details of what *we* know weren't in what went around the village." He detailed what had happened the night that he'd lost Rion temporarily, then continued, "Arbiter Kelsley kept it quiet while we looked into things, but he's about ninety percent sure that it was a vampire that attacked her."

"What *type* of vampire? There's at least three I know of."

"Five, as far as I know," Tobimar said. "We *think* it's the sort called, more formally, the Curseborn."

"*Balance.* They're almost universally monsters, aren't they?"

"Yup," Poplock said, no trace of humor in his voice. "Transfer the curse by blood exchange, feed off of both blood and soul, usually go insane from the transformation, and even if they recover they're usually pretty much monsters from then on. Tough to kill because they're fast, strong, and invulnerable except for a few difficult-to-exploit weaknesses. Helina's description of what she saw could match one that was *very* powerful—a very old one—and that'd be even harder to kill."

"How does Kelsley know it's a vampire?"

"The first and strongest indicator," Tobimar said, "is the signature bite—twin punctures. Kelsley said he found them, er, lower down, where ordinary circumstances would never lead them to be discovered. Then there was her weakness, which Kelsley determined was due to her spiritual energy—her soul—being severely drained of energy, as well as to a significant though not dangerous loss of blood."

"With that as a clue," Poplock said, "I did a little poking around and found that there were at least two other people in Evanwyl—both women—who showed similar symptoms over the last few weeks, before Helina. Though they just claimed they were sick—no one mentioned an attack or anything. They just suddenly got ill, no warning."

Kyri tried to think about this rationally. "So your theory is that Rion is the vampire in question, and that normally he would complete his... feeding and then use whatever mental magic or powers he has to make the person forget they were attacked, but you interrupted him. Right?"

"I am not *entirely* convinced," Tobimar said, with a glance at Poplock. "Helina's story has a couple of inconsistencies if I assume it was Rion who attacked her, the most important being that she claims she heard a shout, and then felt herself falling to the ground as her last memory before blacking out. But she was already on the ground, and had been for at least a couple of minutes, when we came running up to Rion. If her memory is even close to accurate, then whoever shouted as she lost consciousness wasn't us—and would seem likely to have been Rion, as his story would have it."

"Of course, if he *can* mess with minds, he could've already started, and her story *isn't* accurate," Poplock said.

Kyri found the idea that Rion might actually be a monster incredibly painful. It had been so hard *not* to believe in him at first, and now... "Do we have any way of proving this?"

Tobimar frowned. Both he and Poplock were silent for a few minutes.

"I honestly don't know," Tobimar said after a while. "We already knew he was *made* from something dark, at least in part. We've seen what happens when Xavier's blade touches him. But all that means is that his essence isn't entirely human and holy, which tells us nothing we didn't know. He's walked plenty in sunlight, but if he's really one of the *ancients* then walking the sunlight is something he can do pretty well, even though it probably weakens him. And as Khoros once pointed out to me, the fact that a wooden stake kills a man doesn't say much as to whether he is in fact a vampire, so to speak."

"About the only think I can think of that might work is if you directly interrogate him about it using that powerful truth-sense you can get from Myrionar. If you're willing to do it."

A part of her wanted to refuse, but with great difficulty she did not even permit that part of her to voice an objection. *I need to remove this doubt—or reveal the truth—and this is for our good, not just mine. If it truly is Rion, this will do him no harm, and if he is not, it may save us all.* "I will see if he is willing." She stood. "Now."

Poplock and Tobimar both looked relieved, which at least

confirmed that she was making the right decision. *Our general truth-senses have claimed he was genuine, but this will be something more detailed . . . and confrontational. Very,* very *few things could carry off a deception under those conditions.*

They found Rion reluctantly handing Xavier's LTP handheld game console back to its owner. She couldn't quite repress a smile, even under these circumstances. Rion had been bitten *hard* by the fascination of the strange electronic game device, just as Tobimar had during his travels with Xavier. This was another reason that he and Xavier had bonded so much during their relatively short acquaintance. "Rion, could we talk to you?"

"Since when have you had to *ask* to talk to me?" he retorted with a smile. "I recall you sometimes starting a conversation in the middle of the night, when I was trying to *sleep.*"

That was *so* very Rion a response—and so very true—that she wanted to just stop right there. She was so *sure* this was Rion, in all the ways that really mattered. But she refused to allow herself to waver. "Rion, this is serious." As Xavier and his friends started to leave, she held up her hand. "Actually, I would very much like it if you would stay. Just in case."

Gabriel gave one of his courtly nods. "We are then entirely at your disposal, Lady Kyri."

She waited for everyone to be seated. "Rion, you know there are a lot of questions about exactly what you are, and that Poplock and Tobimar caught you out under some very suspicious circumstances. I really, *really* hate to do this . . . but I must ask you to allow me to ask you some questions . . . as the living emissary of Myrionar, with Myrionar's Truth manifest to give me the ability to sense any lies you may tell."

"I . . . see." He looked around, then shrugged and smiled. "And if I said 'no'?"

She'd expected that; Rion would ask it. "Then we'd have to cut you out of any further discussions, keep you confined to the estate, and make sure you were *secured* here—imprison you, to be honest, until we've dealt with Viedraverion and the False Justiciars."

Rion nodded. "Of course you would." He folded his arms, as he sometimes did when preparing himself for a confrontation. "All right, then, Kyri; ask."

She closed her eyes, shutting out the sight of all the others staring at her. *Myrionar, I need your Truth once more. Let me see through lies and disguises, through deceit and misdirection, and come to the knowledge only of what* is.

The golden power flowed up and around her. As she opened her eyes she could see that it bathed the room in an auric glow, and there was awe in the faces of those around her, awe from what they could feel within that power.

At the same time, *she* could tell that the power was weaker than it had been. *Myrionar really is dying. We have to finish this soon, or...*

She buried that thought. *Focus on the present.* "Rion, are you a vampire?"

Rion raised a brow. "I can't say that I'm *not* a vampire. I don't know exactly *what* I am."

The first part could have been a neat evasion, but the second part was a pretty clear statement. Her sense of truth did not show a falsehood. Unless his power was sufficient to mislead Myrionar's power even in direct confrontation, Rion actually did not know what he was. *So if he is a vampire, he doesn't know it.* "Did you attack Helina?"

"I did *not* attack Helina," he said flatly. She was startled to find herself not merely relieved, but *surprised*, when she sensed nothing of falsehood in his statement. *A part of me really* did *suspect him.*

Feeling lighter in her heart, she continued. "Rion, are you truly my brother?"

He looked directly at her. "I am."

"Have you informed anyone of any of the plans we made here, or the discussions we have had on Viedraverion or the False Justiciars?"

"I have not."

She let the power go, feeling the strain on herself and Myrionar, and allowed a huge smile of relief to spread. "Truth."

"Truth," agreed another voice; she saw Gabriel Dante nod. "I sensed nervousness, but no lies."

"Not one hundred percent proof," Toshi said bluntly. "We do not know the limits of our powers, yours, or those of our adversaries. This truth-sensing of yours might be very strong... but we know our adversaries are also very strong."

She sighed, but smiled again. "True enough. But we have done what we can. I asked him questions that were direct, he answered them, I sense that they are true. Should I retain suspicion and allow it to destroy my hope?"

"No," said Poplock. "Sure, he could be fooling us somehow, but . . . well, that turned out to be the case in Kaizatenzei, and somehow we came through it all right anyway. Let's just say he's Rion and not worry about it unless things go south."

She suspected the little Toad would still keep a close eye on Rion, but she appreciated him at least making a public acceptance of her judgment.

Looking around the group, she saw backpacks, weapons, and other equipment assembled. "So . . . you're all really leaving."

"Now that we've settled—as much as we can—whether Rion's a problem? We kind of have to," Nike said. "Fact is, that war's not stopped while we're here, and even if your shortcut's saving us time . . . well, we don't know how much time we actually *have*, so . . ."

"You don't need to explain," Tobimar said. "Khoros brought us together, but he gave you a mission too. For all I know, you've already done whatever he expected you to do here. It's not like we'll all know for sure."

"True enough," Toshi said. "And we're leaving in the evening because most people would expect us to leave in the daytime, if we left at all."

"What about the possibility of spies?" Rion asked. "If you're leaving and you're followed—"

"Leave *that* to me, guys," Xavier said. "Remember, I got us all out of a prison that your people thought was impossible to escape from. And got Tobimar and Poplock past guard posts, too."

Kyri laughed, startled. "You can do that with your whole *group*?"

"If we all keep hold of each other, yeah, for a while at least. If I can do it for a mile or three, it'll be almost impossible to track us. And I'll do it a few more times along our route."

Knowing how utterly impossible it seemed to be to detect Xavier when he used that strange *Tor* ability, she felt he was right. "Is this goodbye, then?"

The cheerful gray eyes were suddenly not so cheerful. "Yeah. Yeah, I guess so." He looked at Tobimar and Poplock. "Um . . . Khoros said that this was the only way for us to get home."

"I know," Tobimar said quietly. "You told us that. All of you were stuck here unless somehow the Great Seal was broken."

"But I guess once it's broken we go home," Xavier said. "I thought I'd be happy about that. Now...well, I *am*, but..."

"I know," Aurora said, and put a hand on Xavier's shoulder. "We felt the same about leaving Skysand. And I guess Toshi and Nike, leaving Artania." She laughed suddenly, a great bell-like laugh that reminded Kyri poignantly of Lady Shae's. "Boy, I was *so pissed* at Khoros when he brought us here, and I would *never* have thought I'd be sorry to go home."

"We all will be," Nike said. "But...we'll all be happy to get home too. Xavier may have a real *mission* at home, but all of us have reasons to go back."

"Then..." Tobimar stepped forward, and suddenly Xavier hugged him fiercely. The two held the embrace for a long moment, and then Xavier picked up Poplock and looked at him; the Toad looked only slightly bemused by the handling.

"Have I ever told you you're kinda cute, Poplock? My sister would think you're adorable."

"Well...fine, thanks. I guess. It's okay for this once, anyway." Poplock's voice was a little unsteady.

Xavier then went to her. "Kyri...you finish your job, okay? Kick that bastard's *ass* for me. Promise?"

She laughed and swept him into a bear hug. "I promise, Xavier."

Rion said nothing, just embraced the boy from Earth, and then shook his hand. But as Xavier turned back to his friends, he spoke. "Xavier?"

"Yeah, Rion?"

"I pray for you to get your vengeance. But...don't leave your family alone."

The smile was brilliant and the gray eyes, so like her own, were happy again. "I won't, Rion. And when I go on the hunt again...well, I'll say a little prayer to your Myrionar, just in case."

Rion smiled back.

The other goodbyes didn't take as long. While Kyri liked all of them—studious, sometimes oblivious Toshi with his razor-sharp mind, analytical, dangerous, yet cheerfully friendly Nike, the ever-charming and talented Gabriel, and strong, awkwardly loyal Aurora—they hadn't shared adventure with Kyri and Tobimar, been part of giving her the first real chance to avenge her family. Finally, the five shouldered their packs, bowed to all of them, linked hands...and disappeared.

For a little while it was hard to accept that they'd left; no door had opened, they had simply vanished in the dining room. But as the much quieter evening began to lengthen, she accepted that the group from Zahralandar—Earth—was gone.

"Well...we're on our own," she said finally to Rion, Tobimar, and Poplock.

"We are," Rion agreed. "But we knew we would be. There *has* to be some way to get to the Retreat."

Tobimar grunted. "So far we haven't had much luck." He yawned. "Look at that. This early?"

"You stayed up late last night," Poplock pointed out, "Hanging out with Xavier, as he'd put it."

"Yeah. Well, I'm going to at least do a little sparring before I wash up and go to bed. Want to join me, Poplock?"

"Why not? You need someone to beat you once in a while."

"How about you, Kyri, Rion?"

Kyri didn't quite feel like sparring. "Not right now. Maybe tomorrow."

"Okay. See you in a bit, then."

She looked back at Rion as the two left. "Well, as they said, we haven't had much luck. I can only think of one possibility, but unfortunately I don't *control* that possibility."

"What possibility is that?"

"If we could somehow get you back your...connection to Myrionar, maybe *you* could find your way there."

Rion tilted his head, puzzled. "But...*you* are a Justiciar, and you can't find the place."

"True, Rion...but I haven't ever *been* there. As a Justiciar, you *were* there. And since Myrionar was the source of your strength, it wasn't through our enemy's power that you could find the Retreat, it was through Myrionar's and the fact that you were already *admitted* to the Retreat."

Rion's mouth dropped slightly open and he stared at her. Then a slow grin spread across his face. "You know...that's just about simple enough an idea that it might just work." Then his face fell. "If it *could* work."

"Rion..."

He stood suddenly, started to walk out. Then stopped. "I want to go for a walk. But you're welcome to come and keep an eye on me, if you want."

"I'm not suspicious of you."

"Your Toad friend still is. And maybe he's right."

They stepped out into the deepening night. The sky was awash in brilliant stars, shimmering in soft colors and sharp, infinitely small and bright points, the great arc of dark-streaked light that the Sauran's called the Dragon's Path crossing the entire sky. She heard the faint trilling cry of a Least Dragon in the distance, the sussuration of insects much nearer at hand. Rion was a black outline on black in the darkness.

"If *we* aren't going to suspect you, do you need to be so hard on yourself, Rion?"

"Kyri, I can't even *touch* holy objects. I'm surprised I can touch your hand without being scorched." He walked towards the rear of the estate—not towards the town; obviously he wasn't taking any more risks. "Can you *imagine* what it would do to me if Myrionar was even *willing* to take me back? I'd explode in fire."

"There *has* to be a way around that." The idea that her brother—that *Rion*—was barred from the thing he had dreamed of, had worked for, had *achieved*—was maddening and tragic. "We'll *find* one. Somehow."

He stopped, the two of them in the deeper shadows beneath the trees that shaded the rear of the estate. Even in that darkness, she saw a phantom flicker of white teeth as he laughed. "And maybe I should just accept that you *will*," he said quietly, laying a hand on her shoulder. "You've been beating the odds all along."

"I try," she said.

They stood that way for a moment. Then Kyri became aware she could *see* his eyes, a faint shade of a shimmer in the darkness. "Your eyes are—"

"Yes, I know. Subtle, but one sign that can remind me of what I am. Is it . . . scary?"

"No," she said with a faint snort of laughter. "I've seen things that were *actually* scary." She concentrated on the faint discs of light. "A little eerie, but I can just about make out the detail— not just a general glow of light for the whole eye. Faint touch of blue in the center."

"Really? You can see that much?"

"Yes." She found herself concentrating on the eyes again. *Wait. Why am I paying so much attention to this?*

But now the eyes were shimmering with yellow.

Oh, Myrionar, NO. "R-Rion..."

"I...I really don't want to hurt you, Kyri. I'm...I'm sorry, but I just realized...I don't have a choice now. I don't know why..."

Desperately she fought to move, feeling the same helpless fury that she had when Thornfalcon had caught her—but made worse by it being *Rion,* by the genuine regret and self-loathing in that voice.

But she could only raise a hand slowly, weakly, as Rion—or whatever it was that wore his face—bent towards her throat.

CHAPTER 22

"This is going to look *so* stupid, Poplock," Tobimar said, settling his swords back into place. "We—"

"I'll take all the blame if it looks stupid. I know that it *seemed* like we pretty much settled it just now, but there's still that chance left, and can we afford it if you're wrong? We can take a little embarrassment, even getting Kyri mad at us, but..."

"Fine, fine. You're right. You generally have been. I just hope we're all wasting our time on this one and that you're going to have to do the apologies."

The brown Toad bobbed his body. "Oh, believe me, I'd *much* rather end up doing abject apologies."

It had been about fifteen minutes; they'd agreed that was the right amount. Of course, if they were misjudging...

"They're not in the dining room anymore."

"That much is obvious, now that we're looking into the dining room." Poplock nodded towards the front door. "If he went back towards the town..."

"Right. She'd go with him, of course."

"Meaning they're alone."

Tobimar strode to the front door and opened it. Another warm night, some ragged, drifting clouds obscuring stars in patches of pure black edged with faint silver, but mostly clear. With a moment to adjust, he could see fairly well. But the pathway down towards the village seemed empty. "You see anything?"

Poplock wobbled side to side, his equivalent of a headshake.

149

"Nothing. So they didn't go this way—I'm sure they'd still be in sight. Around the side?"

"We can do a full circuit. If they're not out here…then they probably went upstairs, and that's okay."

The Toad grunted. "Yeah, if I'm right nothing's going to happen indoors. Too close. Too much chance of someone stumbling on you."

"All this because of her reactions?"

"Don't tell me *you* didn't notice." They started a careful circle around Vantage Fortress.

Tobimar sighed. "Yes," he admitted, speaking in a whisper. "Subtle at first, and perfectly reasonable I guess, but…she's just a little *too* loyal, too accepting, too defensive of Rion."

"Right," Poplock said, matching his quiet tones. "Now, like you say, it *could* be natural—she practically idolized her brother, from everything I've heard—but I dunno; the woman who got tricked once by Thornfalcon, then got faced like the rest of us with the truth about Miri and Shae…I don't see her taking him at face value or losing her caution—or her control—that easily."

"Thus your plan to give him an obvious chance to move, now that our five guests are gone, and before we have a chance to get *new* suspicions."

"Exactly. If he's got anything planned, now's the time to do it, when our suspicions should be at their lowest and our forces weakened."

Tobimar was silent. He liked Rion. He *didn't* like trying to set a trap for him, when he was about nine-tenths sure that Rion was being as straight with them as he could. But Poplock's caution had saved them all more than once; he wasn't going to disregard it.

He almost missed it; the movement was small, in shadow, barely visible, the motion of velvet across ebony. But he belatedly caught it out of the corner of his eye and turned, focusing on that spot.

What the…?

For one incredibly confusing moment, he thought he was seeing a lover's embrace, Rion and Kyri together in a pose too close and intimate for even brother and sister. Then he saw how limply Kyri was standing, and betrayed fury flared up in him. Without even thinking of it, his *vya-shadu* were in his hands and he was sprinting like lightning across the grass. *"RION!"*

The taller figure's head snapped up, and fury now became certainty, for the eerie yellow glow of those eyes was like nothing human. But instead of just dropping Kyri and fleeing, the figure lowered her gently to the ground, coming on guard just barely before Tobimar's swords blazed a silver-green path through the air.

Rion, or whatever it was, parried both blades almost casually, then simply flicked a glance sideways. Tobimar only *just* managed to dodge as a tree branch three inches thick hurtled at him. The longsword tried to bite through Tobimar's armor, and even as he parried *that*, two rocks the size of his fist hammered into his side, sending him staggering. A spray of gravel and sand flew up from the ground behind the false Rion, and Poplock went tumbling away, spitting out dirt and wiping his eyes.

In that instant, Tobimar was startled to see that the impostor chose to run. *He had a perfect opening; I'm* sure *he could have run me through there.*

Instead of taking the opportunity to finish him and Poplock off, Rion sprinted away, heading towards the road, at a speed that astounded Tobimar. *Even in High Center with full strength and speed enhancement I'm going to have a hell of a time catching him!*

But in that moment, five figures simply *materialized* in front of Rion. "You are going *nowhere*, jerk," Xavier said.

"Out of my way!" A fountain of stones and gravel roared towards them—

—and stopped dead in midair. Aurora lowered her hand, and the rocks dropped straight to the ground. "Oh, not *that* easy." Her voice was low and furious; not waiting for her comrades, Aurora lunged forward, leaping up and slamming an axe-kick down.

Rion barely evaded it, but the concussion blew him off his feet and staggered Tobimar, who hadn't yet caught up; a crater ten feet wide and three deep surrounded Aurora, radiating from her foot. *Great* Light, *she's strong.*

The false Rion did not look intimidated, though; strangely, he looked sad. "Then I must fight."

The figure blurred into motion, so fast that Tobimar actually lost track of him. Aurora was suddenly toppling, wincing, and Xavier tumbling backward, one of his swords actually flying from his grasp. Gabriel had *barely* managed to get his own huge blade up in time, and the false Rion was again visible, driving Gabriel Dante back with sheer strength. He disappeared again, speed incarnate, as Nike and Toshi took aim, and Toshi was abruptly defending against strikes that came from every direction.

Concentrate. The power of Terian lies within me now. Call it up. Channel it with the meditation of High Center.

He could *see* his power within, now, a spark of blue-white energy that surged into a flame as he touched it.

Speed *blazed* through him, and he accelerated forward. His adversary was fast, but now Tobimar could follow his moves, track his strategy. Even as his shield smash sent Toshi's bow spinning aside, Rion stiffened and whirled, just in time to catch Tobimar's swords, one with his own weapon, one with his shield, and Tobimar saw him wince as the blue-white aura touched him; a wisp of white smoke rose from the unshielded hand.

His adversary sprang into the air, impossibly high, twenty-five, thirty feet, running through the sky now, heading for the shelter and cover of the trees.

Without warning, the earth *heaved* skyward, stone and soil forming a barrier that was three hundred feet tall in an instant. Rion was unable to completely halt, smacked into the solid obstacle, and then was dashing *down* as bolts of fire, accompanied by sharp, ear-shattering reports, chased barely inches behind him; out of the corner of his eye, Tobimar could see these came from Nike, who was holding a weapon that must be one of the "rifles" that Xavier had told him about once; but the rifle was spitting what looked like solidified flame, cutting holes in the rocky bulwark as though it were a hay-bale.

Tobimar wasn't sure whether it was *wise* for him to reenter the combat. He definitely didn't want to get in the way of either Nike or Toshi, who was now firing arrows at an impossible rate, arrows that shone like the stars and hit like bludgeons. *These five know what they are doing. They're coordinating as well as we do!*

"Don't *kill* him!" Kyri's shout echoed across the battlefield. "Keep him *alive!*"

Rion threw a vial into the air that detonated and sent uncountable metal spikes spearing down. "Easier said than done," Poplock retorted. "He's not worried about *us!*"

At first Tobimar was inclined to agree, but... *High Center. Find the danger, the menace. What is the shape of the battle, the outline of possibility and peril?*

The vision finally began to flow for real, Tobimar now at one with himself, and he could see, not just what was *now* but in a sense what *might be* a few split seconds later, link that with action, and *move*.

And as Rion sent Nike sprawling—*yet with a blow that stunned, not the easier strike that could have killed*—Tobimar was already there, twin swords passing his opponent's defenses, coming to rest on his throat. "Stop."

For just an instant he thought that Rion wouldn't stop—that he'd fight on, let himself be killed, a near-perfect way to maintain his silence. The impostor's eyes flickered to the one direction he might escape in, saw Xavier there, and his shoulders slumped. He let his weapon fall and dropped to his knees. "Then finish me."

"No," Kyri said, anger, confusion, and obvious shock warring for dominance on her sharp features. Blood smeared her face and Tobimar couldn't tell if it was hers or Rion's. "No. You knew so much. You spent so much time with us. You were so much *him*. You'll tell us the truth."

"Or... what?"

Even through the blood, Tobimar saw the teeth flash in a tired, uncertain grin. "A good question. I won't torture you. A part of me *wants* to. Maybe I *should*. But..."

"No," said Toshi, studying the false Rion with an analytical gaze that if anything was sharper even than Poplock's own. "No, he could have killed several of us. Instead I don't think any of us are even seriously injured."

Poplock bounced over and looked up. "Why not show your real face? It's not like there's any point in continuing the lie."

The impostor gazed down, and then he gave a low, tragic sigh. "Yes. The matrix is shredded beyond recovery now. I've failed completely."

With a shimmer, Rion Vantage faded away, replaced by a more slender youth. Long white hair, with perhaps a faint touch of lavender, cascaded down straight and true. The new features were definitely more delicate and defined, almost as pretty as those of Toshi, but in the straightness of the hair and something about the shape of the face there was something that echoed Xavier far more closely.

The eyes were the only inhuman feature, glowing yellow, dark-irised. But the glow was fading, less a lambent threat and now a faint flicker.

"Who are you?"

"My name is Tashriel," he answered.

"Tashriel? Why is that...Oh!" Kyri nodded, even as Tobimar remembered where *he* had heard that name before too. "You were Wieran's assistant. Miri mentioned you, but we never met you."

"So what in the world got you stuck into a bottle pretending to be Rion? That doesn't seem *anything* like what that crazy old man would be doing," Poplock said.

Tashriel hesitated, then shrugged. "You're not going to kill me?"

"I haven't decided yet," Kyri said; her voice was not steady, and Tobimar stepped to her side, put a hand on her shoulder; she reached over and gripped his fingers tightly. "Personally I would like to cut you *apart* for what you've done—this false hope you've given me and taken away. But...you *must* know something about our enemy. If you can tell us something..." Her sword slid back into its sheath. "We'll decide...*I'll* decide...afterward." She wiped her face, looking even shakier, and sat down on a nearby stone.

Tashriel looked around at the whole group, and suddenly gave a low, rueful laugh. "It was *all* a trap. A trick."

"Hey, we'd *always* planned on us coming back after apparently leaving," Xavier said. "Or, to be honest, *Toshi* always planned on that, he's the brains in this outfit. Stood to reason that if their enemies were going to do something, they'd do it when Kyri, Tobimar, and Poplock were basically on their own. Poplock just orchestrated the timing. He figured you'd move as soon as a couple hours had gone by, because *most* people would be expecting you to wait a little longer, maybe a day or two."

Kyri shook her head. "And...And you had guessed he had some influence over me. I can feel it fading away now."

"Not much influence," Tashriel said. "Just...increasing your own reactions, mostly. Exaggerating them." He shook his head. "I'm sorry. I didn't have any choice. But...I'll tell you everything I can about everything I know...what I did with Wieran... what my mission was...and especially what I know about your enemy...about Viedraverion."

CHAPTER 23

Poplock looked at Kyri, who was clearly weakened and shaking with reaction from the attack and shock, and Tobimar standing near her. *Right, I can take this myself.*

"Okay, you've got a chance to talk. Better make the talk good. So you're a demon under Viedraverion's command?"

Tashriel's face twisted in half-amusement, half-misery. "I was...on *loan* to Viedraverion. He made my real master, Balinshar, give me to him for a special project—and used his father to put pressure on Balinshar to do it."

"So the first big question is...why *you*?"

"Because I'm...not really a demon. Not entirely, not in my... what's left of my soul. I was a human being, once. Then I became a vampire, then the demons came for us and they captured me instead of killing me. At the time," another twisted smile, "I almost thought they did me a favor. I was deep in the madness that all the Cursed get when the blood takes hold. I...I think I'd killed some of my own people, it's all blurred, but I know that when I came to myself I really was grateful for a moment. Before I realized they'd simply killed everyone anyway and were making me one of them."

"Interesting," said Toshi. "But you must have had something special about you that made you worth saving."

Tashriel paused, then swallowed, looking at the others. "Yes. It was a huge secret. Balinshar kept that knowledge absolutely hidden from everyone; he figured that I might be a hidden weapon, a blade from nowhere, if he played things right. Realizing that *Viedraverion* already knew about it...that was a shock."

"Well?"

He took a deep breath. "I was trained in *Thanalaran*—I don't know what to call it in your language, exactly. It combined alchemy, sorcery, the powers of the mind, and mechanisms of science, devices—"

"Technomancy!" Xavier blurted out.

"Technomancy? Well...I suppose, yes, that's not a terribly bad way to put it. It was an ancient and secret discipline even in my era, long, *long* ago."

That makes sense. Poplock gave a satisfied bounce. "Okay, so now I understand why you were sent to Wieran. He was doing a lot of that technomancy stuff already."

"I found it almost impossible to believe when I saw it. He seemed to have singlehandedly reconstructed things not seen since Atla'a Alandar. I was there as an assistant."

Gabriel was nearby, leaning against one of the unbroken trees. "Pardon me for saying so, but you're being very pleasant, apparently forthcoming, and so on. If you're such a pleasant fellow, why were you working for these people?"

The yellow gaze dropped, Tashriel's expression went nearly dead. "They...made me what I was. They can...*are*...making me do things. You've beaten me for the moment, I can think and act for myself for a little while...but soon I'll have to go back." He bit his lip hard enough to draw blood with one of his sharp fangs. "I...don't want to. But it's so hard to fight. Now that the matrix is gone and my service to Viedra's failed, I'll have to return to Balinshar, and I don't want to do that. But...I'll have to."

"Not if you're dead," Aurora said grimly. "And you haven't said anything that makes me sure you're leaving alive."

"She's got a point. We still don't know how you got in that tube, and whatever you have to say about Viedraverion."

"I...Speaker's *Name*, this is hard for me! I am fighting... very hard...to try to tell you. If I wasn't sort of between masters, not *formally* returned to Balinshar, I wouldn't be able to act at all!" The white-haired youth's hands shook; he clenched them into fists. "The tube was prepared by Wieran to Viedraverion's precise specifications and secured as you found it. Wieran was simply told to leave it available for later use. *I* was told to enter the tube, and what part I was to play and how I was to disguise myself, when it became clear that the 'endgame,' as he put it, was starting. At that point Wieran would be far too focused on his own work to worry about my location."

"So Master Wieran had no knowledge of this trick of Viedraverion's at all?"

"None. Well...I'm sure he knew that there was a much larger purpose in the tube's presence, but not what it was, nor did he care much."

Poplock saw Kyri's head come up. "How did you manage to play Rion so well? You *knew* things that only he should know. How?"

"That was the 'matrix' I mentioned. Viedraverion transferred it to me when he sent me to Wieran, but didn't *activate* it until I entered the tube. It was..." He met Kyri's gaze; Poplock saw more sorrow there than he had expected. "You had already guessed the essence of it, really. It was a part, a scrap of the real Rion's soul, that I could...well, *wrap around* my own like a cloak and make into a sort of front that reacted on its own, using my soul and strength to translate its echoes of memory. I've never seen *anything* like it; I didn't think it was *possible* to do that so... perfectly. When I spoke as Rion, I almost *was* him. If I didn't let myself *think* too much as myself, if I didn't try to look ahead or behind like an actor, but rather let 'Rion' act...it could be nearly perfect. There were only a few minor gaps in its memory, but you already noticed and discounted those."

"What about our truthtelling? It covered *that*, too?" Kyri demanded.

Tashriel shook his head again, a slow, disbelieving motion. "In truth, I thought I might be discovered then. The matrix was already breaking, I had become too...caught up in it, too interested in *becoming* part of what I saw, for it to remain untouched. I...I didn't want to PLAY the part, I was trying to make the part follow what *I* wanted, and that stressed it too much. It managed to still hide my nature, but I had to be very, very careful about how I answered and literally *force* the remaining matrix to help in the answers. Some of them were...evasive, at the least, such as whether I attacked Helina—I made myself believe it was not really an *attack*, because she was cooperating with me—or whether I was your brother, because I was, with the matrix, the only part of your brother left. But at that point I knew that I had very little time left. Days, perhaps not even that. So..."

"Let's go back. Tell us about Viedraverion. We've heard the name, we know he's a demonlord and a plotter and all, but can you tell us more about *him*?"

Tashriel nodded vehemently. "Oh, yes. Balinshar *hated* Viedraverion, so he made sure I knew all about him, and spent time studying him to find weaknesses and blind spots." He looked at the others regretfully. "But...he doesn't really *have* any.

"Viedraverion is the first son of Kerlamion Blackstar himself. He has served a key role in *many* plans by the King of All Hells. After Atlantaea was brought down and the Sauran Kingdoms shattered, Viedraverion was sent out to scour the galaxy for remnants of the old civilizations and destroy or neutralize them...until there was effectively no chance for anyone out there to learn the truth."

Toshi looked up sharply. "That would have taken nearly *forever*. Galaxies are *big*."

"He knew that too. So—according to the records—what he did was let civilizations rise to a certain level, where they started locating and collecting the relics themselves...and then arrange the civilization to collapse. In effect, he got literally trillions or quadrillions of people to act as his searching parties."

Oh, mud and drought. "He's a *long*-term thinker."

"*Very* long-term. He spent over a hundred thousand *years* on that assignment."

Nike stared at Tashriel. "I know *Khoros* was that old, but I still have a hard time *imagining* something living that long without changing."

"Oh, it can change even Demons some. Balinshar used to *rant* about that; apparently before he spent a hundred thousand years manipulating civilizations, Viedraverion was really bright and manipulative but had a cold, hard approach that tended to drive people away. After he came back, he had learned how to *work* with people."

"I see," said Toshi. "Then when he sent you to Wieran, he had *already* planned your integration with Kyri's party. He was certain they would triumph over all odds, and return here."

"He wasn't *certain*," Tashriel corrected. "He *believed* things would work out as they did—with many, many contingencies prepared for various alternative outcomes." A corner of his mouth curled upward, and the yellow eyes were distant for a moment. "He...it was one of the *good* things about working with him, that I could see something so incredibly...well, *beautiful* as his strategies, laid out like a map of the future, illuminated in gems and gold."

"Screw your admiration for the artist," Aurora snapped. "What had he 'mapped' for *you*?"

Tashriel looked at her and Poplock saw what seemed honest guilt in his eyes. "I was supposed to gain your complete confidence, let you 'help' me regain myself, er, well, *Rion*'s self, and then lead you to the Retreat where Viedraverion and the other Justiciars would be waiting for you."

"Then what were you doing—"

For the first time, color flamed on Tashriel's cheeks. "Rion loved his sister very much. And I was playing him for *months*. But I'm *not* her brother, and those emotions going through me... being near her...I found I didn't *want* to lead her into danger. *I* didn't want to. And my feelings...weren't brotherly, really, not once I started feeling them *myself*. Combined with everything else...I stopped *thinking*."

There was a moment of silence; Poplock could see that most expressions were a combination of sympathy, anger, and revulsion. *Complex situation.* "So," he said, "The important questions: what're his powers, and do you know any weaknesses or quirks he has we might be able to use?"

"Powers are easy. He's...really powerful in most areas. In his natural form—which is about seven feet tall, really broad, gray-skinned—he's phenomenally strong and fast, even for a demon. He's very resistant to most forms of magic and very tough against weapons of all kinds. He's also a *rannon* master—what you call psionics, powers of the mind—with a *lot* of experience in using it to kill, control and so on. Telekinetic, telepathic, self-enhancement, he knows how to use it all at an extremely high level of power."

Tobimar looked grim. "When you say 'extremely high,' what—"

"That big wall of stone Aurora threw in front of me? He could just *think* at it, and it'd fly up a mile and come down on top of you. That's 'extremely high.' And he might be a lot stronger than that."

"Great *Balance*," muttered Kyri. "I...don't know if we can face this."

"Maybe you can," Tashriel said. "If he has any weakness, it is that of all demons: the power of the Gods of Light is a major weapon against them, and you are Myrionar's *only* real representative, now. Tobimar...I know he has true holy power as well. Together you might..."

He stopped suddenly, and his face showed horror and regret that sent a chill of fear dancing along Poplock's skin. "Oh, no. Oh, I'm sorry, Kyri. I'm so, *so* sorry. *That's* why..."

"What? *What's* why? Why what?" Poplock knew that didn't sound very coherent, but it asked the questions he needed answered.

"I...that's why I couldn't stop, why I had to..." Tashriel trailed off, cursing in a Demonic tongue. "No! By the Speaker and the Lady! *That* was why I couldn't stop myself! It was his contingency—he'd made *sure* I would do it!"

"Do *WHAT*?" Poplock bellowed.

Tashriel's face was even whiter than it had been. "I...exchanged blood with her. Some of hers in me, then some of mine to her."

Tobimar's blades whispered from their sheaths. "You monster. You mean..."

"Yes," Tashriel whispered. "She's got the Curse now. In a few days the change will begin. The madness will strike. And even before that...she will be no threat to Viedraverion.

"Because if she so much as *tries* to summon the holy power of Myrionar, it will burn her to ashes."

CHAPTER 24

Kyri found her hand on Flamewing's hilt, the sword already half drawn, before she caught herself. The horrific thought echoed through her, a sentence of death and failure. *Not summon Myrionar's power? Be* barred *from Myrionar? No!*

"That fast?" Xavier asked, unbelieving. "C'mon, she's gotta have *some* time!"

"The Curse is already on her," Tashriel said, the same horror in his voice, and a part of her understood that he *knew* what she felt. "Perhaps she has...a few minutes? A few hours? But no more than a day or two."

She concentrated, called on the power, intending to heal the scratches on Poplock from Tashriel's sandblasting assault.

Gold-fired agony exploded along her skin, danced through her veins like molten steel. She heard her own anguished scream and dropped to her knees. "I...think I have...no time at all."

Tobimar whirled on Tashriel, and it took Xavier, Nike, and Aurora to restrain him. "If we're going to kill him, fine," Nike said, "but not like that. We will do this with justice and judgment, not impulse and hatred. Right?"

"Right," Kyri said, and despite the pain which was slowly ebbing she felt a warm gratitude towards Nike. *I swore to Myrionar that it would be Mercy and Justice before Vengeance, and that is more important for me than for anyone else, because I am the one who will be judged.*

The pain had, strangely, cleared her head, and in its aftermath

161

she felt less anger, more sympathy for the damned boy-demon in front of her. Her instincts told her that Tashriel *was* telling the truth now; it fit with what she knew of many demonic tales, and the way in which she had been told vampires of his sort worked.

But Tashriel was speaking again. "And you—you five—don't have time, either."

"Why not? We could at least take a few—"

"Then you have to kill me *now*," Tashriel said, and a blood-tinted tear ran down his face. "I will have to go back to Balinshar, and if he learns what I know of you, the Black City will be prepared—*Kerlamion* will be prepared, for Balinshar will surely tell him the truth, to ingratiate himself with Father and undermine Viedra."

Kyri heard multiple curses, and knew one of them was hers. As Rion, Tashriel had been present throughout their discussions; he knew the goal of the five from Earth and much about their abilities.

"Maybe we could lock him up, at least for a while," Tobimar said slowly, sheathing his swords.

"*Where?*" Poplock demanded. "If we were in Zarathanton, okay, sure, put him in the Star Cell where they locked those guys up, that'd probably hold him, but there *isn't* a place in Evanwyl that could do the trick. Didn't you *watch* this guy? If he hadn't been holding back, we could've all gotten bad hurt before we took him down."

"The Temple of Myrionar," Kyri said. "Maybe they could—"

Tashriel shook his head. "Arbiter Kelsley is a good man, and honest, but you know as well as I that Myrionar is *very* weak now. Weaker now than mere months agone, despite the works you have done—because Viedra's plan has taken all this into account, to weaken that faith beyond any easy point of return. All of the god's power is bound within or tied directly to you, outside of the simplest powers of the priests. I do not think he could create a sealed prison strong enough to hold me."

"Do you f—fricking *want* us to kill you?" Xavier said in outraged tones. "Because you're like really trying hard to make it happen!"

"I'm trying to keep you *safe*! I . . . he let me stay with you too long, with *her* too long! Don't let me be a weapon against you! I DON'T WANT YOU TO DIE!" Tashriel shouted.

Silence fell in the wake of that agonized declaration, and Kyri saw the bleak choices lying before them. *But only one of them allows mercy or justice.*

"Stand up, Tashriel," she said quietly.

He rose, slowly, eyes fixed on hers. She could read his readiness for the end in the way he kept his mouth clamped shut, tension in the jaw and down the neck clear in the lines of muscle and tendon.

She reached up, let Flamewing rise from its sheath, a foot, two feet—

—and let it drop back with a ringing chime. "Go."

The sight of that jaw dropping, the eyes practically popping from Tashriel's head in Toadlike fashion—an expression echoed by all the others—would have made her laugh under other circumstances; as it was, she managed a smile. "You are someone's tool and weapon, and perhaps in cold, hard policy I *should* kill you. But you were a companion, and I think—from your words, your voice, and your willingness to pass on—that you mean what you say, and thus in *your* heart you are no enemy.

"Were we still in the heat of battle, yes, I might well strike your head from your shoulders; but I will not kill you in cold blood."

"Kyri—"

She looked at Tobimar calmly. "Would you kill him as he stands?"

She saw the lean, dark face go grim; the hands grasped the twin swords. But the swords stayed in their sheaths, and with a curse Tobimar let his hands drop. "No."

"No more will any of us," Toshi said. "Which leaves you, Poplock. If any of us could do it, I think you could."

The little Toad drew his blade Steelthorn and bounced to Tashriel's shoulder. Despite the nearness of the glittering steel, enchanted—Kyri knew—by the spirit mage Konstantin Khoros himself—Tashriel did not move so much as a hair.

"You would *let* me do this, wouldn't you?" Poplock said after a moment. "Just run you through the throat and chop the head off."

"Yes."

"Well, *mudbubbles.* I can't do it either."

"Then we *do* have to leave now," Toshi said grimly. "Can you at least...dawdle on your return?"

Tashriel gave a weak but definite smile. "I promise to drag my feet as much as my compulsion allows. And I have more advice for you."

He turned to Xavier. "Xavier, you are the greatest weapon your group has for this. Not because of your stealth, though I'm not ever going to discount that, but because . . . well, of *who* you are."

"Who I am?"

"I can't say—not for absolutely sure—if it was your father, or your grandfather, or, at most, one of your great-grandfathers, but one of them was—*had* to be—the being that the demons fear above all others. You—and to my surprise, Kyri!—have his eyes, but you have more; you have his face, his build."

"*Whose* face?"

"Torline Valanhavhi, the Eternal King of Atlantaea," Tashriel said. "I met him, once, long ago, when I was living, a child younger than any of you." Tashriel gestured.

The figure of a man appeared, tall, slender, dark-skinned. Kyri stared; except for the appearance of greater age—the man seemed to be about thirty-five—it was like seeing Xavier in a mirror, even to the gray eyes. Before him, the figure held two silvered-green blades identical to those which Xavier carried.

"And you wield blades like his. By your appearance, by your image alone, you will frighten and dismay any demon—up to, and including, the King of All Hells himself. So I say to you that you should remain hidden, even more than your friends. Show yourself only at the end, when you will need *all* advantages, and your adversary is the worst of all."

Poplock had straightened. "You know . . . he's right."

"What?" said Tobimar. "What do you mean?"

"Remember when we got ambushed by those demons, with Xavier? That Lady Misuuma?"

"Yes . . . ?"

"Well, if you remember, she actually bailed on the whole battle right in the middle. I was chasing after her and I heard her saying . . ." The Toad's face wrinkled as he thought, "um . . . 'Those blades and eyes . . . it is worse than she believes. If this new ally is truly what we think—*c'arich!* We must retreat.'"

"She seemed to have a thing about eyes—she was looking at *mine* before—"

Poplock waved that away. "Yeah, we know, but that got cleared up once we saw that you had *Terian*'s blood in you. Terian's eyes are the same color, a pretty weird color for people from your part of the world, so that's what she was looking for. But then they got a good look at *Xavier*, and what'd she do? Flipped right out of her pond, that's what she did, and tried to run out on her own allies—when *she'd* set the trap to catch Tobimar."

"You're right," Tobimar said slowly. "Just the sight of Xavier's eyes and swords were enough to convince her to abort her own mission so she could carry the news back..."

"Except I punched her ticket *canceled*," Xavier said. "And thinking back, there were a couple demons I fought in my own quest that sure looked kinda panicked when I drew the swords and they got a good look at me. Makes sense." He looked over to Tashriel. "Okay, thanks. We'll remember that. But before we go, I've got some advice for you."

Tashriel bowed his head. "I will listen."

"You don't want to work for these guys. You've tried to help us. But then you say you can't fight 'em. I dunno, maybe you're right. But you know what?"

When Xavier didn't continue, Tashriel raised his head, met the Earth boy's challenging gaze. "No, what?"

"I think that's *bullcrap*."

"But I *am* controlled by the Curse! I am bound to the—"

"Bullcrap!" Xavier repeated. "You've got your own mind now, right? You're not formally with one or the other now, right? Okay, maybe it's not gonna be *easy*, but you've stayed here to tell us all stuff I *know* your bosses didn't want you to say, and you know what? You did that because you *fought* to tell us.

"I think you've been so convinced by those bastards that you *can't* fight that you're fighting *yourself* hard enough to keep you imprisoned. My *sensei* told me that there isn't any enchantment that can hold someone forever, if the enchantment isn't binding the person's *will*, their mind. If they can *fight* it, they can *break* it. 'The waves and wind can wear down a mountain, Xavier, and so it is with any binding, any enchantment; with enough time, none can withstand constant work, constant pressure, constant determination. All that is needed is the will to *do* it.' That's what he said."

She saw ages of conviction warring with a spark of hope. "But..."

"Yeah, *but*. But you have to find that will. You have to decide to *do it*, even if that's maybe going to get you killed. But hey, you were willing to die right here. You'll have to make a choice: is your own *freedom* worth dying for, even right after you get it?"

Tashriel stared at him for a long moment, then bowed deeply. "I . . . don't know. I don't know if I *can* believe in what you say. If you're right . . . I've lived as a slave because I bound myself there, as much as they bound me."

Kyri remembered the ancient, ancient tale of the Fall of the Saurans, and the tragedy and redemption of the Hell-Dragon, and its title. "Chains of the mind, Tashriel. Remember the lesson Syrcal learned."

The white-haired youth nodded, face still conflicted. "I . . . will think on this." A smile. "While I drag my feet."

"Still . . . we'd better stop dragging ours." Gabriel looked at her gravely. "But Lady Kyri, how—?"

"I don't know. Perhaps the Temple of Myrionar will have an answer there. But I know there *is* an answer, for I have kept faith with Myrionar, and It told me that always there is a way for me, if only I believe.

"And I still believe."

CHAPTER 25

Arbiter Kelsley wavered on his feet; Tobimar and Discoverer (previously Seeker) Reed caught his elbows, helped him to sit down.

Kyri looked out of the holy circle, and Tobimar felt a phantom pain in his chest as he saw her understanding that even this had failed. "Nothing at all, Arbiter?"

The priest of Myrionar shook his head reluctantly. "I can *injure* her easily enough, Balance save me. But to break *that* curse lies beyond the power granted me by Myrionar; I could feel the power simply *turned back*, dismissed as inadequate. Even with your assistance," he looked at Shasha and Poplock, "I cannot do more than momentarily blunt it, and it recovers any ground I deny it quickly, once I stop fighting."

"Poplock? There's got to be something—"

The little Toad flattened himself in a gesture of perfect despair. "Not that *I* can do. The Cursed are known all over Zarathan. They're not like the Stelati, or the Umbrals, or even the Veridiai— those can, sometimes, be cured by the right invocations, or even by the victim fighting it hard enough, praying well enough. I've *never* heard of a Cursed being cured, even early on. *Wieran* might have been able to do something. The Wanderer. Calladan Wysterios at the Academy. Khoros, if he was around. Idinus, of course. One of the greater gods, directly intervening, if they could. But anyone else? Swimming through thicker mud every minute."

Sasha Raithair simply shook her head. *She can do nothing either.*

Kelsley carefully cut across the lines of the holy enclosure, and the power faded. "We have tried for two weeks. Everything we could think of. I am sorry."

Kyri's face worked, and for a moment there was a glint of alien fury that frightened Tobimar more than anything he had seen in all his travels. "Failed *again?* Are you..."

She went gray with horror at what she was saying and buried her face in her hands. "Oh, Myrionar, is it happening this *fast?*"

"If what Tashriel told you was true—and I am very much afraid it was—he was one of those *there* the day the Curse was enacted. He is one of the actual *ancients* of the Cursed, a vampire half a million years old. His blood, mingled with yours, is terribly potent," Kelsley said, the explanation in a tone of apology and guilt, trying to convince himself that it wasn't his fault that the last and only Justiciar was about to be lost. "It is astonishing that you have remained...yourself...for this long; he thought that the change would be complete in *days*, if your recital of his words was accurate."

"So it *isn't* my imagination. It's not just my being on edge. I'm...turning into a monster."

"Kyri, maybe—"

She made a savage cutting gesture. "*No*, Tobimar. No false comfort. You saw that I couldn't burn it out myself—I can't keep the power going once the pain gets too great. I think...I think we're out of options."

He didn't attempt to hide the tears going down his face. "I wish...wish I had one. But I think Terian's power—"

"—would burn me to ashes even faster." She forced a smile. "But that may be what I'll ask for."

"*NO!*" It wasn't just Tobimar; Poplock, Kelsley, Reed, and Shasha had said it at the same time.

Kyri Vantage took a long breath; it shook with repressed anger. "If necessary, *yes*." She looked at Kelsley. "How...how far is the change now? How long do I have before I go mad?"

"From the records...the time for the madness varies, but tends to be one of the last changes, perhaps *the* last change. It is moving quickly, though. It is evening now. I..." he hesitated. Then the priest's jaw set and he continued, "I...believe that you have seen your last sunrise, Kyri. The sun will burn you tomorrow."

Terian's Light, *no. Not so soon.*

Kyri didn't seem to see them now. He laid his hand on her

shoulder and she reached up, gripped his hand tightly; suddenly she reached out and hugged him close; he embraced her as hard as he could.

"I'm sorry," he murmured to her.

She kissed him, then looked him in the eye; horrific flecks of yellow shimmered within the gray. "It isn't over yet, Tobimar."

Suddenly there was a shout from the sanctum door. "Arbiter! *Arbiter!* Is Lady Kyri there?"

Kelsley glanced at them, shrugged, and went to the door. "She is here, but engaged for the moment."

"I *must* speak with her! It is of the *utmost* importance!"

"Brogan," Kyri muttered, turning towards the door. "That's Brogan, the Watchland's Head of House. Let him in, Arbiter."

The door flew open as soon as Kelsley undid the bolts and wards. Brogan, a tall man with a head bald and polished as an egg and a drooping mustache above a pointed beard, strode in and immediately dropped to one knee before Kyri. "Justiciar Phoenix Kyri," he said. "Thank the Balance I . . . could find you." His voice was clearly breathless.

"What is it, Brogan? What has happened?"

For answer, Brogan reached into his shirt and withdrew a long, sealed envelope addressed to Kyri in an elegant hand. "The Watchland—he's disappeared. Just left without a word or warning, with just this envelope and a note to have it brought to you *immediately*."

"Oh, snakes and dust, *this* doesn't sound good," Poplock said as he bounced back to Tobimar's shoulder.

Kyri had immediately taken the envelope; the seal broke with a flash of light, showing it had been keyed to her. She reached in and took out a letter; she held it so that Tobimar could see it as well.

My most dear and respected Kyri,

If you have this in your hands, then I have gone. I have been frequently seized with the desire to hunt down the one responsible for using me as a puppet and a false face, and at the same time found myself unable to speak of it; merely writing this down has proven nigh-impossible.

You and your friends were right, I fear. Somewhere within me remains the knowledge of how to find our adversary's stronghold, but it will only reveal itself when this compulsion grows strong enough to triumph over my reason and will. This I am sure it will do, for it has only strengthened over each day, without my being able to inform any of this matter.

Rather than be caught by it unawares, perhaps to the detriment of others who might bar my path, I have therefore resolved to fight it no longer. I will prepare myself to confront our enemy as best I can, and let it take me whence it will; I believe, as do you, that this will be the Justiciars' Retreat.

Understand, Kyri, I am under no illusion that I will somehow be able to vanquish this enemy, this Viedraverion. I am a powerful warrior—perhaps stronger than you know— but I am not a Justiciar. But it may be that our enemy will not slay me outright, and so I write this note that you will know what has happened, and—if the Balance should smile upon me—perhaps be able to rescue me once more.

I do not ask you do so purely for my sake, although I certainly do not wish to die. I know you will attempt it no matter what the reasons. However, as your Watchland I give you this one command: do not risk Evanwyl for my sake. I will not be used as a hostage, and I insist that you not accept me as one. I will die for Evanwyl, as I know you would. Rescue me if you can, certainly—but not at a cost I will regret.

The compulsion has begun. I will place this in a sealed envelope to be found in my study, and then leave, locking the room so that—hopefully—I will not be able to undo what I have done here.

In the name of the Balance, I remain,

Jeridan Velion

"Myrionar's Unbalanced Sword!" Kyri cursed. "Brogan, when did the Watchland leave?"

Looking slightly shocked at what Tobimar suspected was great profanity on Kyri's part, Brogan answered, "We cannot be absolutely *certain*, Justiciar Phoenix, because the Watchland sometimes would isolate himself for thought or other private matters for a few days. But we believe he left last night."

Tobimar cursed this time. "That's twenty-four hours ago. We could never catch him, and the trail will be cold. Sand and storm!"

"Add 'drought and freeze' to that, too," Poplock said. "If we'd been able to get on his trail *quick*—within an hour or so, say—I think we could have gotten through the diversion wards. We'd have clear indicators to follow and the wards couldn't change those all that quick. But after this much time? Not a chance."

Kyri's fist had clenched down on the paper, crumpling it into a compressed wad. "Kyri…"

"What? Oh." She slowly relaxed her grip, then nodded. "Thank you, Brogan. I will do what I can. Get back to the estate and let them know."

"I will, Justiciar. Thank you very much."

Once Brogan had left, Kyri straightened. "Come on, Tobimar, Poplock. We don't have time to waste here."

"But, Kyri…in your condition," began Kelsley.

"My condition isn't going to change for the better sitting around here, is it?" At Kelsley's reluctant nod, she smiled. "Then I might as well try to do what I can."

She kissed the priest on the cheek, then bowed, and led the way out.

Tobimar studied her narrowly from behind. "Poplock?"

"Yep. She's not angry. She's…scared. Scared half to death."

"But that note didn't have anything frightening in it."

"I know." The two continued in silence, as Kyri strode ahead of them, through the main temple, towards the doors. "But then why is she so frightened?"

It wasn't obvious to anyone else, perhaps, but he could *see* it—it was in the way she stood so straight, so tense, as rigid and unyielding as the stone pillar she was now walking past. Kyri was deathly afraid of something, and as he walked a little closer to her, he could hear her breathing, a little too quick, a bit too ragged.

Outside, in the night-dark streets of Evanwyl, Kyri turned south. Tobimar quickened his own stride. "What is it, Kyri?"

She didn't pretend not to understand. Her hand reached out, took his. "I believe in Myrionar."

Tobimar didn't quite get what she meant, but her tone showed that she was trying to explain. "I know."

"But…Tobimar, will you trust me? Will you *believe* in me?"

He stopped her, put her hands on her shoulders. "Kyri, I will *always* trust you. I will *always* believe in you. Curse or no. *Always.*"

"Goes for me, too," Poplock said.

She closed her eyes, and two tears fell. "And will you do whatever I ask you to tonight, no matter what?"

"Are you going to ask me to...to end it for you?" Tobimar asked quietly.

The anger of the Curse tried to flare, he could see it in the tension of her arms, the twitching of the lips—but it subsided, left only the beautiful face surrounded by its gold-tipped blue hair, a face that tried to smile and failed miserably. "Not...not now. Not that way. But...something you won't want to do."

He almost started to question her, but an internal voice told him to *stop!*

She's asking me to have faith in her. To believe in her. And I just said I would. "Then yes, I will. No matter what."

Her shoulders slumped in relief. "Thank the Balance. Because I can't do this myself, and can't trust anyone else."

"Since I've agreed...what do I have to do?"

"We have to cure the Curse," she answered.

CHAPTER 26

Poplock stared at her, as did Tobimar; Poplock hopped to her shoulder to talk to her more directly. "Um, that's what we've been trying to do for the last couple of weeks, Kyri. With all the magic I've got, all of Sasha's, and even Kelsley's."

He could feel her pulse, sense it hammering far faster than it should be. "Magic—at least the magic we have—can't do it," she said quietly, still striding towards the south. "The Arbiter can't. Even the power of Myrionar I command can't, because I can't manage to keep the power *going* once I'm hurt enough."

"So?" Poplock asked. "You have another idea?"

"A crazy idea, yes. But it's really the only choice we have. The Watchland's gone. Our friends... if they didn't get caught, they must be almost to the Black City by now. Our enemy *must* be ready to make his move. If I'm gone... Tobimar, I *know* you and Poplock won't leave Evanwyl, you'll stay for my sake... but can the two of you beat him by yourselves?"

Poplock couldn't even try to claim they could. Together, the three of them were deadly. But take away any of them, they weren't nearly as dangerous. He saw Tobimar shake his head. "No. No, we probably can't. And he's got at least three False Justiciars that we know of—Skyharrier, Bolthawk, and Condor." He looked at her again. "Where are we going?"

"There's a hill a little ways outside of town—you must have passed it when you first came here?"

Poplock thought back to the day—which seemed about a

thousand years ago now—they'd first arrived in Evanwyl. "Oh, yeah. Over on the left...well, on the *right* the way we're going now. Nice smooth meadowed slope facing the east, and the river spreading out across from it."

"That's it. Called Trader's Rest."

"What's *there*?"

"My cure...I hope."

Poplock eyed the stars. "Hope you're right. That knoll's about eight, nine miles down the road. Assuming nothing gets in our way, that's still a few hours travel. Be well past midnight, and the sun won't wait."

Kyri nodded. "I know."

They walked in silence for a few moments. "What *is* the cure you think is there?"

"I'll tell you when we get there," she said quickly. "Tobimar... tell me about Skysand?"

"But..."

Even in the darkness, Poplock could see the momentary wide, terrified look in her eyes, a look that silenced Tobimar instantly. *"Please*, Tobimar; tell me about Skysand."

The exiled Prince of Skysand looked at Poplock with a worried, confused expression, but then shrugged, and began to talk.

"Well, it's...it's a big country, we cover a large part of the northeast corner of the continent. But...no, you don't want dry description. Of course not." His smile was forced, but the way he caught and held Kyri's hand was not. "When I stood in my bedroom and looked out, I could see the sun's light slant across the city, the shadows of the Seven and the One stretching towards the horizon, over sand shadowed gray and violet, with nodding green of the trees at the springs just becoming visible in the light of dawn. The roofs would go from a gray to rosy pink and white and light green as the sun sprang up from the sea, and you could look down and see into the central courtyards of most of the houses, squares of deeper shadow with people just starting to move. The Temple of Terian would sound the Dawn Chimes to greet the day, and there would be a whisper of movement, as though the whole city were stretching, rising from its bed. The light would catch the dunes and turn them to molten gold and ruby, sparkling in the sun, and the caravan trails cut through them, lanes still touched with shade in the early morning..."

Tobimar spoke on, telling how he would usually begin his day, describing the great curved sweep of the bay and its blue water, with the wisps of black smoke and ash rising across the endless blue of the sky from the volcanic cone that brooded nearby, naming his sisters and brothers and the people of his household, outlining the city itself in detail—the streets, the sounds, the people. As they walked, Poplock found he was getting a clearer vision of Skysand now than he ever had before. Many of the *facts* he had known already—it wasn't as though he and Tobimar hadn't talked about their homelands before—but Tobimar was now weaving a complete picture, talking for hours without pause, and without letting go of Kyri's hand.

And—at least at times—he could feel that her terror faded, was forgotten as Tobimar spoke, as she focused on distant shores and the love that her companion had for his homeland.

Finally, Poplock could see a dark outline, a curve of blackness against the night that cut through the stars. "I think we're here, Kyri."

He could feel her pulse quicken again. "Yes...yes, we are."

She turned, walked swiftly—almost ran—up the slope, stopping midway, in the center of a broad meadow, barely visible in frosted starlight. She paused, looking outward.

The view to the east was very nice, Poplock had to admit. The river, as he remembered, broadened here, flattening to a shallow ford three-quarters of a mile across. The rippling chuckle of the water over countless stones was soothing, and Poplock's eyes could make out the motion of flow and ripple all the way across. Low bushes dominated the far shore, a flat area that Poplock suspected flooded regularly; trees didn't seem to reappear until near the horizon, a darker darkness in the distance. The horizon itself was a slightly brighter black. *Dawn isn't all that far away.*

"Yes," Kyri murmured. "This is how I remembered it."

Tobimar looked at her. "Now...what?"

Kyri took off her pack and searched through it. "Here we go."

"That's our climbing gear. What do you—"

Her swallow was audible. "Tobimar, I want you to take the stakes and ropes and bind me down. *Hard.* This is shadespider silk, it should hold just about anything, but still, don't take chances."

"Bind you down—" Realization struck Tobimar and Poplock simultaneously.

"Terian and Chromaias... Kyri, you're not—"

"Yes," she said, and her voice shook. "I am."

"That's *suicide!*"

"Maybe... maybe not, Tobimar."

"If Kelsley's right," Poplock says, "it *is*. When the sun rises, you go up in smoke."

"It hasn't got a complete hold on me. Not yet." Kyri put the rope and spikes into Tobimar's hands. "I can't burn it out of myself with Myrionar's power because the pain makes me focus on *it*. I have to stop. But the Sun *symbolizes* purity. I *know* it will burn me—and from my trying to use Myrionar's power I *know* how much it will hurt." Her voice was still unsteady. "Tobimar, Poplock, I *know* how crazy this is. But it's the only thing I can think of, and I have to have faith in Myrionar that I'm right. I will accept the purification of the Sun and hope that the power of... of the *Phoenix*," she managed a smile, "will let me somehow pass through that trial alive."

"And what if it doesn't?" Poplock asked bluntly.

"Then I die *myself*, not a monster. And that's a happier ending than any other I see before me now."

Tobimar stood stock-still for long moments. Then his head bowed. "As you ask, Kyri."

Her voice was filled with relief. "Thank you, Tobimar." She reached up and removed Poplock gently. "I... need to be exposed to the sun for this to work."

"What? Oh. Got it."

The Raiment of the Phoenix flowed off her—all but her helm, the symbolic profile of the bird of prey clear even in the predawn gloom. "Keeping that on?" asked Tobimar, in the most unconvincingly casual tones that Poplock had ever heard, as he began hammering stakes into the ground.

"I do this as Phoenix, not as Kyri Vantage," she said. "The helm... won't make any difference otherwise."

Poplock couldn't argue that. Aside from simple travel support for her breasts and brief underclothes for her lower body, all of her was now completely exposed to the night... and soon to the light. *I feel so completely* useless *here. All I can do is advise Tobimar on how to make sure the bindings will hold her even if she struggles hard. Which she will. No way that she won't when she's burning alive, even with Myrionar's power to keep the pain down.*

Sound of hammer striking metal, looping of rope, more hammering, and the grim, grim look on Tobimar's face deepened. Poplock didn't want to look. But he also couldn't look away. If this didn't work...this would be the last time they ever saw Kyri alive.

Finally, Tobimar straightened. "It...it's done." Multiple stakes surrounded each of Kyri's limbs, but even with many strands of rope, very little of her skin was covered. "Try to break free."

Kyri threw her strength against the bonds. Poplock heard a faint grunt that showed more fear and desperation than Kyri would want to admit. *But that does mean she'll be giving them a fair test.*

But the bindings held firm. Even the Vantage strength could not overcome all of the many loops of spidersilk rope and multiple spikes buried deep in the earth.

Tobimar sighed. "All right. Looks like it will...hold."

The faintest ghost of a smile. "Yes. You...did that well." Suddenly her eyes went wide. "Oh, no, I forgot!"

"Forgot what?"

Poplock found it amusing—and heartbreaking—to see that even in *this* circumstance Kyri was able to look embarrassed. "Um...could you go into my pack and find..." She hesitated, then plunged forward, "find the phoenix and dragon figurines that I have in there?"

"I'll do it. I couldn't do any of the real work." Poplock bounced to Kyri's pack. He remembered the figures she was talking about, and what they meant to her. *The ones she and her brother played with. The figurine she got the name "Phoenix" from, really.*

It only took a few moments. He came back and put one figure in each hand. Kyri smiled at him, though her face was visibly pale in the slowly growing light. "Thank you, Poplock."

"At least it's something." He leapt back to Tobimar's shoulder; there was nothing left to do on the ground, nothing really at all left to do but wait.

He glanced backward. The horizon was lighter. Kyri was now easily visible, bound immovably to Trader's Rest, facing the east. "A few minutes now."

"Yes." She shifted slightly, though the ropes did not allow much movement. "Tobimar...I—"

"*Survive* this," Tobimar said. "No farewells!"

She was quiet, but in the predawn light Poplock saw two tears flowing down her cheeks from beneath the helm.

But then he heard movement behind them, *fast* movement.

Tobimar heard it too, started to turn, but something *smashed* into both of them, an impact like a Dragon's claw. Tobimar tumbled away like a broken doll, striking a tree so hard that the trunk *shattered*, continued on; Poplock leapt clear, tried to roll, but another tree was right there in his path—

The pain was accompanied by the high-pitched greenstick splintering sound of his own bones breaking, despite the defensive wards he'd painstakingly woven into his harness over the last months. Poplock slid from the dented treetrunk, falling limply onto his back. Something was still moving near Kyri, and he tried to rise, to roll to his feet, but he could barely manage to raise one leg before red-tinged pain caught up with him and pushed him down into darkness.

CHAPTER 27

At last I'm here.

Aran looked down over the valley of Evanwyl with a combination of happiness, sorrow, and grim determination that he'd never felt before. *My home. But one I can't really return to. I'm just here to do . . . two jobs.* He smiled bitterly, and felt the acid humor echoed by the Demonshard. *Both for vengeance, and one for justice.*

But vengeance came first. The Phoenix was *near.* He was sure, now. She could not find her way to the Retreat without help. And maybe she never would. He had thought and rethought the plan along the way. Leading the Phoenix and her party to the Retreat carried its own risks; he would have to carry out a letter-perfect act of contrition and redemption in front of the one he'd been hunting for—was it a year, now?—and one who had every reason to believe him fallen beyond redemption.

And that was probably true. He felt the urgings of the Demonshard through him, and it was *hard* to resist, hard to shove the impulses of the black accursed blade to the background of his mind. Many times he'd nearly thrown the thing away, but always the knowledge of how powerful his adversaries were had stopped him. Sometimes he caught a faint amusement from the Demonshard at that. It *knew* he couldn't afford to lose it, even though it was gaining a slow, sure foothold on him every time he used it, despite all his will and dedication.

Focus. The problem was that he *could not* show himself

in Evanwyl. He was a known traitor, a False Justiciar, and he would find no allies below. None to give him advice or aid. He considered disguising himself, asking around for the true Justiciar, but that was terribly risky. If any of his former comrades were still around, they could have assisted, but of course none of them were...

He stopped, wondering. *It just might be possible.*

Stealth was the ally of a Justiciar—or a false one—and once night was falling he called upon all of it to conceal him as he made his way farther into Evanwyl, towards one of the border towns. *I visited there more than once. Now that I know...*

Approaching the clearing, he could see the mansion still standing. *Good. They didn't burn it; needed to keep it intact for searchers.*

The question was how much had been looted, destroyed, or left intact. Revulsion at what Thornfalcon had done had undoubtedly given a lot of people the impulse to destroy everything he'd made, but it *was* a valuable estate, and searching burned ruins was a pain.

The grounds were a mess: dozens of holes had torn up the lawns, and a huge black scar stretched from near the house to the very edge of the jungle. But the front door was mostly intact, and had been mended where it was broken. No lights showed; no one had laid claim to the place or chosen to live here, then, unless they were an early sleeper. Aran opened the door, paused, listened. Cautiously, he made his way into the foyer, stopping every few steps to listen.

It took half an hour or more to make his way through enough of the house to be convinced that there was no one here. Knowing that the house itself couldn't be seen from any other location, he conjured a light and started searching.

The first and most obvious place was Thornfalcon's bedroom, but that had been stripped bare and, by the looks of the symbols placed on various of the walls, purified by everything *but* fire. *If they ever* do *sell this house, I must wonder if anyone will ever use this room again.* The runic pattern the False Justiciar had placed in the floor had been ripped out; whatever powers it had once had were now gone.

What Condor was looking for, fortunately, could be concealed in several places, and might be overlooked by searchers. It wasn't in the basement—which *had* been cleansed by fire, at least to a large extent. *Possibly the Phoenix's doing, since our leader said she'd killed Thornfalcon. If so... incredible control. Such power, yet the entire building remained intact.*

He almost missed it. He had actually entered and searched the room and was about to leave when he suddenly froze, then turned to look across the room. And there it was, in plain sight on the wall of Thornfalcon's ground-floor salon and study. *What incredible arrogance. But then... he almost never had visitors he intended to let live, other than us, so perhaps it simply was his preferred location.*

Aran took the gold and silver scroll and concentrated on it. "I am here."

Minutes passed, and he repeated the call. *He may be busy. I may have to be quite patient.*

Three more repetitions. But Aran had indeed learned a lot about patience, and despite the distant mental chafing of the Demonshard, he simply sat in one of Thornfalcon's remaining undamaged chairs and tried again.

Suddenly the silvery surface cleared, and their Patron gazed out at him. "Why, Condor! I had not realized you had... ahh, of *course*. One of Thornfalcon's mirror scrolls. Clever. What *can* I do for you?"

"How can I locate the Phoenix?"

A broad smile. "Yes, I see. That *is* a challenge for one who cannot question the locals. Small though it is, Evanwyl's very large for one man to search on foot. However, you happen to have the answer to hand."

"I do?"

"The Demonshard, of course. While your so-called Justiciar powers are, ultimately, false, they are quite deliberately made to seem in virtually all ways identical to those of the real Justiciars. The Demonshard can sense other powers—"

Aran felt like hitting his head. Now that their Patron pointed it out, it was *obvious*. The Demonshard had not only been able to sense the power of the Elderwyrm tens of miles away, but instantly recognized *what* that power was. If Aran's power was even *reasonably* close to that of a true Justiciar, surely the Demonshard could look for similar power sources... and there would be only those at the retreat, and the Phoenix. "Thank you."

"It is all in accordance with the plan we discussed. I look forward to seeing you." The scroll went blank.

That simple statement firmed Aran's new resolve. *He's too confident. He's got a plan to deal with the Phoenix.*

And in all honesty... I don't want him in on it. Not him, not Bolthawk, not any one but me. This is my vengeance, my father's honor.

Decision made, he drew his sword. "Demonshard, you know the touch of my own powers, those that I claim to come from the god Myrionar, yes?"

The cold, arrogant thought was instant. *Yes. And that it is a false claim, that too I can see, not only from your mind but from the power itself—though that is a subtle trick indeed.*

"Never mind that. What I want to know is whether you could sense the *true* power of Myrionar at a distance, tell me in which direction I might—"

The sword *laughed*, an eager and malicious sound that echoed through Condor, resonated with the part of him that realized his long hunt was nearly over. *That I can do, yes, for some leagues, even.*

He leapt to his feet. "Then show me. There is but one true Justiciar living, and she is not far from here—a mile, ten, perhaps twice that, but I think no more."

Yes. Yes, I sense a power very like the one you pretend to. It is quiescent, inactive, but I have been with you for long enough that I am certain this is what you seek.

"How far? Where?"

The Demonshard stretched out before him, pointing to the south and west. "There... twelve miles in that direction."

Twelve miles. Twelve miles to finish my quest!

"Then we will do those twelve miles tonight," he said, and sheathed the sword.

Darkness meant little to him. To see through the night was something natural to a Justiciar, and to one who carried a piece of the King of All Hells' sword, it was even less an impediment. He strode through the jungle, shoving aside brush, occasionally using the Demonshard's power to obliterate more stubborn obstacles, and calling on the nigh-infinite power of the blade to support him, to banish weariness.

Even as his heart pounded with eagerness, another part of

him acknowledged how hollow the victory might be. In his travels, Aran knew he had played the part of a Justiciar of Myrionar far too well; he'd even occasionally fooled *himself* into thinking he was one. Now he was accepting the help of the monstrous weapon he'd been given, and he could *feel* it trying—perhaps even succeeding—to take hold of him once more.

Doesn't really matter, another part of him whispered. *Just finish our oath, and then we can destroy the demon himself.*

A smile that was more a snarl of joy crossed his face. If Viedraverion really *was* a son of Kerlamion, as his conversation with the Demon King had implied, then it would be a battle of true irony; a piece of his father's sword would be the weapon used to kill him.

He felt a touch of weariness, drew dark, ecstatic power, strode forward with a smile now, tearing through the jungle. Time passed, but he did not weary.

Then he burst from the forest onto the southern road. Ahead he could see Trader's Rest...

And two figures against the darkness.

He touched the hilt of the Demonshard, caressed it, then drew it slowly, sensuously. "Our time is come, Demon. Tell me I'm not wrong; one of those two is my Phoenix."

You are surely right, Condor, the black sword answered, its tone eager and more respectful. *I can feel her life, her power, she is indeed a Justiciar such as you played at being!*

Buoyed up by the relief and triumph of reaching his journey's end, he broke into a run, calling on the sword's power to silence his movements, cloak his approach, consuming all trace of his coming.

Strange; it appears that the Phoenix is lying on the ground, wearing almost naught but a helm. Why?

It struck him that he might be seeing that most ironic of moments—the Phoenix betrayed and prepared for sacrifice by a false companion. *But there is no way I will let anyone else kill her!*

False companion or true, the standing figure was the only thing in his way. He did not slow, but lowered his shoulder in the charge. The Demonshard protested, screamed at him, but he managed to refuse it to make his arm more than twitch. He had come here to kill one person, and one alone. Yes, if this man faced him again he might be forced to kill, but this time—

The impact was stunning to Aran Condor, enough to make him stumble and fall to his knees for a moment. But his opponent had it far worse: he flew through one tree, two, then collapsed limply to the ground.

He will be out of it long enough, if I have not killed him; but if he was with the Phoenix in the battle against a dragon, I think he will not perish so easily.

Aran rose to his full height and felt adrenalin and joy and an alien, savage hunger rising. Fingers trembling with eagerness, he raised the Demonshard again and strode forward, looked down at the bound figure before him. Dawn was near, now, and he could see that she was a tall woman, as the reports had said, and clearly as well muscled as any he'd ever met. But he could not meet her gaze, for her helm was still on.

"No, murderer," he said, voice shaking. "You'll look on me as I look on you, as I take your *head*, and leave your body for the crows as you left Shrike!"

He reached down and tore the helm from the Phoenix's head, raising the Demonshard for the final blow.

Kyri Victoria Vantage looked sadly up at him.

Aran froze, his brain unable to comprehend what he saw, and his arm began to descend, a stroke of death screaming with howling blue-white fire around a core of night.

"NO!"

With a supreme effort he caught his own arm, shoved the stroke aside, felt the Demonshard's fury at being balked even as the long black blade plunged hilt-deep into the earth with a screaming flare of starfire.

The Demonshard was in his mind now, raging, no longer under control, clawing through his brain, forcing his body upright again, raising the sword again. *She killed your father! She is the one you swore to destroy! She is the Phoenix, the enemy of ALL False Justiciars! Kill her for your justice! Kill her for your vengeance! Kill her as she would kill you!*

But under all the arguments was merely the imperative: Kill. Destroy. Rip asunder bodies and souls and continue to do so. Feel the power of others flow into him, make him more than man, more than demon, something that could destroy the one who tricked him, who thought to control him. The Demonshard promised this, and he knew there was truth in the promises.

But there were eyes of gray—sprinkled with strange, frightening yellow—and long flowing hair, and a tear flowing down the face that was not filled with hate, but sadness.

Impossible. Impossible! It cannot be her! Kyri could never have made it back to Evanwyl in time!

But the power of the gods could make a mockery of time and distance. He *saw* her, and at this range *sensed* her, knew that this was Kyri Vantage, knew how *right* it was that it would be her, sister to Rion, and then he remembered his patron's smiles, his evasions, the denial of knowledge.

He knew! *He* knew *it was Kyri, perhaps from the very beginning! He* arranged *with his allies that I never met her!* Fury burned within him now, but not at the bound figure below him—at, instead, the urbane, smiling mask of a demon. *He made sure I never passed through Evanwyl, had no* chance *to discover the truth! This was his plan all along, to have me destroy her and then be broken by the discovery!*

Even as he thought this, his arm was rising, gripping the Demonshard, moving with a volition beyond his own. Kyri looked up and met his stunned, frozen gaze, and she spoke.

"Forgive me, Aran," she said.

The words pierced through his anger and anguish and self-righteous justifications, reverbrated past even the impassioned and venomous urgings of the Demonshard, shattering the hatred that had squatted, vile and cold and corrupting, in his heart for all this time.

He froze, the Demonshard upraised, fighting the weapon of the King of All Hells one final time. *NO.*

YES! I was created for this! *You will not—you* cannot—*deny me this kill!*

I can and I do. He forced his body to turn—not even an inch, but he turned, turned *away* from the woman he had hunted. *I renounce that oath. I renounce my vengeance. I renounce my oath as a false Justiciar. I renounce it* all. *And most of all, foul weapon, corrupter, Demonshard, monster-blade, I renounce* YOU. *You have no more power over me, for I am no longer Condor. I am* Aran.

I am Aran.

I am Aran!

"I am *ARAN!*" he screamed, and with all his might spun, flinging the Demonshard away. He toppled, rolled down the hill, and lay there, sobbing, feeling both the revulsion at everything he had done and the slow-emerging wonder that he had somehow stayed his hand...and that the Phoenix, the true Justiciar, was by some miracle Kyri Vantage, the one person it *should* have been.

The sun finally sent its first beams across the broad expanse of the world to touch upon Trader's Rest, and for an instant Aran felt it was Myrionar's own symbol, telling him that he had finally, at very long last, emerged from darkness.

But then Kyri began to scream.

CHAPTER 28

"Bolthawk, Shrike, Mist Owl, Silver Eagle, Skyharrier—thank you for coming so swiftly."

Shrike made no attempt to conceal his sour expression. "Aye, but not as if there were a choice."

"Tsk, tsk, Shrike, there *are* still niceties to be observed," it said, wearing the smile he knew they all found most galling. "It is true it would be exceedingly unwise for you to reject my summons, but still, I am not—and I believe you would all agree, have never been—an *unreasonable* being."

"True enough," Bolthawk said, with a sharp glance at Shrike. It was interested to see that after the events of the past year, Bolthawk had become the unquestioned leader of the False Justiciars; even Mist Owl and the old Silver Eagle had accepted him. *Surprisingly capable in the role, too; the crisis brought out something in him that had never come to the fore previously.* "You don't gather us like this without reason, sir. What do you ask of us?"

"It is time for us to prepare to welcome some new guests who will be arriving very shortly," it said.

"You mean Phoenix and her friends," Skyharrier said.

"In a while, yes. But somewhat before that I expect at least one other visitor—an old friend and ally of ours."

Shrike started up. "Condor?" he said, with an eagerness that was utterly at odds with his prior sullen look.

"Indeed, our long-departed friend Condor. He is nearing Evanwyl—in fact, has already entered it. But I am not *entirely* sure that he will be arriving to *assist* us, if you understand my meaning."

Shrike looked up. "He doesn't know who the Phoenix is."

"Not yet, no."

The broad, frowning face suddenly creased in a wintry smile. "Then maybe the lass'll wake him up."

It laughed. "Oh, dear, Shrike! You are *hoping* for my defeat? For your son's *salvation*, after all he's done?" The creature wagged a finger reprovingly at the false Justiciar. "For shame, now. That would just mean that you'll have to kill him *for* me when he comes. You don't want *that*, do you?"

Shrike met its gaze with a sullen glare. "Maybe I'd just fall before him, an' then it'll be *you* he'll be after."

Its hand lashed out, lifted Shrike effortlessly. "You think *he* has the power to defeat me? Even with those allies he has gained? Oh, Shrike, you truly *are* amusing. If you die facing him, I will make *certain* you rise and get to fight him again, until he wearies of slaying his father, or his father wearies of *dying!*"

Tossing the warrior aside casually, it turned away. "I assure you, Shrike, your *best* course of action—for both your sake and his—will be to kill him *swiftly*, before I am actually forced to take a hand in the battle. You know what I can do now. Unless you wish that on your adopted son and the girl who wears Justiciar's armor, you know it would be better they died before that."

It could sense the anger from Shrike, and not just him; all of the false Justiciars were reaching the limit of fear. But then, it only needed them for a short time longer, and having them *break* at the right time would be artistically correct; if it had to either leave them intact, so to speak, or directly deal with them after the rest was done? Not as elegant as the plan demanded, though such an outcome would not directly affect the major goal of the whole plan.

It paused, then turned. "Very well, Shrike; you, Mist Owl, and Silver Eagle may retire to your own rooms. I will not involve you unless it becomes *necessary*."

Bolthawk looked up. "Why not *us*?"

It shrugged, with an easy smile. "Because *you* are known to be alive and in service to me—though they do not, of course, know who I truly am. If *you* are not seen, our adversaries will have good reason for suspicion. If and when Condor appears, ascertain which side he is on before allowing him passage. I would *prefer* no battles within the Retreat itself. I will sense if you require aid soon enough to send the others to you, or come myself. If he is alone, there is a decent chance he is on our side. If not, you will know his intentions.

"All of you ready your weapons, your defenses, your resources of all types. The coming battle will be the last you need be concerned with."

The three he had named first paused in the doorway at that, and Shrike turned. "An'... if we survive this battle... what then?"

It smiled. "Why, then I will have no further need to bind you to me. I will release you—on your sworn oath to never impede me and mine in the future, of course." It turned away again, dismissing the False Justiciars, who quietly filed out and let the door of the inner sanctum close.

Yes, that was the last touch needed. The hope of actual release from my service will balance their hatred and anger towards me. They know they have little chance to kill me, and I have many ways to punish them beyond the merely physical. They—with the possible exception of Shrike, poor man—will fight with everything in their possession to win through and gain their freedom.

It smiled and leaned back in the chair. *Almost all pieces are in place. Just a few last things to arrange.*

It was in the middle of one of those "last things" a few hours later that it heard the door open. But the soul it sensed was not one of the False Justiciars. It passed its hand over the mirror-scroll, erasing the insectoid image, rose from the desk, and turned, grinning.

Watchland Jeridan Velion stood there, a curved, glittering blade gripped in his hands. The point of the blade dipped fractionally as the creature completed the turn. "So. A true duplicate. You and I are as alike as a mirror."

"Necessary, of course," it said, coming slowly out from behind the desk, leaving space between it and the Watchland. "I presume you simply walked past my guards, with an appropriately arrogant pose?"

"Yes. A bit of a hole in your security, others might think. But I believe you *expected* this. You called me here for some reason."

It let the smile broaden. "Indeed, Jeridan. I think you should be here for the *denouement*, as it were." It studied the blade in the Watchland's grip, and raised an eyebrow. "But I compliment you. I had gone to some trouble to move *that* weapon out of sight and mind, even though for various reasons I could not arrange its complete disposal."

"I was able to force some of my foggier memories to the surface," the Watchland replied, blue eyes measuring the creature's pose. "I remembered how the legendary Earaningalane had dwelt on the wall of my chambers for decades, yet I had a vague memory of it being moved, more than once. I knew you *must* have had a reason to make that weapon, of all weapons in the castle, disappear." He raised the blade higher. "I think this can hurt you."

It laughed. "You are *entirely* correct, Watchland. Most weapons of this land would be useless, but that one... ahh, that one was forged by the same hand that made the Raiments themselves, and gifted to the Watchland of Evanwyl in the days the first Justiciars walked the land. Oh, yes, if you can strike me with that blade, I will find it *most* unpleasant."

The Watchland began a cautious advance. "Then why do I have no compulsion to stop?"

"Oh, now, that would be rather unsporting of me, don't you think?"

"Unsporting? Is this a mere amusement for you, then?"

It smiled again, but now that smile was broader, the teeth glinting in a way no human teeth would ever shine. "Oh, indeed, an amusement, little creature. Let us see, then, how long *you* can survive, against *me*."

The look of horror on the Watchland's face as it finally revealed its *true* form was... *inspiring*.

CHAPTER 29

Kyri had *wanted* to stay silent—to suffer the agonies with dignity, without inflicting the pain of her cries upon her friends. But as the fiery agony of the beautiful dawn washed across her, searing like a wave of boiling oil, she found her resolutions impotent; a shriek of anguish burst from her lungs, in that instant sending a minor spike of pain through her throat from the sheer volume of the scream.

Instinctively, desperately, Kyri called up Myrionar's power, and *that* burned too, burned and flamed both cold and hot, even as the glory of the Sun ignited her skin in smoking ruin.

But Myrionar's power was still with her, still answering her prayers, and she begged for one thing, one thing only: *Let me stay myself! Let the pain not drive me mad, nor the Curse take my mind! If I must die ... let me die as* myself!

The agony ebbed, just enough for her to gain control, clamp her mouth shut, reduce the screams to tormented grunts and muffled curses. She saw, in the instants before the torturous, all-destroying, all-renewing light took her eyes, Tobimar stumbling into view, Condor on his knees with horror and contrition, Poplock crawling to his friend's side.

I can't! I can't survive this!

She forced that thought back with desperate will. *I can. I must. I believe in Myrionar. All other cures failed. Only the sun remains.*

But I'm burning away!

She could feel that was nightmarishly true. Though the power

of her god dulled the sensation—barely—the agony was not fading as nerves were destroyed. The pain and erosion extended
throughout her being, consuming her with flame. Her legs were
already blackened, her fingers around the figurines becoming
skeletal. *Myrionar! By the Balance, how can I exist like this?*

But she forced *that* question back, too. That was not faith,
it was not focus. There were—there *had* to be—only two things
in her mind: the first was faith that Myrionar's oath, sworn in
the name of the very power of the gods, could not be a lie. She
had not yet had her justice and vengeance, and thus a way out
for her existed—*had* to exist.

The other was simple: the end of her quest was in sight. She
had kept faith, and Myrionar had provided the last thing she
needed to have her rendezvous with their true enemy.

*I cannot die before I have faced him! Before I have faced
Viedraverion!*

But her body was dissolving like mist before the dawn, corrosive
brilliant fire causing her skeletal hands to collapse, her bones to
begin crumbling. She *felt* that happen, a crushing agony as though
a dozen hammers were pounding on every fiber of her being. She
screamed anew, a horrid dry croaking wheeze that spoke of the
dessicated, charred flesh and cartilage which was now her face and
throat. Myrionar's power was weak, weak indeed now.

Too weak to save her.

She realized that with horrific certainty as she remembered
all the efforts she had put forth through the last months, spend-
ing whatever reserves the god had remaining to it with reckless
abandon in the name of her quest... and now, at this last point,
she could tell that even Myrionar no longer had the strength to
rebuild what was lost. The Curse would be broken, yes... the
moment the last of her mortal form went to ash, then her soul
might be freed, might find some destination beyond. Or might
not, for her oath also bound her, and she had failed. Without
Myrionar to hold the paradise beyond open for her, without the
fulfillment of her oath, she could not be released, nor could see
find refuge; she would be a condemned spirit, fading and weakening, seeking an end to a quest that could never be concluded.

No.

Myrionar had *promised* there was a way out. And even now,
as she heard with ears that were themselves nearly gone the

dry-stick crumbling of her chest, she knew that the god had not—*could not have*—lied to her. She knew that, and refused to give up her hope, to release her faith.

But if Myrionar could not do it—

She thought for a moment of the other gods, allies to Myrionar. Surely Terian had the power. Chromaias, as well, and the Dragons, sleeping though they were, might respond with slumbering might to sweep aside injury and death. Fire burned through her skull, evaporated the remainder of her eyes in pure brilliant torment, and her screams were silent, yet she did not yield her *self* to the pain.

No, the other gods cannot help. By the Balance, the PAIN! I am not sworn to them, and their pact prevents them from acting for those not so sworn. I am the Justiciar of Myrionar, and none other. But soon there shall be nothing left of me . . .

Nothing?

For a moment all seemed still—even the incendiary agony was frozen, distant, inconsequential. *No. Only my* body *will be gone.*

My soul remains.

She remembered Xavier's white-blazing power, Tobimar's senses beyond the physical that guided him through battles of darkness and death; she recalled the moment of a dozen, two dozen, *more* of her ranged about the southern shore of Enneisolaten, all of them as *real* as anything that ever was, and she remembered the cold, precise lecture of mad Master Wieran.

My soul. Our souls, the foundation of the power of the gods, that is given to them in worship, returned to us in blessings. The soul that is our link between the mortal and the transcendant.

If I can find the strength . . .

Even as she thought that, she could *sense*, suddenly, the connection between her and her friends. Tobimar, crying, praying to his own god, entirely of his being *focused* on her. Poplock, golden eyes closed and weeping tears as he, too, prayed for her to the god of his people.

But . . . but there is more!

Condor—Aran—kneeling next to her, his only thoughts being how he had failed her and how he wished it were otherwise. Beyond him . . . Seeker Reed, cleaning the temple, silent yet thinking of her when he glanced at the Sword Balance above; Arbiter Kelsley, isolated in his study, praying for forgiveness for his failures. Lythos, looking into the dawn and wondering if his best student had survived the night, and others, tiny glimpses of the people of Evanwyl sparing a thought for the Phoenix who was also their beloved Kyri Vantage.

And farther: the little girl Hulda, suddenly seized with worry about the Phoenix and her party, offering a prayer to the Light; Zogen Josan, in the small temple of Jenten's Mill, praying and seeing in his eye Kyri Vantage and her party; Miri and Lady Shae, standing together as they watched another tower rising, rebuilt, and thought for moments of those who had led to their salvation.

She reached out to these thoughts and *felt* them, their strength, their spirits, yearning to return to her something that she had given them. And though she did not in her heart think she was truly worthy, still she accepted what was offered, and remembered one more thing:

The warm fire of wings of flame, and the shining eyes of Tobimar Silverun as that moment (and a small Toad) brought them to accept what lay between them.

I will not die!

Her own soul caught those threads of belief, the power of faith, and accepted them, *drew* them in, even in the moment that her last bones were collapsing to dust and ash, and spun them out again, a weave that covered the detritus and charcoal that had been a body.

Myrionar, guide me! I have the power! I believe that WE *have the power! And I have faith that you can show me how to do what no mortal could imagine!*

The answer came to her in a burst of gold, and she *screamed* once more, a cry of tearing agony but of triumph and ecstasy as fire enveloped her very soul now, and the dark, dark cord that sought to bind it broke, tore apart, a curse now impotent and useless against the flames of the living spirit. Her shriek rose to the heavens, a call of vengeance and life, and exploded into pure red-gold flame.

The fire waned, and dancing through her was a feeling of victory. The voice of Myrionar had not spoken to her, and she knew the god was weaker than ever; yet there was surety singing in her veins, echoing through her heart, as she opened her unburned, reborn eyes and saw the awe and wonder in three faces before her, three faces lit by the dawn behind...and the golden fire of rebirth before them.

CHAPTER 30

Tobimar stood frozen with horror and anguish as he watched Kyri burning, literally turning to *ashes* as he watched, the skull trying to scream even as it, too, blackened. *Oh, Terian Nomicon, Light in the Darkness, save her! If she must die, do not let her wander, please, for all I have done, for all I must do, take her to you, so that—*

The black smoke and crumbling ruin before him suddenly ignited in golden fire. The flames *exploded* from the ashes, rising into the dawn, expanding, becoming a mighty firebird that raised its head and gave a screaming cry of triumph, a call to arms and a challenge to the heavens, a Phoenix whose wings spanned the hillside and beyond, mighty pinions sweeping outward in auric splendor to overshadow—and illuminate—the countryside, bringing a second gilded dawn to the land as Sanamaveridion had brought another, deeper dusk.

The golden fire funneled inward, condensed to a figure he knew and loved beyond anything else in this world, and for a moment Kyri Vantage hovered above them all, floating on wings of fire and rebirth, and he could not even *think* the words of his gratitude.

As abruptly as the flame had arisen, she fell, collapsing to her knees as he stepped forward and caught her. She looked up at him with surprise and relief, and Tobimar felt his tears flowing with unrestrained joy. "Kyri...I...by Terian and Myrionar, I thought..."

She smiled, her first smile without care or fear in weeks, and he pulled her closer, ignoring the pain of his own body, just reassuring himself that she was *there* and not a hideous burned husk. "I know. So did I. But I couldn't let that happen, and neither could Myrionar. And now I know beyond any doubt that It spoke the truth: we *can* do this. And we *will*."

She stood, though her knees trembled visibly and he could see how much the shock and fear and relief had taken from her. Kyri looked down at Condor, who still knelt before her in disbelief.

"And you, Aran, will show us the way."

Tobimar turned, ribs grating painfully, to finally look at the man who had ambushed him, and then mysteriously failed to kill Kyri. "Aran...*Aran? You* are the false Justicar Condor?"

The tear-streaked green eyes barely narrowed at the tone, then dropped their gaze to the ground. He nodded shortly, red hair dropping over his face with the motion, and stayed on his knees, not raising his eyes. "Yes. I am."

Poplock gave a wheezing grunt. "Tobimar...healing? *Hello?*"

"Great *Light*. I'm sorry!" His own body reminded him anew that he was far from healed, and while Kyri seemed completely whole, he suspected she had nothing left to give for now. Digging through his neverfull pack, he found some of the healing draughts Poplock and Hiriista had cooked up. "Here, open your mouth." The little Toad complied, even that seeming to cause him pain, and swallowed the powerful alchemical restorative; A green and white shimmer traveled up and down the small, brown-warty body, and Tobimar could see bones straighten, pain fade from his friend's face and posture. The Skysand prince drank one himself, ignoring the excruciatingly bitter taste to be rewarded with a burst of well-being and vanished pain.

Kyri had summoned her Raiment to her and was now fully dressed again; she picked up Poplock and with her other arm hugged Tobimar close. "Thank Myrionar you're all right."

"That *we're* all right?" Poplock's voice was breaking with relief and tears, emotion he rarely let show bringing an answering lump to Tobimar's throat. "You were *burning up*, Kyri! And then the fire...the Phoenix..."

She blinked, puzzled. "Phoenix?"

"You were reborn, Kyri Vantage," Aran said, and his voice was filled with awe. "You crumbled before our eyes to ashes, and then the flames rose up into the semblance of a mighty firebird, screaming victory to the heavens...and you stood anew before us." He still did not raise his eyes. "You *are* the true chosen of Myrionar, and It did not desert you."

Kyri looked down at the false Justiciar, and Tobimar saw a gentler expression than he had expected, given the tales she'd told him. "Aran. Look at me."

Aran Condor took an audible breath, then looked up.

"I hated you, yes. You and all the False Justiciars. But Myrionar instructed me clearly, and I learned well, that the *first* principle of Justice is Mercy. I..." There was a catch in her voice. "I... did not *want* to kill you all, once I had thought it out. I didn't want to believe you were *all* bad, all beyond hope. And it was you, most of all, that I prayed was not beyond redemption."

Aran looked at her with disbelief and hope warring on his face. "You...prayed for *me*?"

"Many times...especially after I killed Shrike. You were coming to kill me, weren't you? Just as I swore vengeance against all of you for my parents and Rion?"

"Yes, I was. It...for a while, I was *mad* with that anger, that *hunger* to find this 'Phoenix' and kill...her. And then..." He looked beyond her, into the woods. "I made a very stupid bargain, and it seemed I had no more choices. But..."

"But you have one last choice, yes."

He chuckled suddenly. "I already made that choice, Kyri. I made it when you..." the pale face flushed suddenly, "...when you asked *me* to forgive *you*."

She did not laugh, just nodded. "And do you?"

Tobimar saw tension in Aran's entire frame, and touched his own hand to the hilt of one sword.

But then all that tension simply drained out, with a relieved sigh. "There is nothing to forgive, Kyri. You were and are the one true Justiciar, and we were your enemies, traitors and liars and murderers all. I doubt Shrike—much as I loved him—gave you any choice. And," his tone was suddenly sharper, "I am *glad* that you killed Thornfalcon."

"I had help in that," she said, gesturing to Tobimar and Poplock.

Aran finally rose to his feet and bowed to them. "Then, my thanks. Aside from...our leader, he was the worst monster I have ever known, even in a group of false heroes."

"It was a genuine pleasure," Poplock assured him.

"Now what, Kyri?" Tobimar asked. "He came to kill you, but seems to have given up on that." Inwardly, he wasn't entirely convinced, but he knew better than to mistrust Kyri's judgment on these things. Her willingness to believe in others had backfired on her sometimes—most obviously with Thornfalcon—but most of the time it had been one of her most potent weapons.

The gentle look faded from her face; instead it became sharp, cold, certain. "Now? Now I must be the Will of Myrionar, Tobimar."

She turned to Aran, and her eyes were the gray of a dawn blizzard; a forbidding, chill aura surrounded her, one of command and doom, and Tobimar felt a momentary impulse to step back. "False Justiciar Aran Condor, do you accept the Judgment of Myrionar for your crimes?" she demanded in tones that rang across Trader's Rest.

Aran swallowed audibly, but immediately dropped to one knee. "I . . . I do."

"Name and own to those crimes, then, and do not hesitate or hold back, for my Justice will see through any deception."

His gaze wavered, but did not drop. "I have taken and used the title of Justiciar of Myrionar falsely. I have professed my faith in the Balanced Sword when I did not believe. I have been a part of plots against the great families of Evanwyl. I have assisted in murder, assaulted the innocent, profited from ill-gotten goods. I have held my tongue when I could have saved lives of others. I have sought vengeance when I did not deserve it. I have knowingly served a demon, and taken a gift of power from the King of All Hells himself."

"Terian's *Light*," Tobimar heard himself curse; he saw a wrinkle on Kyri's brow, but she said nothing as Aran continued.

"I played the part of friend and counselor when I was a spy and a traitor, and even when doing good deeds I have used a name and title which were never mine to use. I have shamed the armor and the name that I wear." He paused. "If this is not sufficient, I will try to name in detail every instance of every crime I have committed, but that will be a list long in the telling."

Kyri studied him, the stormcloud-gray eyes narrow and cool, showing no sign of either sympathy or anger, that impassive aura strong about her. "That will do," she said after a moment. "I am aware of many specifics of your crimes, Condor. I, personally, am the victim of several, and my family more so. Tell me, then: do you have any justification for these offenses?"

He opened his mouth, then closed it and shook his head. "No."

The slightest raising of an eyebrow. "Would there be any to speak for you, in your defense or justification?"

"None that I know, save others as corrupt or more so than I."

"There you are wrong," she said. "I will speak for you, Aran. You were raised by a man already deep in the snares of your patron—a patron we know now to be Viedraverion, first son of Kerlamion Blackstar himself."

Aran's head snapped up at that, surprised. "You know already?"

"We do." She raised a hand and continued. "You were raised to be part of that group, and by the time you knew what you were being asked to do, it was too late to easily escape. I suspect they made a point of showing you just how little chance you had of escape. A child who is raised to be a certain thing has a hard time escaping it. So against your crimes we must set a certain mitigation of circumstance.

"So I ask now: do you *repent* of your crimes?"

"I do." Tobimar could hear the *intensity* of feeling in those two words.

"Will you offer your heart, your soul, your *life* in exchange for those crimes?"

"Those and anything else that I may have to give," Aran said.

Kyri was silent for long moments; her stare neither wavered nor reduced its intensity.

Finally she straightened to her full height. "Aran, you have come to me of your own will, and accepted the Judgment of Myrionar. This speaks well of your sincerity, and there are mitigating circumstances of your upbringing and situation.

"This, then, is my judgment. Firstly, for the offenses against me and mine...I forgive you. I do not *forget* them, but I forgive you, as I have deprived you of your only family in turn. Let the past remain in the past. It is over, it is done."

Tobimar saw Aran blink hard and nod emphatically.

"For your other offenses, you will be pardoned if you perform two services for us. First, that you show us the way to the Justiciar's Retreat, and second, that no matter your fears of, or your friendships for, the false Justiciars and their master, you will fight in the name of Myrionar in truth, on our side, even unto your death if need be. Once our enemy is defeated and the Retreat is cleansed, your debt will be accounted paid."

Aran did not hesitate. "I swear that I will see to it that you reach the Retreat, no matter what, and that I will fight for the *true* Myrionar, on your side, against my old allies, to my last breath if I must."

"Will you swear that oath to three gods?" Kyri asked. "For here before you are three who are witnesses and perhaps emissaries of three gods, and you who were false in naming one will perhaps be less willing to lie to three."

"Name the gods and I will swear to them. To a thousand times three of them if I must."

"Then swear it in the name of Myrionar, of Terian, and," her lips turned up just the *tiniest* bit, "Blackwart the Great."

Aran, on the other hand, was so earnest that his expression did not waver. "Then I do so swear, in the name of Myrionar, god of Justice and Vengeance; in the name of Terian, the Nemesis of Evil, the Light in the Darkness; and in the name of Blackwart the Great, the Golden-Eyed God. May they all witness this, my true and absolute oath."

Tobimar felt something then; a stirring, both within and beyond him, and thought—for just an instant—he saw the same vision of Terian that had appeared to him in Kaizatenzei. He felt Poplock stiffen on his shoulder, and Kyri nodded slowly.

"Then it is done. Your oath is accepted, your penance set." Suddenly the cold, forbidding aura was gone; in its place was Kyri, weary but smiling. She put an arm around Tobimar. Tobimar let her lean just a bit on him and slid his own arm around her waist to brace her. "And since you have repented, and we will see great battle soon enough, I give you leave to continue to wear the Raiment of Condor; it may serve us well in more than one way.

"Now, Aran, tell us—quickly—how you came here, everything from the time you found Shrike, and then everything you can about our enemy. Because tomorrow we go to Justiciar's Retreat."

CHAPTER 31

Poplock listened carefully to the repentant Aran, occasionally catching one of the beetles or flies that now flitted about in the brilliant sunshine, and had to admit, after a while, that there was something to admire in the red-haired young man. *Okay, he made bad choices, but* drought and fire, *he has courage. Traveled to the Black City and faced the King of All Hells himself. That's balls of steel, as Xavier might say.*

And it spoke *very* well of him that he had fought off the influence of the Demonshard—something Poplock had witnessed as he came back to consciousness. *Gotta do something about that, though; can't have cursed demon swords lying around for anyone to pick up.*

"Our leader's always been subtle," Aran went on. "While Thornfalcon was around, we didn't even see him often, and we were *forbidden* from speaking to him when we..." he broke off. "Oh, *Balance*, you don't know. He's really—"

"Jeridan Velion? Actually, we know he was playing that part. Complicated story."

Aran blinked, and then chuckled weakly. "Well. It seems that you already know a lot more than I would have thought. I wonder if I have anything new to tell you?"

Tobimar grinned. "I bet you do. But not the big secrets, more things about him and your remaining companions."

"Hmm." Aran's brow wrinkled. "Well, like I said, he's subtle. He's *always* pleasant to speak to. He always seems to know what you were going to be saying before you say it, even if he does you the courtesy of letting you actually speak first.

"He's a soul-eater. That's not surprising in a demon, of course, but he's something special. He was making Thornfalcon *one* of his people—though I don't know how."

Poplock bounced. "That's why Thorny was such a tough beetle to chew; he was part demon."

"Yes." Aran's face was grim. "Our patron sparred with us once in a while, and it was clear he was *incredibly* good—better than any of us by a long, long bowshot. He has a lot of magical resources, too; you know about his mirrors?"

"Yes," Kyri said. "Miri told us about those, and Tashriel confirmed it."

"Well, I can tell you this: he's been talking with a *lot* of people with those mirrors. Between all of us in the Just...er, *false* Justiciars, we heard bits of conversations with at least a dozen people, and probably that wasn't close to all of them."

"No surprise there," said Tobimar. "We know that Viedraverion was the central planner for everything the King of All Hells was doing—all the revolutions, attacks, all of it."

Aran stared at him, then around at Poplock and Kyri. "What? You mean...*he* was the architect of these wars?" After a moment he closed his eyes. "Of course he was. We should have realized that was why he was in such frequent communication with Kerlamion. Myrionar's Name..." He trailed off. "But that doesn't really matter. Because I tell you that his real goal doesn't have much to do with that."

Poplock sat up straighter. "What? How do you mean?"

Aran opened his mouth, closed it, seemed to be thinking. "It's...hard to explain. I guess the easiest way is to say that it's a matter of the *attitude*, the way that our patron expressed himself with regards to his supposed superiors. I always got the impression that he was *humoring* them, in some fashion, and that Evanwyl *itself* really mattered to him for some reason—that whatever Kerlamion wanted from him he did mainly because he needed something from either the king himself or one of his underlings."

Kyri suddenly looked thoughtful. "You know, that *does* make sense. Didn't Tashriel say something about Viedraverion exerting pressure through Kerlamion?"

"I think so," Poplock agreed, and Tobimar nodded. "So Vie-draverion, your patron, has his own game underway, and he was helping Kerlamion as a means to his end."

"That's...kind of scary," Tobimar said candidly. "Manipulating the King of All Hells *can't* be a safe thing to do. What in the *world* could he be after that would make that risk worth taking? Or has he got some secret that makes it not so much of a risk as it would seem?"

Aran shrugged with an air of apology. "I wish I could say, but I think what's *most* obvious about this is that our Patron maneuvered us and everyone else without letting us know much about what he wanted. I didn't even know his real name, Vie-draverion, until Kerlamion himself spoke that name." He looked at Kyri. "Phoenix Kyri, this isn't much knowledge to go upon. Are you...are *we*...really going to engage them tomorrow?"

"Yes," she said firmly, and Poplock knew that expression; *she's made up her mind and there's nothing in this world that will change it.* "The longer we wait, the worse things will get. For the moment, he doesn't know that you've changed sides. That *has* to be an advantage, but it's an advantage we could lose very quickly if we wait. I am fully recovered..." she smiled with an edge of her own awe and relief, "...fully recovered due to my rebirth, so I will not have a better opportunity. He has, we hope, only two remaining allies at the retreat, so—"

"He may have more," Aran said suddenly. "I just remembered something else that might be important. In his retreat—the inner sanctum we would only enter rarely, with his explicit bidding—he had inlaid ritual circles of various types. He used one such circle, with additional modifications, to send me across Evanwyl to Rivendream Pass."

Poplock saw what he was getting at. "*Mudbubbles.* He's a demonlord; he could be summoning demons to help him."

"I'm afraid so. I wasn't terribly well educated in such things—I'm no magician or priest—but I could recognize some of the symbols and they were definitely associated with demonic works and some I *think* were summoning related."

Kyri nodded slowly. "Then we can't assume it's just the three. On the other hand, that makes it more obvious that we cannot wait much longer. He could keep making bargains and summoning more aid. The longer we give him, the stronger his position."

Poplock couldn't think of a reasonable counter-argument, and by their expressions neither could Tobimar or Aran. The only reasonable justification for *not* going quickly would be if they either had some source for better intelligence against their enemy, or if by waiting they could get more reinforcements. But as far as Poplock could tell, there weren't any more good sources, and their only possible significant reinforcements were in Kaizatenzei, weeks or even months away.

"More importantly, we know Jeridan Velion went to confront him—probably was *triggered* to do so—and may still be alive. I am not going to wait; I wouldn't even delay *now* if it weren't for the fact that we spent all night traveling here, and all three of us are exhausted and need rest. I don't know about you, Aran—"

"I'm fine," he said, though he didn't look happy about it. "I drew full strength from the Demonshard before I went to confront you, and that doesn't seem to have dissipated just because I discarded the blade."

"Hm." She studied him, then glanced at the rising sun. "We need to rest before moving on."

"I'll take a first watch with Aran," Poplock volunteered. "After all, I nap on Tobimar's shoulder a lot while we travel, so I'm not as beat as all of you, now that I got healed up."

Kyri nodded. They moved up the hill, to the shade of the jungle nearby, and set up a small camp. After a brief meal, Kyri and Tobimar lay down to rest; it wasn't long before Poplock heard a gentle snoring from his friends.

"You're smart not to trust me," Aran said in a low voice.

"Ha!" Poplock said, "Not just me, either. If I hadn't volunteered, Tobimar would've stayed up. Kyri...well, she kinda *has* to trust you now that you've accepted judgment. That's the way she is, and me? I don't want her to change. But that does mean people like me have to watch out for her when her approach doesn't quite work."

"Of course." He looked at the two of them, and his expression shifted slightly. Following the line of his vision, Poplock was pretty sure he was looking at how Kyri—even in sleep—was holding Tobimar's hand.

"Yeah, that's the way it is. Sorry, even if you had a chance once, it's gone now."

Aran glared at him for an instant, but then his gaze dropped and he looked ashamed. "I never dared *take* the chance anyway. I would have had to fight... *them* for that chance. Shrike realized I was thinking of leaving, I tried to convince *him* to leave so I could follow her. That's what panicked him, made him bring me to face the truth about who we were *really* serving."

"Viedraverion?"

"Oh, not him. Remember, he didn't *reveal* everything about himself. Although he was *more* than scary enough, draining your power just with a touch, cutting three lines into Thornfalcon's armor as though he were drawing in the sand. No, *that* was when I first saw the King of All Hells." The young man shuddered, making his armor rattle slightly.

Seeing the empty scabbard wriggle reminded him. "Hey, what can we do about that piece of trash you threw away?"

"Oh, *Balance*. I... I'd been trying to forget about it."

"Well, we *can't*. Do you want to—"

"No, I don't. That... thing is more dangerous than you can imagine."

"I dunno, after what we've been through, I can imagine quite a bit."

Aran stood. "Let's find it, at least."

After a few minutes of reconstructing that last agonized moment in which the former Condor had thrown his weapon away, the two entered the jungle at another angle. This did take them away from the camp, but—honestly speaking—Poplock wasn't worried about them, here in what was still part of Evanwyl. Aran was the only real danger he'd wanted to keep an eye on.

The search took a few hours; just like a true Justiciar, Aran Condor had had superhuman strength when he pitched the Demonshard, and it had flown a *long* distance. Finally, though, Poplock noticed the background sounds of the jungle getting quieter, and Aran's head turned. "There. Over there."

The Demonshard was embedded to half its length in the earth, leaning at a sharp angle. Around the blade, everything was black and dead. The weapon hummed louder as Aran approached. The red-haired young man stopped and stared pensively down at the ebony-dark weapon. "Balance take it," he muttered.

Poplock felt a cold, crawling sensation just being this close to the Demonshard. "That's a nasty, nasty weapon," he said quietly.

"You don't even *begin* to know," Aran muttered. "But... it's also the only weapon of any power I own. If we're going into combat against *him* ..."

"You just gave that weapon up. You want to change your mind?"

"I renounced its *control* of me."

"You tried that once before, remember? And it still tried."

"I was still pretending to be Condor, then." Despite the words, Aran backed away from the weapon.

"Take me up again, Aran Shrikeson," said a chill, wavering, echoing voice.

Poplock jumped half a foot in the air from Aran's shoulder. "Blackwart's *Chosen!* That's a creepy voice."

Aran nodded. "Fitting for what it is."

"Your family name is 'Shrikeson'? Sounds like a pretty strange coincidence."

"Not coincidence. I don't know who my real family was," Aran said absently, still regarding the huge black sword with trepidation. "I guess the false Justiciars probably knew it, but there was no point in keeping it and maybe raising questions. Since Shrike adopted me, that's the last name I was given."

"Oh." Now that he could see and sense the Demonshard, Poplock was even more sure this thing had to be dealt with, but he was darned if he could figure out *how.* "Maybe we can just stuff the thing into a neverfull pack."

The blade chuckled eerily as Aran shook his head. "That weapon will cut almost anything even without a hand to wield it, except a scabbard meant to hold it. Kerlamion laid such an enchantment on my scabbard when he gave me the blade. Drop it in such a pack and it might sever even the magical pack, with," he gave a wry smile, "unfortunate consequences."

"You can still fight pretty well without a magic sword though, right?"

Aran nodded. "I am very good, yes. Hand-to-hand I was probably the best of us, even better than Bolthawk. So I don't really need a sword, though without something of real power, I don't know if I'll be any use against a demon." A flash of real humor. "Even though he likes to talk about being sporting, I really, *really* doubt he's going to let me draw on his own power to fight him. And even if I'm forgiven, I'm not even close to being worthy to be a *real* Justiciar."

"And from a few things Kyri said, I don't think Myrionar's got much left to spare, anyway," Poplock pointed out. "Sorry, but really? We were ready to try to take him on ourselves, so you don't *have* to fight the big baddie here. If you're good enough to help keep Bolthawk and Skyharrier off our backs, that'll be good enough."

Aran straightened a little and nodded. "I can do that." He looked back at the Demonshard. "That still leaves *this* problem."

Poplock wrinkled his face, thinking. The problem was that there really *weren't* many options. That blade couldn't just be left here. And while he'd *like* to think that tomorrow they'd head out and triumph, he couldn't be *certain* of that, which meant that it would be ridiculously irresponsible to not deal with it before leaving.

Finally he sighed. "Your scabbard's the only thing that can hold it, right?"

"As far as I know."

"Fine, here's what we do. We put it in your scabbard, then either Kyri or Tobimar will carry it on the way there. When we get close to the Retreat, we can dump it off nearby—no one will find it accidentally, that's for sure, as long as those diversion wards are up around the Retreat. Then we figure out what to do with it after the battle's over."

Aran bit his lip, clearly thinking hard, then nodded. "I guess that's the best we can do for now." He glanced at the little Toad. "Better stay back while I approach it. I've seen it move on its own, and while it might not kill me, since I'm its intended wielder—"

"It won't mind at all doing a little toad-sticking. Fine."

Aran approached the weapon as one might approach a giant scorpion, gingerly, poised to strike or flee at an instant's notice. The weapon stirred slightly as its owner approached, but did not rise from the ground. "Your course is decided, Demonshard," Aran said. "More than once you have fought me and lost; do not attempt to fight me again."

Poplock didn't hear a reply, but sensed the weapon's anger. There was, however, a clear note of defeat in it, despite its prior mocking tones. *The kid has thrown it away on his own, and I guess beat it more than once on its own terms. Not something to laugh at.*

Aran finally reached out, seized the hilt, and in one swift

motion drew it from the earth and slammed it back into its scabbard. The young man shuddered, then straightened again. "Come on, let's get back to camp. I want to be done with this."

Poplock hopped ahead of Aran; he didn't want to sit on a shoulder not more than a few inches from the Demonshard. *Some things are just too creepy-nasty to get used to, and that's one.*

Finding their way back to the camp was easy. Tobimar and Kyri were still asleep, and the sun filtered peacefully through the trees, lighting the camp with gold-touched green. Kyri did stir uneasily for a moment as the surrounding sounds faded with the approach of the Demonshard.

"Better take that off," Poplock said.

"Yes." Aran reached back and the little Toad heard a catch release. The scabbard came free of the armor.

Too late, Poplock noticed that one of Aran's hands was clenched just a little oddly on the scabbard. The hand whipped out and whitish dust sprayed all over the little Toad.

Poplock tried to shout a warning, but his shout was barely a gurgle; as things began to fade around him, the last thing he saw was Aran's face, filled not with triumph but sorrow.

CHAPTER 32

Aran looked down at Poplock, then glanced at the other two. They were still sleeping. He could sense that even the Demonshard was startled. Unlike the three heroes, the sentient sword could sense his emotions, *knew* that he had thrown his lot in with the last Justiciar of Myrionar.

The Toad was completely unconscious. The sleeping powder—ironically enough, made by Thornfalcon many months ago for all of them to carry—had been startlingly effective. It probably wouldn't last very long—nor did Aran want it to—but it would be long enough. Even a relatively few minutes would be adequate. He took out a piece of paper and wrote a swift note, left it under Poplock's nose, and then turned, walking swiftly to the West.

What are you planning, Condor?

"I am not Condor anymore, Demonshard. Just Aran."

An inaudible snort. *Very well, then, what are you planning, Aran?*

"They wouldn't trust me alone. They *certainly* wouldn't trust me while I'm carrying *you*, and I can't blame them. *I* certainly wouldn't trust me. But if I go with them, the moment we appear, the false Justiciars will know I have betrayed them. Kyri and the others said themselves that my great advantage is that our enemies don't know that yet."

I see, the Demonshard said, with a chuckle. *You will go forward and try to be the worm within their apple, to betray them at the moment they spring their trap.* A pause. *Or, perhaps, just to slay those who remain, taking advantage of their trust?*

Aran gave a wordless snarl. "Never. I have sworn to Myrionar, Terian, and the Golden-Eyed. I *mean* to keep that oath. I will not pass judgment and vengeance upon Bolthawk and Skyharrier. But there *is* a promise I made—a promise I made to *you*, Demonshard—that I intend to keep."

A sense of pleased surprise. *Ahhh! You hope to use the weapon of the Demon King himself to destroy his firstborn son!*

"Can you kill Viedraverion? You seemed unsure of an Elderwyrm."

The Elderwyrm had sheer size—and perhaps considerable power above that of even the Firstborn of Kerlamion—in its favor. If you can wield me skillfully enough, I can. Think you that the Lord of All Hells is not cautious of his most powerful children? I have seen through his blade, for I was a part of that blade, and I know Viedraverion well. If you strike him well and truly, he will fall.

"Good enough."

After a few hours, he knew he was approaching the crucial area. He drew the Demonshard and began making random cuts in the earth as he walked.

Stop! What are you doing?

"Making sure that Kyri can follow me even through the diversion wards. Do you think I am so stupidly overconfident that I believe I *must* triumph? That I will *survive*? No. I must do this myself, *for* myself and for all of us who were drawn into that monster's web of deceit . . . and to protect Kyri, if I can. Because it is obvious that Viedraverion *intends* her to find her way here, if she survives. But if I fail, the three who have come so far will at least have their chance, and it may be that I will have weakened him enough."

The Demonshard fell silent.

"Do not think of rebelling against me again, Demonshard."

I will not, it answered, its unvoiced tones both resigned and amazed. *You have bested me at every turn with your will, whether my ways to your mind and heart were direct or as subtle as poison. Even at the last, your will was absolute. I could not force you to complete that oath sworn in fury, that purpose for which I was forged, and while I may still tempt and reason with you, I have found my way to your heart blocked. I know now that which even the King of All Hells did not know, that you will be the master of me, not I of you. Use me to destroy, then, at your will, and if you feed me the soul of the King's Son I shall be well content.*

Aran was startled by this speech, but he could sense the Demonshard meant every word. "Then I promise you that we shall face my patron together, Demonshard, and if you can take his head and soul, do so, and I will ask no more."

He walked on, feeling a faint hope; with the incomparable power of the Demonshard—a power that had shattered a tsunami hundreds of miles long and mountain-high—he just might have a chance to destroy that false-smiling monster and keep Kyri from ever having to face him.

The sun was beginning to drop lower in the sky by the time he approached the Retreat. *Cautiously, now.*

There. He saw Bolthawk, guarding the front entrance. *Skyharrier will be patrolling above...*

He waited. A minute, two, three, and then he saw it, the faintest flicker of motion above. The Raiment of Skyharrier could reflect the sky above it, make the flying Justiciar but a fleeting shadow, a breath of motion scarce to be seen against clouds and blue. He waited again, unmoving. His Raiment, too, could hide him, as could all of theirs; what use stealth if one's armor gave them away with bright colors?

Two more passes, and Condor was certain of the timing. *That's three passes. He will reverse direction now, to make sure that someone trying to guess his pattern will make an error.*

Sure enough, only a moment later he saw the ghostly shape of Skyharrier return, going in the opposite direction. *He will do three more like that, and then do a straight pass across the Retreat and reverse again.*

As soon as Skyharrier was well out of sight, Condor moved, moving around the Retreat until Bolthawk was just hidden by the wall. He waited again until Skyharrier passed once more, then emerged from the jungle, walking swiftly, openly, coming around the corner.

Bolthawk immediately came to the ready. "Condor."

"Bolthawk. Why are you drawing your weapon on me?"

"Have to be sure whose side you're on."

"Whose *side?*" He put as much bitter outrage into that as he could. "I have no *other side* to go to, any more than do you! As well you know."

"Hmph." Bolthawk regarded him narrowly, then shrugged. "Then what news?"

"News I must give to our patron directly, concerning my own quest and our worst adversary."

"You'll find him in the usual place, then," Bolthawk said. For just the tiniest fraction of an instant, his eyes flickered back towards the Retreat.

Aran was already in motion, having hoped and assumed that would be the case; with lightning speed his hand struck, and Bolthawk staggered, stunned, against the wall of the Retreat. Another two blows and his former ally was unconscious. *Possibly dying,* Aran thought with a pang as he dragged the heavy Child of Odin into the doorway, *but not swiftly. If we win out, healing will bring him back to himself. If not . . . he will be free of our Patron, anyway.*

Time was not his ally, now. One or two circuits of the Retreat might pass before Skyharrier realized that his companion's absence from his post wasn't just a matter of a quick visit to the washroom, but no more than that. Skyharrier might be suspicious as soon as the entrance came in view again, which would be only a few minutes now.

But that's all I need.

He moved quickly through the familiar retreat, now quiet with a watchful silence. *Be alert! He may have other guards within.*

And as he came into sight of the doors to the sanctum, he ducked back. *There.*

A massive figure, inhuman, with an insectoid head and chitinous arms, stood impassively before that set of doors. *By the Balance . . . that's a demon of the Mazakh hells . . . one of Voorith's servants, I think. Has Viedra made a bargain with that thing as well?*

He must have, came the unexpected commentary of the Demonshard. *That is one of Voorith's favored guards, of the Sazachil; only his strong allies are given such.*

Well, I have no time or choice.

He came around the intersection striding purposefully, glancing at the demon arrogantly.

"Halt. You may not enter."

"I am Condor, and I have come a long way to talk with our Patron. Stand aside." Even as he spoke he was still approaching.

"Condor? I have been given no instructions regarding you." The creature's eyes were suspicious, and it tightened its grip on the mace it held.

Now, Demonshard.

Power *flooded* into him, black and ecstatic, and he *leapt* from the ground, a bound that took him six feet up and twenty feet forward, slamming into the demon before it even realized he had begun the attack. The mace fell from its grip, but it was recovering—

—not fast enough, as Aran caught the arms that sought to enclose him, spun around, gripping one, pulling, levering it back until there was a crunching *crack!* and a steamkettle whistle of agony. The creature fell heavily against the doors, and Aran dropped to the ground, then leapt again, delivering a roundhouse kick, then a spinning kick that finished bringing the insectoid face back around, and finally springing at it from the wall across from the double doors, both of the Condor Raiment's boots *smashing* into the demon, shattering its armor, driving it into the doors with irresistible strength. The twin portals bowed inward and then burst apart, scattering pieces of the bar that had held them as the demon's twitching corpse skidded across the polished black floor.

Their Patron—*Viedraverion*, Aran thought—merely raised its head as the body slid to a halt near its chair, and slowly closed a book. "Why, hello, Aran. I must admit, I had not expected you *quite* yet."

A chill went down his back at the casual greeting. "You expected me?"

A laugh. "Oh, Aran, of *course* I expected you. Couldn't kill your father's murderer, could you?"

"You *knew* who she was all along."

"Oh, not *quite* all along," it said cheerfully, rising from the chair to face him. Though there were no weapons in evidence, Aran was certain that his opponent was far from unarmed. "I knew *what* she had to be, you understand, but not precisely *who*, until I surveyed the damage after poor Thornfalcon departed our company."

"Knew 'what' she had to be?" He drew the Demonshard now, and it howled distantly, waiting for the strike.

"Of course," it said. "I suppose you already know that my work for Kerlamion was merely...not a smokescreen, precisely, but a project whose purpose was merely to give me access to certain resources, while keeping the King of All Hells and most of his servants too busy to pay much attention to anything else."

"I know that now, yes. Though that must be dangerous, betraying your father, Viedraverion."

"My father?" It smiled, and for the first time there was

something inhuman visible, a glitter from teeth too shiny, too sharp, to be anything human. "Kerlamion has his own interests, but sees only relatively simple goals. I have something much, *much* more important in mind, and the Phoenix is the very heart of it. When she arrives here...oh, now, *then* we shall see something absolutely *unique*."

"What do you mean?" He wasn't quite close enough to dare a quick strike, not when he wasn't sure how fast or tough his opponent might be. Aran edged closer as it replied.

"I *designed* her, Aran. Don't you realize this? Everything I've done, ever since I arrived in Evanwyl, every single one of my efforts has been devoted to producing this last, final, ultimate Justiciar, the last true representative of the god Myrionar, and—as I hoped and planned—one coming directly to me, with the faith of so many upon her shoulders."

Designed? He was at once outraged and appalled. "You planned—"

"—*everything*, yes. There were other possibilities than Kyri Vantage, although once I realized she was the Phoenix it was clear that she was the best possible choice. And now she walks to her doom—a doom I have planned, and which shall give *me* far more than she, or you, could begin to imagine."

"You are never going to *touch* Kyri," Aran said. "And with this weapon, a weapon of the Demon King himself, I will make *sure* of that!"

The Demonshard came down like lightning.

But their Patron *blurred*, moving so fast that the Demonshard passed harmlessly by. A casual backhand from the creature struck Aran harder than a *bilarel* with a club, and he was hurled backwards against the wall, the Demonshard skittering uselessly away across the floor.

Even as Aran felt himself sliding down the wall, his Patron was there, lifting him off the ground like a toy, smiling, chuckling, but the sound was dropping, deeper, now a laugh like rumbling thunder as the shape before him shifted, *ballooned* upwards, seven, eight, nine feet, eyes changing from cheerful blue to a laughing, pupilless, poisonous yellow glow, the face elongating, the mouth becoming a cavernous maw filled with glittering diamond teeth, still laughing, shaggy black-brown fur covering a body of immense, inhuman power, and the hand that held him now gripped him from neck to mid-chest, and every finger was tipped with a glittering claw nigh a foot long.

His heart seemed to stop as he recognized that monstrous shape, a shape of the darkest legends and stories, even as the might of that arm sent him crashing through one of the walls, an impact that drove the breath from him and made red-black pain threaten to envelop his consciousness. He tried to rise, but *again* he was caught up, sent tumbling back through the wall, into and through the great desk, to sprawl helplessly on the floor. *Wrong, wrong, it tricked us even about* WHAT *it was, and now Kyri and the others are coming into its trap!*

"No, no, Aran. You've come here as the perfect bait, you see," the Great Werewolf said, the voice showing it had resumed its human guise. "If the Watchland wasn't enough, surely the repentant Justiciar—who has come here alone to protect her—will ensure that she comes *straight* here. You see, there was still a very small—but measurable—chance that she would choose to withdraw, find stronger allies. The situation is terribly delicate; a delay of weeks, perhaps, surely no more than months, and my entire design would come apart. Now, that chance is essentially zero, and the grand finale is assured."

He could feel a faint coldness near his right hand. *Maybe . . .* "What . . . do you . . . mean to do?"

"Ah, of course, it is so obvious to me, as I've planned it for these centuries, I forget it won't be nearly so clear to you. But it's really quite a simple thing, Aran. Once Kyri Vantage confronts me, she is facing the one who helped corrupt and destroy the very *religion* of Myrionar. She *must* destroy me in turn; it is, in a very real sense, a cosmic necessity, to right the wrongs I have done, to begin the true healing. To do so, Myrionar can—and *must*—invest her with every single trace of Myrionar's power." A shuffling sound, a tinkle of broken glass from something that had fallen on the floor; the monster in the guise of a man was getting closer. "That means that Myrionar's very *essence*—its *self*—will be completely open, utterly vulnerable. All of its existence . . . and all of its *connections*."

Despite his intention to pretend to more weakness than he felt, Aran started half-up to his knees in horror. "You can't—"

"Ahhh, but I *can*. The stakes, you now see, are far, far greater than one minor deity in some backwater realm." It chuckled.

But sitting up had given Aran the chance to see that it stood above him, no more than three feet distant. "You'll *never* have that chance! Be you consumed by the forces of the *Hells!*"

The Demonshard *whipped* into his hand and Aran stabbed upward in the same moment, so close that even that monster's speed could not let it dodge. The black blade *howled* with hunger as it struck out, a shard of a thousand collapsed suns opening themselves to consume even light itself.

But a long-fingered hand *caught* the Demonshard as though it were no more than a child's practice sword. The Demonshard bit deep... but not through, and the arm became huge and monstrous again. To Aran's disbelief, the hunger-song of the Demonshard shifted, became a sound of panic, and the blade vibrated desperately. Aran pulled back, but the Demonshard was held immovably, screaming in fear, its sound *weakening*, fading, the blue glow guttering out like a candle...

And the Demonshard *shattered* in the monster's hand. Aran felt his own life drawn in, his strength fading, as the Wolf gazed down at him. "Did you even *imagine*," it said, "that I would have allowed you *any* weapon that could kill *me?*"

Its laugh was the last thing Aran heard as cold and alien hunger drained his consciousness.

CHAPTER 33

Kyri came awake to something small urgently *bouncing* on her armor. "C'mon, c'mon, *wake up*, Kyri, Tobimar, WAKE UP!!"

She sat up, quickly, seeing a groggy Tobimar doing the same. "What is it, Poplock?"

"That stupid Aran's what!"

She felt a pang of disbelief as Tobimar's face darkened. "He's betrayed us!"

"No," the little Toad said despondently. "Worse than that. He's run off to do the job himself, because he knew we couldn't really trust him. And because his honor's poking him in the stupid places."

She grabbed the piece of paper Poplock held out and read it quickly:

Phoenix:
   I am not forsworn; I will keep my oaths to you and yours. You will find me easily tracked to the Retreat.
   Our patron manipulated us all. I would give him his plans back, on the point of the sword he cursed me with.
   Pray for me.

                              Aran Shrikeson, once Condor

She closed her eyes, seeing that pained face before her mind's eye. "Of course. Of course he'd feel he had to do this. *Great Balance*, I should have had you tie him up!"

"Too late to argue what we should have done," Tobimar said. "How much time have we lost, Poplock?"

The Toad squinted up at the sun. "Hmm...About an hour, I'd guess. No more."

"Then the trail's fresh, and if he's telling the truth, it won't be hard to follow."

"Are you guys ready?"

Kyri forced herself to pause, to consider. "How long was it before he knocked you out?"

"Well...took a bit of searching...A couple hours, maybe three."

So three or four hours total. Well, I've worked days with less. "I don't think we can afford to wait, do you?"

The bounce-grunt was an obscenity. "No, I guess not. By *Blackwart*, I wish we could summon Miri or Shae. Or both of them."

Kyri found an involuntary, but very welcome, smile at the thought. "So do I. You didn't happen to grab any of those summoning crystals before we left, did you?"

"Hey! I know you think I'm sneaky, but I'm not stealing vital resources of a kingdom that just got pounded by a dragon." Poplock paused. "I *did* think about it, though. *Chosen*, but that would have been a great thing to have as a backup."

"And Xavier's hundreds of miles off that way...maybe even *at* the Black City by now," Tobimar said. "No backup from him or his friends this time." He shivered visibly. "Kyri, we may be going to face *one* demon now, but those five children, they—"

"We're not *that* much older than they are, Tobimar," she said. "And just the little we've seen of them...I think old Khoros knows what he's doing. Those five are going to do just fine." Inwardly, she said a prayer to Myrionar she was right. They'd helped the five on their journey to a place no one should ever go; if it got them killed, she might not forgive herself.

"Terian's *Light*, I hope so."

"Guys, worry about *us* right now. Aran's an hour ahead of us, and even if we pick up the pace as much as we can, he's gonna be having his head handed to him long before we get there. We'd better be ready to make sure his stupid, stupid gesture isn't wasted."

Kyri nodded, and strode forward as fast as she could without breaking into a run. *Have to conserve most of our strength. Running to get there will be self-defeating.* "How about the diversion wards?"

Poplock squinted forward, although there wasn't much to see other than more jungle. "Well, if Aran's being straight with us—and I think he is, honestly—he's not going to be hiding his trail. Might even be making it a *lot* easier to follow when we get to the warding area. I told you we could probably have followed the Watchland if we'd got on his trail right away; we've got a chance now, especially since he *wants* us to follow; that's got to affect the ward, since they're usually designed to allow people to lead in allies and such."

"Let's hope so," Tobimar said. "Otherwise we're going to spend the day running in circles."

It was easy to follow Aran's trail, as Poplock had expected. The former Condor Justiciar was moving in as straight a line as he possibly could, plowing through bushes, chopping away thicker impediments, leaving crisp, heavy bootprints across clearings.

"We're making very good time," Tobimar said after a while. "He's cleared the way for us as well as leaving a trail. We *must* be catching up to him."

"I would presume he *wants* us to. He wanted to get there first, but probably not be there alone for very long. Either he'll succeed in killing Viedraverion . . . or he'll be dead or captured very fast." She didn't like to think about that.

"Whoa! Stop!" Poplock shouted suddenly.

"What is it?" She looked around.

"His trail's *that* way," the Toad said, pointing to her left.

She saw they had, indeed, departed from Aran's trail. "Strange, he was going so straight. I wonder why he turned so suddenly."

Poplock looked at her silently, then gave a derisive croak. "He *didn't* turn. *You* two turned."

"What? But no, his trail turns—"

She gestured, and then felt her eyes and mind rebelling as she tried to follow the path. One part of her could see, clearly, that Aran's path went straight as an arrow, and that she and Tobimar had simply curved swiftly away from it; but another part of her saw that Aran's trail curved sharply in the other direction. Yet when she focused on any individual *section* of the trail, it looked perfectly straight!

Tobimar was evidently having the same problem. "Great Terian's *Light*. My head hurts. This is a diversion ward, then."

"No doubt about it. Powerful one, too."

She finally forced her eyes to simply focus on the nearest portions of Aran's trail—some of it random, blackened cuts through the forest floor, evidently done by the demonic sword he carried—and walk forward with careful, measured strides, studying only the forest in front of her feet. "Why isn't it affecting you, Poplock?"

"Oh, it's affecting me, I'm just not doing the *walking*, so I can focus all my brain on watching the path, no matter how the spell tries to mess with my perceptions. It's strongest on people trying to move, not just those sitting still, and from *my* point of view I'm sitting still, the ground's just moving away under me."

"Amazing," Tobimar said, also using painstaking caution in every step. "You can even manage to confuse *spells* with your logic."

The humor caught Kyri by surprise; she managed to turn her giggle into a snort. "It's *incredibly* strong," she said after a few minutes. "I *know* that Aran's going as straight as he can, but my eyes and brain keep insisting that he's turning somewhere, and I keep getting a feeling that I should keep going straight."

"With 'straight' meaning 'curving around so I can't get where I'm going,' yeah," Poplock agreed. "Sorry, but we're going to lose some time here. I don't know how thick the wards are; maybe we're almost through, maybe we'll have to do a mile or more of this."

"Just keep your eyes locked on the trail and stop us if we start to go wrong," Tobimar said. "I have a feeling that if we ever actually *lose* the trail we'll never find it again."

Poplock bounced in a subdued way. "You're probably right."

It was impossibly hard to keep on the trail against the power of the diversion ward, a subtle and deviously stubborn trick that was made even more difficult by the fact that it did not care *how* you went wrong, so it would shift the direction it was trying to lead you in at any moment, seizing the advantage when you were forced to turn to the right when going around a large tree, switching back to the left if you tried to skirt a boulder, even forcing you to glance backward with the conviction that you'd somehow gotten turned around and were going *away* from your destination. Kyri trudged forward, one foot in front of the other, sometimes reaching out to pull Tobimar back in line, at other times feeling his arm dragging her in the right direction, and both of them often being corrected by the increasingly strained voice of Poplock Duckweed.

Just as she felt her head would *burst* if she had to take one more step against that senseless antagonist, the pressure on her mind *broke*. It was so sudden that she actually stumbled forward as though an actual barrier had given way before her.

Tobimar also nearly fell, and then did collapse on the ground, holding his head and muttering a prayer of thanks to Terian. She sat down beside him, letting her whirling brain settle back to normalcy. "Great *Balance*, that was an ordeal! At least Rivendream Pass ran *straight*."

"No argument there," Tobimar said, then heaved himself back to his feet. "Come on, we can't take the time."

"You're right, of course." She followed suit and started moving along Aran's now obviously dead-straight trail. As they walked swiftly forward, without any impediment, her mind cleared. "How long *was* that, anyway?"

"Straight-line distance? I think it was close to a mile. We've got a lot of time to make up," Poplock said grimly. "I think that took us more than an hour and a half, guessing by the sun."

Myrionar's Blade. Aran may already be dead, depending on how much farther it is to the Retreat.

Still she did not allow the urgency to stampede her. March fast, but no faster than endurance would allow. At Tobimar's glance, she shook her head. "This is the end of my quest, Tobimar. Don't you think I want to go as fast as possible?"

"I could simply draw on the power of Terian," Tobimar pointed out.

"And I could do the same from Myrionar. But I do not know how much my god has left to give, and we do not yet know the limits of the power you have inherited from Terian and the broken Sun."

"She's right, you know," Poplock said. "We've gotta assume Viedraverion's as tough a nut to crack as Shae and Miri, maybe even as bad as Sanamaveridion—even if he's probably not that big. You *saw* what Tashriel could do, and the way he talked, he didn't even *rate* on the scale of someone like Viedraverion. You guys are going to have to be at the top of your game."

Kyri looked at the little Toad. She knew he didn't have any deific powers, just some clever magical tricks and a lot of luck. "What about you?"

"Hey, I've got some pretty potent pick-me-ups in my pack. Me and Hiriista did a lot of work before we left. He knew what I was going into. Once we're at the Retreat, I'll be able to keep up for at least a bit. But both of you, remember: this guy has played *everyone*. You can bet that he's ready for us. He may not know *everything* that happened, everything we can do...but maybe he does." The golden eyes held hers. "I know you don't have a choice—you've *got* to face him down now that you can reach him. And no way are we letting you do it alone.

"But by Blackwart's Chosen, we can do it as smart as possible."

She smiled at Poplock and gave him a quick pat. "You're right. And we'd *better* do it smart, because like you said, our enemy's been very, *very* smart for a long, long time."

Tobimar nodded, and took her hand.

They continued forward, stride by stride, together, as the sun began to sink towards the horizon.

Abruptly Tobimar halted. "Look. This is actually starting to turn into a path."

Kyri saw he was right. Slowly but unmistakably, the traces of Aran's passage were growing less, but not because he was suddenly hiding those traces. The ground was harder, flatter, with less and less growth, packed and pounded flat by the passage of many feet over a period of months or years. The path become more and more obvious as they continued to the west.

And then she could see a lighter space ahead, with something dark and tall just visible. They slowed and moved off the path, none of them needing to say anything; a glance, a gesture, each of them understood. Kyri crept forward through the jungle brush, slowing even more, going a few inches at a time, until finally she could peer out into the clearing.

Before her was a broad sweep of cleared land, covered with bright greenery like a lawn, and beyond that a large, tall building of dark stone, entranceways and galleries supported by graceful white columns of stone, a wide-flung construction with multiple wings sprawling over acres; carvings and inlay around the building added touches of color, dominated by blue, silver, and gold. And at the very center of the roof that sloped gently towards the center of the complex stood a great symbol, towering high above the forest surrounding it: a mighty two-handed blade suited to a giant thrusting high into the heavens, gleaming pure silver in the sunlight; a razor-sharp pivot upon which rested a sparkling sky-blue sapphire bearing supporting a pair of golden scales.

The Balanced Sword.

CHAPTER 34

"No doubt about where we are," Tobimar said. He gripped his sword hilts for reassurance, looking at the huge symbol of Myrionar, silver, blue, and gold shining atop the building before him. "We've reached the Retreat."

"Yes." Kyri's face was a shade paler. "Tobimar . . . this is really it. The end."

He took her hand; to his surprise her hand was *cold*, cold as though she'd been holding ice, and it shook in his own. "What . . . Kyri, are you *afraid*?"

"All of a sudden . . . yes, I am." She sounded as surprised as he was. "But I think we should be."

"Bet your last coin on that," Poplock said in a low voice. "Viedraverion set all this up. He *has* to know we're on our way. He's been *watching* us most of the way with various agents. I dunno *why*, but this guy *wants* this confrontation. He's *waiting* for us to come try to take him down, and near as I can figure it, this is the end of *his* plan too."

Tobimar frowned, and suddenly *he* felt a chill go down his spine. "For what purpose? Terian and Chromaias, what *possible* reason could there be for this? If he wanted to destroy Myrionar's faith . . . he could have killed Kyri *way* earlier, wiped out Arbiter Kelsley. With the revelations about Thornfalcon? That would have finished what all these centuries started."

"No, you're right," Kyri said, and he could hear the trepidation in every word. "That *can't* be his goal. I think we don't

223

understand our enemy, and if I had any choice I'd be turning around right now, leaving, only coming back once we'd gotten Miri and the entire Unity Guard to help, and even then only if I'd figured out what he was up to."

He looked at her face, drawn sharp in profile as she stared with fierce intensity at the Retreat. "But you really don't have any choice, do you?"

"No. That's the other thing that's scaring me. I made an *oath* to do this, and Myrionar swore an oath to me—in the name of all the gods and their power. I can't back out on it, and now that we are so close to the architect of that betrayal...I can't even turn around."

He took her other hand and pulled her to face him. "He can't have planned for *everything*," he said firmly. "Someone else was planning here, too. Khoros. The Wanderer. Myrionar. Maybe even Terian and Blackwart. *They* want this confrontation too. Whatever Viedraverion thinks he's getting out of this...we're here to send him back to the Hells, and I don't think they'd have *let* us get this far if that was impossible."

"And," Poplock said, looking at her from Tobimar's shoulder, "you've got *us*. And so far, that's been a pretty darn bad combination for anyone that's gotten in our way."

Suddenly her gray eyes lit up and she caught him up in a crushing embrace. "That it has, Poplock," she said, unshed tears in her voice. "That it has. And you're right, Tobimar; they wouldn't have let us get here if it wasn't time. And I still have my faith."

She straightened and looked at the retreat, the determined look back. "Poplock, I need you to do a quick reconnoiter of the area. I *think* that doorway ahead looks clear, but if there's any hidden patrols or traps, well..."

"...there's no one better to find them or avoid them than a Toad," Poplock finished. "I'm on it."

He bounced to the ground and scuttled off through the brush; even in the clearing the greenery grew high enough to mask the little Toad quite well. Even knowing he was there, Tobimar quickly lost sight of the faint movement that showed where his friend was.

They waited, still and silent, for several minutes, watching keenly for any sign of life.

"I don't see anyone," he finally murmured.

"Neither do I," Kyri said. "Of course, Aran's arrival might have gotten everyone to come inside. But I haven't heard anything, either."

"That can't be good. If he'd won and was in any shape to move, he'd be out here to greet us. If he was still fighting, we'd have heard *something*. So..."

He didn't finish, because her expression showed she understood perfectly. Aran was captured, dead, or very badly injured somewhere inside.

"Nothing!" a voice said from near his boot, making him jump.

"Nothing?" he repeated as he reached down to pick up Poplock.

"Not a mud-stuck *thing*. No wards on the nearby door, no patrols in the air or on the ground, the defense wards under the grass are down—and not broken, either, just not active—"

"There's a defense ward there?"

"Oh, yeah, big thing, just not visible under the grass, probably goes all the way around the Retreat. It's not active, though, and there's not even a seeing crystal I could find. As far as I can tell, we can walk right through that door and no one will even know we're coming. There isn't even an *alert* charm on that door!"

Tobimar narrowed his eyes. "Well, we *know* bad trouble's waiting inside. As Xavier used to say, this gives me the creeps. I'm getting myself ready before we go in."

"You and me both," Poplock agreed, and they saw Kyri nod as well.

Tobimar focused on the meditations he had drilled into himself over the years, and had refined and practiced even more over the time he had been with Kyri. The scene about him sharpened, became brighter, yet somehow removed, as though he stood outside himself, outside the the world, and every movement was showing itself in its entirety—what had been and what was to come. The High Center was his, and he was now aware of the warp and weft of possibility, the geometry of risk and reward that followed every step.

From within that source of vision and certainty he reached *within*, found a glittering blue-white spark at the core of his being. He grasped it with his mind, felt it waiting, ready to ignite into power beyond dreams at the simple touch of his will.

"Ready," he said.

He saw Poplock putting away a bottle. The miniature Toad

had also changed from his simple harness into a shining metal jacket covered with brilliant gemstones.

Kyri smiled as she, too, opened her eyes and saw what Poplock was up to. "Ready to do a little Gemcalling, I see."

"Doesn't work quite as well on this side of the mountains, but I made sure they were as ready as possible before we came back." Poplock took out multiple other objects—a miniature wand, his clockwork crossbow that Hiriista and he had vastly improved, an assortment of bottles filled with liquids, powders, and shifting vapors—and then put them carefully back, obviously focused on memorizing location and order. "I'm set."

With Poplock's assurance that there were no watchers, stealth was pointless, at least for the moment. They walked quickly through the grass to reach a paved walkway that encircled the Retreat, and then followed that to the doorway that had been just visible from the forest's edge.

Kyri regarded the door with obvious suspicion. "There may not be an alert on the door, but someone could be waiting just on the other side."

"No way to tell . . . unless . . . Tobimar?"

Tobimar reached out with his senses as he also reached out for the door handle. Grasping it, he had no sudden sense of peril drawing near, as he had when Thornfalcon had suddenly appeared. Shrugging, he turned the handle and threw the door open.

A long corridor, leading deep into the Retreat, was revealed. A corridor that was completely empty except for a few doorways and lightglobes at intervals.

"Nothing again."

Kyri gave an impatient snort. "Fine. I think he's just waiting for us to find him. Probably in the center of the complex, this inner sanctum that Aran mentioned. We *want* to find him anyway. Enough of this sneaking around; I am the Phoenix Justiciar and I have come to *cleanse* this place!"

He found himself nearly running to try and keep up with her long, rapid strides, but didn't protest. This was her moment, as purely *hers* as his encounter with the Sun of Terian, and she was drawn forward as irresistibly as he had been then.

The corridor went straight as a bowshot into the complex. If his guess about its shape was right, that inner sanctum should be straight ahead, if there were no obstacles. But there probably were.

Sure enough, he saw that it ended in a cross-corridor. Kyri, however, didn't even pause; she turned left, her Raiment's armored boots rapping out a metronome rhythm of determination, and Tobimar followed, glancing the other way to make sure they weren't ignoring anything. But there was nothing to see; the Retreat seemed as empty as though abandoned for centuries.

A corridor appeared to the right and Kyri took it, her helm down, a predatory bird diving on its prey through the empty hallways. Her stride had quickened again, and now he *was* jogging to keep up. Another intersection, another turn, and then up ahead finally something different, a doorway with scattered pieces of wood nearby, as though the door had been broken.

It *had* been broken; he could see remnants of the shattered door still hanging from bent hinges as they got nearer, and a faint sense now of something nearby told him that Kyri's instinct had led them truly.

And as they reached the doorway and turned, a voice spoke.

"At last you've come," said the voice of Jeridan Velion.

The inner sanctum was a vast circular room, well over a hundred feet across and rising to nearly forty feet in the center. In the middle of that wide floor stood the speaker, who also looked like Jeridan but wore a wide, mocking smile utterly unlike the Watchland's usual expression. To either side of him stood Bolthawk and Skyharrier; Bolthawk's fists were raised in a combat-ready pose, and Skyharrier had his golden bow drawn and centered on the Phoenix as she entered.

Behind them, lying as limp as discarded dolls, were Aran Condor and what had to be the real Watchland.

"At *long* last you have come," the false Watchland said, and smiled, spreading his arms. "And now we begin the final act."

CHAPTER 35

Poplock studied the three figures before him. *Even with my senses up I get* nothing *off the guy in the middle. Looks like Jeridan, senses like an ordinary human. Which he definitely isn't if he's running the show.*

Bolthawk and Skyharrier, on the other hand, felt pretty similar to the way they had in the Temple of Myrionar, way back when Kyri had revealed the truth to everyone in Evanwyl. *Maybe a little stronger, but they're no stronger than Kyri was when we first met her, I'm pretty sure.* That was good news, overall, although that still meant they weren't going to be pushovers.

"I welcome you, Kyri Victoria Vantage, the Phoenix; far-wandering Tobimar Silverun; and you as well, Poplock Duckweed."

Darn, he knows. But I really expected he would.

But Kyri was already acting; she swept her helm off and looked at the False Justiciars. "Bolthawk and Skyharrier, are you *really* ready to kill me? You who walked my family's halls, who ate at our table, who called me little sister?"

Poplock saw a momentary aching sadness appear on Skyharrier's face, and Bolthawk swallowed, tightening his fists.

"Join us instead," she said, not even bothering to look at the false Jeridan. "He believes *he* orchestrated this confrontation, but he is not the only one playing the game. It is my turn, *Myrionar's* turn, and I will be the one judging you at the end. You *know* you have been on the side of darkness while speaking words of light. I do not believe you are like Thornfalcon. I believe you would like to have *meant* those words."

"Damnation to you, Kyri," Bolthawk said through clenched teeth. "You think it is so easy, so simple?"

Poplock was watching the false Jeridan—presumably, the demonlord Viedraverion. He was making no move to stop the conversation, merely smiling and watching. *He's pretty sure what's going to happen ... or else he doesn't care which way they go. Either way, not good for us.*

On the other hand, it seemed that their main enemy was concentrating on this exchange. Poplock decided to try at least slipping out of sight. Being unseen was always better than being seen. Once he was halfway down Tobimar's back, he used an invisibility charm layered over a camouflage amulet effect. Two layers of "you can't see me" were always better than one.

"Neither I nor Myrionar say anything of it being *easy*. I know it will be hard. I also have no doubt he has a hold of some sort over you. But I also have no doubt that both of you were *worthy* of being Justiciars, and if you have the courage to prove it, you can stand with me, as we cleanse the Retreat."

Poplock dropped to the ground, scuttled away towards the side of the room farthest from Kyri. Neither of the Justiciars seemed to note anything; their leader ... did the gaze flicker in his direction for a second? Poplock couldn't tell. *But hey, if he's going to let me get away with it, maybe I can still make it my advantage.*

This wasn't just a tactical maneuver to get a better shot at the bad guy; Poplock had more goals in mind.

Skyharrier finally spoke. "If only I could believe you stood a chance, Kyri ... Phoenix. But I have seen nothing save weakness from Myrionar, and nothing but power from our patron."

Kyri laughed. "Such weakness that I have traveled to Moonshade Hollow and found the secrets hidden within. So weak am I that I have survived a confrontation with the Elderwyrm Sanamaveridion!" The two false Justiciars started. *Hmmm. So Viedraverion hasn't actually told them all the details of what we've been up to?*

She drew herself up and pointed her sword at first one, then the other. "Myrionar itself swore an oath to me, in the name of the very power of the gods, that if I held my faith, then there was a way for me to triumph."

The central figure *did* react to that, although by now Poplock couldn't see his face. But the false Jeridan had straightened, tensed as though this news were either very welcome, or very *unwelcome*.

"I hold that faith within me, Skyharrier, Bolthawk. By Myrionar's name, I say to you that this false-faced creature, this demon, Viedraverion son of Kerlamion, will fall this day!"

Their enemy burst into laughter, even as the two false Justiciars each took a hesitant step forward. "Ah, Phoenix, you truly exemplify the teachings. Myrionar could not have found a more fitting emissary!"

Well, he may know I'm here, but he's not doing anything! That could be very bad, of course—if that was the case it either meant that Viedraverion knew what he was up to and knew it wouldn't matter, or that it was a trap specifically made for Poplock.

Still, he was now within a few feet of both Aran and the real Watchland. *Now the question is if my next trick backfires on me, or works as intended . . .*

"Face me yourself, puppetmaster. If you are Viedraverion, architect of the wars and corrupter of my temples, you shouldn't need to hide behind others. Draw your blade, summon your powers, prove yourself stronger than the Phoenix of Myrionar." Kyri put her helm back on, readied herself for combat.

The other laughed again, but there was a hint of an inhuman backtone in the voice. "But of *course*, Phoenix. I have never planned on anything else. We shall . . . we *must* . . . settle this between ourselves. I simply didn't want my *other* guests to feel neglected. I am, after all, known to be an excellent host." The false Jeridan gestured, even as Poplock readied his first Gemcall. "Thus two Justiciars for your two companions—perfect correspondence, don't you think?"

"I like less even odds, myself," Poplock said, and Called to the Eönae's Tear on his right side.

Gold-green light jetted outward like shining water and engulfed the two unconscious figures, vanishing into them as if they were sponges. Jeridan Velion and Aran Condor instantly gave great gasps and shoved themselves to their feet, already trying to orient themselves as their injuries faded away. *My biggest healing trick used up, but if I'm right . . .*

In that instant, their main enemy charged, and Phoenix's sword parried his; the impact sent a shockwave through the room that sent Poplock tumbling nose over rump. *Wow, they're not starting small!*

At the same time, the two Justiciars started for Tobimar—although, from what Poplock could see as he righted himself, they didn't seem to be *happy* about it.

Kyri ignited in red-gold flame and she was suddenly a *blur*, evading her adversary's strikes like a wraith, and raining down blow after blow with Flamewing. Even as the real Watchland and Aran steadied themselves and stared with amazement, Poplock saw one of the blows penetrate her enemy's defenses, smash into and partly through the light armor he wore, send him flying into the wall with an impact that cracked the marble like glass.

Kyri gave a wordless cry of triumph and unleashed a sun-bright bolt of energy, an insubstantial yet irresistible talon of flame that pinned the false Watchland to the wall, struggling and writhing against the Phoenix fire that seethed around him, melting and burning the armor, making the hair ignite. The Phoenix Justiciar's power burned higher and Poplock could see her literally *throwing* more of her power against the screeching, struggling creature—

"*NO! Phoenix, STOP!*"

The shout of utter desperation cut across the sound of ringing blades and roaring god-fire, and made every eye turn to Aran Condor.

The pillar of flame hesitated, shrank, though it did not dissipate, still keeping its target pinned. "Do you want me to show mercy?" Kyri asked, disbelief in her voice.

"No, by Myrionar, but you're . . . you're not hurting him at all! He's not what you think!"

Kyri's eyes widened, and suddenly Poplock saw the flames . . . *accelerate*, as though they were not merely being thrust at their target, but *drawn* to it, like a boat being caught up in a rapid river, heading for a cataract. "What in the name of the Balance—"

And the figure was stepping away from the wall, walking towards Kyri, hair and clothing reforming, urbane white smile now shining with inhuman brilliance, as the godsfire flowed *into* him.

"Stop, Kyri, stop it!"

"*I CAN'T!*" she shouted with consternation, even as the red-gold flames sped up even more. "What's happening? He's . . ."

"He's not a demon! Kyri, he's a *Great Wolf!*"

Oh, crap. Poplock's mind locked for a moment. *I thought we ruled those out! They don't work with . . .*

But then, this one *hadn't* really been "working with" anyone, had it? Just playing all sides against each other.

And they're only vulnerable to...

The little Toad bounced forward, reaching into his pack. *This is gonna suck.*

He found what he was looking for, whipped it up and around, and hurled the small sack directly into the stream of golden godsfire.

There was a detonation of gold and black that rocked the room, and the concussion was enough to almost knock Poplock out despite all the enhancements he'd put on himself. But he could see, blearily, that Kyri's power was no longer pouring into the false Watchland.

The false Watchland shook his head. "Oh, well done, little Toad. Toss silver into the stream, so that my power is broken and she regains control. *Brilliantly* done."

Even Tobimar and the two Justiciars had halted their battle, staring. "You're...not Viedraverion?" Tobimar said, with the tone of a man desperately trying to make sense of things that made no sense at all.

"Well, in a sense, I *am*. In the sense that I killed him a long time ago, consumed his essence, and took his place, so I've *been* Viedraverion longer than even his dear father would have believed." The smile was broader, and the teeth were sparkling diamond blades, still in a mostly human face. The creature glanced around, raised an eyebrow as it saw Skyharrier raising his bow, not towards Tobimar or Kyri, but towards it. "Oh, my. Changing sides now, are we?"

Skyharrier's bow was shaking. "The Great Wolves help no one but themselves. You have no intention of releasing us, no matter what the outcome."

"Tsk, tsk, Skyharrier," it said, that monstrous smile widening— and all the more monstrous because the figure of Jeridan Velion was otherwise unchanged. "I have *always* played the game fairly with you all. Point your bow in the right direction, and there may well still be freedom for you."

This guy likes to talk. Poplock looked at Aran, pale, and the Watchland beside him. *He let me bring these guys back...*

Kyri shook herself, then raised Flamewing. "So power is unwise to use against you, without the right preparation. But this sword, forged by the Spiritsmith in my own presence, has silver worked throughout the blade. So, too, the blades of Tobimar Silverun. And of all things, only two can harm a Great Wolf: soul-consuming powers, like unto their own...and silver. Now that I know you for what you are, I can kill you."

It grinned. "Then by all means...do so."

Like I thought. "Watch it, all of you," Poplock said. "He's not just after Myrionar's power. This is still *part* of his plan."

The creature's head tilted. "Oh?"

Poplock waved his hand around at the room. "You didn't have to leave these guys alive. I think you *knew* I was going to wake them up. You *wanted* them to reveal your secret, after you'd gotten a taste of her power. But this whole confrontation...you've got it all mapped out, right down to your speeches, your delays... maybe even *mine*, for all I know." He watched the figure, which simply stood there, waiting. "You *wanted* her to find out before you finished draining her power. You probably figured someone would find a way to disrupt that trick. I don't know what you're *really* after, but it's more than just taking her power."

Aran nodded. "He...needs something else. Something associated with Myrionar's connections to the other gods."

Kyri's body tensed. "That may be true. But does it really change what we have to do?"

"Oh, certainly not," the creature wearing the Watchland's face said, with a chuckle. "Nothing will change that. You *have* to face me, Phoenix. Not only is that my intention, but it is your oath."

It looked around, the smile mocking. "But I must say, the odds have become a bit lopsided. Even if my good friends Bolthawk and Skyharrier choose the wiser path and help me, they'll be far too busy to properly accommodate all of you. But let it never be said I was a poor host."

It flung its arms outward and shouted something rough and incomprehensible.

Instantly two massive, demonic forms materialized, one at each end of the room; vaguely humanoid, scaled, with heads of an insectoid aspect.

At the same time, the sound of armored feet came from the doorway, feet running as to a summons, and through the doorway came three figures. Poplock heard himself give a stunned croak, and both Tobimar and Kyri took a step back, pale and disbelieving.

Before them, grim in their shining raiments, were Shrike, Mist Owl, and Silver Eagle.

CHAPTER 36

For an instant, the tableau was frozen. Aran felt as though the room was swaying under his feet even as everything else was motionless, as he recognized the face of his father, the man who had raised him... a face unmarked, as though a piece of his own axe had not impaled him through the skull—a piece of the axe that Shrike now held, whole and raised and ready.

He could bring us back from the dead? He said nothing of that! He never brought any of the others back! Why? How?

With a tremendous effort he threw off his paralysis and started forward, just as the frozen scene dissolved into chaos.

Kyri lunged, engaging their patron, the Great Wolf, no longer using the power of the Phoenix but just her great glittering blade that sang and rang as it spun and whirled and dipped in geometries of death, parried by crystal claws that appeared and vanished on the false Watchland's hands. Tobimar charged one of the two summoned demons, even as Bolthawk and Skyharrier began circling the other three false Justiciars.

Where Poplock was, Aran had no idea. The little Toad excelled at disappearing.

The Watchland glanced at him. "Aran, we must engage the other demon!"

The fact that the Watchland said this without the slightest hesitation—showing him the trust of a companion, the trust he had lost long ago—brought him back fully to himself. "Yes!"

But as they started towards the huge thing, which looked

something like a *bilarel* crossed with a warrior ant—he noticed something. "Sir . . . your sword?"

"On the far side of the room, I am afraid. I would never reach it." A dueling sword and a dagger appeared in his hands in a flash of light. "But a wise man is never completely unarmed. What of you? Your sword was destroyed, and weapons without magical virtue will avail little against that monster."

The demon loomed over them now, as Aran allowed himself to give a hunter's smile. Ducking beneath taloned arms, he delivered two mighty blows to the thing's midsection, staggering it backwards. "I still wear the Raiment of Condor," he said, as the thing snarled in pain and anger. "And that is magic enough for any demon!"

"Ha! Well struck, Aran, and well said!"

The room shuddered, then, as Kyri smashed the Great Wolf headlong through one of the walls; the Justiciar of Myrionar charged after her adversary. Tobimar was holding the other demon off well enough, and the other false Justiciars were trading half-hearted blows while arguing at the top of their lungs.

As Aran managed to catch and hold the demon's massive arms for an instant, Kyri flew back through the hole, crashing to the ground and skidding fifty feet across the smooth polished stone. Aran did not allow this to distract him, and the Watchland used the demon's momentary immobility to run it through with his narrow rapier. It roared and staggered, but the wound was starting to close already. *Won't be that easy.*

The Great Wolf leapt after Kyri, now transformed to a nightmare shape of claws and fur, crystal-death smile and blank, glowing eyes of green malice. Her blade Flamewing met it in mid-leap, carving a red valley across its chest, but it rolled and weaved enough to evade the killing strike.

I would give a great deal for the Demonshard back, he admitted to himself as he used a leaping kick to drive back the insectoid monster. *Perhaps it would be no use against* him, *but these demons? They would be nothing.*

Blue-white fire blazed out behind him, and the demon staggered back, shielding its eyes, calling out in furious pain. Aran wasn't sure what *that* was, but the demon of Voorith was vulnerable now; together he and the Watchland drove it back, smashed it in a dozen places, and rammed blade and fist through its head. It spasmed and then lay still, wounds no longer closing. Aran looked around quickly.

The other false Justiciars had been staring in horror at the Great Wolf, now alternately snarling and laughing as it traded earthshaking blows with the Phoenix. Across the room, Aran's gaze met Shrike's.

For a moment it was as though they stood alone, not a part of the battle; just seeing each other as they had many times before, father and son, allies and friends. Shrike glanced down at the weapon in his hands, then back to Aran, and without warning the pain and doubt and anger faded away, replaced with a certainty.

Shrike spun and charged, axe drawn back, heading straight for the Wolf.

Their patron sensed his approach—as the source of their power, Aran doubted it was *possible* for them to truly surprise it. But it was hampered by the fact that it was already facing a powerful foe indeed, and though it struck Phoenix aside and began to turn, it could not quite be fast enough.

Windclaw caught the Great Wolf full on the side of its mighty chest, plunging haft-deep into the monster. Its roar of pain shook the entire Retreat, and it staggered.

Kyri fairly *flew* from the floor and Flamewing impaled their patron completely, a foot and a half of cold-glittering metal emerging from its back. At the same moment a backhand from an immense hand armed with glittering claws sent Shrike careening across the floor, trailing blood. Aran heard himself scream his father's name, dove to catch him, even as the monster sagged to its knees, grasping at Kyri's sword to prevent her from withdrawing it.

Shrike looked up. "Good ... t' see ye again ... lad ..."

Aran couldn't say anything, saw the whole scene wavering through tears.

"Finally ... got to hit ... the arrogant bastard," he said, but there was red froth on his lips, the Raiment of Shrike was carved across in three places, and blood was pooling on the ground. "Mayhap ... I helped end it."

Then the creature began to laugh.

Aran's head snapped up, even as it rose to its feet, hurling Phoenix and her blade aside like straws. "What a *heroic* thing to do, Shrike," it said, grinning with its mouth of crystal blades, blades that *shrank* and *grew* and *moved* as it spoke. "To try to expiate your crimes by such a courageous act! And such *timing*! You truly were a *fine* warrior, Shrike, that you could so assure that both your strike, and hers, went true!" Its tone shifted to a cloying sympathy. "What a shame that I had already so much power from the Phoenix's first assault that even those strikes meant *nothing* to me!"

Tobimar Silverun came into view, shimmering with the blue-white radiance that had blinded the demon, and his sharp features seemed cast of dark stone. "Yet they struck you, monster, and something of you must have been hurt. Kyri is not harmed, and your reinforcements have died or become *ours*."

Even through his grief at a second parting from his father, Aran found a proud wonder in his heart as he saw the others—Bolthawk, Skyharrier, Mist Owl, and even the old Silver Eagle—forming into a line facing their Patron, weapons drawn, faces grim but somehow with a simple joy beneath—the joy of doing, for once, the *right* thing.

"And so it ends, monster," Kyri said, once more standing with Flamewing in her hand. "Great Werewolves are fearsome indeed. But my grandfather once killed one, and others have fallen before other heroes. We know you now, know what you are, and we have weapons to harm you, for all things the Spiritsmith wrought have included that touch of silver you fear. Some of us may fall...but *you* shall fall before the last."

It looked at her and the others, its wounds already gone, and suddenly it chuckled again. "You *know* me? Oh, child, you have not yet asked my *name*."

Aran felt a knife of ice impaling his heart, and saw understanding belatedly flare in Kyri's suddenly horrified gaze, as the monster drew itself up, towering nine feet and more, laughing loudly enough make the air itself shake with fear. "I am no mere 'Great Wolf,' little Justiciar. Who do you think could *direct* the actions of other Wolves, send one of them to infiltrate and assassinate the Sauran King, to whisper poison words of advice in the guise of the friends and advisors of a dozen countries, could himself live and walk within the court of Kerlamion himself and none suspect a thing?"

Tobimar's blades dropped lower, his blue-white power fading, and the false Justiciars were ashen.

"Only *I* command *my people*, little Kyri Victoria Vantage. Only I, the Slayer of Gods, the Hunger without End, that whom the Saurans and Demons name Lurlonimbagas, the Lightslayer, the King of Wolves." The monster's smile filled the world with glittering death. "Only I... *Virigar*."

CHAPTER 37

Even as the truth was revealed, part of Poplock's mind was simply saying *of course*. He remembered how they'd mentioned—and dismissed—the Great Wolves as the suspects, because they worked with none and for none other than their King, and there were many others—demons and otherwise—involved. He remembered the spectral shape that had surrounded Thornfalcon when he had drawn on the power given him, and saw how perfectly it compared with the fearsome glowing-eyed, shaggy nightmare before them. He remembered Kelsley having suffered wounds to his soul, and Kyri's tale of how her brother's had been shredded. *Of course.*

So their King was the mastermind, and his people his tools, as he manipulated even the King of All Hells, set Miri and Shae dancing like puppets! Poplock found he could do nothing but stare, sitting all the way across the room from the monster where he'd been making sure that the demon Tobimar had chopped to pieces stayed that way.

"And as for your weapons?" Virigar continued, that smile impossibly wider. "Do you believe you will ever *touch* me with them again?"

He spread taloned arms wide and roared again... but this time a subliminal ripple of... *something* rolled out from him.

Kyri fell to her knees immediately, trying to rise and failing. Tobimar's remaining blue-white fire guttered and went out, the last traces streaming towards the towering, dark figure of Virigar. Aran Condor collapsed over his father's bleeding body; the Watchland and the other False Justiciars sagged to the ground.

Even from his distance, Poplock felt a faint tug on his very soul, a chill hunger that sought to take all energy and spirit from him. *What? Blackwart's* Chosen, *he can drain energy from a* distance? *Not by touch, not by being within an arm's reach, or by you stupidly throwing the energy* at *him so he can get a hold of it, but just by* wanting *to take it?*

The legends hadn't said anything about *that*. The ability to appear to be anyone, so perfect that no magic or god could sense the truth behind the mask, and to slay anything with those crystal claws, that was more than enough. But now Virigar was killing Poplock's friends without even *touching* them!

I've got to do something!

He thought of his clockwork crossbow. But even if he could get good aim at a range of over a hundred feet, he doubted a silver needle would be more than a slight annoyance. It sure wouldn't stop Virigar from killing all of them. Maybe he'd stop on his own—the monster had certainly shown he liked to play deep games—but Poplock couldn't afford to wait and see!

He cast about desperately. *I can't get closer to him. I can't throw a spell or a Gemcall at him, he'll just* eat *them.* The demon nearby had nothing useful; it wasn't silver-coated and it didn't use weapons.

Wait. What's that?

Against the wall was a long, slightly curved sword, glittering whitely in the lightglobes; the far side of the room, by contrast, was going dark as even the lightglobes there lost the magic within them.

A sword. He bounced over in three great jumps and looked at it. *That workmanship . . . it might be . . . no, it* has *to be the Spiritsmith!*

And if that's true . . .

Poplock concentrated, summoned up the magic, wove a spell of levitation, of movement, of *flight*. The blade stirred, then rose into the air, swiveled around to point directly at the massive shaggy-haired figure standing over Kyri as she started to drop from her knees towards the ground.

Gotta do it right the first time . . .

He concentrated, reached deep within himself to encompass the magic that he'd learned to wield. *Blackwart, I'm probably going to have to use it all. Hope this works.*

He threw all his strength into the spell, *willing* the sword to fly through the air as fast as it could.

As the sword sped through the air, closer and closer, keeping it aloft took more and more power, the energy *draining* out of Poplock like water pouring from a slashed waterskin, but he paid no attention, just *pushed* as hard as he could, pushed with will and magic until suddenly there was nothing left.

But while the magic was gone, the mundane power of momentum still ruled, and the little Toad's spell had accelerated the Watchland's blade to a tremendous velocity. Point-first it slammed into Virigar just below his left shoulder and drove completely through the Werewolf King.

Virigar gave a startled roar of pain and shock, staggering, nearly falling. At the same moment the oppressive *Hunger* lifted, the others rose to their feet and scrambled away, backing off; those like Skyharrier who had ranged weapons kept them drawn.

The Werewolf King was suddenly facing Poplock, without turning; somehow his back had become his front. A taloned hand reached up, yanked out the sword, threw it aside. "I . . . confess, that did rather sting. And it's now clear that none of you will allow Phoenix and myself to complete our personal business without interruption unless I give you something to *really* keep your attention." He was back in human guise, and bowed ironically in Poplock's direction. "So I think I should let you talk to an old friend—one who's really been quite looking forward to the opportunity."

"Oh, this isn't a good thing," Poplock muttered.

The King of Wolves bent and touched an inlaid circle in the floor. "By my name and power I complete the summoning. Abide by the pact—*Voorith!*"

A column of inky black smoke erupted from the ground, spread, grew wider, became more solid. A nightmarish head, like that of a praying mantis the size of a castle tower, emerged, followed by a semi-humanoid body armored with chitin and scales, forelegs for ripping and crushing yet also with armored, powerful hands, one of them gripping a staff that seethed with energies more than merely magical. The glittering eyes sought and found him, and Poplock felt himself shudder.

"*Poplock Duckweed*," the *Mazolishta* chittered. "I have been waiting for you."

CHAPTER 38

Tobimar had barely recovered from the shock of learning their true enemy's identity, and then having his power snuffed out like a small candle in a breeze. But the name *Voorith* brought him to his feet immediately. *Terian's Name... that* Mazolishta *Demonlord has a direct and personal grudge against Poplock!*

"Now, Voorith, I want you to keep them *all* busy," Virigar said cheerfully, waiting as Kyri forced herself to stand. "The Phoenix and I have a private little war here, and I want it to *stay* private."

"By 'busy' I hope you mean 'dead,'" the nightmarish head buzzed.

"Dead is perfectly fine, if that's what you wish. Just keep my guests entertained."

Voorith nodded, and with a single gesture, a cloud of biting, stinging insects appeared about him. They flew towards the others, driving them back, ignoring blows, curses, even a few abortive attempts to use fire merely redoubling the attack. Tobimar realized that the whole purpose of this assault was to get them out of the room. He sprinted across the floor, forcing more strength to rise up from his mind, and caught up Poplock. A buzzing rattle warned him that the swarm was after him, too.

"*Drought*, this is bad!" Poplock said as he grabbed tightly onto Tobimar's shoulder.

"Bad enough."

And getting worse, he realized; they were heading for a solid wall, and behind the rising sound of the swarm were swift, inhumanly hard and sharp strides. *Voorith's after Poplock above everything else. He'll get us too, but he wants my friend first!*

"Don't slow down!" Poplock snapped. The Toad threw a crystal sphere ahead of them, calling out "*Come forth!*" The sphere shattered into a prismatic cloud and a small, stocky, reptilian form entirely composed of rock materialized just before the wall.

"*Open the way!*" Poplock shouted.

The creature...*melded* with the wall, and the wall abruptly parted like water, a gap just large enough for Tobimar to dive through. Scarcely was he through than the wall was whole again.

"That was...a *Light*-good trick, Poplock!" he said; finding one of the corridors he thought led out of the complex, he kept running; he was under no illusions as to how long that would balk a *Mazolishta*.

"Got good connections with nature, we Toads," Poplock said, without quite his usual self-satisfied tone. "Lucky I had one that was Earth; I'd been arguing with myself that I should drop that one and get another Salamander. I—*look out!*"

The very air before them had coalesced into the figure of Voorith, crouching low to fit in even these high corridors. Rather than slackening his pace, Tobimar dove forward, swords extended, and slid right between the reptile-scaled insect legs, his weapons forcing his opponent to jump away—behind them—or be impaled in a *very* delicate location. With a swift roll, Tobimar was back on his feet. *Got to keep my senses tuned to their highest pitch.* He needed to get to a position where he could *focus* for a moment.

A howling, whining swarm of black bees with the heads of giant warrior ants screamed out of nowhere. Poplock answered this attack with a fan of orange flame that momentarily parted the hungry curtain. *Is that a door? Please let it be to the outside!*

Bursting through the door, he found that it was...in a sense. They were in a pleasant, green courtyard, probably one of several spaced around the core of the Retreat. High above them, the Balanced Sword stood, an ironic witness to the unholy below it. Grasses and bushes dotted the enclosure, with three trees planted at the corners of the generally triangular space.

Almost at the same time Tobimar realized where they were, a door across from them flew open and the other Justiciars— Bolthawk, Skyharrier, and Silver Eagle half-dragging a screaming

Aran Condor sprinted into view, with the Watchland stumbling along behind, pushed by a pale Mist Owl.

"Oh, *Balance*, we've been herded," Bolthawk cursed.

"Precisely, Justiciars," Voorith said, in a voice like howling winds and swarming death. "I am nothing if not...*reliable*. I made a pact, and I will ensure that none of you interrupt our host."

On cue, the entire *complex* shuddered, and Tobimar thought he heard a high, chiming sound over that, the sound of the Spiritsmith's art clashing with crystal claws.

"Quick, back inside!" Silver Eagle said. "We need to..."

He trailed off. Tobimar, who'd had the same thought, saw why: in an instant, the stone of the complex had simply...erased the doors. Nothing but solid, featureless stone surrounded them.

They were trapped in a courtyard no more than fifty yards across.

"To the sky!" Skyharrier shouted. His armored wings whipped out, and the other Justiciars nodded.

But only Skyharrier rose into the air. The others leapt...and fell back to the ground. Even the *Valkyrnen* Justiciar seemed to rise slowly, with effort, not with the smooth speed that Tobimar had seen from Kyri.

Oh, no.

"Did you think that your patron would continue to support you with power when you had betrayed him?" Voorith laughed, a hideous sound like a hundred dry sticks scraping on stone. Then the demon gestured.

Skyharrier's wings beat desperately, but the black swarm was faster to climb, rose above him—and came down. Tobimar turned his head away.

"That...was the second time...I left my father behind." Aran was turning towards Voorith, and his face was dark with rage. *"He was dying again, and you made me leave him!"*

"No, don't—"

To Tobimar's astonishment, Aran actually *reached* Voorith before the *Mazolishta* reacted; perhaps it simply didn't expect anyone to do anything that *stupid*. Aran's fists slammed heavily into the demon's leg at the knee—and though his false-Justiciar power was gone, still he was wearing the Raiment of Condor, and the gauntlets on his hands had been forged by the Spiritsmith.

Voorith gave a steel-ripping shriek of pain; his taloned arm lashed down, caught up Araṇ Shrikeson, and hurled him away with such force he flew *over* the wall, to crash into another part of the complex with an impact audible in the courtyard.

The others, Tobimar with them, began their own charge. *He's hurt; we'll never get a better chance.*

But even as they started forward, Voorith's leg straightened, and the praying-mantis head with wide-flung mandibles turned towards them, fanged mouth sneering behind the carapace. "You have no advantage, little creatures."

Tobimar felt himself grabbed, held. The grasses had darkened, lengthened, and were twining around his legs. Nearby, a bush uprooted itself, rose higher, and began to shift from a harmless leafy shape to something of thorns and rough, wirelike stems. Farther away, he could see the trees themselves starting to twist and move.

Poplock gave a terrified squeak as he realized that Tobimar couldn't move, and he didn't dare jump down. Vaguely, Tobimar could hear his friend muttering a rare heartfelt prayer.

"I am *Mazolishta*, mortals. I am more than *demon*. I am a *god*, one of the five, Voorith, Yergoth, Windego, Zaoshiss, Uluroa." It picked up Silver Eagle despite all the man's desperate struggles, like a man grasping an insect, and then tossed him aside. The black swarm dove and caught the false Justiciar, and Tobimar was glad the swarm was so thick he could not see what happened. The swarm had dropped Skyharrier, and when the Raiment of Skyharrier hit the ground it came apart, filled with nothing but bloody bones, the skull fixed in a scream.

"I am the Bender of Nature, the Shaper of Life. There is no escape from me on any living world."

Bolthawk's face was blotchy with white and red, horror and fury and shock warring for control, while Mist Owl's *Artan* visage was possessed of the unnatural calm of a man at the moment of his execution. The Watchland was slashing desperately at the vegetation around him, but it was a losing battle. Tobimar had managed to hack himself free for a moment, but that was but a short reprieve.

I have to find a way out soon, or we're all dead.

"Throw me away," Poplock said hopelessly. "He's after me first. Maybe..."

"I will *not* do that. He'll kill us all anyway." He remembered staring at a Dragon the size of a mountain. Though almost infinitely smaller, Voorith *radiated* power, power perhaps as great as that of Sanamaveridion.

But he's a demon.

Suddenly he remembered the demons he and Xavier had met, and other conversations across the months.

Maybe...

He reached down within himself, even as the monstrous gaze was turned upon him. *I had not drawn upon nearly all of my power before. Maybe...*

Glittering deep within him he could see with his heart and mind a blue-white star. Ignoring the Demon's deliberate, lethal strides, he reached out, in, down...

Starfire of silver and sapphires exploded around him, turning the warped grasses and approaching corrupted plants to ash. Raising his head, Tobimar extended his swords and then brought them up, parallel across his chest in the same pose that he and Xavier had been taught.

And Voorith halted in his tracks.

"Come then, Demon," Tobimar said, and lifted his gaze to the faceted orbs that now held a trace of doubt. "But know that I am Tobimar Silverun, Seventh of Seven. I have faced an Elderwyrm and I still live. I have fought a Demonlord before, and emerged the victor. I am the Heir of the Lords of the Sky, wielder of the Light of Terian. And," he lifted the swords a hair, "I have been trained in the ways of *Tor* by Konstantin Khoros."

Voorith took an involuntary step back.

Tobimar instantly lashed out with both swords, mind and spirit focused to perfect and implacable intensity.

A shockwave, a symmetric double-crescent, of raging blue-white fire streaked outward from the twin blades. Voorith's black swarm of demonic insects was instantly before its master, but the power of Terian incinerated them almost without notice.

Voorith threw up its arms with a demonic invocation and ebony fire enveloped the *Mazolishta* a split-second before a blaze of azure-argent light momentarily erased the world with a shockwave that knocked Tobimar flat and blew down two of the three walls surrounding the courtyard. Poplock was thrown from his shoulder, tumbling away end over end.

Tobimar forced himself to his feet; he saw the Watchland

and Bolthawk doing the same from within the wreckage of part of the complex. *They're tough, those two, and Mist Owl seems to have simply evaded the shockwave.* But he kept most of his attention focused on the cloud of smoke and dust. *Did it work? Or did it fail?*

The obscuring veil was suddenly blown away by a shrieking wind, and Tobimar felt his spine turning to ice more cold than the peaks of the Khalals.

Voorith emerged from the smoke and ash. The *Mazolishta* was far from unscathed; one clawed arm was gone to the shoulder, and the other was scored deeply with black burns, and the smooth stride had become a dragging limp; more, the wounds did not seem to be healing swiftly.

But the eyes burned with a yellow-green flame. "Oh, mortal spawn of the Light, you have achieved your aim; now, surely, I shall slay *you* before that accursed Toad, and he shall witness every moment of your pain!"

CHAPTER 39

Virigar. The King of Wolves.

Disbelief warred with absolute terror within Kyri. Only her training, her bone-deep experience of battle, kept her circling, cautious yet watching for an opening. *Godsbane, the Soul-Eater.* The monster before her had those names and a dozen more, all names of shuddering legend.

She drove the fear back with sheer will. *I have to control the battle now, or he will end me. The only thing protecting me right now is the silver in my armor and weapon, what little there is, and the fact that for some reason he's still not really* trying.

"Why the elaborate ruse?" she asked. *He likes to talk. Maybe if I can keep him talking I'll find out something I can use.* "Playing at being Viedraverion, manipulating the King of All Hells, setting country against country...all while you claim your real goal was *here*? What possible point was there to killing the Sauran King, or arranging an attack on Skysand? You've no real interest in politics; you and your people are hunters and killers, not conquerors."

Lightning-fast claws struck; she parried them with desperate speed and Lythos' training, and even together they were barely enough. But her opponent was grinning, a wall of sparkling death that spoke. "I suspect you guess some of it; but I am afraid you have made something of an error in your evaluation.

"It is true," he said, and once more there was an exchange of claw and blade that sheared off a part of the Phoenix's Raiment as though it were pasteboard, "that my *people* are, in essence, lone hunters, generally uninterested in the motions of the prey beyond that needed for safety. But that, you see, is because I *want* them to be that way. The more of them that develop a taste for rulership, the more start to wonder if perhaps *they* might be better suited for ruling our people. This causes me inconvenience, so I...discourage it." The shining, cold crystal smile left her no doubt as to *how* he discouraged such behavior. "But *I* have many interests beyond the hunt.

"In particular, I have an interest in *destruction*. I enjoy it—done artistically, done well. Assisting Kerlamion in bringing such destruction, such *coordinated* destruction upon the world? Now, *that* was most worthwhile effort."

It's a game *to him. The wiping out of the* Artan *was just another amusing move. What a complete monster.* She used that fury, the outrage against the injustice of this thing's very *existence*, to push herself into concentrating solely on Virigar. She saw an opening, feinted and then dove and swung, nearly chopping one of the huge legs, but Virigar leapt swiftly over the stroke, and the diamond-bladed kick nearly carved her in half. *Balance, he's fast. And my strikes...he's already healed all the damage he's taken from everything. I need to hit him harder, with something that has more silver...and I don't have anything.*

"But you aren't terribly interested in the generalities of destruction. You want to know why my *main* plan seems so convoluted. But really, it isn't, if you follow it back far enough." He was now suddenly back to being a copy of Jeridan Velion, evading her blows with unsettling ease. *Is he really that much better than I am?* "Still, why should I tell you at all?"

Kyri stopped trying to strike; she might be able to speed up again, but she needed to figure out how to really *hurt* her adversary, here in the middle of...

In the middle... They *were* in the middle. The *center* of the complex.

If I can somehow manage this...Myrionar, guide me!

The important thing was to keep Virigar amused, talking, angry only when *she* needed him angry. "Yes, that *is* the question. Why should you? Why are you even wasting the time talking to me?"

The so-human smile widened a bit.

"Poplock said you've planned *everything*. But I can't believe that. You can't *possibly* have known every single thing we would do. I don't believe you could have predicted that Poplock would show up to meet Tobimar, and both of them would come to rescue me just in time." She ducked under a clawed attack from a suddenly monstrous arm, risked slamming into the otherwise-human form with her lowered shoulder; the impact actually sent Virigar tumbling away for a moment, but she didn't quite dare follow up with a charge; she'd seen how fast the monster was, and she had a larger plan. "You couldn't have known that we would defeat Sanamaveridion, let alone *how*. There are so many ways your plan could have failed."

She continued to circle, but out of the corner of her eye she was marking locations, places where the flow of battle would have to take her and her opponent if she was going to have even the smallest chance of victory, and once more focused on Lythos' teachings: *Speed of East, Guidance of Spring, Light of South, Circle of Summer, Wisdom of West, Flow of Fall, Hardness of North, Cleansing of Winter.* "I don't think you have a perfect oracle," she went on, feeling herself trembling on the edge of the Ninth Wind, and knowing that to *think* about that would lose her that chance. "So there have to be things you don't know... or things you're improvising."

The false Watchland laughed approvingly as he rose to his feet. "An interesting gambit to open, Phoenix. It is possible, of course, you are underestimating me; after all, while I am not generally accounted a *god*, when one has killed and consumed the essence of enough gods, one *does* gain some advantage from it. And I do, as it happens, possess an oracle which is, indeed, perfect... although quite perilous for me to consult with any frequency."

She gave a sudden, full-power lunge, directly for Virigar's chest, but that incredible speed took him *just* out of harm's way, causing her to smash into and partly through the wall. Only an instinctive reverse-roll kept her from losing her head, as diamond blades slashed the air and then finished the job she'd started, tearing a huge hole in the wall.

Virigar continued as though there had been no interruption at all. "But you are correct... and so is Poplock. I planned much of the entire sequence of events, but I did so with many, many contingencies, as I am sure Tashriel must have told you, and often the precise *details* did not matter at all. I didn't need, for example, *you*—Kyri Victoria Vantage—to become the Phoenix; I needed *someone* to be chosen as the final Justiciar by Myrionar, to have the god commit fully and finally to one representative. In point of fact, I didn't know that the Phoenix was *you* until I examined the aftermath of Thornfalcon's defeat. I had other candidates higher on my list, but once I realized who you were, well, I knew you were a perfect choice."

This time Virigar leapt at her, transforming instantaneously into the hulking, clawed monster that was his true form. She instantly called on her power for speed, and *more* speed, and it was just barely enough, as the King of Wolves bit, slashed, stomped, sometimes nicking her armor, often ripping great holes in floor or walls, but always, always coming within hairsbreadths of death.

But he's just physically *attacking. He could try that distance-draining thing again at any time. Why doesn't he? I'm stalling for time, yes, but is he? Is my plan...part of his plan?*

How many layers do I have to think on?

"But you did systematically destroy the faith of Myrionar. Why not stamp it out entirely?"

"Ahhh, why indeed? Instead, I was pleased to see you performing miracles in a manner that created *new* temples. Why is that, Phoenix? What am I accomplishing? Come, come, don't make me tell you, why don't *you* tell *me?*"

The last sentence ended with the false Watchland grasping and hurling a gigantic piece of rubble at her; she cut at it with both strength and Phoenix-power, shattering the missile and a twenty-foot length of the far wall. "I'm finding it a bit difficult to think while you try to kill me."

"Just another challenge." He smiled at her, a sunny, cheerful smile that seemed utterly without malice, and she shuddered. *If I ever lost sight of him, how would I ever be able to know if I was facing Jeridan Velion...or Virigar?*

As his next strike jabbed at her, she took a terrible risk, caught the outstretched arm, amplifying strength and speed, and then threw Virigar into and through the nearby wall. *Building's really taking a beating...*

But he wants me to solve the riddle. If I keep thinking about it, he'll keep staying not-quite-serious about this fight. That's about my only chance. "All right, I accept the challenge."

He bowed. "Then say on, Phoenix."

Vaguely from outside she heard a tremendous explosion, and the floor shook. *Please let that be Tobimar attacking, not Voorith.* She drove that worry from her head too. "All right. What have you accomplished? That's got to be the clue. You wiped out all of the other temples. Until I went to Kaizatenzei, as far as I know Arbiter Kelsley's temple was the only temple of Myrionar left in the world. Now there's at least two others, one in Jenten's Mill and one in Valatar." During this speech they had traded some blows, but it was clearly just for formality; neither came close to injuring the other.

"I will confirm that you were correct in your surmise that there was indeed no other temple of Myrionar left in the world until your journey to Kaizatenzei."

She leveled a blow at Virigar that he once again ducked easily, but though the sword carved through stone again, she wasn't disappointed. It was all a matter of keeping up appearances. "It can't just be for Myrionar's power as such, because most gods—including Myrionar—gain more power from more worshippers, more temples, more *significance*..." She trailed off with a sudden chill of understanding.

Her arm blocked the lightning-fast stroke with nothing at all to spare; as it was, the Raiment on her arm was torn to pieces and she found herself sliding painfully across the floor, face scraped by dust and fallen stone from above. Somehow she was on her feet, Flamewing pointed at Virigar, halting his follow-up charge.

But the monster was still smiling. "And? You seem to have had a thought, Phoenix."

"Worship," she said, and felt the blood draining from her face. "You've...your plan, my course across the world...the way I confronted the Watchland and revealed the False Saints...the temples in Kaizatenzei..."

"Ahhh, perhaps you *do* begin to understand!"

She remembered that moment of rebirth. "Even Arbiter *Kelsley* isn't thinking of the Balanced Sword now when he prays. They're all thinking about *me*. And that means that if I die, with Myrionar focused entirely on me..."

"...there is truly *no way* for Myrionar to be reborn. Ahh, excellent reasoning, Phoenix Kyri," Virigar said, changing once more into the massive black-brown nightmare shape, facing her casually from the center of the room. "That is, after all, one of the problems of facing a god; unless the god be incarnate on this world, they have...

an anchor, even if they throw all that they are into the assault, a connection to the realm of the divine which can be rebuilt if their worshippers remain true." He chuckled. "But if the worshippers are focused overly much on the *vessel* and not its *contents*, then that belief... dissipates, and the god is well and truly lost."

Kyri glanced towards the door. "But now that I know, Myrionar knows. It will not commit so much of itself as to be destroyed."

Virigar shook his immense head slowly, his smile lethal with crystal blades. "You know better, Phoenix. Your own words have told me that Myrionar swore you this chance in the name of the very power of the gods. Myrionar can no more go back on that than you could forgive me and walk away, leaving me to my other work.

"And you, too, dare not leave this confrontation. Once we have parted ways, once I am no longer in your view... how will you know whether the friend you speak to is your friend... or myself?"

Kyri stared at the monster for a moment, as he simply smiled wider and waited, perhaps for her to charge, perhaps merely to watch all the emotions play across her face.

Virigar was right. She couldn't turn back. And Myrionar would commit everything it was to this attack. "You're right. So you intend to destroy *everything* that Myrionar was, not merely wound but obliterate the god. Which leaves me only one choice." As she spoke, one of her hands dipped into a pouch at her side.

Virigar began a slow, pacing walk forward, claws lengthening. "And that is...?"

"Win."

As she spoke, Kyri hurled a handful of pure silver coins at Virigar—and sent her power raging *through* the coins, vaporizing and pushing the vapor of the metal *ahead and within* her assault.

This time Virigar could not simply absorb the energy. He was driven back against his full strength, the silver-touched fire ripping and blasting his body, momentarily stunning him. And as he halted, she raised her sword and the Phoenix-fire shattered the ceiling overhead, tore outward, found what she sought, and touched it just enough to guide it in its fall.

Virigar's face was a burned ruin, eyes flaring red and green with fury, as he shook himself. Masses of stone fell around them both, but abruptly the King of Wolves' gaze snapped upward.

Just in time to throw up his arms as the point of the Balanced Sword drove straight between his eyes.

CHAPTER 40

Poplock rolled himself upright, thinking furiously. *Got to distract Voorith.*

Tobimar was backing up. There was, at least, more room, if he could manage to negotiate the rubble strewn everywhere, since that blast had blown down the enclosing wings on either side, and cracked the curved wall of the central building.

But Voory's healing now. Concentrating a lot of his power to do it, which is probably why he's not attacking yet. The *Mazolishta* clearly had limits—limits that were considerably lower than those of, say, Sanamaveridion—probably because *as* a god he was still subject to that pact of the gods. *He was summoned as an avatar; you can't just pull the whole incarnate god into this world under that pact. If we had a few more allies we just* might *be able to beat him.* For at least the tenth time that day he found himself wishing for Miri and Shae.

There wasn't much point in continuing to think about it right now, though. First order of business was to split the demonlord's attention. He emptied a bottle of prepared oil in a circle around him, then took careful aim at Voorith with his clockwork crossbow, and, just as the insect-reptilian thing began to move towards Tobimar more quickly, unleashed a barrage of needle-sized death.

Alchemical fire and explosions stitched their way up the black carapace and across one of the huge eyes. Voorith shrieked in anger and gestured, making the grass and brush nearby turn hostile. *Hate it when he does that!*

However, Poplock had expected that; he muttered off a quick spell and then flicked his fingers, producing a tiny flame; with a low *whoomp!* the volatile oil around him ignited.

Demon-transformed grass and brush hissed and rattled, writhing in agony and fury as the fire engulfed them. The fire charm he'd placed on himself, on the other hand, made the flames just feel a little warm.

At the same time, Tobimar had reversed and leapt from the highest block of stone. Voorith blocked the assault, but only barely, and Tobimar slashed out again as his feet touched the ground; the Demonlord staggered. Poplock heard himself gasp as Tobimar just barely avoided a mantislike strike, then bellowed out "Look *out!*"

From the ground boiled a mass of writhing maggots, covered with scales, blind heads questing about and hissing, mandibles also armed with snake-fangs. They began slithering after Tobimar with shocking speed.

"Your *stings* are nothing, Toad, Silverun," Voorith said contemptuously. "And of stings I know a great deal indeed. You think to fight me on your terms?" It spread great sparkling wings and leapt into the ruddy glare of the setting sun. "No, you will die on *my* terms."

Tobimar incinerated the first wave of lizard-maggots, but more were oozing out of the ground—and not in one place but in dozens. Poplock sent a spray of fire up at Voorith, but realized he couldn't reach the monster now, not if he insisted on flying.

He reached back, grabbed another handful of needle-sized bolts and dropped them into the crossbow. Fire and explosives still seemed like the best choice, but the monstrous things, some longer than Tobimar's arm, were so *many*...

A glittering arrow streaked from one side to strike Voorith just beneath a wing. The Demonlord screeched in rage and pain and dropped clumsily to the ground. Startled, Poplock glanced around.

Aran Shrikeson stood atop a crumbled column; in his hand was Skyharrier's bow, and a few silver-gold arrows lay before him. "*That* was for Skyharrier," he said.

Tobimar did not hesitate, but unleashed another blue-white crescent fire that also eradicated maggots on its way. Distracted by Aran's reappearance, Voorith barely evaded the blast, and dodged straight into Bolthawk's path. The stocky Child of Odin plowed into Voorith at full speed, hammering with his fists, a crunching sound of splintering chitin accompanying the assault; Mist Owl simply *appeared* from the other side, rammed his blade home.

But it made no difference. Voorith snarled and batted the false Justiciars aside like toys. "*Enough!* I will tolerate this no more."

Aran's next arrow rebounded from empty air, and Tobimar's sapphire-touched argent bent but did not break the insubstantial barrier that had appeared about the Demonlord.

"Grow," Voorith commanded.

The maggots suddenly froze, expanded, became pupae the size of men. *Oh, this isn't good…*

"*Awaken,*" the Demonlord said.

From the pupae burst dozens—*hundreds*—of gigantic wasps, black and poison-green, but with the fanged heads of serpents and armored along their body with thick scales. Their forward legs were armed with sharp, bladed points for clawing and impaling, and they also sported a long, gleaming sting.

Crap.

Instantly the voorwasps took to the air and began circling, diving, harrying the others, as Voorith strode implacably towards Poplock. "I think knowing your friends are going to die is suffi-cient," he said coldly. "Now I will repay you for your interference."

It was not an idle boast; even as Voorith finished speaking, four of the hideous creatures hammered Mist Owl, tore him from the ground, and ran him through too many times to count with their sword-long stings, ignoring Bolthawk and Aran's screams of rage and horror. Poplock saw Tobimar glance in his direction, but they were too far apart for Tobimar to do much. Still, even as he started backing away, Poplock mimed a gesture of gripping something and throwing it. Tobimar's brow furrowed, then cleared and he nodded, even as he incinerated two of the monsters and evaded a third.

"Hey, not *my* fault your cultists were sacrificing my people."

"True," the insectoid face answered, "but you also refused my offer, and thus I was barred entry into the world for *years.*" It paused, tilting its head. "Yet I can be merciful."

The screams and curses of Aran, Tobimar, and Bolthawk provided a backdrop for the word *mercy* that Poplock didn't care much for. But he was too busy arranging things in his pack while seeming to just talk to look. "How so?"

"For symmetry and for my own amusement...if you swear fealty to *me*, I will even spare your friends. Having one of your kind as a vassal and ally? The one that opposed me now belonging to me, rejecting the Golden-Eyed? One who has achieved so much? That would be most useful *and* amusing."

And swearing such an oath would bind *me to a Demonlord.* Poplock knew that much. Even if he swore it meaning to dump the oath right away, the magic of swearing fealty to a Demonlord wouldn't permit it. "As my friend Xavier says, 'in your dreams!' I'm not swearing any oath except to see you sent back to the Hells!"

Voorith loomed over him now, and one of the great striking talons was lashing out—

And over the din of the battle, Tobimar's voice shouted, *"Come forth!"*

It was a kind of... *bubbly* sensation, being yanked from one point to another, but Poplock materialized right in front of Tobimar, the pieces of his own summoning crystal still falling to the ground around him. *Please, Blackwart, please let this work...*

A tremendous detonation shook the air and the voorwasps staggered; a column of black smoke, mixed with acid green and choking yellow and flame-orange, crackling with brilliant electrical discharges and spreading both flame and frost before it, enveloped the spot Poplock—and Voorith—had been a moment before. Debris rained down, some pieces smashing the flying abominations to the ground. Tobimar stared at the place where Voorith had been. "What in the name of the Light..."

"Dumped out every single explosive, poisonous, thundershock, or otherwise nasty thing from my pack in one place; you snatched me out, and Voory hit the pile."

The wasps were renewing their assault, but still Tobimar looked hopeful. "Maybe that was enough to—"

"TOAD."

Green flame streaked from within the expanding cloud, and went straight *past,* not *through,* the shield that Poplock threw up to protect himself, as though the shield hadn't been there at all. It slammed into his gemcalling armor and vaporized it, blowing the Toad fifty feet away. *Mudbubbles... think that just broke most of the same ribs that Aran broke earlier!*

Voorith limped from the roiling holocaust, but once more his injuries were healing with horrific speed. "I will pursue you no matter your tricks or traps, Poplock Duckweed." The voorwasps were beginning to overwhelm Tobimar and the others by sheer numbers, and a single sting or bite could weaken them swiftly. "You have no other allies. Run. Run as far and fast as you may. I will be following, and I will teach you *fear.*"

Suddenly Voorith was ahead of him, no pause, no sign of effort. "And there is, truly, nowhere for you to run."

Poplock felt the agony in his chest only distantly. Seeing the monstrous wasp-things tearing into his friends, hearing the *Mazolishta's* slow, deliberate steps approaching, simply drove personal concerns from his mind. *I'm not running.*

He drew Steelthorn and faced Voorith. "Then I'll finish it here. And just maybe stick you in a really tender spot." He glanced back quickly. *Maybe if I can keep his attention, they'll be less coordinated in their...*

The voorwasps lifted up without warning, backing away. Poplock glanced back, and suddenly he grinned. "Or maybe I've got one more ally."

"Then I shall slay them as well," the Demonlord said; then he, too, noticed the wasps' behavior, and tilted his head in confusion.

"I don't think so," Poplock said. "You wanted to teach *me* fear, but as I might say, you should—"

"FEAR ME," thundered a voice so deep and powerful that the rocks all about them vibrated like sand on a drum.

Voorith whirled, to see towering up behind him a gargantuan Toad, black as night, with glowing golden eyes and mouth gaping wide in a humorless, hungry grin.

And at that moment, as a screech of furious terror started from the *Mazolishta's* throat and its minions scattered to the four winds, the central dome of the Retreat shuddered, split, and collapsed; the Balanced Sword fell, the gigantic blade rotating, and plunged straight down to strike with earthshaking force.

CHAPTER 41

Kyri called the power of the Phoenix to shield herself, to keep the rest of the collapsing Retreat from crushing her. *Myrionar and Chromaias, this is hard!*

For a moment, she thought she might have failed, but somehow, from deep inside, managed to drag out one more ounce of strength, shove the massed rock above her aside *just* enough.

She collapsed to one knee, panting. The power of the Phoenix... of Myrionar... was very nearly gone now. Her battle with Virigar had drained almost everything she had; even though the monster had not been trying to steal her power at range, even the slightest touch of his claws or body had been enough to suck away energy at a frightening rate.

But there were still sounds above, shouts, curses, alien roars. Kyri forced herself up, clambered over the piled stone with the strength of pure will. *They're fighting a* Mazolishta *out there! I have to help!*

But as she cleared the top of the mountain of rubble, she halted in astonishment.

Voorith was there... but so was a titanically huge Toad, and the two were locked in combat that shook the ground; the heap of stone on which she stood shuddered and began to collapse. She sprang away, rolling on impact and coming slowly to her feet. A cloud of monstrous wasp-creatures was darting about and harrying her friends, even as the two gods settled a duel that must have been ages in the making.

261

Taking a deep breath, Kyri called on what might be the last of the power she could reach, and raised Flamewing over her head, igniting it and herself in gold fire.

The light caused all eyes to turn towards her—and gave the great Toad the opening she had hoped. With a tremendous lunge, Blackwart the Great was upon his enemy, mouth gaping wide, and half of Voorith disappeared into that immense maw. There was a crunching sound, the crushing of bones and chitin, and with a dark flash the *Mazolishta* was gone. In the same moment, the wasp-things disappeared as well.

All movement ceased; all those remaining, from Aran and Tobimar all the way to the God of Toads himself, stared motionless at her.

Then the gigantic Toad gave the smallest of smiles and lowered himself in a bow, then hopped into Elsewhere without a word.

"Kyri! You did it!"

Tobimar was sprinting towards her, Poplock clinging on for dear life, the Watchland only a little behind them. Aran helped a limping Bolthawk move towards her as well.

She caught Tobimar in a huge hug and kissed him, then kissed the little Toad on his head, and laughed. "I . . . I think I did!"

"You did indeed," the Watchland said, looking up at the gigantic sword-hilt jutting from the wreckage.

"You used the Balanced Sword," Aran said with awe. "Pure silver around a forged-steel core. They say over a ton of silver went into that blade."

"I was thinking that I needed more silver, and then I remembered seeing it in the sunlight, and suddenly I was *sure*. Here, at the Retreat, they would never have settled for *less* than real silver."

"With a never-tarnish charm," Poplock said. "Or it'd have been about as black as Aran's old blade."

She laughed. "Yes, with a never-tarnish charm, I'm sure."

Then she turned to Aran and Bolthawk; both saw her changed expression and immediately went to their knees.

"Aran Shrikeson, once Condor," she said.

"Yes, K— Phoenix," he answered.

"You have fulfilled the conditions of your parole and pardon. You are no longer an enemy of the Balanced Sword. You have shown . . . a bit of foolishness in the way you attempted to charge ahead, but even there you made sure to lead us here, and," she grinned, remembering her own actions in the past, "I cannot claim to never have chosen poorly, either. But stay, if you would, for I have another charge for you."

Aran nodded and did not move, so she turned her gaze to Bolthawk.

"Bolthawk, I have never known your true name."

"Hittuma," the Child of Odin answered in low tones, not meeting her gaze. "Hittuma Thorvalyn, Phoenix."

"Then, Hittuma Thorvalyn, once Bolthawk, you have committed grievous wrongs against us, against others, against the very faith of Myrionar. In the end, you sided with us—but that could be explained by choosing what you thought might be the winning side."

"No," he said immediately. "I thought you...I did not believe in Myrionar. I did not believe in *you*. I just was...tired of being on the side I had come to hate."

"And do you believe in Myrionar *now?*"

The broad face rose and looked her in the eyes. "Yes, Kyri Vantage, the Phoenix of Myrionar. Now I believe, and I reject my old words, my old doubts of the strength of the Balanced Sword."

"Then first you must name to me, before us, your crimes." She knew that he must do the same as Aran if there was to be any chance for true forgiveness and redemption, but she would give him that chance—especially for the others who were now fallen, and who would not have that chance.

Bolthawk, like Aran, did not hesitate, but recited a litany of dark deeds, and accepted her right to judge him, even unto death.

Kyri nodded, feeling the knot of tension within her—a knot, she realized, that had been there since the day she discovered that the Justiciars had been the murderers of her family—slowly beginning to ease.

"Then to you, Bolthawk, I have a command, if you would redeem yourself; and while Aran requires no further redemption to go free, if he would prove himself more than merely forgiven, I would lay the same command on him."

Aran nodded. "Whatever tasks you set for me, I will do."

She smiled at him. "I had hoped as much, for you will help Bolthawk on his journey. The two of you will—"

A deep, echoing chuckle rolled out from the fallen Retreat. "Oh, Phoenix, let us not be *premature* about these things."

The Balanced Sword was flung upward a hundred feet, to come crashing down a few dozen feet away.

Kyri felt her body going numb with shock. *No. Myrionar, no...*

Virigar stood atop the wreckage, smiling down at them. "And *now* all truly *is* ready."

She could not take her gaze from the glowing, blank eyes, now yellow, now green, now blue, nor stop herself from saying, "But...how...?"

"How did I survive? Oh, Phoenix, that was a master-stroke, I give that to you. Stunning me with silver and power, then bringing down the Sword! A perfectly marvelous plan, and such *symmetry!* I brought down the entire faith of Myrionar, and you would defeat me by literally bringing the Balanced Sword down in vengeance.

"Unfortunately for you, I was able to get my hands up *just* in time, and prevented the thing from entirely splitting me in twain." Virigar held up his hands, which were blackened and scored deeply; there was also a deep scar down his face. "This may actually take some moments to heal."

"Then let's not *give* you those moments," Tobimar said coldly. Instantly he was springing *past* her, charging with both swords before him. On his shoulder, Poplock gestured and sent silver coins streaming out ahead of them from one of Tobimar's pouches.

Aran was charging too, and Bolthawk heaved himself up and lumbered forward, limping slightly but still undeterred, and the Watchland was leaping nimbly upward as well.

Even as she forced herself to move, broke her paralysis, Virigar *roared*, and the others were cast aside, crumpling with weakness or falling from the sheer impact of sound that was like a bludgeon. "Child of Skysand, you have no say in the matter," the King of Wolves said, stepping over Tobimar, who tried to move but failed to do more than raise his hand. "This battle has always been intended to end in one way, and one way only: the last Justiciar against me, falling by my hand, under these *exact* circumstances."

Kyri summoned as much power as she could, but it was nowhere near enough. Even in the moment she felt her perceptions speed up, Virigar streaked the last few feet and caught her up about the throat.

For an instant, she felt despair; but then she refused it. *I haven't done anything wrong here; I've done the best I could. I've kept faith. There is—there has to be—a way out of even this.*

"So end it, then," she said. "You hold the last of Myrionar's faith. That's what you were after."

"In part."

"In *part*?"

The crystal grin widened. "You still have not quite solved the riddle? Yet it was you, yourself, who assured me that my plan would come to fruition; your own words told me it was all prepared."

"What?" Desperately she searched her memory for something she could have said that would have told Virigar anything of the sort.

"You said that Myrionar had sworn an oath *to you*—in the name of the very power of the gods. Is this not so?"

"Yes..."

The King of Wolves waited, then shrugged. "I suppose you lack the proper perspective to solve this riddle. Master Wieran would have understood, I think.

"Simple enough, then. So far, what I have told you was the truth, just not *all* of the truth. I did, indeed, need everything focused upon *you*, so that no...ideal, no *symbol*, of Myrionar was strong enough to serve as another anchor for the god in this moment, not even in the minds of those who had opposed the god directly but who believed in its existence—which is, naturally, why all the false Justiciars needed to be either dead or focused entirely upon you. No symbols; only *you*, only the focus of all that remains. Even now, that oath *binds* Myrionar's last power to you. An oath that *connects* Myrionar to the power of the gods, specifically to the power of its allies."

She felt the blood drain from her face. "No."

"Yes! Oh, *now* you see!" The face before her was the Watchland's again, but a Watchland holding her like a doll in one hand. "If I consume the very *essence* of Myrionar, with that oath *still in force*, I can consume—I can *duplicate*—those connections, and through them, I can slowly and surely consume *all of Myrionar's allies*...and they will never be able to stop it from happening, because the very power of the gods creates that connection, they can no more undo it than they can act against their own natures. I will have *become* Myrionar, and they will be *bound* to me!"

Kyri felt as though time had frozen with the pure, absolute horror of that revelation. Even Myrionar was just a tool for him. "And Myrionar..."

"...was the only reasonable choice. Such connections among the gods exist at all levels, of course, but there would be no way for me to, for example, eliminate all the priests and knights of Terian, or even of Thor or of the Three Beards. But Myrionar's faith, *that* still had a single, singular source, could have its outlying temples pared down, its worshippers diverted to other faiths, could be slowly reduced until I could distill it down to a single, ultimate defender, who would become the god's perfect and final vessel."

Virigar laughed, and as he laughed she felt the last strength starting to ebb away. The King of Wolves was going to win the final prize, and no justice would be done, no vengeance would be hers.

No justice?

Though her strength was fading like morning mist before the sun, her mind grasped at that thought in outrage. *No. That isn't possible. After all this, with everyone believing in Myrionar—in me—I can't fail them.* Myrionar *can't fail them.*

And then she saw it, through shock and fading consciousness, and even though a part of her recoiled with disbelief, the rest of her simply said *of course.*

Justice and vengeance. These were the very *foundation* of Myrionar. And as Virigar had said, *the gods could not act against their natures.*

Yet Myrionar *had.* Myrionar hadn't given a single *hint* to Arbiter Kelsley about the true nature of their adversary, when Myrionar *had* to have known. Her parents and her brother had gone unavenged, no justice done for them. All the others who had died in Evanwyl of Virigar's schemes, of Thornfalcon's malice, they had died without justice or vengeance.

But a god cannot act against its nature.

And what was it that Virigar had done?

Replaced the symbol of the Balanced Sword.

The part of her that denied the revelation turned back, and brought forth another recollection, as she had spoken to the Wanderer:

"A prophecy. You have a prophecy."

"*Not . . . precisely. Though, perhaps, close enough for your purposes.*"

And then, she finally remembered one other thing:

A voice that seemed both as unfamiliar as a stranger on the street, yet so familiar that she felt she had always known it.

Kyri opened her eyes, and Virigar's laugh paused, for she was *smiling*.

"Injustice," she said.

"What?" The blue eyes flickered to blank, glowing yellow.

"It is impossible for a god to act against their nature. Yet Myrionar allowed so much injustice. I believe in Myrionar, and Myrionar *swore* that there was a way out for me, and that means that there was a *reason*. There was something else, something so important that even the loss of the Justiciars, the destruction of the very *faith*, was less important."

As the wolf-eyes narrowed, she finished, "and what could that *possibly* be, except the god's very existence itself?"

"But then it should have acted earlier, unless—" Virigar's eyes flew wide, wells of pure white shock. "No."

But his tone said *YES*.

"*This is the day that Myrionar was BORN!*" Fire burned through her, fire sweet and pure as justice itself, and she felt the focus of a thousand prayers upon her as Kyri Victoria Vantage spoke her final words. "*I AM Myrionar!*"

CHAPTER 42

Tobimar realized he, himself, must have the same expression as he saw on Virigar's face in that instant: a paralyzing, stunned disbelief... a disbelief that was founded on a vastly stronger, bone-deep *belief*, for that deepest part of him *understood*, and he heard Poplock and the Watchland both murmur "Of course," next to him.

Kyri Vantage detonated in golden fire.

Virigar was flung away like a doll, the flood of power so immense that it was clear that all he could do was *blunt* it, even with his soul-consuming Hunger. He was blown *through* the mountain of rubble that had been the Retreat, to fetch up against the trunk of a massive tree, staring up as a mighty red-gold firebird rose into the sky... and then transformed into the blazing symbol of the Balanced Sword, a symbol from which walked Myrionar, Kyri Vantage burning with the power of a newborn god.

The world was silent for a moment then, save only for the subliminal hum of absolute might that vibrated from Myrionar, potency vastly greater than any Tobimar had sensed, save perhaps only that of Sanamaveridion himself, dwarfing even the power of the Golden-Eyed God. Virigar rose slowly, eyes wide enough that Tobimar could see the whites against the darkness of the false-Watchland's face.

Then a smile like lightning burst across Virigar's face, and he threw back his head and laughed, a laugh like a man told that his lost children had come home, that his daughter had become a hero of the land. Tobimar stared in confusion as the laughter continued, and then Virigar shouted in a voice that shook the earth, "*MAGNIFICENT!* Oh, magnificent, wonderful, superlative! To play the game across time and space itself, to make the trap of the hunter your own creation and salvation!"

Virigar spread his arms wide, as though to embrace the sights before him. "My plan is entirely destroyed, for you are a *new-born* god, and none of the connections you had forged before exist."

"Exactly," she said. The voice was still that of Kyri Vantage, but more powerful, more certain, and the energies of the god seethed about her weapon, energies much harder to drain when the god was aware and incarnate.

He shook his head. "Still, I can barely take in the *perfection* of the plan. And once more, your *timing*! Your *symmetry*! To have made *my belief* the final trigger of your apotheosis... MY belief, my realization and certainty of the truth, making you stronger, oh, *vastly* stronger in every possible way than you could have been otherwise." He chuckled, still shaking his head in admiration. "This wasn't just Myrionar's work, oh no. Khoros *must* have had a hand in it, and the Wanderer perhaps. Terian, almost certainly, and maybe even the Golden-Eyed God."

"The Wanderer, certainly," Tobimar said slowly. "He knew... knew what *was* to come. What had already happened, in Myrionar's future."

The King of Wolves nodded, rubbing his hands together as though anticipating a most marvelous present. The whole scene sent creeping chills down Tobimar's spine. *He seems surprised, yet happy. This can't have been his plan!*

"And," Virigar went on, "as you have just been born, created here, you are *native* to Zarathan, you exist here and *only* here. The ban of the gods does not apply. Oh, I say again, *magnificent*. Not in a thousand thousand *centuries* have I been so completely gulled, so maneuvered by others while maneuvering myself." He bowed deeply. "My compliments and admiration to you and your fellow artists, for this is art of the *highest* degree."

Then he transformed to his true form. "All I can salvage, then, is to take the soul of a pure, newborn god!"

"Not even that," Myrionar said, and her voice reminded Tobimar of what she had said, that Myrionar's voice seemed both that of a stranger and utterly familiar. *Of course it would. We do not sound to ourselves as we sound to others. So she spoke to herself, secure in the knowledge that she would never imagine it was her own voice.*

"Not even that," Myrionar said again, and raised her sword. Light blazed across her body, transforming her armor so it shone pure silver in the sun. "For how could I have arranged this, gone back to the beginning of my faith and founded it, if I were destroyed here? Your ending is foreordained, Virigar. You have only the choice of flight or of death."

Virigar tilted his immense, alien head with its impossible crystal maw, and then smiled, a fearsome and eerie sight. "Oh, now, not at all."

The world shuddered as he raised his arms, talons a foot long standing up from his curled fingers, and a darkness swirled about him. "Think you that you understand what you face, little godling?" Virigar said, and though he spoke softly, the words carried the force of a Dragon's shout. "I am the Godsbane, Myrionar New-born, and even *time* has no hold on *ME*, paradox is neither barrier nor threat! Ask your heart, born from the ashes of your defeat, ask your allies, call for Chromaias' word, ask the wisdom of Terian, and they will tell you that the outcome is far, *far* from certain."

Tobimar rose. The shock had worn off now, and he had regained High Center. Even around Virigar he could see the weaving of peril and possibility—terrible peril, miniscule possibility, but even there, even there against the legend of the death of legends, there remained a spark of hope, a chance of victory. And about Myrionar, the weave of strength and will was still strong. "She will not be your only opponent, King of Wolves." He called up Terian's power, and wove it into his body, through his swords, but not outside himself, where the Werewolf could easily reach it. On his shoulder, he felt Poplock—pained, broken, weary—lift his tiny sword defiantly.

"No, she will not," the Watchland said. He bent down, reached into the rubble, and pulled forth Earaningalane. "The Sword of the Watchland is returned to me, thrown forth from the wreckage in the moment of your plan's dissolution, and it will strike at least a blow or two for our true patron . . . and truest daughter."

Aran said nothing, and neither did Bolthawk, but both brought up their hands in readiness.

Myrionar smiled and gestured, and into all of them poured gold-fire power. "If you would stand with me, then you will not lack for speed and strength...nor for health," she said, and rose from the ground on burning-gold wings, preparing to strike from above.

"Ooo, now *that's* gonna help!" Poplock said. "I fight lots better without broken bones."

"So be it," Virigar said, his smile undimmed, his teeth growing and shrinking with each word, serving in a macabre way as lips. "But it will come to the two of us in the end, little Phoenix who was, Myrionar who is, and I have slain more gods than you could count."

"It will end here," she said. "Justice demands it."

The monster said nothing. For a moment, all of them were still as statues, knowing that the next movement would signal the beginning of a combat that would decide the fate of Evanwyl and beyond.

Then, without so much as a twitch of warning, Virigar streaked across the ground, a howling wind of death.

Even with Terian's power increasing his speed and strength, Tobimar would have been dead in that instant, except that—just as on that far-off day in which Thornfalcon had nearly taken his head—the web of possibility had drawn to a single point of certainty. The swords forged by the Spiritsmith crossed before him in the very instant two mighty taloned hands slashed down, and caught the crystal claws perfectly. In the same moment, Poplock sent a fountain of silver coins into Virigar's mouth. The Werewolf King gagged, but his immense strength shoved Tobimar away, sent him rolling down the slope of broken masonry.

That, however, had slowed Virigar *just* sufficiently. Bolthawk and Aran each caught one of those mighty arms, and the Watchland proved as good as his word: Earaningalane's silver blade struck hard and true in a powerful overhand blow that carved through the crystal-fanged head. Myrionar appeared above, and drove her own sword down, straight into Virigar's body, six feet of Sauran-forged, silver-alloyed metal.

It wasn't enough.

Tobimar had just that tiny bit of advance warning to throw himself flat before the mangled body gave a gurgling roar and *stripped* every ounce of power from those surrounding him—save only Myrionar, and even she wavered in the air, pulling back in consternation as Virigar's head and body reformed. Tobimar felt the extra energy gifted to him vanish, and even part of Terian's strength faded. *He... he is something completely different, on an utterly higher scale, than we have ever faced.*

He saw the same expression on Myrionar's face, and knew that she, too, was not sure they would leave this place alive.

CHAPTER 43

She was not sure how to think of herself now; a part of her was still firmly Kyri Vantage, but there was a new, vaster part that was Myrionar, that saw farther, saw *more*, understood more, could *do* more than Kyri had ever imagined possible.

And it still might not suffice.

The living Hunger of Virigar tore at her strength, at the power that was her essence; it was a battle of her will against that of the Godslayer, and even as she was—for the moment—winning the battle, still she was going to lose the war if she could not find another path to victory.

"Oh, come now, Myrionar," Virigar said, and gestured an invitation for her to land. "Let us complete this saga."

"It seems you cannot *fly,*" she said. "Why, then, should I not stay up here, beyond your reach, and shred you with silver borne on my fire?"

Virigar raised a rough-furred eyebrow at that. "I *could* point out that I could finish your companions, and force you to land that way. But . . ."

Abruptly the monster's form wavered, twisted, and launched skyward, a bat-winged, crystal-fanged nightmare, Virigar in the shape of a Dragon. "Cannot *fly*? Child, child, I am the Unseen Death, the Shadow within Shadow. There is no shape I cannot take, no power you can use to escape my pursuit. Face me on the ground, face me in the air, face me within the seas. It matters not, for in all places I remain the Lightslayer."

Forced to confrontation, she reinforced the silver armor she had created about herself, and met Virigar's charge with a head-on strike.

A shockwave blasted out from the point of impact, blowing trees flat for a half-mile around, hammering her friends down, and she realized that mere *proximity* to this battle could—and would—kill them.

But the impact, with the strength of a newborn god behind it, *had* been enough to send Virigar sailing back, flaring his wings to recover, and that gave Kyri-Myrionar a moment to gesture, to send healing life and shielding power to cover them. She was still unsure of the extent of her capabilities, but such a shield would protect them from the simple consequences of combat.

Nothing would save them from Virigar's direct assault. She had to win, she had to defeat this monster somehow, even though the more she thought, the more she wondered if it was even *possible*. In that blank glowing-eyed grin she read the simple truth of the King of Wolves' words: he *had* been the death of many a god before, deities experienced, aware, knowledgeable of what they were, what they could do, had consumed every energy, every power, every thought, every trace of their souls, their *selves*, and made them part of the King of Wolves.

But maybe that gave her a chance. Lythos had once said to her, "The greatest swordsman in the world does not fear the second-greatest. But he may well fear the worst, for the worst swordsman may do something so foolish that the greater warrior would never expect it, and so be felled."

I don't know what in the world I'm doing as a god. So just maybe, I'll make a decision he doesn't expect.

She flew higher, circling, evading Virigar's hurtling assault, then dropped back to the earth. *I know best how to fight here; the only battle I've fought in the sky was against something the size of a mountain, not a power-draining monster that lives by stealth, misdirection, and guile as much as by sheer strength.*

And the silver was helping to protect her. She could feel, as his claws missed her by inches, that the glittering armor she had created was refusing his Hunger, preventing him from reaching within and tearing her soul out.

Another passage at arms, another detonation that stamped the earth down as though a giant's club had struck it and sent shattered trunks of trees flying. Virigar, having resumed his accustomed form, skidded to a halt, circled her again. "A fine duel on a fine day, Myrionar. And how clever you are to gird yourself in silver." His head tilted. "Yet . . . perhaps not clever enough."

He pointed a clawed finger, and his Hunger tore at her—

No! Not at HER . . . At the armor.

And the silver faded away, replaced with the red-gold pattern of the Phoenix. "Ah," Virigar said cheerfully. "*Much* better."

He sprang with the speed of thought.

But she was a god now, and though she was only barely beginning to grasp what that meant, still it gave her speed beyond speed, enough to bring Flamewing up and parry the diamond blades that sought her essence. But to her consternation she saw those water-clear claws *gouging* Flamewing—small gouges, but still damage, *cuts* into the edges of the invincible. *He can—he will—carve apart the rest of my armor and even my sword if I cannot stop him!*

But he had dismissed even the silver that had protected her, as though it hadn't existed, as though her power was, literally, *nothing* to him, just . . . just another meal, an amusing chase before the kill. Virigar was the cat, and she, god or no, was nothing but a mouse trapped in a wide, open field.

Another clash, sparks flying a thousand yards, energies of conflict shattering the outbuildings of the Retreat. Virigar spun away, the cut she had managed through his guard healing at visible speed, and she had felt a wave of weakness pass through her. *He's using my own strength to recover from any blow I land.*

Hopelessness warred with determination and rage and the desire to be avenged upon this unspeakable monster, destroyer of her friends, her family, her *faith*, and she found another surge of power, flashed across the ground, slammed into Virigar and hurled him across the land, towards the Balanced Sword, lying flat across the heaped remains of the Retreat.

The Werewolf King twisted his body at the last instant, rolling across the silver instead of being impaled by it. Smoke and vapor sprang out from his form at the contact with so much of the sacred metal, but his speed carried him past and clear, to the other side of the wreckage—and out of her sight.

Oh no.

She moved as fast as possible, yet by the time she reached the other side of that hill of broken stone, Virigar was nowhere to be seen. *He said he can assume* any *form . . .*

The thought solidified just one split-second too late.

One of the blocks of stone nearest her transformed, lashing out a taloned arm the size of a small tree-trunk, batting her aside like a rag doll, Flamewing flying away into unguessable distance and her armor shattering. Even as she tumbled to a halt, the King of Wolves was upon her, catching her once more about the throat, dragging her to a halfway-upright position, as Virigar towered up above her. She felt even her new-born power now running out of her like water.

"And *now*," Virigar said pleasantly, with a twinkling of water-clear blades for a smile, "*Now* it will end, Myrionar. Not with a final clash of blades, nor with a cry of vengeance, nor of mercy, nor even the calm certainty of justice. Just with the fading of your strength, the quiet of the grave, and the silent thrill of your power becoming *mine*."

And he was right. She couldn't speak, could barely keep herself half-standing before the monstrous figure, as he drained her power, *drinking* it like the freshest, coolest water on a hot, hot day.

No.

Anger and hopelessness combined with outrage and desperation, and suddenly she was calm, *calm* in a strange way, feeling herself like chilled steel, like the silver of the distant moon, high and distant, above all things, seeing them in its light equally. *Justice must be done.*

How many thousands—hundreds of thousands, *millions*—of lives had the King of Wolves claimed?

How many homes destroyed by the war he had designed for Kerlamion?

How many children screamed for their parents, parents cried for their children?

How many defenders watched helplessly as all they sought to defend fell?

Justice must be done.

But her power flowed away, her will only slowing it, not stopping that impossible, implacable drain. She *was* Myrionar now, she could not *tolerate* this failure, yet even *silver* had failed her, been erased as though her power was...

And then she remembered a long-ago conversation—the Spirit-smith leaning over his forge, talking of the creation of metals and the reason for his work—and knew there was one last possible chance.

CHAPTER 44

The power of Myrionar flowed into him, and Virigar smiled. *This has* truly *been a fine, fine day. Even if my ultimate goals have been rather put back.*

As he had intimated to Bolthawk, the problem with immortality and power was *boredom*. To encounter a surprise, something *new*, this was worth a great price, and the complete and utter reversal of his plan into something that *birthed* the very enemy he had reduced to nothingness? There was surprise indeed.

Kyri-Myrionar struggled weakly, both physically and in her will. The flow hesitated, but did not stop; his smile broadened. *She will fight, yes. As long as she retains consciousness, she will fight. And that, too—her anger, her fear, her hopelessness—these things also feed me.* That was, of course, the other of the primary reasons he did *not* simply kill his enemies outright. Not only did that remove the chance for his adversary to either surprise or amuse him, it also reduced the variety in the meal.

And the dying struggles of a god? That was a *banquet*, one to be savored slowly and carefully, as a human might linger over a magnificently prepared meal with a carefully chosen wine, not something to be bolted down in three bites so one could, metaphorically, run out the door to the next appointment. He had done this many times—with gods, and things greater—and the few times he had been forced to end it quickly were some of his greatest regrets, in a life that had very few regrets indeed.

There was a sudden shift in the flow of power, and he braced himself—but wait! That was not an attempt to fight him again, but the flow had been released, a *FLOOD* of energy fountaining into him, a reversal so unexpected that for an instant—the barest moment—he had to pause, to adjust—and he felt some of that power flow *away* from Myrionar, not towards him, not an attack, just a flow of power—

And the flow was cut off as sharply as though a guillotine had dropped across it. In the same instant, an armored knee drove straight up between his legs.

A knee armored in pure silver.

The agony and power of the impact buckled him over, and a fist—glittering with pure silver—drove upward, sending him flying. *What . . . ?*

And as he rose, he saw Kyri Vantage, Myrionar, also rising, clad in pure silver, raising a silver-gleaming sword. He reached out with his Hunger—and found it *rebuffed.* Then he looked over her shoulder and saw the fallen Balanced Sword . . . and a large section of that blade now bare, no longer gleaming, just steel support where silver blade should have been.

Not created *silver! Not silver I can erase by disassembling the magic that tries to counterfeit the true metal! She has* exchanged *the metal in her armor for pure silver, silver through which courses her power, out of reach, out of reach!*

From behind the silver beak of the silver helm of the Silver Phoenix, amid the golden fire of her power, Kyri Vantage's voice spoke, with the echoing power of Myrionar making the air quiver:

"JUSTICE MUST BE DONE."

With a joyous snarl he leapt to the attack, catching the deadly blade's stroke with his own claws, feeling actual *pain* still radiating from the first rude strike and second followup, and still he laughed. "Then let us *see* your *justice,* Myrionar! For this, surely, is your final surprise for me."

But as they came together, there *was* another surprise for him, after all.

The entire *world* shuddered. A dimness that had been barely visible, yet had weighed upon the senses beneath perception, flickered, faded, *lifted,* and all of Evanwyl—all of *Zarathan*—seemed to blink, to breathe.

"The Black City is banished," Myrionar said in a voice of vindication and certainty. "The Five who were chosen have completed their task; Kerlamion is vanquished, and the Great Seal is broken."

For the first time in literal ages, Virigar felt his mind go momentarily blank with shock. *The Black City banished? The Great Seal... BROKEN?* His stunned incomprehension was so great that he missed a parry, and the great silver sword of Myrionar ripped in cold agony across his chest.

And in the distance... or near as a heartbeat... he heard a single ringing chime, the jingling of a staff in the hand of his oldest, most beloved enemy. *Khoros.*

Now, truly, all there *was* left was to finish off this young god. There was nothing here on Zarathan to hold him, no reason to stay. With the Great Seal broken, the power held in abeyance for half a million years would be unleashed, thundering across light-years and through the spaces between reality to return to the world that had not known its touch since the Fall—and he had to be there before that happened!

He spun, ducked, feeling his wound healing, denying the power of silver with the dark power that was his own, evaded a strike, another, caught the blade between splayed crystal claws. Yet... yet he did not sense the rage, the thirst for vengeance. There was only...

... only a calm, calm determination. A certainty placid and implacable as a glacier, and through the silver helm he saw eyes.

Eyes the color of stormclouds and steel, cold and grim with barely a trace of doubt or fear or hesitation, and a chill went through his soul.

Were these exactly *the eyes?*

He could not be quite certain, and then he was sure. *No. Not quite. But close, oh, so very, very close.* But Kyri's blade was yanked from his grasp, came about again, and again he barely parried the stroke.

Enough of this. I have no more time to waste. A magnificent day, still, yet now I must end it in haste.

He flipped backward, concentrated, brought all the power he had stolen to bear, and increased his speed beyond any limit. The world froze about him, the debris of their clashes suspended in air as though frozen in ice, the breaths of Kyri's friends and allies halted, the very *sound* crawling so slowly that he could *sense* the sluggish, sluggish rippling of the atmosphere, such that he could have counted to a thousand and it would barely have moved a hair's breadth.

Like a bolt of lightning he strode through the unmoving world and brought his claws down to cleave Myrionar from head to toe.

Silver rocketed across his perceptions, smashed into his face, a bludgeon of flaming cold agony. He rolled, dodged a gold-blazing blade, swung, was *parried*, even at this impossible speed, and then another strike. *Fast! Faster than* I*! That's impossible!*

And the golden Phoenix fire was changing. The fire *itself* was shimmering, blazing to a cool liquid white, sparkling, silver flame that drew its strength from the foundations of the earth, from the source of silver itself, a past lost in time and memory even for him. She struck him again, and *again*, and he impacted the ground with a force that sent a wave rippling out, and he *tried* to regain his bearings, yet she was *there*, in front of him, even before he could *blink*, and her eyes blazed gray and silver as the power that tore into him, shredded his essence like his own Hunger had rent so many other souls asunder!

Impossible, his thoughts repeated. *What is she?*

But...he knew that light. He had seen it *before*.

And then the memory broke through, from the place it had been hidden by his own will when first he began this game, and for the first time in ages *beyond* ages he felt a touch of fear.

Virigar turned and *fled*, and the silver-blazing avatar of Justice was close on his heels. *No, no chance to match this, not now, it would take long, far too long, to unbind that which lies within, to retake that which I have hidden! By the time that could be accomplished, I would be dead, torn apart by that which I have created!*

He knew what was happening, and why, and fear warred with laughter at the absolute *perfection* of this, the final surprise. His only hope was his knowledge that it was a *unique* event. If she could be interrupted, even for a few moments...*I must escape. I can* NOT *allow her to complete this apotheosis!*

He ran, focusing all his power now into speed, and slowly, *slowly* he drew ahead, feeling the silver fire still burning in his wounds, knowing that he was defeated in truth.

There! Evanwyl, the town before me!

He spun then, whipped savage claws around, sent a surge of his Hunger *screaming* at her, separated that part of himself in the veriest *instant* before it struck, and then streaked away, shedding his power, his shape, everything, as he dove into the one shelter he knew could protect him.

CHAPTER 45

The black-consuming Hunger clawed at Her, and She met it with silver and calm, certain will.

Even as Her blade struck, She realized that it was *not* Her enemy; a part of him, a piece thrown aside as a distraction, as a lizard might shed its tail to divert the hawk, an octopus relinquish a tentacle that it might regrow later. She understood this, but even that did not upset Her tranquil certainty, absolute conviction, pure Justice. She *was* Justice now, only vaguely aware She had ever *had* another name, silver burning through Her like shimmering cool water with the power of the sun dancing along it at dawn, and She no longer thought of vengeance or fear or anger, no longer worried about friends or enemies, only of the *one* Enemy, the Enemy that had been behind all other enemies.

She cleared Her vision, dispersed the foul darkness of the distraction, and sped forward through air as solid as stone to Her feet, seeking that final confrontation with the King of Wolves.

But here was a village, a small city. A part of Her knew it was Evanwyl, the center of a faith dedicated to one small aspect of Justice.

And Her enemy was gone—hidden, She could be absolutely certain, within this village. For that was Virigar's most potent talent, his ability to hide, to be unseen by any. He was here—as one of the townsfolk, as a dog, perhaps even a stone.

But he would *not* escape. Justice *demanded* his destruction, a destruction earned eons before She could even truly recall or understand, and She answered that call, raised Her Sword, called the silver flame of Justice and Retribution to kindle above Her, a silver sphere the size of a mountain. It would eradicate all beneath it, and even the Lightslayer could never escape.

No.

It was the tiniest of voices, an echo of a hint of a memory lost within the vastness of what She was becoming, had very nearly become.

Mercy before Justice. Justice before Vengeance.

Yet the deaths and destruction that the Wolf had caused towered up in Her knowledge, some the result of others who had stayed their hand, been unwilling to strike against the King of Wolves because he held others hostage, and so let him flee, let him destroy again, and *that* blood was then on *their* hands, not on his alone. She firmed Her resolve and began to call upon the Silver Fire to descend.

No. Justice can never be done by expedience. The voice was Hers, yet it was not. It was a quieter voice, a *human* voice, but it strengthened.

The sacrifice of innocents is never *Justice.*

She wavered, confused. What the voice said was true. Yet She also knew that the monster below had *used* that to escape, had been responsible for deaths, for corruption, for evil utterly beyond measure on a thousand thousand worlds in a thousand thousand realities, and he was so *close*, so *vulnerable*, and voices forgotten for years out of mind called to Her to *strike!*

NO.

It was a human voice, and it was *Her* voice, and She suddenly *saw* Evanwyl beneath Her, and remembered Lythos and Arbiter Kelsley and the little twins in the temple, afraid, and most of all remembered herself, crying, holding her brother's body. *If I do that to another, there is no Justice, no matter what monster I may strike down.* And with sadness, She knew it to be true, and lowered her sword, let the Silver Fire return to her from above.

"No," she said to herself, and with fear and wonder realized that she was finally remembering who she *was*, that she had lost herself in something that had lain beyond rage, beyond vengeance, beyond even Myrionar, and now was returning, returning from the high, implacable *otherness* that was even now fading from her understanding. The silver fire guttered down, faded, transformed back to the red-gold flame of the Phoenix, and Kyri looked down on her home, seeing the faces of all the people looking up at her in awe and welcome.

And then she remembered the others and the battle that had raged about them. With a spurt of perfectly human fear that she *embraced* after that passage at inhuman coolness, she streaked away, back, back to the devastated forest, the fallen Retreat, feeling her heart beating, her limbs trembling, chest rising and falling, and taking back her *life* that she sensed had been within a knife's edge of vanishing utterly into something else.

Kyri-Myrionar looked down, and then breathed a sigh of relief. For there in a mostly undamaged circle, still shimmering with traces of her own red-gold flame, were Tobimar, Poplock, Aran; the Watchland, smiling up at her with vindication; and Bolthawk, collapsing with stunned relief to the ground.

All about lay destruction; the Justiciar's Retreat was an almost unrecognizable mass of pulverized stone, buckled steel, burning trees and wood, shattered glass. Even the remains of the Balanced Sword were broken, some of the silver taken by her in that last, desperate maneuver, some of it simply stripped and crumpled by multiple impacts.

The sight weighed on her heart. *It took twenty years to build it, it was said. And in a few moments, it's been destroyed. Corruption had come here... but these halls were not to blame.* The thought that even the Justiciar's Retreat was gone, the great Balanced Sword thrown down, no home remaining for even the last Justiciar unless Evanwyl were willing to dedicate itself once more for decades to rebuild it? One more injustice that wrenched at her heart.

But then she saw the wonder in the eyes of her friends, and suddenly remembered that, somehow, impossibly, she *was* Myrionar, was the living god of Justice and Vengeance and, she knew now in her heart, Mercy... and a god incarnate in the world did not always have to heed its limitations.

Kyri laughed, and reached out into memory with golden Phoenix-fire. Flames leapt up throughout the clearing, flames that sparkled like gold and danced like joy, and the wreckage quivered, chimed, began to move. Kyri-Myrionar called to the remains of the Retreat, to the elements that made it, to the magic that still lingered, and reminded it of form, recalled to it strength, told it the tale of proud, high walls and strong doors and songs sung and stories recounted, of laughter and oaths sworn and victories celebrated.

With the fire of the Phoenix the Justiciar's Retreat rose from its ashes and wreckage, windows reforming, great halls rebuilding themselves out of broken stone that became whole and solid once again, and finally the great Balanced Sword rose up, its blade pure and shining silver, balancing two great pans of gold upon a solid bearing of imperishable sapphire.

The shattered and burning forests flickered, and the burning became brighter, became auric flame as bright as the sun, a flame that did not consume but *healed*. Green grass followed golden fire. Brown, seamed trunks sprang anew from the earth and burned for a moment with gilded power that faded to emerald leaves that rustled quietly, *joyously*, in the untainted breeze.

Kyri landed before the others, and they all—from Tobimar on down—dropped to their knees before her, save only for Poplock, who bowed as low as his squat body would permit and cast his golden eyes down.

She reached down, drew Tobimar up. "Never kneel to me, Tobimar. Or you, Poplock." She looked at the others. "Nor you, Watchland." She gave a sudden grin. "Aran, Bolthawk—you can do it once in a while."

Tobimar burst out laughing, and his brilliant blue eyes shone at her as they had the first day she'd realized she loved him. "You're... still yourself. I wasn't sure."

She remembered those brief silver moments and shivered, then took his hands in hers. "I wasn't, either. But now I am."

He embraced her so hard her armor creaked, and she returned the hug fiercely. "Now I am."

CHAPTER 46

Poplock felt his heart *finally* returning to something approximating a normal rhythm as he saw Kyri and Tobimar embrace. "Glad to hear that," he said. "But, um, what about Virigar? Is he dead? Is it *over*?"

Kyri let go of Tobimar, and her joy faded. "I . . . no, he's not dead."

"But it is, indeed, *over*," said a deep, sonorous voice, accompanied by a chime.

Poplock jumped and whirled to face the sound, as did the others.

A tremendously tall man stood not ten yards distant, gripping a staff whose crystal headpiece rang softly. A five-sided hat with mysterious symbols shaded his face, but Poplock could see a smile on the mouth beneath.

"Khoros!" Tobimar exclaimed.

"Greetings to you, Tobimar Silverun, and you, Kyri Vantage. And of course to you, Poplock Duckweed."

"Nice to see you again," Poplock said. "Steelthorn did pretty well for me after you put that charm on it."

The smile broadened, showing white teeth. "More than a mere *charm*, I assure you, but you are welcome."

"So," Kyri said. "Is it *really* over?"

"This particular war? Yes. Virigar has been utterly defeated, deprived of essentially everything he hoped to win in this war. He can, of course, be vengeful—but only when it suits his purposes. In this case, he has realized that his best choice was to, as a gambler might say, cut his losses. You may face him once again—in fact, I would be certain of it—but that will not be soon and it will not be here."

Aran spat. "I can't call that a victory."

Khoros' voice was grim, devoid of his usual humor. "That, young Aran, is because you have no perspective in the matter. Together you have denied him all his objectives. You have saved uncounted innocents he would have slain with the power he sought, and more, prevented him from corrupting and consuming the highest and brightest of the gods. That trick is the sort that works only when others are unaware of it. He will not try it again, and even were he to do so, it will take him many centuries, millennia in fact. You have faced the King of Wolves and you yet have your life, your health, your sanity, and even some of those you might call friends. That is something few enough have ever achieved, especially when he has chosen a guise of such power and guile."

Poplock found himself agreeing, despite his normal cynicism. "Aran, he meant for all of us to die, for Kyri to serve him up a god on a platter, and end up destroying not just your faith but about a dozen others, if I guess right about Myrionar's connections. And if I heard what he said earlier, the *rest* of his plans came apart too."

Khoros nodded, and so did Kyri. "I felt it," she said. "When the Black City's presence here was broken, I could *feel* it, as though a leaden blanket had lifted from the whole world. And somehow I *knew* that it was the Five—our five friends, Tobimar, Poplock, *Xavier's* friends!—that had somehow beaten Kerlamion himself!"

"Terian's *Light*. They did? The five of them? As simply as that?" Tobimar looked stunned, and Poplock couldn't blame him.

"It was neither easy, nor simple," Khoros said. "They had passed through great trials before they gathered here, but none as great as the one that nearly destroyed them in the heart of the Black City, but pass it they did."

"And...begging your pardon, sir," the Watchland said, "did I also hear aright that the Great Seal is broken?"

"It is. Kerlamion is not only defeated this day, his greatest work was unmade, and can never be restored." Khoros bowed to them. "But *your* battle was at least as crucial to the fate of the world, and all unfolded as it was hoped."

Poplock squinted at him. "Hoped? I thought you and the Wanderer knew how this all played out."

Khoros looked off in the direction Virigar had fled. "Virigar does not make idle boasts, Poplock Duckweed. Yes, Myrionar had taken me and the Wanderer and a select few others into confidence, given us more or less knowledge of Its past—which was also Its future—and begged with us to assist It in ensuring Its birth.

"And that was, itself, a bold and risky undertaking, for it meant, as you now know, allowing Virigar to work his entire plot effectively to fruition, and never, *ever* tampering with any aspect of the timeline beyond that which we had reason to believe we had already done in that future."

Bolthawk grimaced. "My head was *already* hurting after today. This is not helping."

A deep laugh rolled out. "I cannot blame you. Such tricks with time are not easy to follow, even for those more versed in it.

"But in the end, it was not certain. Once Myrionar was created—with the help of Virigar's own realization—Myrionar had to face Virigar herself," another white flash of a smile, "not, note, *Itself* now. And *that* outcome, despite what we *knew*, was not certain."

"That makes no sense," Poplock said. "Paradox. If Myrionar hadn't gone back in time, you—"

"Not quite. First, I am unsure of Virigar's true nature, even now. I do know this: the legends of something that must *be* him go back as far as anything the gods will tell me, anything the Dragons can recall. He is ancient, ancient, a destroying force that even the gods have always feared. And that implies, of course, that he has some means of evading even the final judgment of time that some of the gods would otherwise bring down upon him.

"More importantly, the very nature of our counterplan was such that *it could only work if it did not disturb Virigar's own plan*. That is, every significant event involved *would happen in either case*. Thus, the only 'paradox' would be Myrionar's existence...but gods have been known to transcend time previously, so this itself was not a guarantee; it would simply mean that we would all have lost the knowledge that Myrionar had brought back, and would have suddenly found Virigar's plan complete and irrevocable."

Poplock bunched himself up in a shudder. "I'm glad I don't have to fully understand that. But I guess it means we *did* win."

Khoros bowed deeply before them. "You won indeed, and have my gratitude, and that of Terian, Chromaias, the Wanderer, and many others—even if some of them know it not. You have saved Kaizatenzei from a threat it never knew, salvaged souls born to darkness, and defeated a creature that expects to see defeat less than once in a Chaoswar's time. Instead, you have handed Virigar his second defeat in a year—and yours a far more comprehensive one."

He bowed again. "And, too, Kyri Vantage, you have saved not only those precious to you here, but those precious to you in the past."

Her head snapped up, and Poplock saw a dawning, disbelieving hope. "What . . . ?"

"Myrionar has not fallen, Kyri Victoria Vantage. Myrionar was, and is, and shall be. And those who *trusted* in Myrionar, who were *dedicated* to Its Justice and Vengeance, will not have been forgotten. Virigar did not take what he sought, and so that place beyond death where Myrionar and Its allies gather the souls that are theirs still waits."

Tears welled up in her eyes, spilled over, and she dropped to her knees as Poplock watched with a chill of awe. "Mother? Father? *Rion?*"

"In the lands beyond the end that the gods rule, yes. For they were not felled by the hand of the Godslayer, nor his children, and though Rion's soul was sorely torn by one who *would* have been a child of Virigar, still . . ." Khoros smiled briefly, "we did take that much of a risk, and Myrionar's allies caught what Thornfalcon did not take."

Kyri stepped forward and without warning threw her arms around the tall mage.

Khoros stood frozen; Poplock thought, by the stiffness of his stance, that this of all things was something he had neither foreseen, nor prepared himself for.

"Thank you," she murmured, then stepped back.

Khoros was silent a moment, and Poplock saw one of the long-fingered hands rise up, pass over the invisible eyes, and was there a trace of moisture upon that hand? Then the ancient wizard straightened. "Thank yourself. Thank your allies." He turned. "I assisted, yes . . . but it was for my own and broader purpose. Give thanks to those who truly deserve it."

He stepped away, and his figure became indistinct, as though journeying a thousand miles in a stride without even moving; but he paused on the threshold of the infinite, and turned his head the slightest bit. "But...you are welcome, Kyri Victoria Vantage, the Phoenix, Myrionar who is, and the world is a far, far brighter place with you and your friends in it. It will warm me...to know you are here."

And he was gone. For a moment, all of them stood still, staring at the empty space.

Then Poplock bounced back onto Tobimar's shoulder. "C'mon, people. Let's get back to Evanwyl and let 'em know—we've won!"

Bolthawk and Aran hesitated.

Kyri looked at them, studying the two with eyes that glinted with more than mortal power. "Aran, you I trust without reservation now. And Bolthawk, you could have chosen to flee, and did not. You have much to expiate, many crimes to make amends for...but on this day, you have done well, and you will come with us, and they will know that I remember the most important part of the faith is not Justice, nor Vengeance, but Mercy."

Tobimar reached out and took her hand, and they walked—with Poplock balancing in his comfortable, accustomed place—towards the distant city.

CHAPTER 47

"I can scarcely take it all in," Arbiter Kelsley said, shaking his head. "Kyri? *You* are...Myrionar?"

She laughed, hearing the priest's disbelief echoing her own. "I can't believe it myself, really, but...yes, I am."

They were seated around a (relatively) small table in the Watchland's private rooms. Kyri knew that a grand celebration was in preparation, probably to happen in the next two days, but for now, a quiet, private dinner to relax and talk with her friends and oldest advisors was what she really wanted. That and to go to bed soon and sleep for maybe a week.

She looked over to Lythos, who had sat quietly throughout the recital of their final adventures, his expression scarcely wavering from its usual calm attentiveness. Lythos nodded thoughtfully, and took another bite of the pastry in front of him.

This reminded her that she was still hungry—it had been a busy day—and she dug into the flashfry dish the Watchland's cook had prepared for her. "Watchland, I hope your cook's very happy, otherwise I may steal her."

"Yalina has always seemed very pleased with her position and treatment here, and I assure you I will match any offer you might make her," Jeridan answered with a smile. "Unless you cheat and offer her something only a god could manage."

She shuddered. "Someone please warn me if I *ever* start showing signs of being willing to use my power for such petty reasons."

"I'll bounce on your head for sure," Poplock promised. "That should do it."

"Fear him," agreed Tobimar. To her newly sharpened senses, he seemed unusually tense, given the fact that they seemed to have won a complete victory, but then, maybe he was just finding it hard to relax. "He'll have no more respect for you as a god than he did before."

"By the Balance, please, don't *any* of you treat me differently—"

"That," Lythos interrupted, "is not possible, Kyri, and it is extremely naïve of you to believe otherwise. We will endeavor to remain your friends and counselors insofar as we can, but you *are* changed, and over time I believe this will become more, rather than less, obvious, as you become accustomed to the new role that has become yours."

Kyri felt an irrational spark of anger at Lythos' correction, but forced that down. He was right; the *Sho-Ka-Taida* usually was. *I'm . . . a god. I'm my own god.* An embarrassed giggle escaped from her lips.

Tobimar looked at her. "What?"

"I just realized that this means . . . I've been *worshipping myself* for my entire life! Does that make me the most self-centered person who ever *lived*?"

Even Bolthawk burst out laughing at that. "Nay, Kyri, it makes you no different than ever you were," the Child of Odin said. "And glad I am of that."

"I must admit, however," Kelsley said hesitantly, "that I am still unclear on a few things. I understand—although only in a limited way—how Myrionar was able to arrange its own birth, and that this explains why Myrionar did not, and could not, act to stop the outrages the false Justiciars perpetrated." The others nodded, and Kelsley went on, "but what I do not understand is what the King of Wolves believed was happening. He *must* have had some reason that *he* believed Myrionar could not act, and obviously it could *not* have been the same reason that we now know was the truth."

"I spent a lot of our trip back here thinking about that," Poplock said.

"I thought you spent a lot of it sleeping and eating bugs," Tobimar said.

"Hey! That trip was like eight hours, I had plenty of time to do all three. Don't interrupt!"

Chuckles sped around the table; Poplock raised a tiny glass to the others, took a drink, then continued, "Anyway, a lot of the pieces fell into place once I started connecting things Condor—I mean Aran—said with other things we saw.

"See, Virigar's whole plan obviously relied on the gods not knowing what was happening, right?"

"Right," Kyri said. "Khoros confirmed as much, that if they knew about the plan it probably wouldn't work—if for no other reason than that the gods wouldn't swear such all-encompassing oaths to mortals until the danger was over."

"Right. And Virigar's biggest power is to hide himself, right? His form *and* his power, right?"

She remembered, dimly, that even the vast silver Someone she had almost become had lost the King of Wolves. "Definitely."

"Well, let's fit all those pieces plus what we already knew together. Virigar had all these false Justiciars—people that he chose and carefully corrupted over the last couple of centuries, anyway, after he had whittled away the rest of the faith. We *know* he was providing them with the powers to act *just like* the Justiciars. We also know that—with the exception of old Thorny—all the Justiciars we know of started out worthy, at least reasonable candidates to be Justiciars."

"I see," Lythos said. "You're saying that he insinuated himself into the process while Myrionar was, in fact, still choosing the Justiciars. He could extend his power out and into other people—concealing, perhaps, shortcomings their minds or souls might have from Myrionar."

She was finally starting to grasp the *subtlety* of Virigar's power, and in some ways it was more frightening than the vast soul-ripping reality of his power in battle. "He would *take over* the support of the Justiciars when they were doing things that Myrionar wouldn't approve of...and he could *hide that* from even the god!"

"Gotta be the way it worked," Poplock said with a bounce-nod. "Even the legends didn't tell us a *fraction* of what that monster really could do, and he as much as told us that we didn't understand. Aran, even the Demonshard couldn't tell the difference, could it?"

Aran nodded. "Not really. Being in my hands and feeling my power, it could use that to detect Kyri's power miles away.

It implied there was a subtle difference, but that could just as easily be because she was the Phoenix and I was Condor, and our powers aren't identical."

Kelsley rubbed his chin. "I think I see. Myrionar would not even be able to *see* events that the Werewolf King concealed, would not know if and when the false Justiciar power was being used. Perhaps Myrionar even was supporting the false Justiciars for much of their career."

"A brilliant strategy," the Watchland agreed slowly. "Myrionar would become aware of injustices associated with the Justiciars but only peripherally, and could not ascertain the truth even with all the god's powers—as clouding the truth is and was Virigar's primary power. The loss of its strength due to the destruction of its other temples, and the association of these events with members of its own corps, would mean that it literally could not be sure as to which members of its own *worshippers* were the enemy. It had to try to act, while being unable to be sure who it could trust, which meant that its own central power of Justice limited its ability to act. Myrionar would be paralyzed by its own principles."

"And eventually forced to act by choosing someone out-side of the entire structure," Poplock said. "Preferably a devout worshipper who had no connection to the prior events except, possibly, a negative one—that is, the known unjust events had injured them in some way. That's how Virigar knew what kind of final representative Myrionar would have to choose, and how that would play out."

"Great Balance," Kelsley said. "Alas, I had such faith in Myri-onar that the idea it could be tricked—"

"Arbiter, *none* of us realized just how far and deep deceptions could go," Kyri said. "Now that . . . now that I am Myrionar, well, I can understand that even a god has limits, and when there are many powers equal to your own . . . they can be fooled exactly as we can, it's just on a higher level, so to speak. And Virigar had many other allies, or rather puppets, running around to confuse the issue. Myrionar probably suspected any of a dozen other demonlords or dark gods, which made it that much easier to continue the charade."

"Yup," the Toad said, cramming several berries into his mouth. "Mmph. Probably we'll be figuring out more scary details of his plans for years. Not so sure that some of them won't be giving us problems later on; it's not like he cleaned up everything for us. But that's for later."

"Much later," Tobimar said firmly. "Right now, I just want to enjoy the fact that it's all over."

Kyri smiled, and took his hand. "So do I."

There was something odd—strained—about the smile he returned to her, but he did grip her hand, maybe even more tightly than usual.

The door burst open; Samni, the Watchland's Master of House, stood there, eyes wide. "Watchland! An emergency!"

Everyone had jumped to their feet at the sudden entrance. The Watchland's brows came down over the blue eyes. "Emergency? What is it?"

Shouldering past Samni was Devran Thalinde, one of the Eyes; he was breathing heavily. "Something...coming out...of Rivendream Pass. *Lot* of somethings. That's why I came straight here, Helsa and I didn't dare engage that group, or even get too close."

"How many?"

"At least two dozen, judging by the lights I saw moving with them. Moving in formation, too."

"Balance! We haven't had an incursion that large in a generation and a half!"

"We're on our way," Kyri said. "You muster the Eyes and Arms, but the three of us—"

"Should be more than enough, I would think," the Watchland said. His eyes finished his thought: *and if not, there are no forces sufficient.*

No rest. *Is this, perhaps, something Virigar left as a final attack, something like Thornfalcon's last trap?*

She emerged into the night of Evanwyl and looked towards Rivendream Pass, and to her shock she could *see* a gathering of lights approaching swiftly. *They must have been moving at a tremendous pace already.*

"Kyri, do you think—"

"I don't know, Tobimar, but we have to expect the worst."

No point in revealing anything we don't have to. The three set out at a run to intercept the fast-approaching mass of...something.

As they got closer, Kyri could hear footsteps. *Marching* footsteps. *No, it couldn't be—*

Crystal-bright light suddenly bloomed in front of them, a singing luminance that showed a column of troops in shining metal and crystal armor, and at its head—

"Phoenix!" Miri called out with a joyful laugh. "The Unity of Kaizatenzei has found you!"

CHAPTER 48

Tobimar was momentarily speechless, stunned by the sight of the golden-haired Light of Kaizatenzei and the arrayed Colors, Hues, and Shades behind her, people he had not expected to see again for months, perhaps *years*.

Then the paralysis of startlement broke, and he sprang forward, for once beating Kyri by a step, and caught Miri up in his arms, swung her around, laughing, to have both of them grabbed in Kyri's crushing embrace. "Miri, what in the name of the Infinite are you doing here? We thought—"

"—that we were too busy rebuilding Kaizatenzei?" she finished. "Yes, we thought that at first too. And then one day, I looked up at the same time Shae did, and we both knew what we were thinking: that you'd saved our country—saved *us*—and we'd sent you off to face *Viedraverion* without so much as one Shade to help."

"But that made perfect sense, Miri!" Kyri said, easing up on the hug but still holding the diminutive Light's hand. "You—"

"It made sense, but it was *wrong*!" Miri said bluntly. "Our hearts should have known—*did* know—better. So what if rebuilding the city took a little longer? The greatest threats were *gone* thanks to you, and we'd given you *nothing*! So once we realized that, we called for twenty-five of the Unity Guard to volunteer to come on a fast march through the Pass of Night to your aid, and of course every single one of the Guard volunteered. And so I chose my twenty-five—"

"Twenty-*six*," said a calm, precise, hissing voice. "For you could not persuade me *not* to come."

"*Hiriista!*" Poplock sprang from Tobimar's shoulder with such force he was momentarily staggered, and Hiriista caught up the Toad, hissing and rippling his crest in delight. *How strange to see a* mazakh *and a Toad so happy to see each other. And how wonderful.* Once Poplock had jumped to the Magewright's shoulder, Tobimar stepped up and grasped Hiriista's claws and bowed. "We're glad to see you too, as you can see."

Kyri followed suit, laughing. "This is *wonderful*, Hiriista, Miri," she looked behind, saw others they had seen, and some they hadn't, but all smiling, all overjoyed to have found the ones they sought. "... *all* of you, how wonderful and welcome!"

Miri laughed as well. "As I was saying, I gathered them all and we came as fast as we could, to help if you needed it, to congratulate you if you didn't, and," she looked momentarily grim, "to avenge you if you were beyond help."

She brightened again. "But obviously that didn't happen, and since you came so swiftly at our approach, I venture a guess that you have either defeated your enemy, or found no good way to—"

She broke off with a gasp, as Jeridan Velion rode swiftly up on his sithigorn, the sound of many other feet in the distance heralding the approach of Evanwyl's Eyes and Arms.

Miri's blades were in her hands, and she began to shimmer. "*You!*"

Tobimar flung himself between the startled Watchland and the furious Light of Kaizatenzei. "No, wait, *wait*, Miri! This is not our enemy!"

She paused, then glanced from him to Phoenix, who nodded; Miri then returned her stare to the Watchland. "You are not Viedraverion?"

"I am not the one who was using that name, no," Jeridan said. "Though I was a pawn of his, and he used my face when it suited him."

Miri gave a sigh of relief. Her knives returned to their sheaths, and a rattling whisper of blades caused Tobimar to look up in surprise. The entire force of twenty-five Unity Guards was sheathing its weapons as well, and Hiriista was letting one of his many jeweled bangles drop back to his chest; they must have all drawn at the same moment as Miri. "That is well, then. We have come too late to aid you in the battle, but it seems you needed no aid." She paused, tilted her head. "You said 'the one who was using that name'; do you mean to say that it was *not* Viedraverion? I assure you, I knew Viedra quite well."

"Oh, you could have known him better than his father and it *still* wouldn't have done you any good," Poplock said. "since it was the Werewolf King doing the playacting."

The color drained completely from Miri's face. She wavered, half-fell—would have fallen, Tobimar thought, if Kyri hadn't caught her. "The *Lightslayer*...?" she said.

"Ahhh," Hiriista breathed. "Yesss, of course, the Eater of Light, the Hunter Unseen. *That* makes sense of your entire story!"

But Tobimar was more concerned with Miri, who was shaking, eyes wide, filled with terror and revulsion. "Miri? Miri, what *is* it?"

"*I saw him!*" she said, voice breaking with remembered horror. "In the castle...when I went to get the mirror! He was *waiting* for me, talked with me, trapped me with his power, making me *forget* everything, so I couldn't reveal the clues..."

Kyri hugged her, as the others gathered around. "We know what he was like, now. We faced him and defeated him, but it was a *very* near thing, Miri. I would rather have faced Sanamaveridion again, once I realized what he truly was."

"Second that," Poplock said, hopping down and sitting on the still-shivering Light's lap. "Believe me, he's the scariest thing I have ever, *ever* seen. You didn't have a *chance* if you didn't know what you were up against."

The Toad glanced up at Hiriista. "Hmm. But if he could *act* through that mirror..."

"...that implies that the mirrors have even more capabilities than we suspected. A secure communications method, yes. Open to mental, magical, or verbal communication, yes. But I did not think they could be used as gateways."

Miri forced herself to her feet; color was slowly returning. "They can; I can recall it now very clearly." She looked up, gripping Phoenix's arm. "You're *sure* he is defeated? Not waiting, not—"

Tobimar touched her shoulder. Those who didn't *know* Miri— and the Werewolf King—might mistake her current behavior for weakness, but Tobimar remembered that blank-glowing crystal smile and knew it was anything but. "We were assured that the war was over by Konstantin Khoros himself."

Miri blinked. "By my Father... *Khoros* was here, too?"

"The whole thing was a battlesquares competition between a *lot* of sides," Poplock said. "But hey, instead of standing around outside, why don't we all go back to the Watchland's? If," the Toad said with an offhand glance at Jeridan, "that's okay with you."

"I have not been properly introduced," the Watchland said, sliding down from his sithigorn and letting the giant bird stride a ways off. "Welcome, travelers, to Evanwyl. I am Jeridan Velion, Watchland, nominal ruler of this country. Who are you that grace our land with your presence?"

Miri straightened, and her smile held much of its usual brilliance as she then did her spread-armed bow. "I am Miri, Light of Kaizatenzei, emissary of Lady Shae, the Lady of Light and our ruler. This is Hiriista, finest Magewright of the land, and these are others of the Unity Guard, whom I will introduce in detail later."

"I have already heard much of you, Light Miri, and we are honored to receive you here. As our friend and mighty hero Poplock suggests, let us return to my home, where your people can refresh themselves, partake of my table, and find lodging appropriate to your station and your mission. We were in fact in the midst of hearing the account of Kyri's victory when you arrived."

"We would be most honored to do so," Miri said formally, then waved to the Unity Guard. "Come on, everyone! We've missed the war, but it looks like we're still in time for the celebration!"

"Tonight's just a little private meeting," Tobimar said as they started off towards the Watchland's fortress. "Tomorrow or the day after, pretty much all of Evanwyl's going to be at the party, though."

"And you and your people are of course invited," Kyri said immediately. "The celebration will be at Vantage Fortress."

"Vantage... but that would be *your* home, yes?" Miri said with a puzzled tone. "Surely the others would be—"

"Unless I miss my guess, Light Miri, *you* know our Kyri well enough to guess why," Jeridan said, echoing Tobimar's own thoughts.

Miri looked at her friend with narrowed eyes that still twinkled with mirth. "Oh, yes. Yes, indeed. You're far too *uncomfortable* with people celebrating you being a hero, so you want to celebrate *them* instead!"

"Well, it's not that I'm... *uncomfortable*..."

"Lessee," Poplock said. "You would've run straight out of

Jenten's Mill if they hadn't basically asked you to help found a Temple of Myrionar. Lady Shae practically had to beg you to do the service for Tanvol and the others. We ducked out of every other town we helped pretty much as fast as you could make your excuses. Either you're really uncomfortable with the idea of being called a hero, or you're afraid they're gonna catch you stealing the silverware."

Everyone burst out laughing; even Kyri joined in after a moment of looking mortified. "Oh, all right, *yes*, it's completely embarrassing. I don't feel any different than anyone else!"

"Which is nigh-inexplicable to most others," Hiriista said. "And, also, very likely the reason that you *are* a hero."

"But it *is* a somewhat unusual trait in an adventurer," Tobimar mused. "Most of us may not want to be constantly paraded around, true, but we all look forward to the cheers and celebration when we've done our jobs well."

Kyri nodded at that. "Put that way, it *is* odd, I guess. I remember my daydreams of being a Guilded Adventurer, and there certainly were scenes of the people cheering me after I'd put down one of the Nine Kings or something like that."

"Reality has a way of being rather different—in ways both good and bad—from our dreams," Jeridan said, leading his sithigorn rather than riding it so he could speak with them on the level. "And I will be the first to admit that your position in this case is vastly different than that of an ordinary adventurer, and the stakes were...a bit higher than most."

The mention of *different* reminded Tobimar of something he'd been trying to avoid thinking about. *Different indeed. Kyri...in a very real sense isn't Kyri anymore. She's a god now, and I can't believe that this won't change her.*

Will it change us too?

Tobimar tried to push those questions aside. *God or not, she's still Kyri. At least now. And by asking these questions, I might be changing myself. Do I want to lose her because I'm asking foolish questions?*

But on the other hand...were the questions foolish? There were reasons that people worshipped gods and not other people, in general. He stole a glance at Kyri, talking animatedly with Miri, then remembered the transcendant look in Myrionar's gray eyes. *Maybe foolish. Maybe not. But by the Light, try not to dwell on it!*

The doors of the Watchland's Fortress opened as they approached, a glow of cheerful light making a golden pathway leading them inside. "Welcome again, all of you. Rest and refresh yourselves, and prepare for a true celebration on the morrow," Jeridan said. "A celebration now not merely of victory over evil, but of a meeting with friends from the pass that before has shown us only evil; may this be an auspicious omen indeed."

He raised his voice. "Samni! *Samni!* Apologies to all, and there will be double pay for this night, for we have *twenty-seven* honored guests arriving from beyond Rivendream this night, and I want them to appreciate the hospitality of the Watchland!"

As they approached, they saw Samni raising one of her white eyebrows. "Twenty-seven? On the road through *that*? They'll want baths and rooms *and* food, and all of it quickly. Thrice pay, I think."

"You know best how to keep the household running. Thrice, then."

She bowed, and immediately turned, striding inside, her voice carrying with the authority of a Master of House. "No rest yet, all of you! Guests such as we've never had, and we'll outdo ourselves! Thrice pay, and I want at least thrice the speed and thrice the service!"

Tobimar forced his useless musings away, smiled to hear the enthusiastic response from within. "You have a fine household, Jeridan."

"I do, the finest in the land, I would hope. Except that of Vantage Fortress, not for lack of trying; I simply couldn't entice either Vanstell nor Lythos to come here."

"You old fraud," Poplock said. "You wouldn't replace Samni for anything, and Vanstell wouldn't know what to *do* as anything but a Master of House."

Jeridan laughed. "Your words are as true as they are sharp." He turned and bowed at the threshold. "Enter, all of you, and be welcome."

CHAPTER 49

"Good night, thank you so much for coming!" Kyri said for what seemed the thousandth time.

The door finally closed behind Minuzi and Arbiter Kelsley, and Kyri breathed a sigh of relief. "That's all of them."

"Well, all except our little group," Poplock said. His voice was somewhat muffled as he was currently stuffing a silverpeach slice into his mouth.

Tobimar stared at the little Toad. "Sand and *wind*, Poplock, are you still *eating*? I swear, you're either going to explode or turn into a ball."

"Hey, this is good stuff. I'm making up for the months on the road. You weren't exactly holding back tonight either," the little Toad answered, bouncing to Tobimar's shoulder.

Kyri stopped, looking into the huge banquet hall. "Oh, *Balance*, it's such a mess." She started in.

"Young lady, you go right to your friends in the family hall," Vanstell said. "This isn't the first party we've cleaned up after, nor even the twentieth. I appreciate your desire to help, but I am not that decrepit yet, and I'm not alone. Treidi and Riderin are already at work, and we hired the Fandre brothers a few weeks ago, if you recall." As if on cue, he raised his gaze to a medium-sized young man with dark, curly hair who was cleaning up the table. "Raltu! Do *not* try to overdo it, young man! Better to make five trips and break no dishes than three trips and break five!"

"Come on, Kyri," Tobimar said, putting his arm around her. "Let the man do his job."

She leaned against him as they walked. "*Balance*, this is going to be a long, long day."

"It was a long day by the time the sun rose," Poplock said. "What with getting this banquet prepared and all. It's only been a day and a half since you went to burn out the Curse and we ended up chasing Aran to the end of our quest."

As they reached the room, they saw Hittuma—the former Bolthawk—and Aran standing outside the door. The two knelt as she approached.

"Aran, Hittuma, why are you out here instead of in there?"

"Because you have not yet finished laying your commands upon us, Myr—"

"*Please* don't call me that!" Kyri said earnestly.

"But it *is* who you are," Aran said. "Do you expect us to forget it? Forget what we *saw*?"

"I . . ." She glanced at Tobimar, but he could see she sensed that he had his own questions in that area. "No, I guess not. But I am still Kyri Vantage, too, and the Phoenix. Call me Phoenix, and that's close enough, for I was also the rebirth of Myrionar."

"Phoenix, then," Hittuma said. "You have not yet finished laying your commands upon us, Phoenix, and . . . and I find that I do not wish to wait. I felt the eyes of the people upon me, and while they mostly withheld their open scorn, I could see that they only tolerated me for your sake."

As she began to speak, he continued, "I *know* this is deserved. I knew what I would see, and indeed there was less hatred shown me than I deserve. But I would have your commands upon me, that I might know my path."

Tobimar hid a smile; others might not be able to tell, but he could see that Kyri wasn't at all ready for this; understandably, she hadn't given the issue much thought in the past couple of days.

"Is there another reason?"

Hittuma Thorvalyn nodded. "I have lost my brother and friend. Skyharrier and I were almost as were Condor and Shrike. I have heard his screams in my dreams, and I have no stomach for celebrations now. We served evil, and we knew what we served, and still I wish it could have ended differently."

"So do I, Hittuma," Kyri said quietly.

Aran stood. "I have a...suggestion as to how we might start, if you would hear it?"

Kyri looked at him gratefully. "Of course, Aran. Does it have to do with where you went this morning?"

"Yes," Aran said. "I went to the Retreat and searched the area; you renewed the Retreat itself," and his eyes echoed Tobimar's own awe at that memory, "but other remains of the battle... were still there.

"I have recovered the Raiments: my own, of course, Bolthawk's, but also that of Skyharrier, Silver Eagle, Mist Owl and," his voice broke but continued, "Sh-Shrike. Thornfalcon's is held in the Watchland's vault.

"I would propose, then, that our first quest be to seek out the Spiritsmith and give him the tainted Raiments, that they be either destroyed or purified."

Kyri's brows rose, and then she smiled. "That is well-thought, Aran. With the war over, the Spiritsmith will return to his forge, and reaching his forge will, itself, be a trial. The Spiritsmith may himself require something of you also, simply for intruding on his forge with uninvited presences. If so, you will accept whatever commands he places upon you. Afterwards, you will return to me, and we shall see what other expiation will be in store for you."

There was no question of *whether* there would be more. While Aran was forgiven, he had chosen to share Bolthawk's fate, as the only other of the former Justiciars still living, and Bolthawk had been a false Justiciar even longer than Condor.

"It shall be done. But..." Hittuma hesitated, and then dropped to his knees once more, "I ask of you one boon, M— Phoenix."

She looked surprised, but nodded. "You may ask."

"Aran has retrieved the Raiments...but the remains of our fallen comrades he has left behind, for we knew not what should be done with them. I ask...I beg of you that they not be cast aside as worthless husks but given a proper sending, however you might say it should be done."

Tobimar was startled. "Kyri?"

Her face was a shade paler; she looked at Aran, who swallowed but nodded. "Aran...you even left your father there?"

"They were all traitors to the Balanced Sword," he answered, voice rough but no accusation in his eyes. "It was not for me to judge whether they deserved, or could ever receive, forgiveness even in death. Only *you* can judge that."

She beckoned to Tobimar, and they moved a ways down the hall, leaving the two former Justiciars to wait. "Tobimar, what do I do?"

"Why are you asking me? Terian's *Light*, you *are* Myrionar, Kyri! You have to accept that these kind of questions *are* your problem!"

"But..." she chewed her lip, thinking. "they were in service to Virigar. There's nothing to have a service *for* in that case."

"Maybe not," Poplock said. "They turned on him, and he dumped 'em. They lost their powers. Maybe that means he didn't get their spirits. Shrike hadn't died quite before Voory chased us out of the room, and he'd sure made *his* position clear."

"I can't believe we're advising a god as to how to deal with the dead," Tobimar muttered. "Even if she wasn't a god before. Kyri, don't you *know* how to handle this?"

She gave a nervous giggle. "I... sort of do, and sort of don't. It's not like I was given a bunch of training in whatever gods *do*, and really, I'm a new-born god. However Myrionar handled it before, I'm going to have to figure it out myself, because *that* version of Myrionar *ended* then. Now I have to live on into the future and someday when I know how, I go back and close the loop. Maybe. I don't think even *that* is guaranteed, somehow."

"Voorith might have tried to grab at least one or two of their souls, but he got kinda interrupted by Blackwart," Poplock said, continuing his train of thought. "And at the end, Virigar was fighting for his life, so I'm pretty sure he didn't have the *chance* to go grabbing for people who were dead or dying."

"You're saying that their souls just might still be waiting on the threshold, and if I don't do *something*, they could get taken by something else. Or start wandering, go revenant, that kind of thing."

"Kyri... the conditions under which they died were horrific. Tailor-made to cause something very bad to happen if their souls don't get to move on in some manner," Tobimar said.

She was silent a moment, then looked at him with her gray eyes wide and serious. "Tobimar... what would you think if—"

"Stop." He held up his hand. "You're *Myrionar*. Maybe you don't know all of what that means, but *you* have to make your decision. Don't base it on what *I*—or anyone else—will think. You are the judge. And *only* you, for things having to do with your temple and faith, and if this isn't about your temple and your faith and your people...I don't know what is."

She looked at him, and then nodded her head slowly. With a deep breath, she turned around and strode back to the others. "Hittuma Thorvalyn, I will grant you—and Aran Shrikeson—this boon," she said, and her voice shook the hall; silver, gold, and sapphire light shimmered about her, and even Tobimar was seized with a momentary impulse to kneel.

Kyri—Myrionar—went on: "Your comrades—Shrike, Mist Owl, Skyharrier, and Silver Eagle—fell defending their friends and fighting against my greatest enemy, no longer in service to the power that ensnared them. In the name of Mercy, I give you leave to have them sent on in My name, and if their spirits still linger, they shall come to the Fortress Beyond and I shall judge them fairly."

Bolthawk and Aran both bowed to the ground, and Bolthawk said, with a trembling voice, "Thank you, Phoenix."

She knelt before them, and the fearsome majesty was gone. Only Kyri Vantage reached out and took their hands. "You've lost your father twice, Aran. Go put him to rest. And Bolthawk—Hittuma—send your friends to a far better place. No matter how they may be judged...it *will* be better than what he would have given them."

"Aye," Hittuma said, voice still unsteady. He gripped her hand tightly. "As Shrike would have said, aye, that it will, even if you send them to dark judgment indeed. I thank your mercy...the same mercy my little sister always had."

He stood suddenly and bowed. Without another word, he set off down the hall, face working; Tobimar saw tears as the Child of Odin passed him. Aran pressed Kyri's hand once more, bowed to Tobimar, and hurried after his friend.

Kyri shook her head. "I don't *feel* so different...except when I do. Tobimar, how am I supposed to handle this?"

Tobimar tried to laugh, failed miserably. Instead, he just stared at her silently for a moment. Finally, he said, "How am *I* supposed to handle it? I love you, Kyri Vantage, Phoenix, but can a mortal man love a god?"

Kyri opened her mouth, but she, too, fell silent. For long

moments they stared at each other, and Tobimar felt a chill fall over him. She didn't know the answer any more than he did.

A loud snort made them both jump. "Oh, *mudbubbles*, both of you. Gods fall in love with mortals *all the time*," Poplock said with exasperation. "Look at Aegeia; they say half the population can trace their ancestry back to one of the gods or another! Blackwart's *NAME*, look at your own family, Tobimar—how do you think Terian's blood ended up *in* your family line?"

Poplock bounced on Tobimar's head hard enough to stun him, leapt to Kyri's shoulder and smacked her gently in the side of the head. "Stop *worrying* about these things, you two. You aren't different people, you've just got different powers and some new problems, and you really just need to stop overthinking this!"

And suddenly the nebulous fear that had held him since he first saw the Phoenix become the Balanced Sword lifted, and he laughed, and saw her laughing, laughing so hard that suddenly she had to lean against the wall.

"Oh... ohhhhh, Tobimar, ow, my ribs, that hurts..." she finally gasped. "But... once again..."

He reached out and embraced her. "Yes, once again... we should just do what the Toad says."

CHAPTER 50

"I'm so terribly sorry, Watchl—"

"You need to get out of the apology habit, Kyri," Jeridan said, looking up from his place at the smaller table in the Vantage private chambers. "No one here will demand you keep to a schedule, and I assure you that I have been far from bored talking with Light Miri and Hiriista."

Kyri opened her mouth, realized that she was about to apologize for apologizing, and then—for the second time in about ten minutes—found herself laughing so hard her sides hurt. Tobimar put an arm around her, grinning broadly. Poplock bounced down, landed on the table, and started rooting around in the various snacks.

Finally she recovered, and took her seat next to the Watchland. "What have you all been talking about?"

"Mostly about Kaizatenzei," Miri said. "You told him the story of your adventures, of course, but the Watchland has a greater interest in our country as such, so he's been, well, *interrogating* me on everything about it—purely in a friendly manner, of course," she put in hastily, "but . . . you know, sir, you're forcing me to actually realize that I wasn't paying as much attention to the country as I thought." She tilted her head. "I suspect that Lady Shae could answer your questions better."

"Most certainly," Hiriista said. "Lady Shae administered the country, while you were more her troubleshooter—even if, as we later discovered, you were technically the mastermind."

"Well, she *thought* she was the mastermind," Poplock said, nibbling on something. "But Master Wieran was running that show by the end, and of course the big V was the top of the scheming pyramid."

The Watchland glanced around. "Where are Hittuma and Aran?"

"On a personal mission," Kyri answered, and explained briefly. "That was one of the things that delayed me."

"That and seeing off the rest of the few hundred guests, yes," the Watchland said. "It is well. And I will certainly give them Thornfalcon's Raiment to take with them. That was an excellent suggestion on Aran's part. What do you think the Spiritsmith will do?"

Kyri thought back to her interactions with the Spiritsmith, the many conversations she'd had with him, and what had happened afterwards. "Honestly? I think he's going to probably dismantle them completely and forge new Raiments as new Justiciars are selected. The old Justiciar's *names* are tainted, too."

Tobimar nodded thoughtfully. "I hadn't thought about that, but you're right. A new Myrionar, a rebuilt Retreat, makes sense to have new Justiciars."

"You have anyone in mind?" Poplock asked.

"You volunteering?" Kyri asked with a grin.

"Oh, no no no no! Not me. Definitely not my kind of thing. Now maybe *Miri* over there..."

Miri blushed a lovely shade of rose, something Kyri had to admit she somewhat envied; that light skin color was so rare, and Miri carried it well. "I...no, I really can't, at least, not now. Still so much to do in Kaizatenzei—I'm going to have to go back soon, now that we know you're not in danger anymore."

"I wouldn't say that," Jeridan said gravely. "The great war may be over, in the sense that the coordinated attacks have ended, and the Black City banished. But unless I greatly miss my guess, it will be a long time before peace as we knew it before returns to Zarathan as a whole."

The truth of his words fell over Kyri like a sodden blanket. *Dalthunia's still held by...whatever took it over under Kerlamion and Virigar's plan. I haven't any idea how badly the Army of the Dragon, or the forces of the Archmage, suffered in their siege of the Black City, but they couldn't have escaped unscathed. No one knows what happened in Aegeia yet. Artania's going to be rebuilding for years.*

Then she forced herself to sit up a little straighter and banished that dark line of thought. "You're probably right, Watchland—but then that just makes Miri's presence even better. It's time we *cleaned out* Rivendream Pass. It's time that it become Heavenbridge Way again, as it was before the last Chaoswar severed our connections."

"Now that we know that Justice and Vengeance are just the other side of our mountains, yes!" Miri said. She frowned suddenly. "But with the Sun and Stars all gone..."

"I know," Kyri said. "But all the good that is there isn't going to vanish overnight, and—if I'm right—a lot of the corruption in the surrounding forest came from Sanamaveridion, yes?"

"Almost certainly," Hiriista said. "Now that there are no longer secrets being kept from me, I was able to delve into the surviving archives, including some of the materials that Poplock salvaged during our evacuation of Wieran's laboratory and kindly gave to me to study. The power of the Stars and Sun effectively sealed Sanamaveridion's power and influence away, forcing them underground and water to, in effect, flow back to the surface outside of the established barrier. Thus the corrupt forest and the Pass of Shadows, what you call Rivendream.

"But Sanamaveridion has, himself, been removed. There is no longer an active force of great evil sealed beneath Enneisolaten. The combination *should* mean that if we remain strong and true to the principles of the Light, we should be able to maintain Kaizatenzei much as it is, at least for some decades."

"But we do need allies. And so do you," Miri said, smiling at the Watchland. "I'm so *happy* to find out that you're actually on our side! I'd been *sure*, from what we'd learned, that at *best* we'd be coming to a country without a ruler."

"It could easily have been exactly that. Or worse," Jeridan replied. "And I agree that I much prefer it this way, especially as it gives me the opportunity to open relations with such a wondrous land. I must travel there myself, meet with your Lady Shae. In fact, I would say I should do so very soon."

Thinking about the situation in Kaizatenzei reminded Kyri of something she had been worried about. "Miri, I hate to bring this up—but you and Shae have basically betrayed everything that

Kerlamion represents. Won't he be, to put it mildly, extremely displeased with you? And if he can't take out his displeasure on the Werewolf King..."

Miri laughed, and there was the sharp edge to her smile that showed the dangerous warrior that hid behind the sparkling façade. "Oh, Father is undoubtedly furious with us beyond measure. But... Kyri, you have no idea what a defeat he has just been given! The Black City forced back against his will? The *Great Seal* shattered by a handful of *children* in his throne room?"

She grinned again. "We still have a few...lines of communication we can use, and the cost of this setback was tremendous; half the city is severely damaged, and several of Father's most important generals are either dead from the action, or have disappeared, perhaps fleeing from expected punishment or merely deciding that this complete fiasco indicates that even Kerlamion is not eternal. Voorith and Yergoth of the *Mazolishta* were killed in their manifest forms and will take a long time to recover, Balgotha hasn't been heard from at *all* since the battle and some suspect he suffered the final death, Kurildis simply went silent, and even Balinshar's disappeared."

She shook her head. "No, while he is undoubtedly furious with us, Kerlamion will not be able to spare energy or time to move against us for a long time. I wouldn't be surprised if some of the others actually try a coup, Erherveria especially, as for once the urgings of his true nature and the Curse of Blackness will be completely in accord on the need to throw down the ruler of All Hells and take his place."

"Well, that's great news!" Poplock said.

"Good news indeed," Lythos said, entering. "There is evil enough in the world without the Lord of All Hells intervening."

"But, Miri—what about the Five? The children you mentioned, our friends? What happened to them?" Tobimar was tense, which wasn't surprising. Kyri was worried about that too, but Tobimar and Poplock had always been closer to Xavier than she was.

Miri looked down. "No one saw or heard anything else from them. They...they might have—"

"No, they're okay," Poplock said with certainty.

"You're sounding confident on that. Why?"

"Well, two reasons. First, Khoros was pretty darn self-satisfied about that part of his plan. I could tell. And even if he *is* willing to take whatever means he can to get to his end, I don't think he'd have been happy about sacrificing them all. Second, when they told us their stories, one thing they mentioned was that Khoros said they couldn't go *home* until the Seal was broken. Something about the way they were brought here.

"So I'm thinking that as soon as the seal broke, they ended up going home."

Tobimar looked as relieved as Kyri felt. "Makes sense. And now that you mention it, didn't Xavier say that Khoros promised him he'd be able to complete his hunt for the person that killed his brother?"

"Yep. So obviously he'd have to have survived that mess to be able to go home and do the job. With the seal gone, maybe they'll even be able to come back and visit sometime."

Lythos nodded. "It is possible. Their world will be changing, and perhaps, with luck, we will have the opportunity to help them."

There was something more pressing in Kyri's mind, though. "Miri? You...haven't said anything about Aegeia. Do you know anything?"

Tobimar gripped her hand; he knew that her little sister Urelle had decided to emulate her big sister and go off to be a hero, following their former bodyguard Ingram Camp-Bel to his homeland of Aegeia, and Aunt Victoria had set off immediately in pursuit.

Miri frowned. "Not as much, unfortunately. Aegeia was Viedra...I mean, Virigar's own project too. Or rather the person who was overseeing it was under his direction, not Kerlamion's. But," she said, seeing Kyri's expression, "but we do know that things didn't go the way they wanted. No one has details, but despite what was described as a Godswar, it seems that the Lady of Wisdom remains incarnate."

"I have to get there soon," Kyri said after a moment. "And even though we know the demon siege was broken, I know you need to get home to Skysand, Tobimar."

Tobimar brightened. "Yes. With good news. The *best* news." His smile faded a touch. "That will be a *long* trip, though, and... well, Kyri, I had hoped you could come with me. I know Poplock will, but—"

"Of *course* she will come with you," the Watchland said firmly. "Now that you have dealt with the rot at the heart of our land, Kyri, Tobimar, Poplock, the safety and strength of

Evanwyl is *my* responsibility, not yours. I can neither command
Myrionar, nor Myrionar's Justiciars, and certainly not someone
who embodies both."

Kyri felt a rising hope, a lightness and joy that was completely
unexpected, and wondered. *What...?*

And suddenly she realized that, inside, she had been sure that
Evanwyl would be, would *remain* her responsibility, or worse, that
as a god she would be forced to leave the world, to ascend...
elsewhere, wherever the gods went, and that Tobimar's fears had
more foundation than even Poplock wanted to admit.

But the Watchland was telling her *that is not true.*

"I...can," she said slowly. "I can leave Evanwyl...and come
back any time I choose."

Jeridan raised an eyebrow, and then laughed. "You truly thought
you *couldn't*, didn't you? That being who you were *bound* you?"

"Oh, Kyri—you're an *incarnate god*," Miri said, shaking her
head. "You're the least bound of any of us—unless you bind
yourself. The oaths of the gods have no hold on you, and even
less the requirements of mortality."

*And that probably scares me more than anything else. I have
power I don't understand, and absolutely nothing and no one
except myself accountable for it.*

But then she looked at Tobimar, and realized that she'd had
the same fears all along. *And as long as I worry about that, I'm
probably going to be all right.*

"The world's still going to be at war for a while," she said,
and reached out and took Tobimar's hand. "All the more reason
that these three adventurers not stay in one place."

Tobimar surprised her with a sudden embrace and a kiss.
"Then—"

"—Then we should get ready to go," Kyri said, a completely...
normal excitement and nervousness that felt so very *right* starting
to flood through her. "After all...you need to introduce me to
your family, don't you?"

The room filled with laughter, and Kyri suddenly knew that
she'd been wrong.

She wasn't someone else. She was Myrionar, but that didn't
mean she was not Kyri Victoria Vantage, because Myrionar was
also her. She wasn't less herself.

She was just *more.*

CHAPTER 51

Tobimar felt his heart hammering in his chest as he paced the deck. *This is ridiculous. I've faced dark dragons and monsters and the Slayer of Gods himself. And I'm shaking like a tent in a sandstorm at the thought of coming home.*

But no Skysand in exile had *ever* come home. The exile was for twenty-four years... but twenty-four years of delving into dark secrets had apparently ensured that none would return.

I'm coming home in triumph! *Why am I...*

"You're gonna wear a hole in the deck, and then that old Sauran's gonna kick you off the boat," Poplock said from the railing nearby.

That did get a faint smile. "If thousands of years sailing haven't put holes in this deck, I don't think I'm going to manage it." He looked up, seeing T'Oltha standing high on the bridge deck above. *As my journey started, so it ends. Sailing on the* Lucramalalla.

Of course, it had taken a lot less time. Kyri had helped... cheat. Teleportation and gateways were still uncertain things, but being a god, even a new god, gave her leeway. She couldn't cross the Khalals—apparently the disruptions there were intense indeed—but in great flashing jumps, one every few days, they had bounded across the face of Zarathan, from Evanwyl to the Odinsforge, bypassing the patrols of Dalthunia, from the Odinsforge to T'Tera, from there to Zarathanton, and finally to Shipton, where they had found the *Lucramalalla* completing its loading on the docks.

It would have been far swifter to have taken a ship from Tor Port in the Empire of the Mountain, but none of them had ever been there, or anywhere near it, so Kyri had no image, no real

317

vision of that place, to use as a guide. He suspected that if she exerted her powers she could probably have found a vision of it that could guide her, but Kyri clearly didn't want to abuse her powers overly much, and was still learning their extent.

He could understand that, and approved of it, really. He didn't know anything about his *own* limits, now. The power of Terian had been awakened in him and was not disappearing. He had probably used up the extra...boost that the Sun's energy had given him, but the star-blue power still waited within him.

Really, it should have been a *good* thing that it took time. It *was* a good thing. He and Kyri had finally been able to spend time with each other, talking deep into the night for weeks, standing at the rail just watching the sea together, occasionally being called to assist the crew when something threatened the ship—for the seaways had become more dangerous with the unleashing of the powers in the great war.

And he'd stood by her side and just held her as they sailed past Aegeia, which had not yet opened itself to the world. Whatever had happened to Urelle and Victoria, Kyri would not know for some time yet.

But at the same time...sailing left him with too much time to think. When you were travelling cross-country, you had plenty of things to keep you busy. And knowing what had happened at home...knowing that Terimur and Sundrilin would not be there to see him, to welcome him home, that many of the people he knew had fallen defending Skysand while he was away...

"I think I see something, Tobimar," said Kyri quietly.

His head snapped up instantly, and he found himself halfway up the rail, staring, looking...

Yes.

A spire was there, just becoming visible over the horizon. *The Great Tower, the One within the Seven Lesser.*

The towers are still standing.

Somehow just seeing that, knowing that at the least the towers stood, released some of the tension. He could *see* Skysand now, see that no matter what the ravages of war, it was still there, still standing defiantly against the strength of the desert. The Smoking Lighthouse also rose up to one side, the mostly quiescent volcano at the head of the port sending a thin trail of steam and vapor high into the air.

"Is that it?"

"That's it. That's Skysand, Kyri. My home."

"Then let's not wait any longer."

He looked at her in surprise, and she smiled. "Oh, Tobimar, I can see you're so tense you're going to snap like a frayed bowstring if we wait. And now that I can see where I'm going, it's not a problem."

"Well..." He suddenly laughed. "All right, Kyri, you know me. Let's go get our things together."

It didn't take more than a half-hour to pack everything; after everything they'd gone through, they were in the habit of leaving as much packed as possible, just in case. Poplock, of course, was waiting for them impatiently. "Can't wait to see what kind of a table your family sets," the little Toad said.

"So that's your ambition, to eat your way across Zarathan."

"I can think of worse! But I've never been here, so I'll bet there's all sorts of new delicacies. And probably new bugs to eat, too. Never tried a scorpion, but one of my second cousins once said—"

"Enough about your stomach!" Kyri gave Poplock an affectionate rap on the head. "I know you're almost as nervous as we are. This is a huge event for your people, isn't it?"

Tobimar nodded. "The biggest, really."

"Then stand straight and *be proud*, because you know they will be."

Tobimar concentrated, and with not a little effort brought up the meditations of *Tor*. His heart slowed, he saw more clearly, more surely, and realized that in truth he was more worried about things more personal than just his homecoming.

Which was ridiculous; was there even the *faintest* possibility that his mother, the Lord of Waters, would disapprove of Kyri? Of course not. Yet the nervousness remained, and he suddenly grinned at himself. *And the adventurer is reminded that he is still human.*

He turned to look up. "Captain, we are departing a bit ahead of schedule."

T'Oltha nodded. "The fact that you return tells me that I will have good fortune. I will expect a celebration by the time we make port, yes?"

"I...would not be surprised. And you are invited, personally. I began this journey with you, and it was you who sent me to the First City, when I would have chosen elsewhere."

The huge Sauran gave a complete Armed Bow. "Then I accept, with honor. Go, then."

He grasped Kyri's hand. "Can you tell exactly *where* you're going?"

"I can see . . . the seven towers around the one you described. I could put us anywhere there, or in the city around . . ." Kyri's eyes shimmered with blue-gold fire.

Silver, blue, and gold . . . the colors of Myrionar. I wonder why *those colors.* "Put us in front of the Great Tower, then. The Lord of Waters will be holding court there now."

She nodded and closed her eyes.

Golden fire bloomed around them, a fire that invigorated and warmed and did not burn, and then blazed like the sun. When the light faded, Tobimar saw the great double doors, set in a frame that curled upward like a flame or the shape of the tower's peak itself, the doors of pure black set with silver runes and the single golden sigil of Terian, the doors of the palace flung wide for petitioners and friends.

The doors of home.

All around them were startled people, staring; and then a voice called from the steps, "Tobimar? *TOBIMAR?*"

Murmurs sprang up as Vancilar, his oldest brother, sprinted down the steps. "Tobimar? It *is* you! But how . . . why? You know you cannot—"

"Vancilar, I know. I know the traditions as well as any of us." He looked into his brother's dark-brown eyes, waited until he had his full attention. "The youngest of the Skysand knows full well what is demanded of him, and says to his oldest and wisest of brothers that he must be brought immediately to speak with the Lord of Waters."

As he had expected, the formality cut off the questions. This was not something to be discussed on the threshold, but only in the presence of the ruler of Skysand.

Vancilar nodded. "Then I bid you follow, Tobimar, and if your companion would as well, for the Lord of Waters holds court today."

As they mounted the steps and entered the Great Tower, Tobimar saw the others waiting glance back, see Vancilar and Tobimar and Kyri, and step aside. The whispers and mutters increased, and there was a fearful edge in some of those glances, a hopeful tinge to others' voices, for they knew that Tobimar's return could mean only one of two things.

The doors to the Throneroom of Fountains were also flung wide, and from within Tobimar could hear a voice so familiar that it brought tears to his eyes, his mother's voice, calm and reasoning, dissecting some problem brought before her and showing her people the way to its solution.

She glanced up—her hair now pure white, not a trace of the few black strands that had been there five, six years ago when he had departed—and froze, staring at him in shock, fear and hope momentarily clear on her face before she regained control.

She straightened in her throne, and gestured for the way to be cleared.

Now they walked across the black and gold polished granite of the Throneroom, and their steps echoed in the startled silence. He stopped precisely eight steps from the throne and then knelt. "The youngest and least of her sons greets the wise and ageless Lord of Waters, and begs that she will hear him at this time," he said. Beside him, he felt Kyri duplicate his gesture, saying nothing. Poplock, of course, merely balanced and watched.

There was a pause, then his mother spoke. "May the Spring of the Court flow ever for you, my son. The Lord of Waters must indeed hear you, and grave indeed is the occasion, for you have returned to this land far before the term of your Seeker's Exile. Rise and speak."

He rose, heart once more hammering, but now with anticipation. *I daydreamed about this. I think all of us did as children. Mother did, I know. And now...*

"O Lord of Waters, what you say is even so. But I say to you that this is because my term is ended."

Her eyes widened, blue eyes so like his own shimmering with disbelieving hope. "Then—"

With a great laugh, he abandoned formality, leapt up the stairs, caught his mother's hands. "I have found that which was lost, Mother! I know from whence we came! I have faced our enemies and touched the Sun, and the power of Terian itself has touched me!"

He raised his hand, turning to face the crowd, and let a blaze of blue-white godsfire ignite like a torch of stars. "The curse is lifted, the ban is broken!"

"The ban is broken, and Mother...Mother, I have come home!"

GAZETTEER FOR ZARATHAN

NOTE: Some elements of the Gazetteer are spoilers for *Phoenix Rising* and *Phoenix in Shadow*.

Overview

Zarathan (more properly Zahr-a-Thana, World of Magic) is a planet of generally Earth size and composition. It is presumed to be the source of all magic in all universes. The main continent (and the only continent commonly known) stretches approximately four thousand, eight hundred miles north to south and, at its widest, is about the same east to west (it averages between two and three thousand east-west over most of its extent, however). It can be generally divided into three regions: Southern Zarathan, which is most of the continent south of the Khalal mountain range, Northern Zarathan which is everything north of the Khalals plus the very large island/miniature continent of Artania, and Elyvias, a subcontinent peninsula shaped something like a gigantic Cape Cod and separated from Southern Zarathan by the Barricade Mountains.

The history, geography, and peoples of Zarathan are all affected greatly by the apparently cyclical "Chaoswars" which bring periodic conflict to the world and are associated with massive mystical/deific disturbances which, among other effects, distort or erase memories and even records of prior events—up to and including those of the gods. Thus, while the generally known history of Zarathan stretches back over half a million years, clear records are rarely available for anything older than the most recent Chaoswar, and even the gods themselves can only partially answer questions pertaining to events beforehand.

Countries

There are several countries on this continent, but it should be made clear that "country" on Zarathan is not quite the same as "country" in the modern civilized world of Earth. Most of the area claimed as a country's territory is actually relatively wild and untamed and dangerous; only cleared areas around cities and major roads tend to be safe for travel. The overall population of the countries is therefore much lower than might be expected, given that the average standard of living is closer to that of twentieth-century Earth in many ways than it is to the medieval era that one might first assume, seeing no factories and noticing that the sword is still a common weapon. Following is a list of the important countries of Zarathan (there are others not listed, but these are the ones significant either overall, or specifically for the *Balanced Sword* trilogy):

STATE OF THE DRAGON GOD

Called variously the *State of the Dragon God*, *The Dragon-King's Domain*, *The State of Elbon Nomicon*, and other appellations, the actual name for this country is a very long string of Ancient Sauran words that boiled down means something like "The Country founded in the days of the Dragon-God's First Creation, That Endures Eternally." It is the largest country on the planet, stretching from the western edge of Southern Zarathan all the way to the Barricade Mountains in the east, and from the southern coast all the way to the Ice Peaks in the north. In a governmental sense, the State of the Dragon God might best be described as a theocratic libertarian state.

The capital of the State of the Dragon God is called in Ancient Sauran *Fanalam' T' ameris' a' u' Zahr-a-Thana T'ikon*, but commonly (and to the Saurans and Dragons, painfully) called simply "Zarathanton." It is the most ancient city, and the largest, on the continent, with some buildings over five hundred thousand years old and a population of roughly 200,000 inside and immediately outside its walls. Other important cities within the State of the Dragon God borders include T'Tera (also called the Dragon God's City), Artani (a city of trade with the *Artan* of the Forest Sea), Dragonkill, Bridgeway, Odinsforge (also the name of the mountain range in which it is set), Salandar, Thologondoreave (an independent city of the Children of Odin), Shipton (known to the Saurans as *Olthamian' a' ameris*) and Hell's Edge.

THE EMPIRE OF THE MOUNTAIN

Nearly as large as the Dragon God's country, the Empire of the Mountain actually straddles the Khalals, claiming much of the territory north of the Ice Peaks to the Khalals and some territory to the north and east above them. Ruled in unbroken power for hundreds of thousands of years by the God-Emperor Idinus, most powerful wizard ever to live, the Empire has always had an uneasy relationship with its neighbors. While Idinus is not, strictly speaking, evil, he has motives and goals that are unclear to others and this has led on occasion to war on a titanic scale. The capital of the Empire of the Mountain is Scimitar's Path, at the base of Mount Scimitar—tallest peak of the Khalal range at sixty thousand feet. There are several other cities, the most important of which are Kheldragaard to the west and Tor Port in the east. It is an ironclad theocracy ruled directly by the Archmage himself from atop Mount Scimitar—where he remains virtually always.

DALTHUNIA

Dalthunia used to be an ally state to the Dragon God, a modest-sized country which broke away from the Empire due to a very bad set of mis-steps by some of the Empire's local rulers, eventually triggering a local revolution. For some reason the Archmage—after a short demonstration of his power which showed that if he wished, he could take Dalthunia back at any time—allowed Dalthunia to remain independent. At the time of the story, however, Dalthunia has been a conquered state—whether by internal revolution or some subtle external invasion is unclear—for a couple of centuries, and very little is known about it other than that they do not welcome visitors. They clearly have powerful magic and probably deific patrons, because scrying and ordinary espionage have not been effective. The capital of Dalthunia is Kymael, named after the instigator of the revolution.

EVANWYL

A small country between the northeastern portion of Hell's Rim, the Khalals, and the Broken Hills, Evanwyl is an almost forgotten country at the time of The Balanced Sword trilogy; its great claim to fame used to be its connection to the civilization that lay on the other side of Heavenbridge Way, the only useful pass through the Khalals. But that was before something happened during the last Chaoswar, something that turned the other side to the monstrous Moonshade Hollow and the Heavenbridge Way into Rivendream Pass. Now Evanwyl's only function is keeping the things that exit from Rivendream Pass from entering the larger world.

Governmentally, Evanwyl is a monarchy (ruled by the Watchland) with the monarch's power moderated by his subordinates and advisors the Eyes and Arms, and by the powerful influence of the faith of Myrionar, the Balanced Sword, especially as embodied in the Justiciars of Myrionar and the high priest called the Arbiter. The city of Evanwyl is the capital; its population is between four and five thousand people in total.

Evanwyl is the focus of the trilogy overall, as it is the homeland of Kyri Vantage and the place where the three heroes first join forces...and to which they must return.

SKYSAND

Situated on the far northeast corner of the continent, Skysand is a country which is mostly desert with considerable volcanic features and with some interior and coastal oases (around which are built its few cities). A theocratic monarchy, Skysand is ruled by the Silverun family under a complex set of rules administered and watched over by the temples of Terian, the Mortal God; the capital is also named Skysand and is situated in a natural harbor with a periodically active but generally harmless volcano on the southern side. Cut off from the rest of the land by the high and volcanic Flamewall Mountains, Skysand trades by sea with other countries around the continent, its most prominent exports being magical gemstones which are found in great quantity and diverse assortments in the desert and mountains.

ARTANIA

A huge island or small continent a thousand miles long and a few hundred wide, Artania is the claimed homeland of the youngest of the major species on Zarathan, the *Artan* (sometimes called Elves). Few other than the *Artan* are allowed beyond the capital city, Nya-Sharee-Hilya (which means "Surviving the Storm of Ages"); this city is run on rather militaristic lines but it's uncertain as to whether this reflects the overall government, or the fact that the city is often the focal point of invasion attempts.

WHITE BLADE STATE

Located in a circle of mountains in the far northwest of the main continent, the White Blade State is a rotating monarchy, with rulership cycling regularly between the ruling families of the five main cities. How the individual cities determine their ruling families varies, making governmental changeovers... interesting at times. Naturally this also means the capital city changes with regularity. The "White Blade" is a symbolic, but extremely powerful, sword which is held by the current ruler; it is said to be the gift of the patron god of the White Blade, Chromaias, and each of the five cities are devoted to and named after one of the five gods of that faith (Chromaias, Stymira [Thanamion], Amanora, Taralandira [Mulios], and Kharianda).

AEGEIA

A small country walled off from the rest of the continent by the mountain range called Wisdom's Fortress, Aegeia is a theocratic state which is ruled much of the time by a council of twelve nobles, but at other times by the literal incarnate Goddess of Wisdom, Athena, in the capital city of Aegis.

ODINSFORGE RANGE/THOLOGONDOREAVE

The Children of Odin claim this as their homeland, and politically the entire mountain range is treated as a sort of neutral ground with the Children of Odin having priority in disputes. The area immediately surrounding the general location of Thologondoreave ("Cavern of a Thousand Hammers") is acknowledged to be sovereign territory of the Children of Odin; as the exact location of Thologondoreave is a well-kept secret from most people, with powerful enchantments and even deific protection, in practice this makes most of the Odinsforge Range their country, an island in the middle of the State of the Dragon King.

PONDSPARKLE

Possibly the smallest country in the world, Pondsparkle consists of one small city and the surrounding area near a small lake a few miles in extent. Pondsparkle is the permanent home for a large number (several thousand) of the Intelligent Toads and the site of the first and still primary temple to their god, Blackwart the Great.

KAIZATENZEI

A country unknown to the outside world until *Phoenix in Shadow*, Kaizatenzei is a country set in the midst of Moonshade Hollow—and is every bit as beautiful, fruitful, and pleasant as Rivendream Pass and the outer part of Moonshade Hollow are monstrous, corrupt, and deadly.

The name of the country translates to "The Unity of Seven Lights," with the Seven Lights of the name being seven cities or very large villages which served as the center of safety and power against the evil surrounding them, and who began working together once they discovered each other's existence. The discovery of what was called the Light of Unity caused them to found a reasonably central capital city called Sha Kaizatenzei Valatar, which means something like "soul-light heart city of the Unity of Seven Lights."

The creation of Kaizatenzei was originally guided by two demonlords, Emirinovas and Kalshae, who were instrumental in the downfall of the Lords of the Sky and the imprisonment of the Elderwyrm Sanamaveridion, whom they had tricked into being one of their weapons in the initial assault. However, in the process of attempting to extract the power of the "Seven Lights," aka the Seven Stars of Terian, they created a powerful land of purity which eventually affected them; now simply called Light Miri and Lady Shae, the events of *Phoenix in Shadow* transformed them into agents of the Light. *Phoenix Ascendant* begins with our heroes still in Kaizatenzei.

Other Locations

ELYVIAS

Not, strictly speaking, a country, but a subcontinent, Elyvias used to be a larger portion of the continent, with additional area extending up nearly to Tor Port, but according to legend a battle between Elbon Nomicon and the Archmage Idinus caused a cataclysmic restructuring of the whole area, sinking a large chunk of the continent and creating the distorted conditions within. Elyvias has several countries and significant cities within its borders (Firestream Falls, Shuronogromal, Thunder Port, Thelhi-Man-Su, Zeikor, Artilus) but is severely cut off from the rest of the world both by the physical barriers of the Barricade Mountains, Blackdust Plateau, and Cataclysm Ridge, and by the mystical disruption called the Maelwyrd which surrounds the entire peninsula to a range of up to forty miles, with only a mile or two of clear-sailing space inside the Maelwyrd, near land. Magic also tends to work differently in Elyvias and the civilizations there have developed differently in the last several thousand years.

THE FOREST SEA

Stretching from the Great Road and the Odinsforge Range in the east to the Barricade Range in the east, the Forest Sea presses against the Ice Peaks and surges around them in the east, up into the Empire of the Mountain. Stretching for three thousand miles, the Forest Sea is broken only by tiny enclaves within it and by the narrow clear-cuts around the cities and Great Roads. Somewhere within is hidden the Suntree, which the *Artan* on the main continent use as temple and center, but most of it is utterly unexplored, filled with danger and possibility.

"HELL" AND HELL'S RIM

Created, it is said, from a cataclysmic mystical confrontation between the powerful Demons and the Great Dragons in the days before human beings walked the planet, the region called "Hell" is a place of twisted, distorted magics, impossible conflicting terrain, and monsters found nowhere else. No coherent picture has emerged of the place within, and few even attempt to go there;

passing Hell's Rim, a steep barrier of high peaks, would be too much effort for most anyway. The only pass through those peaks is sealed off by the fortress city, Hell's Edge, which exists almost solely as a barrier between "Hell" and the rest of the world.

ICE PEAKS

Like "Hell" and Elyvias, the Ice Peaks are a reminder of one of the conflicts of history, though long enough ago that the precise nature of the event isn't known. The Peaks are magical, solidified ice for the most part, meaning that they are beautiful, transparent or translucent, and very, very hard to pass, given they have nothing growing on them. They form one of the natural borders between the State of the Dragon God and the Empire of the Mountain.

People of Zarathan

Many different species share this continent—many relatively peacefully, others... somewhat less so. Following is a summary of the most significant peoples of this world.

HUMANS

Human beings on Zarathan are basically the same as they are on Earth. Generalists, humans are something of the chameleons of the civilizations, showing up in any profession, any part of the world, in large numbers. They are probably the most common of the intelligent species.

INTELLIGENT TOADS

Called the *Sylanningathalinde*, or "Golden-eyed," by the Saurans, the Toads claim to be the oldest of the intelligent species, even pre-dating the Dragons and Demons. They are in general a fun-loving but insular people, and mostly stay near to the pond they are born and raised in. Toads are given one name in their larval (tadpole) stage and, when adults, choose a significant second name. They vary tremendously in size, from dwarfed individuals a few inches long up to some four feet from nose to rump and weighing two hundred pounds. Some small number of them do find that the "ground chafes their feet," or in other words have wanderlust; these tend to be quite effective adventurers.

SAURANS

Averaging eight feet in height with massive bodies, armored tails, heavy, clawed feet and arms, and a head sporting a very large fanged mouth, Saurans resemble nothing so much as a miniature Godzilla. They claim to be direct descendants of the Great Dragons, and the Ancient Saurans—somewhat larger and clearly superior in many ways—are supposedly ranked as equals with the Dragons. There are very few Ancient Saurans left. Generally even-tempered, and a good thing, since when angered they are terribly dangerous.

ARTAN

Very humanlike, Artan tend to the delicate in appearance, with hair and eyes of exotic colors; they are extremely controlled in emotional displays as a rule. They often live in wilder areas—forests and mountains—but not, despite some assumptions, because they like to live "close to nature"; they prefer to be hard to find and have a sort of racial paranoia that they are still being hunted by some nameless adversaries who supposedly chased them from beyond the stars to Zarathan. The Rohila are technically the same species, but are otherwise separated from them in culture, behavior, and associations, aside from being also isolationist.

CHILDREN OF ODIN/ODINSYRNEN

Short, broad, tough as stone, these appear to be—and in many ways are—the classic dwarves. However, they are not a species of hard-drinking and fighting warriors, despite appearances and the fact that their patron pantheon includes Odin and Thor. According to their legends they were literally created by Odin, who forged them in Asgard from the heart of a world, using Thor's hammer to do the striking. While their greatest city is indeed underground, the Children of Odin are equally at home above ground and are nearly as flexible in choice of profession and environments as human beings.

WINGED FOLK/SAELAR

Generally human in appearance but with a set of huge but compactable wings, the Saelar are almost certainly the result of some mage's experimentation a few Chaoswars ago. The records are, however, lost, and they breed as true as any, so they are now an uncommon but widely-spread species, most heavily concentrated in the region of the Broken Hills.

MAZAKH

Often called "snake-demons," "snake-men," and other more deroga-
tory terms, the *mazakh* were originally the creation of the demons
they worship (the *Mazolishta*) who literally constructed them from a
number of other species. In appearance they are actually somewhat
less snakelike and more like small raptorian dinosaurs. Generally
raised in a hostile culture that trains them for warfare and lack of
empathy, the *mazakh* are still not inherently evil and some leave
the service of the *Mazolishta* and join the greater societies above;
these are called *khallit*. The few *mazakh* living in Kaizatenzei are
unaware of their origin and share their civilization and behavior
with the mostly-human natives of that country.

SHELLIKAKI

Relatively rare, Shellikaki are essentially intelligent land-dwelling
hermit crabs. Whether they were the creations of some sort of life-
sculpting mage from many Chaoswars ago, or the result of "natural"
magical evolution is unknown. Slow in movement, the Shellikaki are
known for both their immense strength (most prominent in their
foreclaws, which can crush steel armor with ease) and their ability
to perform extremely delicate and precise operations with the small
manipulators around their mouths. Gantrista-(unpronounceable),
usually called Gan, is the only active Shellikaki warrior in Evanwyl.

Gods and Beings of Significance

The gods and their choices affect nearly everything on the
planet. There are, literally, hundreds if not thousands of deities
worshipped on the planet; for purposes of The Balanced Sword,
only a few are of great significance, however. In this section are
also included a few individual beings who may not be, strictly
speaking, gods, but who have influence on that level.

MYRIONAR

God of Justice and Vengeance, Myrionar is at the heart of the
action here. In the grander scheme of things Myrionar is a fading god whose influence is vastly reduced from what it was, but
that may be changing. Represented as a set of scales balanced
on the point of a sword.

TERIAN

The Nemesis of Evil, the Light in the Darkness, Terian is also called Infinity as he is referred to in prophecy as "The Length of Space." A deity of unswerving good, Terian is also ranked as one of the most powerful of deities on anyone's scale. Represented by a human figure mostly in black with a cape or cloak clasped with a golden sidewise-eight figure and head blurred/concealed by a blaze of light.

CHROMAIAS AND THE FOUR

Generally portrayed as good, the Chromaian faith is extremely... flexible, especially as it manifests all aspects of magic and power. Symbolized by a four-pointed jacklike object with crystals of four different colors at the points and a clear diamond at the center.

EÖNAE

Goddess of the world(s), Eönae's focus is on nature, with control over the natural elements (earth, air, fire, water, and spirit) the common manifestation of her power. She is commonly allied with **Shargamor**, a demon of water turned to the light, who is mostly focused on storms, streams, rain, and so on. Symbolized either by a woman (young, medium, old) with green and brown hair, or by her signature creatures, the **Eönwyl**, which are essentially god-empowered winged unicorns.

ELBON NOMICON AND THE SIXTEEN

One of the most ancient pantheons, the head of this group of gods is Elbon Nomicon, Teranahm a u Gilnas (Great Dragon of the Diamond), supposedly father to all Dragons and a being of almost incalculable power. The Dragons tend to slow, long duty-cycles on Zarathan, either sleeping for ages or travelling to other planes of existence, with only a few physically present on Zarathan at any given time; it is, however, rumored that Elbon Nomicon's own home is at the center of the Krellin mountains at the extreme southwest tip of the continent. The symbol of each dragon is its chosen gemstone; Elbon's personal symbol is a stylized lighting bolt with rays extending out from it, made of course of diamond. The Great Dragons have some sort of mystical cycle of hibernation which alternates with that of their opposite numbers, the Elderwyrm.

THE ELDERWYRM

Where there is light, there is shadow, and the Elderwyrm are said to be the shadows that Elbon and the Sixteen have cast onto creation. Sanamaveridion, one of the Elderwyrm, is seen at the end of *Phoenix in Shadow*; many others are awaiting their time to rise, which is implied to be very soon indeed. This is obviously one of the worst features of this Chaoswar, as it means that one of the most powerful pantheons for the forces of good will become mostly inactive while a very powerful force for evil rises.

KERLAMION

The Black Star, King of All Hells, Kerlamion is one of the most powerful of the gods as well as one of the original Demons. He symbolizes destruction and conquest and thus attracts only the worst sort of worshippers; he is however often quite active and those who please him may often get material aid. His symbol is, predictably, either a black starburst or a humanoid outline of pure black.

THE MAZOLISHTA

Great Demons who are the patron gods of the mazakh and other creatures of darker natures, there are several Mazolishta whose names are rarely spoken; the only one appearing directly in The Balanced Sword is **Voorith**, whose focus is life, forests, and such—in a corruptive and destructive sense. The others are **Yergoth**, a corruptive representation of water, **Windego**, a dark and malevolent spirit of air, space, and dimensional distortions, **Zaoshiss**, a master of the destruction and corruption of the solid representations of earth, and **Uluroa**, patron of the destructive aspects of fire.

BLACKWART THE GREAT

God of Toads (and anything else he happens to like), Blackwart manifests as a gigantic black toad, hence the name. While not powerful on the scale of many of the gods, he is much more savvy than many give him credit for (just like his people). He is symbolized by a stylized set of pop-eyes and a smile, or by a black toad figurine.

THE WANDERER

A supposedly human wizard, the Wanderer is a figure of popular legend across Zarathan; stories about him go back at least one and possibly two, three, or even four Chaoswars. An extremely powerful magician, the Wanderer is most known for his unorthodox approaches and apparent immunity to destiny; it is said he originally came from Zaralandar (Earth) which may explain his unique nature. Even the "he" is somewhat in doubt as the Wanderer has appeared in dozens of different guises throughout history, men, women, children, and even occasionally *Artan*, Child of Odin, or other species.

KONSTANTIN KHOROS

The most powerful spirit magician known, Khoros is regarded with trepidation, awe, and fear by almost all beings of power. He is a master manipulator, whose goals may be good but whose methods are at best harsh and at times dark indeed. He has devastated the plans of demonlords and kings, of gods and villains, often without being himself physically present. In The Balanced Sword, Khoros is known to have had contact with all three of the main characters and be directly involved with some of their actions, which has caused others aware of this to have no little trepidation in dealing with them.

THE SPIRITSMITH

An Ancient Sauran with a history stretching back at least half a million years to the Fall of the Saurans, the Spiritsmith is the greatest known artificer on the planet, and the one asked by gods and heroes for the mightiest weapons and strongest armor. He forged the original Raiment for all the Justiciars.

VIRIGAR AND THE GREAT WOLVES

Not, strictly speaking, a god by the standards of Zarathan, Virigar is the King of the Great Werewolves, or Great Wolves, which are the most individually feared monsters on the planet. Great Werewolves (seen in their weakest form in *Paradigms Lost*) are soul and energy eating shapeshifters whose only vulnerabilities are silver or powers similar to their own. Virigar himself is the most ancient and powerful of their race, and is a bogeyman to even the gods themselves; one of his appellations is "The God-Slayer," and he has apparently earned this title multiple times in history.